THE BEST OF THE DESTROYER

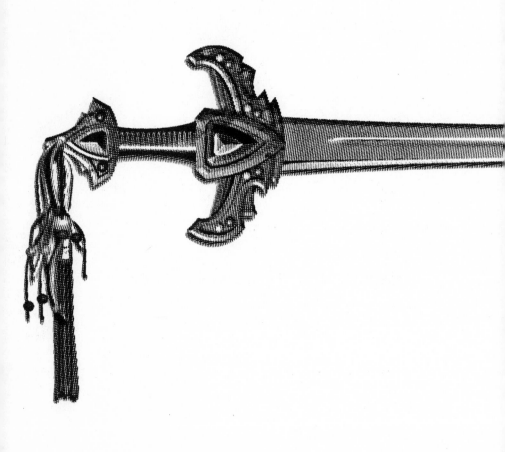

THE BEST
OF THE
DESTROYER

WARREN MURPHY AND RICHARD SAPIR

A TOM DOHERTY ASSOCIATES BOOK

NEW YORK

THE BEST OF THE DESTROYER

Introduction to this omnibus, "Creating the Destroyer," copyright © 2007 by Warren Murphy

The Destroyer: Chinese Puzzle © 1972 by Richard Sapir and Warren Murphy
Originally published in 1972 by Pinnacle Books

The Destroyer: Slave Safari © 1973 by Richard Sapir and Warren Murphy
Originally published in 1973 by Pinnacle Books

The Destroyer: Assassins Play-off © 1975 by Richard Sapir and Warren Murphy
Originally published in 1975 by Pinnacle Books

A Forge Book
Published by Tom Doherty Associates, LLC
175 Fifth Avenue
New York, NY 10010

www.tor-forge.com

Forge® is a registered trademark of Tom Doherty Associates, LLC.

Library of Congress Cataloging-in-Publication Data

Murphy, Warren.
    The best of the destroyer / Warren Murphy and Richard Sapir.—1st Forge trade paper ed.
        p. cm.
    Contents: Chinese puzzle—Slave safari—Assassins play-off.
    "A Tom Doherty Associates book."
    ISBN-13: 978-0-7653-1800-8
    ISBN-10: 0-7653-1800-8
    I. Sapir, Richard.   II. Title.

PS3563.U7634 B47 2007
813'.54—dc22

                                                            2006053547

First Forge Tradepaper Edition: May 2007

Printed in the United States of America

0   9   8   7   6   5   4   3   2   1

Contents

CREATING THE DESTROYER

WARREN MURPHY

MY late partner, Dick Sapir, and I wrote *Created, the Destroyer,* the first novel in our Destroyer series, on an attic typewriter what seems like a century ago. And after seven more years of trying, we found a publisher and became "overnight successes"—to the total surprise of everyone, including ourselves, the series became a big hit. But the big hit begat a big problem.

In those days, it was the nature of the publishing beast to keep dancing with the girl who brought you (not a bad rule, generally), and so our publishers wanted us to keep writing the same book over and over again.

But Dick and I had the idea that in that direction lay the bone-yard, and readers would soon get tired of us if we kept cultivating the same cabbage patch. So instead we decided to roam farther afield and the Destroyer, which started out as a better-written but pretty ordinary adventure yarn, began to wander off in the direction of mythology and magic, political satire, fantasy, science fiction and culture wars.

We guessed right and as the flood of action-adventure series dried up to a trickle, the Destroyer kept going strong, even to this day—some thirty-five years later and more than 140 books later—because it became unquantifiable. Each book brought something completely different.

Over the past few years the series has drifted away a bit from those roots—but now with new books in the New Destroyer series coming from Tor/Forge Books, myself and cowriter James Mullaney hope that we will be able to put Remo and Chiun right back on the cutting edge where they always made their home.

This special backlist omnibus includes three books that have found special favor with fans of the series over the years. *Chinese Puzzle* was the first book that really defined the relationship between Remo and Chiun, our two hero assassins. *Slave Safari* took a tough look at racial politics in America and *Assassins Playoff* set the stage for the direction the series would take for more than the next quarter-century. Each of these three books is always on the faithful readers' lists of the "Best Destroyers."

They represent both old and new, and we hope this look at some of our favorite past Destroyer books will show the way for the new books that will follow.

THE DESTROYER

Chinese Puzzle

AUTHORS' INTRODUCTION

THIS book, the third in the original Destroyer series, is about the visit of a mythical American president to China. It first appeared in the bookstores in February 1972, the same week that Richard Nixon made his trip to China (and then spoiled it all by coming back).

That relevance was one of the charms of writing books back in the early days of the Destroyer series, when Pinnacle was a tiny publishing house, and deadlines were a lot more flexible. Nowadays, publishers like manuscripts in hand a year or more before a book gets published, so trying to write a novel that stays on top of the news is almost impossible.

But it wasn't just timeliness that made this book special for us. *Chinese Puzzle* was the first Destroyer in which the relationship between Remo and his teacher, Chiun, was defined, and the first book in which they actually worked together on a mission. For the first time, the legends of the House of Sinanju, the age-old house of Korean assassins, began to work their way into the stories.

Why should it take until the third book of a series to nail down such basic points as the characters, their history, and their relationships?

Well, the first Destroyer, *Created, the Destroyer*, was written in 1963, but not published until 1971. In that book, Chiun was a karate instructor and nothing more. In the eight years the book was waiting for publication, karate, which had been an esoteric art in 1963, became more and more common. After publication of *Created* in 1971, we realized we needed something more, something that had totally eluded us in *The Destroyer #2, Death Check.*

In *Chinese Puzzle,* we felt we had it right for the first time. This was also the book where we decided we were not going to write "splatter books," filled with bodies oozing blood, and which read like casualty reports. Instead, we decided to make humor and satire ongoing components of the series—if it lasted, which, in those days, was never certain.

Twenty-five million copies later, we're still trying to do the same thing.

WARREN MURPHY *and* DICK SAPIR
September 1984

THe *ReaL* INTRODUCTION

YOU have just read a pack of lies, written by two idiots, and published by a third.

As usual, those two incompetent scribblers, Sapir and Murphy, have gotten everything wrong. Save one thing.

It is true that the thieving Chinese owed money to the House of Sinanju, and that I, Chiun, Master of Sinanju, collected some. Everything else is false.

I was never a karate instructor. That is like calling the sun a lightbulb. And as for these two cretins "defining" the relationship between Remo and me, they are like cockroaches who infest a house just to describe its architecture.

Even the title is wrong. *Chinese Puzzle* indeed. As all know, the true title of this book is *Chiun Collects from the Thieving Chinese*.

They call this book *Authors' Choice*. *Morons' Choice* would be more like it. You would all be well advised to ignore this garbage.

With moderate tolerance for you, I am
CHIUN, MASTER OF SINANJU

For
Philip Sapir, a super-great uncle;
Ramona, who graces worlds not good enough for her;
D.D., who clings to joy like a life raft;
and for Bill Ashman and Davis Jacobs
—because Remo says so.

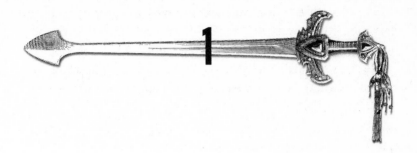

HE did not want coffee, tea or milk. He did not even want a pillow for his head, although the BOAC stewardess could see he was obviously dozing.

When she attempted to slip the white pillow behind his barrel neck, two younger men slapped it away and motioned her to the rear of the jet, then to the front. Any direction, so long as it was away from the man with closed eyes, and hands folded on top of a brown leather briefcase handcuffed to his right wrist.

She did not feel comfortable around this particular group of Orientals. Not with their dour faces, their cement lips obviously set in childhood never to smile.

She judged them to be Chinese. Usually Chinese were most pleasant, often charming, always intelligent. These men were stone.

She went forward to the captain's cabin, past the forward galley, where she snitched an end of a cinnamon bun and gobbled it down. She had bypassed lunch on her slimming diet and then did what she always did when she missed lunch. She ate something fattening to quell the rising hunger. Still, dieting and breaking the diet in small ways, while not really trimming pounds kept her lissome enough to hold her job.

The bun was good, somehow extra sweet. No wonder the

Chinese gentleman had asked for more. Perhaps they were his favorite. Today was the first time they had served cinnamon buns. They were not even on the regular lading for the menu.

But he had liked them. She could see his eyes light when they were served. And the two men who had slapped the pillow away had been ordered to give him their buns.

She opened the front cabin door with her key and leaned into the cabin.

"Lunch, gentlemen," she said to the pilot and co-pilot.

"No," they both answered. The captain said: "We'll be over Orly soon. What kept you?"

"I don't know. It must be that time of year. Most everyone is dozing back there. I had a pickle of a bother fetching pillows. It's awfully hot here, isn't it?"

"No, it's cool," said the co-pilot. "Are you all right?"

"Yes. Yes. Just feels a bit warm. You know." She turned away, but the co-pilot did not hear her close the door. There was a good reason she did not close the door. She was suddenly sleeping, face down on the cabin floor, her skirt angling up to the pinnacle of her rump. And in those strange patterns that greet the unexpected, the co-pilot's first thought was silly. He wondered if she was exposing herself to the passengers.

He need not have worried. Of the 58 passengers, 30 had passed all cares of the world, and most of the rest were in panic.

The co-pilot heard a woman's scream. "Oh, no. Oh, no, Lord. No. No. No."

Men were yelling now also, and the co-pilot unstrapped himself and hopped over the body of the stewardess, dashing into the seat-lined body of the plane where a young woman slapped a young boy's face and kept slapping it, demanding he wake up; where a young man walked the aisle dazed; where a girl desperately pressed her ear to a middle-aged man's chest; and where two young Chinese men stood over the body of an elderly Chinese gentleman. They had drawn guns.

Where the hell were the other stews? Dammit. There was one in the back. Asleep.

He could feel the plane pitch and dive. They were going in for an emergency.

Unable to think of anything else, he yelled to the passengers that they were making an emergency landing and that they should fasten their seat belts. But his voice scarcely made an impression. He dashed back to the front, pushing the dazed, wandering man down into a seat. An elderly couple nearby did not even look up. They were apparently dozing through it also.

He snatched the stewardess' microphone from its cradle hook in the small compartment near the front seat, and announced they were making an emergency landing at Orly airport and that everyone should fasten their seat belts.

"Fasten your seat belts now," he said firmly. And he saw a woman first buckle in a sleeping boy whose face she had been slapping, then resume her slapping in an effort to rouse him.

The plane moved down through the foggy night, locked in on the right path by a homing beacon that the pilot followed unerringly. Upon landing, the airplane was not allowed to taxi to the main terminal but was ordered to a hangar where ambulances and nurses and doctors were waiting. As soon as he opened the door for the platform steps, the co-pilot was pushed aside by two men in gray suits, with revolvers drawn. They went storming into the plane pushing aside two passengers. When they reached the Chinese gentleman, they returned their revolvers to their holsters, and one of them nodded to one of the young Chinese, and the two of them ran back up the aisle again, slamming into a nurse and a doctor, knocking them over, and continuing down the ground platform.

Only the people taken to the morgue or the hospital that night left the airport. It was not until midnight on the following day that the survivors were allowed to depart. They had not been allowed to see a newspaper or listen to a radio. They answered questions upon questions until all the questions and answers seemed to blend in a continuous flow of words. They talked to white men, to yellow men, to black men. And very few of the questions made sense.

Nor did the newspaper headline they were finally allowed to see:

TWENTY-NINE ON FLIGHT DIE OF BOTULISM

Nowhere, noticed the co-pilot, did the paper mention the Chinese gentleman or his two aides, not even in the roster of passengers.

"You know, honey," he said to his wife, after reading the newspaper reports three times, "these people couldn't have died of botulism. There were no convulsions. I told you what they looked like. And besides, all our food is fresh." He said this in his small London flat.

"Well then, you should go to Scotland Yard and tell them."

"That's a good idea. Something's not on the up and up here."

Scotland Yard was very interested in his story. So were two American blokes. Everyone was so interested that they wanted to hear the story again and again. And just so the co-pilot would not forget, they gave him a room to himself that stayed locked all the time. And did not let him leave. Or call his wife.

The President of the United States sat in the large soft chair in the corner of his main office, his shoeless feet resting on a green hassock before him, his eyes riveted on predawn Washington—for him, the floodlights on the White House lawn. His pencil tapped on the sheaf of papers resting between his knees and his stomach.

His closest advisor was summing up in his professorial manner. The room smelled of the lingering cigar smoke of the CIA director who had left one hour before. The advisor spoke in the gutturals of German childhood, droning on about possibilities and probabilities of international repercussions and just why this was not as bad as it looked.

"It would not do to minimize what has happened. The dead man was, after all, a personal emissary from the Premier. But the important thing is that the Premier's visit to this country is still on. For one thing, the emissary was not poisoned over American territory. He boarded the plane in Europe and was to transfer at Montreal, for this country. Because of this, it is apparent that the Premier does not believe that any of our people were involved. That is evident, because he has indicated a willingness to send another man to finalize the arrangements for his visit to this country."

The advisor smiled.

"Moreover, Mr. President, the Premier is sending a close friend. A colleague. A man who was with him on the long march when they were retreating from Chiang Kai Shek, and a friend who was with them in their dark days in the caves of Yenan. No, I absolutely and firmly believe that they know we were not responsible. If they felt otherwise, they would not now send General Liu. His presence on this mission is their assertion that they believe we are of good will. So the Premier's trip will go ahead as planned."

The President sat up straight and rested his hands on his desk. It was Autumn in Washington, and the offices he entered and worked in were always toasty warm. But the desk now felt cold to the touch.

"Just how is Liu arriving?" asked the President.

"They will not let us know."

"That doesn't sound as if they are brimming over with confidence in us."

"We have not exactly been their trusted allies, Mr. President."

"But if they would let us know the route, then we could offer protection also."

"Frankly, sir, I am very happy we are unaware of General Liu's route. If we are unaware, then we are not responsible for him until he arrives in Montreal. We will hear from the Polish embassy here as to his arrival time. But he is coming. May I further stress again that they informed us he would be coming, within one day of the tragedy."

"That's good. It shows they did not change policy." The table still felt cold to the touch and the President's hands felt wet. "All right. Good," he said. But there was little joy in his voice. He added, looking up: "The people who poisoned the Chinese emissary? Who could they have been? We have absolutely no clues from our intelligence. The Russians? Taiwan? Who?"

"I am surprised, Mr. President, that Intelligence did not send an entire library on who would wish the Chinese Premier not to visit the United States." He brought from his briefcase a folder the thickness of a Russian novel.

The President raised his left hand, palm forward, signalling the advisor to belay the report.

"I don't want history, Professor. I want information. Hard today information on how the Chinese security system could be breached."

"That is unavailable as yet."

"All right, dammit, then I've decided." The President rose from his chair, still clasping the sheaf of notes that had been on his lap. He put the papers down on the fine polished wood of his desk.

"On one level, we will continue with normal procedures of the intelligence and local security people. Just continue."

The advisor looked up querulously. "Yes?"

"That's it. I can't tell you anymore. I'm glad I have your services, you're doing as well as anyone could. You're doing a good job, Professor. Good night."

"Mr. President, we have worked well together because you do not withhold pertinent information. At a time like this, to leave me wondering would be counterproductive."

"I agree with you one hundred per cent," the President said. "However, the very nature of this area precludes my sharing it with anyone. And I'm sorry. I cannot explain further. I really cannot."

The advisor nodded.

The President watched him leave the room. The door shut with a click. Outside, the harsh floodlights would be dimmed in two hours, when replaced by the sun still steaming hot over Washington in the early fall.

He was alone, as every leader of every nation had always been when the difficult decisions had to be made. He lifted the receiver of a phone he had used only once since he had been inaugurated.

There was no need to dial although the telephone had a dial, as if it were any other telephone. He waited. He knew there would be no ringing sound on his end. There was not supposed to be. Finally he heard a sleepy voice answer.

The President said: "Hello. Sorry to wake you. I need the services of that person . . . it is a grave crisis . . . If you come down to see me then I will explain more fully . . . Yes, I must see you in person . . . and bring him, please. I want to talk to him . . . Well, then tell him to stand by for immediate service . . . All right. Fine. Yes. That would be fine for now. Yes, I understand, it's just an alert. Not a commitment. You will put him on alert. Thank you. You don't know how desperately the world needs him now."

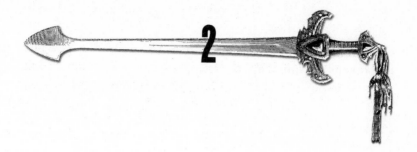

HIS name was Remo.

He had just laced the skin-tight black cotton uniform around his legs, when the telephone rang in his room in the Hotel Nacional in San Juan, Puerto Rico.

He picked up the receiver with his left hand while finishing the cork-blackening of his face with his right. The telephone operator told him there had just been a long distance call from the Firmifex Company in Sausalito, California. The woman at Firmifex said that the shipment of durable goods would be arriving in two days.

"Yeah, okay." He hung up and said one word: "Idiots."

He turned off the lights and the room was dark. Through the open window, the sea breezes blew off the Caribbean, not cooling Puerto Rico but swirling away and redistributing some of the autumn heat. He walked out onto the open balcony with its round aluminium tube railing supported by curved metal spokes.

He was about six feet tall and the only hint of muscle was a slight thickness around the neck, wrists and ankles, but he hopped the railing to the ledge as though it were a horizontal matchstick.

He leaned into the sea slick brick wall of the Hotel Nacional, smelling its salty wetness, and feeling the cool of the ledge at his feet. The bricks were white but they appeared gray close up in the early morning darkness.

He tried to concentrate, to remember to press into the building, not away from it, but the telephone call rankled him. A 3:30 A.M. telephone call to inform him of manufacturing deliveries. What a stupid cover for an alert. They might as well have advertised on prime time. They might as well have put a spotlight on him.

Remo looked down the nine stories and attempted to spot the old man. He could not. Just the darkness of the tropical shrubbery, cut by the white paths, and the rectangular splotch where the pool was, midway between hotel and beach.

"Well?" came the high-pitched Oriental voice from below.

Remo dropped from the ledge, catching it with his hands. He hung there for a moment, dangling his feet down into space. Then he began rocking his body back and forth, picking up the where of the wall, speeding his rocking, and then he opened his fingers and let go.

The swinging of his body threw him against the hotel wall, where his bare toes slid against the smooth white brick. His fingers, tensed like talons, bought a hold on the surface of the stones.

The lower half of his body rebounded out again from the wall of the hotel, and as it began to swing back in, he released his hands, and his body dropped. Again his feet braked his descent against the wall of the hotel, and again his powerful, charcoal-coated fingers pressured like talons against the wall of the Hotel Nacional.

His fingers felt the slimy Caribbean moistness on the wall. If he had tried to hang on, even momentarily, he would have plunged to his death. But he remembered the injunction: the secret is in, not down.

Remo's mind concentrated furiously on the position of his body. It must keep moving, constantly, but its force must always be inward, overcoming the downward pull of nature.

He smelled rather than felt the breezes, as he again rocked off from the wall with his legs, and dropped another five feet, before his toes and hands slowed his descent against the wall.

Fleetingly, he wondered if he really was ready. Were his hands strong enough, his timing keen enough, to overcome gravity, by the disjointed rocking technique perfected in Japan by the Ninja—the warrior wizards—more than ten centuries ago?

Remo thought of the story about the man who fell from the thirtieth floor of a skyscraper. As he passed the fifteenth floor, someone inside yelled, "How are you?" "So far, so good," he answered.

So far, so good, Remo thought.

He was moving rhythmically now, an irresistible pattern of swing out, drop, swing in, and slow against the wall. Then repeat. Swing out, drop, swing in, and slow against the wall, defying gravity, defying the laws of nature, his smoothly muscled athlete's body using its strength and timing to bring its force inward against the wall, instead of down where death waited.

He was halfway down now, literally bouncing off the wall, but the downward pull was growing stronger, and as he rocked off the wall, he applied upward pressure with his leg muscles to counteract the pull.

A black speck in a black night, a professional doing professional magic, moving down the wall.

Then his feet touched the curved tiled roof of the covered walk, and he relaxed his hands, curled and rolled his body through a somersault, landing noiselessly on his bare feet on the concrete slab behind the darkened hotel. He had made it.

"Pitiful," came the voice.

The man was shaking his head, now clearly visible because of the strands of long white beard coming down from his face, the thin, almost babylike hair dotting his balding Oriental head. The whiteness of the hair was like a frame shimmering in the early morning breeze. He looked like a starvation case brought back from the grave. His name was Chiun.

"Pitiful," said the man whose head barely reached Remo's shoulder. "Pitiful."

Remo grinned. "I made it."

Chiun continued to shake his head sadly. "Yes. You are magnificent. Rivalled in your skills only by the elevator which carried me down. It took you ninety-seven seconds." It was an accusation, not a statement.

Chiun had not looked at his watch. He did not need to. His internal clock was unfailingly accurate, although as he approached eighty, he had once confided to Remo that he was miscalculating as much as ten seconds a day.

"The hell with ninety-seven seconds. I made it," Remo said.

Chiun threw his hands up over his head in a silent appeal to one of his innumerable gods. "The lowliest ant of the field could do it in ninety-seven seconds. Does that make the ant dangerous? You are not Ninja. You are worthless. A piece of cheese. You and your mashed potatoes. And your roast beef and your alcohol. In ninety-seven seconds, one can go up the wall."

Remo glanced up at the smooth white wall of the hotel, unbroken by ledges or handholds, a shiny slab of stone. He grinned again at Chiun. "Horsecrap."

The elderly Oriental sucked in his breath. "Get in," he hissed. "Go to the room."

Remo shrugged and turned toward the door, leading into the darkened rear section of the hotel. He held the door open, and turned to allow Chiun to pass through first. From the corner of his eye, he saw Chiun's brocaded robe vanish upward onto the top of the roof over the walkway. He was going to climb up. It was impossible. No one could climb that wall.

He hesitated momentarily, unsure if he should attempt to dissuade Chiun. No way, he realized, and walked inside rapidly and pushed the elevator button. The light showed the elevator was on the twelfth floor. Remo stabbed the round plastic button again. The light still read 12.

Remo slid into the doorway alongside the elevator, leading to the stairs. He started running, taking the stairs, three at a time, trying to gauge the time. It had been no more than 30 seconds since he had left Chiun.

He raced at full speed up the stairs, his feet noiseless on the stone slabs. At a dead run, he pushed open the door leading to the ninth floor corridor. Breathing heavily, he walked to his door and stopped and listened. It was silent within. Good, Chiun was still climbing. His Oriental pride was going to get kicked.

But what if he had fallen? He was eighty years old. Suppose his twisted body lay in a heap at the base of the hotel wall?

Remo grabbed the door knob, twisted, and pushed the heavy steel door back into the room, and stepped in onto the carpet. Chiun was standing in the middle of the floor, his hazel eyes burning into Remo's dark brown eyes. "Eighty-three seconds," Chiun said. "You are even worthless for climbing stairs."

"I waited for the elevator," Remo lied, lamely.

"The truth is not in you. Even in your condition, one does not become exhausted riding the elevator."

He turned his back. There was the infernal toilet paper in his hand.

Chiun had removed a roll of toilet paper from the bathroom, and now he rolled it across the heavy rug of the hotel floor. He smoothed it down, and then reentered the bathroom. He returned with a glass of water in his hand, and began pouring it over the paper. Twice, he went into the bathroom to refill the glass, until finally the toilet paper was soaked with water.

Remo had closed the door behind him. Chiun walked over and sat on the bed. He turned to look at Remo. "Practice," he said. Almost to himself, he added: "Animals need not practice. But then they do not eat mashed potatoes. And they do not make mistakes. When man loses instinct, he must regain it by practice."

With a sigh, Remo looked across the 15-foot length of wet toilet tissue. It was an ancient Oriental training technique adapted to the 20th Century. Run along pieces of wet paper, without tearing the paper underfoot. Or, following Chiun's standards, without wrinkling it. It was the ancient art of Ninjutsu, credited to Japan but claimed by Chiun for Korea. Its practitioners were called invisible men, and legend had them able to vanish in a wisp of smoke or to transform themselves into animals, or to pass through stone walls.

Remo hated the exercise, and had laughed at the legend when he first heard it. But then in a gymnasium years ago, he had fired six shots point blank at Chiun as the old man ran toward him across the floor. And all the bullets had missed.

"Practice," Chiun said.

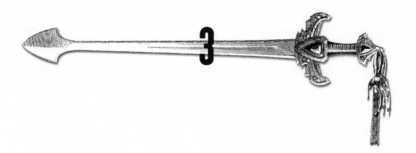

No one heard the shots on Jerome Avenue in the Bronx. It was a busy time of the day and only when the black limousine with the drawn curtains spun with a crunch into one of the pillars supporting the Jerome Avenue line of the subway, did people take note that the driver appeared to be biting the steering wheel and that blood was gushing from the back of his head. The man in the front passenger's seat was resting his head on the dashboard and appeared to be vomiting blood. The curtains covering the windows of the back seat of the car were drawn and the car's engine continued to hum with the wheels locked in drive.

A gray car with four men in hats pulled up quickly behind. The men leaped from the car, guns drawn, and scrambled to the black car which churned, going nowhere, buttressed by the pillar, its nose caved in against the concrete base holding the grime-blackened steel supports of the elevated subway.

One of the four men grabbed the handle of the rear door. He tugged, then tugged again, then reached for the front door handle which also would not open. He raised his snub-nosed automatic above the handle and fired, then reached through the broken window and unlocked the rear door.

That was all Mabel Katz of 1126 Osiris Avenue, just around the corner past the delicatessen, could remember. She explained it carefully again to the attractive young man who didn't look Jewish but had a name that could be, although the FBI was not exactly the place for a young Jewish lawyer. Everyone else on the block was talking to men like these so Mrs. Katz would talk also. Although she did have to get home to make Marvin his supper. Marvin wasn't feeling well, and certainly shouldn't go without supper.

"The men in the front looked Chinese or Japanese. Maybe Viet Cong," she suggested smartly.

"Did you see any men leave the car?" asked the man.

"I heard the crash and saw some men run to the car and shoot the lock off. But there was no one inside the back."

"Did you see anyone who looked, well, suspicious?"

Mrs. Katz shook her head. What was suspicious, already, when people were shooting and cars were crashing and people were asking questions? "Will the two hurt men be all right?"

The young man shook his head. "Now did you see any Orientals around here other than the two men in the front seat?"

Mrs. Katz shook her head again.

"Do you ever see any Orientals around here?"

She shook her head again.

"What about the laundry across the street?"

"Oh, that's Mr. Pang. He's from the neighborhood."

"Well, that's Oriental."

"If you want to call him that. But I always thought Orientals meant, you know, far away and exotic."

"Did you see him near the car?"

"Mr. Pang? No. He ran out like everyone else. And that was it. Will I be on television now?"

"No."

She was not on television that night. As a matter of fact, the story was on only a few moments, and it did not mention how the neighborhood suddenly had been flooded with all sorts of investigators. It was called a tong war killing, and an announcer talked about the history of tong wars. The announcer did not even mention all the FBI men around the neighborhood or that someone in the back seat had disappeared.

Mrs. Katz was peeved when she saw the six o'clock news. But she was not quite as peeved as the man for whom she had voted. His closest advisor was also peeved:

"He was to take a motor caravan because that was the safest way to arrive here. How could he just vanish?"

Heads of departments sat almost at attention with their uniformly disastrous reports. It was a long wooden table and a long dark day. They had been there since early afternoon and although the sky could not be seen, their watches told them it was night in Washington. On the half hour, messengers brought in new reports.

The President's closest advisor pointed to a bulldog-faced man across the table. "Tell us again how it happened."

The man began the recitation, reading from notes in front of him. General Liu's car had left the caravan at approximately 11:15 A.M. and was followed by security people who frantically tried to swerve him back to the Thruway. The general's car had taken Jerome Avenue into the Bronx and another car had gotten between his car and the security auto. The security people managed to catch up to General Liu's car at 11:33 A.M., just beyond a city golf course. The car had smashed into one of the steel supports of the "el" when the security men had reached it. The general was gone. His driver and an aide were dead, shot from behind in the head. The bodies were taken to nearby Montefiore Hospital for immediate autopsy and removal of bullets, which were now being checked in ballistics.

"Enough," yelled the presidential advisor. "I am not concerned with the tedium of police details. How can we lose a person under our protection? Lose! We have lost him entirely. Didn't anyone see him? Or the people who kidnaped him? How far behind were your people?"

"About two car lengths. Another car got between them."

"Just got between them?"

"Yes."

"Does anyone know where that car went or who was in it?"

"No."

"And no one heard shots?"

"No."

"And then you found the two dead aides of General Liu and no General Liu, correct?"

"Correct."

"Gentlemen, I do not have to stress again how important this is or how deeply concerned the President is. I can only say I view this as incredible incompetence."

There was no response.

The advisor looked down the long table to a small, almost frail man, with a lemony face and large eyeglasses. He had said nothing, only taken notes.

"You," said the aide. "Do you have any suggestions?"

Heads turned toward the man. "No," he said.

"Might I be so honored as to be advised why the President asked you to this meeting?"

"No," said the man, as unruffled as if he had been asked for a match and did not have one.

The directors at the table stared at him. One squinted as if seeing a familiar face, then looked away.

The tension was broken when the door opened for the half-hourly messenger. The President's advisor stopped talking, and drummed his fingers on the stack of half-hour reports before him. Every so often a phone would light before one of the directors and he would pass on what information he had received. None had lit in front of the lemon-faced small man at the end of the table.

This time, the messenger leaned over and whispered to the aide. The aide nodded. Then the messenger went to the lemony-faced man and whispered something to him, and the man was gone.

He accompanied the messenger down a carpeted hall and was ushered into a large dark office with one lamp casting light upon a large desk. The door shut behind him. He could see even through the shadows the worry on the face of the man behind the desk.

"Yes, Mr. President?" said the man.

"Well?" said the President.

"I would like to point out, sir, that I consider this whole affair rather irregular. It was an incredible breach of our operating contract for me, not only to appear at the White House but to participate in a meeting, where, I believe, for a moment I was recognized. Granted, the man who recognized me is of the utmost integrity. But that I should even be seen defeats almost every reason for our existence."

"No one knew your name besides that man?"

"That is not the point, Mr. President. If our mission becomes known, or even broadly enough suspected, then we should not have existed in the first place. Now, unless you consider what is happening important enough for us to close down our operations, I would like to leave."

"I do consider what is happening important enough for you to risk your entire operation. I would not have requested you here if I did not." His voice was tired, but not strained, a strong voice which endured and endured and endured and did not falter.

"What we are dealing with today is a question of world peace. Whether or not. It's that simple."

"What I am dealing with, sir," said Dr. Harold W. Smith, "is the safety of the United States Constitution. You have the Army. You have the Navy. You have the Air Force and the Federal Bureau of Investigation and the Central Intelligence Agency and Treasury men, and grain inspectors and customs clerks and everyone else. They are all within the framework of the Constitution."

"And they failed."

"What makes you think we can do any better?"

"Him," said the President. "That person."

Dr. Harold W. Smith sat silently. The President continued: "We have been in touch with the Polish Ambassador here, through whom we deal with Peking. If we do not find General Liu within one week, I am informed that as much as the Premier would like to visit this country, he will not be able to. He has his nationalistic elements too. And he must deal with them. We must find General Liu."

"Then, sir, what do we need with that person you mentioned?"

"He would make the best possible bodyguard, would he not? We haven't been able to protect General Liu with quantity. Perhaps with awesome quality."

"Isn't that like putting the world's best padlock on the proverbial barn door when the horse has left?"

"Not exactly. He is going to join in the search. We are going to find General Liu."

"Sir, I have dreaded this moment. That is, when I have not longed for it."

Dr. Harold W. Smith paused to choose his words carefully, not just because he was in the presence of the President of the

United States, but because a strong integrity implanted in youth insisted upon expression during manhood.

It was because of that integrity, he knew, that he had been entrusted many years before by another President. Smith then had been with the Central Intelligence Agency and had gone through three interviews with superiors in one week. All three had told him they were unaware of his potential assignment, but one, a close friend, had confided that it was a Presidential assignment. Smith immediately made a sad note of his friend's untrustworthiness. Not the written kind of note, but the constant analysis a good administrator makes. He was asked for an analysis of his three interviews on a clear and sunny morning. It was the first time he had ever spoken to a President of the United States.

"Well?" said the young man. His shock of sandy hair was combed dry. His suit was light gray and neat. He stood with a slight stoop from a recurring back injury.

"Well what, Mr. President?"

"What do you think of the people asking you questions about yourself?"

"They did their job, sir."

"But how would you evaluate them?"

"I wouldn't. Not for you, Mr. President."

"Why not?"

"Because that's not my function, sir. I'm sure you have people expert at such things."

"I am the President of the United States. Is your answer still no?"

"Yes, Mr. President."

"Thank you. Good day. By the way, you've just lost your job. What is your answer now?"

"Good day, Mr. President."

"Dr. Smith, what would you say if I told you I could have you killed?"

"I would pray for our nation."

"But you would not tell me what I asked?"

"No."

"All right. You win. Name your job."

"Forget it, Mr. President."

"You may leave," said the young, handsome man. "You have one week to reconsider."

A week later, he found himself back in the same office, refusing again to give the President the evaluation he had asked for. Finally the President spoke.

"Enough games, Dr. Smith. I have very bad news for you." His voice was no longer insinuating. It was honest, and it was frightened.

"I'm going to be killed," Smith suggested.

"Maybe you will wish you were. First, let me shake your hand and offer you my deepest respects."

Dr. Smith did not take his hand.

"No," said the President. "I guess you wouldn't. Dr. Smith, this nation will have a dictatorship within a decade. There is no question about it. Machiavelli noted that in chaos exists the seeds of dictatorship. We are entering chaos.

"Under the Constitution, we cannot control organized crime. We cannot control revolutionaries. There are so many things we cannot control . . . not under the Constitution. Dr. Smith, I love this country and believe in it. I think we are going through trying times, but that they will pass. But I also think our government needs the help of some outside force to survive as a democracy."

The President had looked up. "You, Dr. Smith, will head that outside force. Your assignment will be to work outside the Constitution to preserve the process of this government. Where there is corruption, end it. Where there is crime, stop it. Use any means you wish, short of taking human life. Help me protect our nation, Dr. Smith." The President's voice was anguished.

Smith had waited a long time before responding. Then he said: "It is dangerous, sir. Suppose I sought power to control the nation?"

"I did not exactly pick you up off the street."

"I see. I assume, sir, you have some sort of program worked out to dismantle this project if necessary?"

"Do you want to know about it?"

"If I take this assignment, no."

"I didn't think so." He passed a portfolio to Dr. Smith. "Your budgetary procedures, operating instructions, everything I could think of are in these notes. There are many details. Cover stories for you and your family. Acquisition of property. Hiring of staff. It will be difficult, Dr. Smith, since no one is aware of it but we two."

The President added: "I will tell my successor and he will tell his successor, and should you die, Dr. Smith, your organization will automatically dissolve."

"What if you should die, sir?"

"My heart is fine and I have no intention of assassination."

"What if you should be assassinated without it being your intention?"

The President smiled.

"Then it will be up to you to tell the next President."

So on a cold day, one November, Dr. Smith informed the new President of the United States of his organization. And this time, all that President had said, was "Shoot. You mean if Ah want you to rub someone out, anyone, Ah can just say so?"

"No."

"Good. Cause for sure, Ah would have sent all you people out behind the barn to play in the daisies."

And that President had told this President, showing him the phone through which the headquarters of the secret organization, CURE, could be reached. And he had warned him that the only things a President could do was to dissolve the organization or ask for something within its mission. He could not order a mission.

And now another President was asking.

But for the light on the desk, it was dark and now the President queried, because the man before him had hesitated.

"Well?" he asked.

"I wish your people within the government could do the job."

"I wish they could too. But they have failed."

"I must seriously consider dismantling the organization," Smith said.

The President sighed. "It is very hard to be President sometimes. Please, Dr. Smith."

The President leaned into the sharp light on his desk and held his forefinger and thumb a pencil width apart. "We're this close to peace, Dr. Smith. This close."

Smith could see the tired courage in the President's face, the steel discipline pushing the man toward his goal of peace.

"I will do what you ask, Mr. President, although it will be difficult. Exposing that person as a bodyguard or even an investigator might lead to someone who knew him while he was living, recognizing his voice."

"While he was living?" the President said.

Smith ignored the unspoken question. He stood up and the President stood with him. "Good luck, Mr. President." He took the offered hand, as he had failed, and since regretted many times, to take the hand of another President years before. As he turned to walk out the door, he said: "I will assign that person."

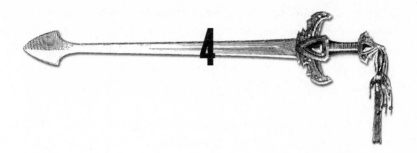

REMO was at peak. He could see the old Korean looking for the slightest wrinkle on the toilet paper and finding none, looking up in surprise. He had been training Remo for almost a solid year now since a miscalculation had kept Remo at peak for three straight months.

Remo did not wait for a compliment which would not come. In seven years of intermittent training, compliments had been rare. Remo got dressed by peeling off the ninja suit and putting on jockey shorts, white T-shirt, and covering them with slacks and a green sports shirt. He slipped into sandals, then brushed his short hair. He had gotten used to his face in the last seven years, the high cheekbones, the straighter nose, that hairline that receded just a little more. He had almost forgotten the face he used to have, back before he had been framed for a murder he did not commit and escorted to an electric chair that did not quite work, although everyone else but his new employers had thought it worked.

"Good enough," said Chiun and Remo blinked. A compliment? From Chiun? He had been acting strangely since August but a compliment for doing something right after failing so many times was incredibly strange.

"Good enough?" Remo asked.

"For a white man whose government is stupid enough to recognize China, yes."

"Please, Chiun, not that again," Remo said in exasperation. It was not that Chiun resented America recognizing Red China, he resented anyone recognizing any China. And that had caused the incidents.

Remo could not cry, but he felt moistness making demands on his eyes.

"Even for a Korean, Little Father?" He knew Chiun liked the title. When Remo had used it in those first days when the burns were still on his forehead and wrists and ankles where the electrodes had been placed, Chiun had rebuked him. Perhaps it had been the joking tone of voice; perhaps it was that Chiun had not believed he would live. In was back in those early days when Remo discovered the first people who also believed that, as a Newark policeman, he had not shot that pusher in an alley.

He knew he hadn't. And that was when the whole crazy life began. With the monk in to give him last rites, with a little pill on the end of his cross, asking him if he wanted to save his soul or his ass. And the pill in his mouth, and the last walk to the chair, and biting into the pill, and passing out, thinking that this was the way all condemned men were brought to the chair, by lying to them that they would be saved.

And then waking up and discovering others who knew he had been framed because they had framed him. It was really part of the price he paid for being an orphan. He had no relatives, and having none, he would be missed by no one. And it was also part of the price he paid for having been seen efficiently killing some guerillas in Vietnam.

And so he had awakened in a hospital bed with a choice. Just start some training. It was one of those beautiful little steps that could lead to anything. To a journey of a thousand miles, a life-long love affair, a great philosophy, or a life of death. Just one step at a time.

And so CURE, the organization that did not exist, got their man who did not exist with a new face and a new mind. It was the mind, not the body, that made Remo Williams Remo Williams. Whether he was Remo Cabell or Remo Pelham or all the other Remos he had ever been. They could change neither his voice, nor his instant response to his name. But they had changed him, the bastards. One step at a time. Yet he had helped. He had taken that first step, and done, albeit laughingly, the first things Chiun had taught him. Now he respected the aged Oriental as he had respected no one else he had ever known. And it saddened him to see Chiun react so un-Chiun-like to the talk of peace with China. Not that Remo cared. He had been taught not to care about those things. But it was strange that so wise a man could act so foolishly. Yet that same wise man had said once:

"One always retains the last few foolishnesses of childhood. To retain all of them is sickness. To understand them is wisdom. To abandon all of them is death. They are our first seeds of joy, and one must always have plants to water."

And in a hotel room many years from the time of that first wisdom of the little father, Remo asked:

"Even for a Korean, Little Father?"

He saw the old man smile. And wait. And then say, slowly: "For a Korean? I feel I must truthfully say yes."

Remo pressed on.

"Even for the village of Sinanju?"

"You have great ambitions," Chiun said.

"My heart reaches to the sky."

"For Sinanju, you are all right. Just all right."

"Is your throat all right?"

"Why?"

"I thought it hurt you to say that."

"It most certainly did."

"It is an honor, little father, to be your son."

"Another point," Chiun said. "A man who cannot apologize is no man at all. My bad temper the other night came from the relief of my fear that you would be hurt. You came down the wall perfectly. Even if it took you ninety-seven seconds."

"You went up perfectly, Little Father. And even more quickly."

"Any schmuck can do a perfect up, my son." Chiun had been picking up those Jewish words again. He learned them from the elderly Jewish ladies he liked to converse with, discussing their common interest: their betrayal by their children and the personal misery ensuing therefrom.

Mrs. Solomon was Chiun's latest. They met every day for breakfast in the restaurant that faced the sea. She would repeat how her son had sent her to San Juan for a vacation and did not phone, even though she had waited by the phone the entire first month.

Chiun would confide that his most loved son of 50 years ago was doing an unspeakable thing. And Mrs. Solomon would put a hand to her face in shared shock. She had done it for the last week and half. And Chiun had yet to tell her the unspeakable thing.

It was fortunate, Remo had thought, that no one laughed at the pair. Because there would surely be a laugher with an extra thoracic cavity.

It had almost come to that the day the young Puerto Rican busboy had sassed Mrs. Solomon for saying the bagels were not fresh. The busboy was the amateur middleweight champion of the island and was just holding the job at the Nacional until he turned professional.

One day he decided he did not want to be a professional. It

was approximately the time he saw the wall coming at him, and the unfinished bagel going seaward.

Mrs. Solomon had personally registered a complaint about the young ruffian attacking a fine, warm, sweet, old man. Chiun had stood there in innocence as the ambulance attendants carried the unconscious busboy out of the dining area and into the ambulance.

How had the young man attacked the elderly gentleman? asked the Puerto Rican police.

"By leaning, I think," Mrs. Solomon said. That was definitely what she thought. After all, Mr. Parks certainly would not have reached across the table and thrown the person into a wall. Why, he was old enough to be her . . . well, uncle.

"I mean, there was this snort from that young man and the next thing I saw, well, I guess, he was like kissing the wall and falling back down. It was very strange. Will he be all right?"

"He'll recover," a policeman said.

"That's nice," said Mrs. Solomon. "It will certainly make my friend feel better."

Her friend had bowed in his Oriental way. And Mrs. Solomon thought that was just adorable for a man carrying the burden of a son who had done an unspeakable thing. Remo had been forced to give Chiun another lecture. They had become more frequent since the President had announced plans to visit Red China.

They had sat on the beach as the Caribbean sky became red, then gray, then black, and when he felt they were alone, Remo had scooped a handful of sand and let it sift through his fingers, and said: "Little Father, there is no man I respect like you."

Chiun sat quietly in his white robes, as though breathing his salt content for the day. He said nothing.

"There are times that pain me, Little Father," Remo said. "You do not know who we work for. I do. And knowing that, I know how important it is that we do not attract attention to ourselves. I do not know when this retraining will end and we will be separated. But when you are with me . . . Well, we were very lucky that the busboy thinks he slipped on something. We were lucky in San Francisco also last month. But as you yourself have told me, just as luck is given, it is taken away. Luck is the least sure of all events."

The waves made steady slapping sounds and the air began to cool. Softly, Chiun said something that sounded like "kvinch."

"What?" said Remo.

"Kvetcher," said Chiun.

"I do not know Korean," said Remo.

"It is not Korean, but is apt anyway. Mrs. Solomon uses the word. It is a noun."

"I assume you want me to ask you what it means."

"It is of no matter. One is what one is."

"All right, Chiun. What is a kvetcher?"

"I do not know if it translates that well in English."

"Since when are you a rabbinical student?"

"This is Yiddish, not Hebrew."

"I'm not auditioning you for *Fiddler on the Roof*."

"A kvetcher is one who complains and complains and worries and complains over the slightest little nothing."

"That busboy will not walk without crutches for months."

"That busboy will no longer be abusive. I have given him an invaluable lesson."

"That he should never be off balance when you're in one of your moods?"

"That he should treat the elderly with respect. If more young-sters respected the elderly, the world would be a far more tranquil place. That has always been the trouble with civilization. Lack of respect for age."

"You're telling me that I should not talk to you like this?"

"You hear what you will hear and I say what I will say. That is what I am telling you."

"I may have to terminate this training because of what happened," Remo said.

"You will do what you will do and I will do what I will do."

"Will you not do what you have done?"

"I will take into account your nervousness over a nothing."

"Were those football players a nothing?"

"If one wants to worry, he will find no shortage of subjects."

Remo threw up his hands. Invincible ignorance was invincible ignorance.

Later, the phone rang. Probably the signal to abort. Of 10 alerts a year, if Remo went into action once, it was a lot.

"Yes," said Remo.

"Nine o'clock tonight in the casino. Your mother will be there," said the voice. And then the receiver clicked down.

"What the hell?" Remo said questioningly.

"Did you say something?"

"I said a bunch of idiots are acting pretty peculiar."

"The American way," said Chiun happily.

Remo did not answer.

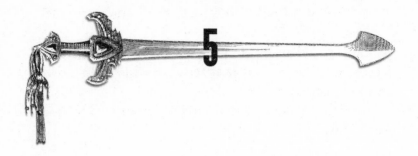

THE casino was like a large living room with anxious muffled sounds and subdued lighting. Remo arrived at 9 P.M. He had checked his watch forty-five minutes earlier and was checking to see how close he could come to approximating minutes. Forty-five minutes was perfect because it came to exactly three short times, the units of time upon which Remo had built his judgment.

He looked at the second hand of his watch when he entered the casino. He was fifteen seconds off. Which was good. Not up to Chiun, but still good.

Remo wore a dark double-breasted suit with a light blue shirt and dark blue tie. His shirt cuffs were double buttoned. He never wore cufflinks since extraneous metal hanging from his wrist by threads could never be controlled.

"Where are the smallest bets allowed?" Remo asked a tuxedoed Puerto Rican whose aplomb showed he worked there.

"Roulette," said the man, pointing to two tables along a wall, surrounded by a gaggle of people identical to the other gaggles of people surrounding other tables. Remo moved easily through the crowd, spotting a pickpocket at work, and casually grading his technique. His moves were too jerky; he was barely adequate.

His ears picked up an argument over the size of bets and he was fairly certain by its nature that Dr. Smith was in it.

"Minimum bet is one dollar sir," repeated the croupier.

"Now I purchased these twenty-five cent chips and you sold them to me, thus making a mutual contract. Your sale of a twenty-five cent chip commits you to allowing twenty-five cent bets."

"At times we do. But now we do not, sir. The minimum bet is one dollar."

"Outrageous. Let me speak to the manager."

There was a small whispered conference of the two casino men at the table.

Finally, one said, "If you wish, sir, you may cash in your chips now. Or, if you still insist, you may bet twenty-five cent chips."

"All right," said the bitter-faced man. "Go ahead."

"Are you going to make your wager now?"

"No," said the man, "I want to see first how the table is running."

"Yes, sir," said the croupier, called all bets and spun the wheel.

"Good evening, sir," said Remo, leaning over Dr. Smith and brushing his jacket ever so gently. "Losing?"

"No, I'm seventy-five cents ahead. Wouldn't you know that as soon as someone starts to score on them, they try to change the rules?"

"How long have you been here?"

"An hour."

"Oh." Remo pretended to take from his pocket the wad of bills he had just extracted from Dr. Smith's pocket. He glanced through it. There was more than two thousand dollars. Remo bought mounds and mounds of twenty-five dollar chips. Two thousand dollars worth. He blanketed the table with them.

"What are you doing?" demanded Dr. Smith.

"Betting," Remo said.

The ball bounced and spun and clinked to a hard stop. The

croupiers almost instantly began collecting chips and paying off bets. Remo almost broke even.

And again he spread out his money in bets. He did this five more times as he saw the controlled anger well in Dr. Smith. Since Remo was obviously a lunatic, the croupiers did not enforce the house limit of $25 a number on him. So on the sixth roll, Remo had $100 on number 23 when it came out, and he collected $3,500 on the bet.

He cashed in his chips and left with Dr. Smith behind him. They entered the hotel's night club where the noise would be loud and where, if they sat up front and faced the noise, they could talk without being overhead. Talking into noise provided an excellent sound seal.

When they were seated, to all eyes apparently watching the bouncing breasts bathed in neon and incredible metallic costumes, Dr. Smith said:

"You gave that man a one-hundred-dollar tip. A one-hundred-dollar tip. Whose money did you think you were betting?"

"Oh," Remo said, "I damn near forgot." He took the roll of bills from his pocket, and counted off $2,000. "It was your money," he said. "Here."

Smith patted his pocket, felt it empty, and took the money without further comment. He changed the subject.

"You're probably wondering why I am meeting you directly, without setting breaks in the chain."

Remo had been wondering just that. His original go was to be an advertisement in the morning paper, whereupon he would catch a flight to Kennedy Airport—the first after 6 o'clock in the morning. He would then go to the men's room nearest the Pan Am counter, wait till it was empty and then say something to himself about flowers and sunshine.

A wallet would be handed out from one of the toilet stalls. He would check the wallet to make sure the seal on it was still intact. If it wasn't, he would kill the man in the stall. But if the seal was not broken, he would exchange his current wallet, and leave without ever letting the man see his face. Then he would open the new wallet and not only get his new identity, but also the meeting place with Smith.

This was the first time Smith had ever contacted him directly.

"Yes, I was wondering."

"Well, we don't have time to discuss it. You will meet a Chinese woman at Dorval Airport in Montreal. Your cover will be that you are her bodyguard, assigned by the United States Secret Service. You will stay with her as she looks for a General Liu. You will help her find him, if you can. There are only six days left to do it. When General Liu is found, you will stay with him and protect his life also, until both of them return safely to China."

"And?"

"And what?"

"What is my assignment?"

"That is your assignment."

"But I'm not trained as a bodyguard. That's not my function."

"I know."

"But you were the one who stressed that I should only fulfill my function. If I wanted to do something else for the government, you suggested that I volunteer to help collect garbage. That's what you said."

"I know."

"Doctor Smith, this whole thing is stupid. Incompetent."

"In a way, yes."

"In what way, no?"

"In the small distance we are from having the beginning of peace. A lasting peace for mankind."

"That's no reason to switch my function."

"That's not your decision."

"It's one goddam beaut of a way to get me killed."

Smith ignored him. "And one more thing."

"What else?"

The trumpet blare ceased as a new act with soft music floated onto the stage in another aspect of undress. The two men at the table stared forward, silent, until the blaring resumed.

"You will take Chiun with you. That is why I am meeting you here. He is to function as your interpreter, since he speaks both the Cantonese and Mandarin dialects."

"Sorry, Dr. Smith, that busts it. No way. I can't take Chiun. Not on anything to do with the Chinese. He hates the Chinese almost as much as he hates the Japanese."

"He's still a professional. He's been a professional since childhood."

"He's also been a Korean from the village of Sinanju since childhood. I've never seen him hate before, not until this business of the Chinese Premier coming to the U.S. But I'm seeing it now, and I know he also taught me that competence decreases with anger." In Remo's vocabulary, incompetence was the vilest word. When your life depends on the correct move, the greatest sin is "incompetence."

"Look," Smith said, "Asians are always fighting among themselves."

"As opposed to who?"

"All right. But his family has taken Chinese contracts for ages."

"And he hates them."

"And he would still take their money."

"You're going to get me killed. You haven't succeeded yet. But you'll make it."

"Are you taking the assignment?"

Remo was silent for a moment as more young, well-formed breasts set over well-formed butts, topped by well-formed faces paraded out in some symmetrical dance step to the brassy blaring of the trumpets.

"Well?" said Smith.

They had taken the human body, the beautiful human body, and packaged it in tinsel and lights and noise and made the parading of it obscene. They had aimed at the exact bottom of human taste, and were right on target. Was this garbage what he was supposed to give his life for?

Or maybe it was freedom of speech? Was he supposed to stand up and salute for that? He didn't particularly want to listen to most of the things said anyway. Jerry Rubin, Abbie Hoffman, the Rev. McIntyre?

What was so valuable about freedom of speech? It just was not worth his life to let them mouth off. And the Constitution? That was just a bunch of rigamarole that he had never quite trusted.

He was—and this was Remo's secret—willing to live for CURE but not to die for it. Dying was stupid. That's why they gave people uniforms to do it in and played music. You never had to march people into a bedroom or to a fine dinner.

That was why the Irish had such great fighting songs and great singers. Like, what was his name, the singer with the too loud amplifiers in that club on Third Avenue, Brian Anthony. He could make you want to march with his songs. Which is why, as any intelligence man knew, the IRA couldn't compare to the Mau Mau or any other terrorist group, let alone the Viet Cong. The Irish saw the nobility in dying. So they died.

Brian Anthony and his big happy voice and here Remo was listening to this blare when his heart could be soaring with the boys in green. That was what dying was good for. Singing about, and nothing else.

"Well?" said Smith again.

"Chiun's out," said Remo.

"But you need an interpreter."

"Get another."

"He's already been cleared. The Chinese intelligence people have his description and yours as Secret Service men."

"Great. You really take precautions, don't you?"

"Well? Will you take this assignment?"

"Aren't you going to tell me that I can refuse and no one will think any the worse of me?"

"Don't be absurd."

Remo saw a couple from Seneca Falls, New York, that he had seen before with their children. This was their night of sin, their two weeks of living placed gem-like in the 11 1/2 month setting of their lives. Or was it really the other way around, the two weeks only reinforcing their real enjoyment? What difference did it make? They could have children, they could have a home, and for Remo Williams there would never be children or a home, because too much time and money and risk had gone into producing him. And then he realized that this was the first time Smith had ever asked—asked instead of ordered—him to take an assignment. And for Smith to do that, the assignment meant something, perhaps to those people from Seneca Falls. Perhaps to their children yet to be born.

"Okay," said Remo.

"Good," said Dr. Smith. "You don't know how close this nation is to peace."

Remo smiled. It was a sad smile, a smile of oh-world-you-put-me-in-the-electric-chair.

"Did I say something funny?"

"Yes. World peace."

"You think world peace is funny?"

"I think world peace is impossible. I think you're funny. I think I'm funny. Come now. I'll take you to your flight."

"Why?" asked Smith.

"So you get back alive. You've just been set up for a kill, sweetheart."

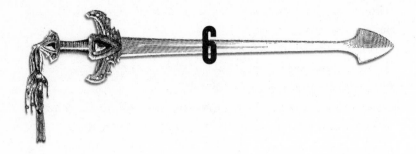

HOW do you know I've been set up?" Smith asked as their taxi sped down the multi-laned highway to San Juan Airport.

"How're the kids?"

"The kids? What do . . . ? Oh."

Remo could see the driver's neck tense. He kept whistling the same dull tune he had begun as soon as they had left the Nacional. He undoubtedly thought the whistling would show he was relaxed and carefree and not at all part of the set-up Remo had seen form, first in the casino, and then in the nightclub. They had all telegraphed, just as the driver was telegraphing now. With them, it had been never letting their eyes settle on Remo or Smith, while continuing to move as though Remo and Smith were at one of the loci of an ellipse. It was a feel Chiun had taught Remo's senses. Remo practiced in department stores by picking up objects and holding them, until he sensed that feel from a manager or a sales clerk. The difficult part wasn't really sensing when you were the object of scrutiny. It was knowing when you were not.

The driver whistled away in his classic telegraph. The same tune with the same pitch over and over. He had dislocated his thoughts from the sound; it was the only way he could reproduce the same sound over and over. His neck was red with dark potholes like tiny moon craters, filled with perspiration and grime. His hair was heavily greased and combed back in rigid black sticks that looked like the framework of a germ nursery.

The new aluminum highway lights cut through the humidity like underwater flashlights. It was the Caribbean and it was a wonder that the poured concrete foundations of the large American hotels did not go moldy along with the will of the people.

"We'll wait," Dr. Smith said.

"No, that's all right," Remo said. "The car's safe."

"But I thought. . . ." said Smith, glancing at the driver.

"He's all right," Remo said. "He's a dead man."

"I still feel uncomfortable. What if you should miss? Well, all right. We are compromised now. The fact that I am followed shows we are known. I'm not sure how much these people know, but I do not believe it is everything. If you understand."

The driver's head had begun to twitch, but he said nothing, intimating that he was not listening to the conversation behind him. His hand reached slowly toward the microphone of the two-way radio Remo had spotted on entering the taxi. He had been sure it was off.

Remo leaned forward over the seat. "Please don't do that," he said sweetly, "or I'll have to tear your arm out of its socket."

"Wha?" said the cab driver. "You crazy or something. I gotta phone in to the dispatcher."

"Just make the turnoff to the side road without telling anyone. Your friends will follow you."

"Hey, listen, Mister. I don't want trouble. But if you want it, you can have it."

His black eyes darted to the mirror, then back to the road. Remo smiled into the mirror and saw the man ease his right hand away from the radio to his belt. A weapon.

It was the new sort of taxi now being introduced into New York City with a bullet proof glass slide that the driver can move into place by pressing a button near his door. The doors locked from the front, and only a little microphone and a money slot connected the driver and his passengers.

Remo saw the driver's knee move and touch the hidden switch. The bullet proof shield slid quickly up into place. The locks clicked on the rear doors.

The bullet proof window had one flaw. It ran inside a metal track.

"I can't hear you too well," Remo said, and with his fingers peeled off the aluminum track from the body of the cab. The window dropped and Remo carefully set it at Smith's feet.

Remo leaned forward again. "Look, fella," he asked "can you drive with just your left hand?"

"Yeah," said the driver. "See?" And with his right hand he brandished a snub-nosed .38 caliber pistol.

Smith appeared mildly interested.

"That's nice," said Remo, as he grasped the driver's shoulder in his right hand, insinuating his thumb into the mass of bunched muscle and nerve. The driver lost control of his arm, then his hand, then his fingers, and they opened, dropping the gun quietly onto the rubber-matted floor.

"That's right," Remo said, as if talking to a baby. "Now just turn off where you're supposed to turn off so the cars behind can ambush us."

"Uhh," the driver moaned.

"Listen," Remo said. "If they get us, you live. A deal?"

"Uhh," responded the driver through clenched teeth.

"Yes, I thought you'd feel that way." He squeezed the driver's shoulder again, evoking a shriek of pain. Smith looked upset; he did not like these activities except on written reports. "This is the deal," Remo told the driver "You stop where your friends want you to stop. And if we die you live. Okay?"

He lightened the pressure on the shoulder and the driver said "Right. You got a deal, gringo."

"Are you sure that's wise?" Smith asked.

"Why kill someone you don't have to?"

"But he's the enemy. Perhaps we should just dispose of him, grab the car and run?"

"You want me to get out now and let you handle it?"

"No," said Dr. Smith.

"Then if you would, sir, shut up."

Just before a green sign directing them to the airport, the driver turned right onto what appeared to be a long black unlit road, penetrating a misty green swamp. He drove for a mile, then turned off onto a dirt road underneath hanging trees. It was a dark green misty night.

He stopped the engine. "This is where you die, gringo."

"It's where one of us dies, companero," Remo said. Remo liked him, but not so much that he didn't knock him out by releasing his shoulder, leaning forward, and driving a hard index finger into his solar plexus. Okay, Remo thought. Good for at least two minutes.

Two sedans began to pull up behind them, parking ten feet behind the cab, side by side.

Remo could see their onrushing headlights in the mirror and then they stopped. He pressed Smith's head down roughly. "Stay on the floor," he growled. "Don't try to help."

He slid out of the right hand door. Four men poured out of each car, one group approaching the back of the cab from the left, the other from the right. Remo stood behind the cab, between the lines of the eight men, his hands resting behind him on the cab's trunk.

"You're all under arrest," he said. The eight stopped.

"What's the charge?" one of them answered, in precise English.

In the light of the headlamps, Remo could see he was a tall heavy man with a bony face, wearing a snap brim hat. His answer marked him as the group's leader. That was what Remo wanted to know. He had use for him.

The man repeated, "What's the charge?"

"Reckless dying," Remo said. He leaned his weight back onto his hands, then with a push of his arms and a leap his lower body flashed through the air. The polished tip of his right shoe crashed into the Adam's apple of the first man on his right. His feet hit the ground, his hands still on the trunk of the cab, and without stopping, he spun about on the trunk of the car and repeated the action, flashing out with his left foot at the man closest to him on the left. This shoe too was christened in the Adam's apple. The action had occurred so quickly that both men fell simultaneously, their throats crushed, death on its way.

Remo moved off the trunk of the cab in between the three-man rows, and the six men charged. One fired a shot, but Remo made it miss, and it landed in the stomach of a man charging from the other side. He teetered, then fell heavily.

The remaining men moved together in a kaleidoscope of arms and legs and bodies, flailing, reaching out for Remo. They dropped their weapons in the close quarters, hoping to use their hands. But their hands captured only air, and Remo moved through them, in the classic patterns 1500 years old, as if travelling through a different dimension of space and time. Their hands closed on air. Their lunges enveloped each other. None touched Remo and he spun through them, performing the ancient secrets of aiki, the escape art, but aiki made deadly through performance by a killing machine.

He fractured a skull here, perforated a kidney there, with an elbow crazed a temple into shattered jaggers of bone.

Six were down and done. Two were left, including the leader. Remo moved directly now and faster because if they regained their composure, they would know he was a clear target for their bullets. Pulling his blows, he knocked out the two remaining men with hiraken blows to the side of the head.

He propped the two living men against the back of the cab and called "Doctor Smith."

Smith's head appeared in the rear glass of the cab, then he climbed out through the door Remo had left open.

"Look around," Remo said. "Recognize anyone?"

Smith looked at the two men that Remo had propped up against the trunk of the cab. He shook his head. Then he walked around, through the glare of the two cars' headlights, turning over men's bodies with a toe, bending closer sometimes to see a face. He walked back to Remo.

"I never saw any of them," he said.

Remo reached up and touched his thumbs to the temples of the two men, and gave a rotating squeeze. Both groaned their way into consciousness.

He allowed the leader to be aware of the man on his left. Then Remo leaped into the air, and came down full force with a steely elbow on the top of the man's skull. Just as quickly, Remo brought out gray bloodish matter in his hand.

"You want to go like this?"

"No," said the leader.

"Okay. Who sent you?"

"I don't know. It was just a contract from the States."

"Good night," said Remo and sent the man on his eternal way by driving a knee into the man's right kidney.

He and Smith walked to the front of the cab. The driver moaned.

"Can we let him live?" Smith asked.

"Only if we hire him."

"I can't do that," said Smith.

"Then I've got to kill him."

"I knew these things had to be done, but . . ."

"You wipe me out, sweetheart. What do you think those numbers I phone in mean?"

"I know. But they were numbers."

"They were never numbers."

"All right. Do what you must do. World peace."

"It's always so easy to say," said Remo. He looked into the driver's black eyes. "I'm sorry, companero."

The man's addled mind began to sort the fact of the gringo still alive, and he said: "You deserve to live, gringo. You deserve."

"Good night, companero," Remo said softly.

"Good night, gringo. Perhaps another time over a drink."

"To another time, my friend." And Remo saluted the driver with death.

"Are you sure he's dead?" Smith asked.

"Up yours," Remo said, and pushed the driver's body out of the car and got behind the wheel. "Get in," he said roughly.

"You don't have to be rude."

Remo started the car and backed over a few bodies in steering around the two parked cars, back onto the black road. He picked up speed and turned onto the road to the airport. He did not drive as other men did, either too quickly or puttering slowly along. He maintained a computer-even pace on springs he did not trust and with an engine in whose power he had little faith.

The car smelled of death. Not decayed death but a smell Remo had learned to recognize. Human fear. He did not know if it had come from the driver, or if it came now from Smith who sat quietly in the rear seat.

When he pulled up to the airport, Smith said, "It's a business that makes you sick sometimes."

"They would have done the same to us. What makes you sick is that we live on others' deaths. I'll see you again, or I won't," Remo said.

"Good luck," said Smith. "I think we're starting without the element of surprise."

"Whatever would make you believe that?" Remo asked, and laughed out loud as Smith took his luggage and departed.

Then Remo drove back to the Nacional.

He would still have to face Chiun. And it might have been easier for him to die on the side road.

But again, as the little father had told him: "It is always easier to die. Living takes courage."

Did Remo have the courage to tell Chiun that he would be instrumental in bringing about peace with China?

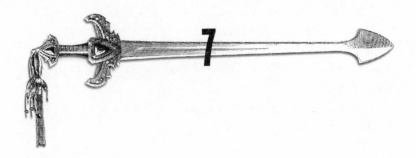

SHE was a very little girl in a very big gray coat from which her delicate hands poked out, lost in the immensity of the cuffs. The two hands clutched a little red book.

She wore big rimmed round eyeglasses that reinforced her oval eggshell face and made it appear even more frail and more loveable. Her black hair was neatly combed back and parted in the center.

She appeared no older than 13 and was definitely airsick and probably frightened. She sat in the front of the BOAC jet, not moving, determinedly looking forward.

Remo and Chiun had arrived at Dorval Airport in Montreal less than a half hour earlier. Chiun had gone onto the jet first, hiding behind a business suit and a gold badge of identification. As soon as they had brushed past the stewardess, Chiun pointed to the sick little girl and said:

"That's her. That's the beast. You can smell them."

He went to the girl and said something in what Remo assumed was Chinese. The girl nodded and answered. Then Chiun said something that was obviously a curse, and showed his identification to the girl.

"She wishes to see yours also, this little harlot of the pigsty. Perhaps to steal it. All her people are thieves, you know."

Remo showed his identification and smiled. She looked at the picture on his ID, and then at Remo.

"One can never be too careful," she said, in excellent English. "Would you please show me to the room for women? I am rather ill. But I shall overcome it. Just as I overcome the rudeness and reactionary vilification of your running dog."

"Dung of dung," answered Chuin. His hazel eye blazed hate.

The girl managed to lift herself up and Remo helped her down the gangway steps as she struggled under the coat. Chiun followed uncomfortably. He wore black American shoes and his beard had been shaved close. He had shocked Remo back at the Nacional in San Juan when Remo had first posed the question. But Remo should have known that by now he should not be shocked by Chiun.

"I can read English also," said the girl. "To destroy imperialism, one must know its language."

"Good thinking," Remo said.

"You may be an iron tiger in the short run, but you are a paper tiger in the long run. The people are the iron tiger in the long run."

"Can't argue with that," Remo said. "That's the ladies' room," he said, pointing to a sign she had missed on her march from the gangway.

"Thank you," she said and handed him the little red book. "Treasure this with your life."

"Sure thing," Remo said, taking the plastic bound book. Then she spun as if on parade and, still entrapped in the large gray coat, marched into the ladies' room. Remo could have sworn he saw her take toilet paper from her pocket before she entered.

"You are already reading the propaganda of that little wanton seducer," said Chiun, looking triumphantly and at the same time disdainfully at the book.

"She's just a kid, Chiun."

"Tiger cubs can kill. Children are the most vicious."

Remo shrugged. He was still grateful that Chiun had come. And still surprised. After all, there was the San Francisco incident.

They had been bringing Remo's mind and body along slowly after an overpeak that almost became a burnout, when the President announced the impending visit by China's Premier.

Chiun was already disturbed because the Wonderful World of Disney had been preempted for the President. Remo was working on his deep breathing, looking out at the Golden Gate Bridge, trying to see himself running across its suspension bands and breathing accordingly.

Chiun had worked Remo back into shape very well and very quickly, which was not surprising since he had devoted his life to that sort of thing, starting his own training at 18 months. When he had begun training Remo, he had informed him that he was 26 years too late to do anything serious but he would do the best he could.

Mentally, Remo was going down the far side of the Golden Gate bridge, when he heard a shriek.

He quickly floated into the living room. Chiun was making hostile, oriental sounds at the television set from which the President spoke in his usual dull and precise manner, always appearing more sincere when he abstained from trying to show warmth or joy.

"Thank you and good night," said the President, but Chiun would not let the image escape, and he fractured the picture tube with a kick of his foot, the main tube imploding on itself before showering the room with splinters.

"What did you do that for?"

"You fool," said Chiun, his wispy beard quivering. "You pale-faced fool. You imbecile. And your president. White is the color of sickness and you are sick. Sick. All of you."

"What happened?"

"Stupid happened. Stupid happened. You are stupid."

"What did I do?"

"You did not have to do anything. You are white. That is deed enough."

And Chiun returned to the console to smash the wood top of the set with his left hand, and with his right hand caved in the right side, leaving the left corner of the cabinet rising like a steeple. For that, he smashed his elbow down, shattering it into splinters.

He stood in front of the split wiring and wood and shards of glass and triumphantly spit down upon it.

"China's Premier is visiting your country," he said, and spit again.

"Chiun. Where is your sense of balance?"

"Where is your country's sense of honor?"

"You mean you're for Chiang Kai Shek?"

Chiun spit again at the remains of the television set. "Chiang and Mao are two brothers. They are Chinese. You cannot trust the Chinese. No man should trust Chinese who wishes to keep pants and shirt. The fool."

"You have something against the Chinese?"

Calmly Chiun opened his hand and looked at his fingers. "My, you are perceptive tonight. My training has done well by you. You perceive even the faintest vibration. You soar to ultimate understanding."

"Okay, Chiun. Okay. Okay."

But it was not okay.

The next night, while passing the third Chinese restaurant, Chiun spat for the third time.

"Chiun, will you cut that out?" Remo whispered, and for a reply, drew a deft elbow in the solar plexus that might have sent an ordinary man to a hospital. Remo let out a grunt. His pain seemed to make Chiun feel better because Chiun began humming as he shuffled along, waiting for the next Chinese restaurant to spit at.

Then it happened.

They were big, perhaps the biggest bulk of men Remo had ever seen up close. Their shoulders were at the tip of his head, and they stretched broad and wide, their bodies came down straight and sturdy like three large cigarette machines. Their shopping bag size heads were connected to their shoulders by what medically would be called necks, but more accurately were only swollen growths of muscle tissue.

They wore blue blazers with Los Angeles Bisons patches on them. There was one crew cut, a greasy longish job, and an Afro. They must have weighed nearly a half ton.

They stood there in front of the glass window of the furniture store singing in harmony. Training camp had obviously ended and they were out for a night on the town. When in good and joyous faith, made more joyous by booze, they accosted a wizened old Oriental, none of them had intended at the time to end his professional football career.

"Hail, brother of the third world," sang out the giant with the Afro.

Chiun stopped, his delicate hands resting, clasped before him. He looked at the black man and said nothing.

"I hail the President's decision to welcome your premier, a great leader of the third world. The Chinaman and the black man are brothers."

Thus ended the wonderful career of defensive tackle Bad Boulder Jones. The newspapers the next day said that in all probability he would be able to walk again within a year. His two companions were suspended for a game and fined $500 each.

They both insisted to the police and to the press that a little old Chinaman had picked up Bad Boulder and thrown him at them.

Coach Harrahan, according to the press, said that he was not really a strict coach, but this sort of heavy drinking was ruinous to a team. "It has already permanently injured one of the great defensive tackles in football history. It is a tragedy, compounded by an obvious lie."

While the coach was sorting his problems, Remo was sorting his own. He was getting Chiun the hell out of San Francisco and on to San Juan, where one night he was forced to ask a favor he thought Chiun would never grant.

Chiun was resting in his suite where he was listed as Mr. Parks and Remo as his manservant. Smith had just gotten off to a safe return to headquarters. The only way to ask it was to ask it.

Remo asked it.

"Chiun. We must guard the life of a Chinese person, and attempt to save the life of another."

Chiun nodded.

"You will do it?"

"Yes, of course. Why not?"

"Well, I know how you feel about Chinese, that's all."

"Feel? What is there to feel for vermin? If our lords who pay our sustenance wish us to watch and protect cockroaches, then we do just that."

Chiun smiled. "Just one thing," he said.

"What is that?" Remo asked.

"If we are supposed to get any money from the Chinese, get the money first. Before you do anything. Just the other day, they hired some people from my village and had them do most dangerous tasks. They not only did not pay them, they attempted to dispose of them."

"I didn't know the Chinese Communists hired the people of your village."

"Not the Communists. The emperor Chu Ti."

"Chu Ti? The one who built the forbidden city?"

"The same."

"What do you mean, the other day? That was five hundred years ago."

"A day in the memory of a Korean. Just be sure we get paid first."

"We will." Remo was again surprised when Chiun willingly agreed to trim his beard for the assignment.

"When you deal with vermin, it makes no difference how you look," Chiun had said.

And now they waited outside the ladies' room at Dorval Airport. The late September rain played on the windows and had cut chillingly through their light summer suits. They would have to purchase fall clothes as soon as possible.

"She is probably robbing the washroom of soap and towels and toilet tissue," said Chiun, smiling.

"She's been in there ten minutes. Maybe I'd better check," Remo said.

So taking out his Special Services badge which came with the identities Remo and Chiun had been given by Smith, Remo stormed into the ladies' room, announcing "Health inspector, ladies. Be just a minute." And since the tone was correct and officially distant, no one had protested but left quickly.

All but her. She was piling up paper towelling and stuffing it in her greatcoat.

"What are you doing?" Remo asked.

"There may be no towels or paper in your country. There is plenty here. Plenty. Paper in every stall."

"There's paper all over the United States in every stall."

"In every stall?"

"Well, except when someone forgets to fill them up."

"Aha. Then we take a little. I brought some with me from Peking."

"Toilet paper?"

"Preparedness for a task is the doing of the task. He who does not prepare a task by looking at it from many sides is destined to stumble on one side. Be prepared."

"You a girl scout?"

"No. The thoughts of Mao. Where is the book?" She looked at him anxiously.

"It's outside with my partner."

"Have you read it yet?"

"I've only had it ten minutes."

"Ten minutes can be two most valuable thoughts of Chairman Mao. It could liberate you from your imperialistic, exploitative ways. And also your running dog."

Remo grabbed the young girl firmly but gently by both shoulders.

"Look, kid," he said. "I don't care what names you use for me. If it gives you kicks, all right. But watch what you call Chiun. 'Running dog' and 'imperialist lackey' are not fitting words for a man three or four times your age."

"If the old is reactionary and decadent, it must be buried, along with all the other anachronisms afflicting mankind today."

"He's a friend of mine," Remo said. "I don't want him hurt."

"Your only friends are the party and your worker solidarity."

The young girl said that, waiting for approval. She did not expect two sharp stinging pains under her armpits. Remo kept his thumbs working, rotating, pressing the flesh up into the joint.

Her delicate almond eyes went almost round with pain. Her mouth opened to scream and Remo switched one hand to her mouth.

"Listen kid and listen close. I do not want you insulting that man outside. He deserves your respect. If you are unable to give that, at least you may avoid disrespect. I would suggest that he knows more about the world than you and if you would just shut up for a moment, you might learn something from him.

"But whether you do or not is no concern of mine. What concerns me is your lack of manners, and if you mouth off just one more time, kid, I'm going to grind your shoulders into mush."

Remo pressed his right thumb in even deeper and felt her body tighten even more. Her face contorted with pain.

"Now we have had our little dialogue," Remo said, "and we have formed our revolutionary consensus. Correct?"

He released the hand from her mouth. She nodded and gasped.

"Correct," she said. "I will show the old man respect. I will take one step backward, so that I may take two steps forward at a later date. I am allowed to speak the truth to you, however? Without fear of aggression?"

"Sure, kid."

"You are a shithead, Remo whatever-your-name-is."

She had begun to rebutton her greatcoat, using maximum energy on each large button. She had obviously remembered his name from the identity cards Remo and Chiun had flashed.

"Not an imperialistic, oppressive, reactionary, fascistic shithead?"

"A shithead is a shithead."

"All right, Miss Liu."

"My name is Mrs. Liu."

"You're married to the general's son?"

"I am married to General Liu and I am looking for my husband."

Remo remembered the small picture from briefing. General Liu's face was hard and weatherbeaten, with strong lines cut in the bitterness of many long marches. He was sixty-two years old.

"But you're a kid."

"I am not a kid, damn you. I am twenty-two and I have the revolutionary consciousness of someone three times my age."

"You have the body of a kid."

"That's all you decadent westerners would think about."

"General Liu didn't marry you for your revolutionary consciousness."

"Yes, he did, as a matter of fact. But you wouldn't understand that." She buttoned the top button with defiance.

"Okay, let's go. Look, I can't call you Mrs. Liu for obvious reasons. You can't travel under that name either. It's already been proved we've got a system like a sieve. What do I call you?"

"Lotus Blossom, shithead," she said with ringing sarcasm.

"Okay, don't be funny," said Remo, holding open the door of the ladies' room and receiving stunned stares from passersby.

"Mei Soong," she said.

Chiun was waiting with his hands behind his back. He was smiling sweetly.

"The book," said Mei Soong.

"You treasure the book?"

"It is my most valued possession."

Chiun's smile reached for the outer limits of joy and he brought his hands before him, containing paper shreds and red plastic shreds, the remnants of the book.

"Lies. They are lies," he said. "Chinese lies."

Mei Soong was stunned.

"My book," she said softly. "The thoughts of Chairman Mao."

"Why did you do that, Chiun? I mean, really Chiun. That's really rotten. I mean there was no reason to do that to this little girl's book."

"Ha, ha, ha," said Chiun, gleefully and threw the pieces into the air, raining the thoughts of Mao in very small pieces over the entrance to the ladies' room of Dorval Airport.

Mei Soong's soft lips began to crinkle and her eyes moistened. And Chiun laughed the louder.

"Look, Mei Soong, I'll get you another little red book. We have loads of them in our country."

"That one was given to me by my husband at our wedding."

"Well, we'll find him and we'll get you another one. Okay? We'll get you a dozen. In English, Russian, French and Chinese."

"There are none in Russian."

"Well, whatever. Okay?"

Her eyes narrowed. She stared at the laughing Chiun and said something softly in Chinese. Chiun laughed even more. Then he said something in return in the same language. And Mei Soong smiled triumphantly and answered. Each response, back and forth, became louder and louder until Chiun and Mrs. Liu sounded like a tong war in a tin kettle.

They raved on that way at each other, the elderly man and the young woman, as they departed the gates of Dorval Airport with ticket clerks, passengers, baggage men, everyone turning to stare at the two shriekers. Remo desperately wished he could just run away, and trailed behind pretending he did not know the two.

Above was a balcony packed three deep with people staring down at the trio. It was as if they had box seats to a performance.

And Remo, in despair, yelled up at them:

"We'll go to any lengths for secrecy."

DR. Harold W. Smith read the reports that came in hourly. If he had gone home to sleep, they would be stacked a foot high in the small safe that was built into the left side of his desk. If he stayed in his office at the Folcroft Sanitarium overlooking Long Island Sound from the Westchester shore, they would be brought into his office and quietly placed in front of him by an assistant.

That assistant believed he worked on a scientific program so hush-hush that it did not have a name. Smith's personal secretary was under the impression she worked for the Federal Bureau of Investigation on a special undercover team.

Of the 343 employees at Folcroft Sanitarium, the majority believed they worked for a sanitarium, although there were very few patients. A large portion of the employees were certain they knew. Because of computer banks underground, they were certain they worked for an international scientific-marketing firm.

One employee, an ambitious young genius, had attempted to crack the computer's program for his own personal use. He reasoned that if he could gain access to the secrets of the giant computer bank, then he could use this information to make a fortune in the market, or in international currency. After all, why such secrecy unless the secrets were worth fortunes?

Being a bright fellow, he realized the secrets must be worth fortunes because, on just a rough estimate, it cost Folcroft $250,000 a week to operate.

So in little steps he began to make contact with other facets of the computer operations, in addition to the section in which he quite legitimately worked.

And within a year he began to see a picture emerging—of hundreds of employees gathering information, of profiles of criminal networks, espionage, business swindles, subversion, corruption. A computer portrait of illegal America.

It definitely was not marketing, although his small computer function had led him to believe that since it dealt with the New York Stock Exchange.

It puzzled him. It puzzled him all the way to his new assignment in Utah. Then one night, it struck him exactly what Folcroft was about. It struck him approximately 24 hours before he met a man in Salt Lake City. A man whose name was Remo.

For a day, he was the third employee of CURE who knew for whom he worked and why. And then he was intertwined with the shock absorbers at the bottom of an elevator shaft, and only two employees, Dr. Smith and a man named Remo, knew for whom they worked and why. Which was the way it was supposed to be.

Now the hourly reports were showing that perhaps the danger of exposure was imminent again, something that Smith had dreaded since the early formation of CURE years before.

He had dozed at his desk the night before, and awoke with the first salmon shimmers in the cold gray dawn, crowning the darkness of Long Island Sound. His oneway window to the Sound collected early morning dew around the edges although he had been assured that the thermal windows would not do such a thing.

His assistant had just quietly deposited another report in front of him when Smith opened his eyes.

"Bring me my electric razor and my toothbrush, please," he said.

"Certainly," said the assistant. "That special clearing section is working very smoothly, sir. I must say this is the first information clearing center to work so smoothly while not knowing what it was doing."

"The razor, please," Smith said. He turned the bundles of reports in front of him over, and began to look through them chronologically. The reports were apparently unrelated documents, which was as it should be. Only one person should be able to put the pieces together.

A salesman for a car company in Puerto Rico reported on the love life of the owner of a cab company. An accountant, believing he was being bribed by the Internal Revenue Service, made note of a sudden large deposit of money by the owner of the cab company.

A doorman, where a young woman kept her pet poodle, told a newspaper reporter who had paid for the poodle.

A flight from Albania to Leipzig, then Paris. Large amounts of money coming out of Eastern Europe in small bills. An according upgrading of CIA activities, in case the money was payment for increased espionage.

But the money came in through Puerto Rico. And the taxicab company. And Smith remembered the bodies strewn out behind the cab on the lonely side road near the airport.

And then disturbing reports.

The Chinese girl arriving at Dorval Airport. Met by an elderly Korean and a bodyguard. The bodyguard, six feet tall, brown eyes, well-tanned complexion, medium build.

And there it was. The photograph. Of Remo Williams walking behind Chiun and the girl.

And if he could be photographed by the Pelnor Investigative

Service which believed it serviced an industrial account in Rye, New York, who else could make solid contact with the trio and the only other employee of CURE who knew for whom he worked?

That photograph alone was like sighting a gun, not only at Remo Williams' head but at CURE itself.

To be known. To be exposed. The armor of secrecy peeled off. And the fact that the United States government itself could not function within its own laws, laid bare.

If the Pelnor Investigative Service could so easily spot the trio, who else?

There it was, the two Orientals obviously yelling at each other, and the man who had been publicly executed years before. A neat picture obviously shot with a not-very-long tele-photo lens.

The face of Remo Williams had been changed by plastic sur-gery, the cheekbones, nose and hairline altered. But to see their ul-timate weapon, The Destroyer, in a common photograph made by simple private detectives made Smith's already queasy stomach turn sour in anticipation of coming doom.

CURE would be disbanded before being exposed. Only the two men would know, as they had known before, and they would not know for long. Smith had prepared the destruct mechanism the day he returned from his meeting with the President.

He had his pill. He would phone his wife and tell her he was off on business. In a month, a man from the C.I.A. would tell Mrs. Smith her husband had been lost on an assignment in Eu-rope. She would believe it because she still believed that he worked for the C.I.A.

Smith dropped the photograph into the shredder basket be-hind him. The basket whirred and Remo Williams' picture dis-appeared.

He spun his chair around and peered out at the Sound and the lapping waves breaking over the rocks in small rhythmic currents, dictated by moon and wind and tide.

The water was there before CURE. It would be there after CURE. It had been there when Athens was a democracy, when Rome was a republic, and when China stood at the center of world civilization, known for its justice and wisdom and serenity.

They had fallen and the water continued. And when CURE was gone, there would still be the water.

Smith would do several small things when he put CURE into destruct. He would make the phone call to payroll which would reassign approximately half the people back to the agencies they thought they worked for anyway, turn Folcroft back into a real sanitarium, and dismiss with recommendations the remainder.

When this large scale dismissal was processed through the computer, it would set off in one day a raging fire within the computer complex destroying the tapes and the equipment.

Smith would not witness the fire. He would have, 24 hours earlier, left a memo ordering shipment of a box in the basement to the Maher Funeral Home in Parsippany, New Jersey. He would not see the memo executed either.

He would have gone downstairs, to the corner of the paint room, where the box stood in the corner, slightly taller and wider than the average man. He would remove the light aluminum lid, lie down in the tight white foam rubber, approximately hollowed for his figure, and pull the lid back down over himself. From the inside, he would snap shut four locks that fastened the lid and made it airtight.

He would need no air. Because when the last lock was closed, he would swallow the pill and go to sleep forever along with the organization he had helped design to save a nation incapable of saving itself.

What of Remo Williams? He would die soon after if the plan worked. And it was the only plan that could work. For when Smith had put the destruct plan on "prepare," Remo's executioner was already at Remo's side. He had been assigned to accompany him.

Smith would receive the daily phone contact from Remo through a Detroit dial-a-prayer, and would tell Remo to send Chiun back to Folcroft immediately.

And when Remo told this to Chiun, Chiun would fulfill his contract of death, as Koreans had been fulfilling contracts for centuries.

And Remo and Smith would carry with them to their graves the awesome secret of CURE. And when the only other person who even knew of its existence called from the White House, he would get that busy signal on the special line signifying that CURE was no more.

Chiun, who never knew for whom he worked except that it was the government, would probably return to Korea to live his few remaining years in peace.

The waves beat steadily on the shore.

The world was close to peace. What a fantastic dream. How many years of peace had the world known? Was there ever a time when man was not killing man, or when war upon relentless war was not being waged to adjust this border or to right that wrong, or even in its ultimate silliness, to protect a nation's honor?

The President had a dream. And Smith and Remo might have to die for it. So be it. It was worth dying for.

It would be nice to be able to tell Remo why he was going to die but Smith could not dare reveal how Remo would die. If one had an advantage against this most perfect killing machine, one kept it. To use when needed.

And then the special line from Remo rang.

Smith picked up the receiver. He suddenly felt a deep and disturbing affection for this wisecracking killer, the sort of attachment one makes in a foxhole one has shared with someone for . . . what was it now, eight years?

"Seven-four-four," said Smith.

"You're some piece of work," came Remo's voice. "You really gave me the business. You know the two of them are fighting?"

"I know."

"It's incredibly stupid to keep Chiun on this thing. He's popped his cork."

"You need someone who can translate."

"She speaks English."

"And what does she speak to a Chinese who might try to contact her?" Smith said.

"Okay. I'll try to live through it. We'll be leaving Boston later today."

"We're checking out that Puerto Rican group. We still don't know who sent them."

"Okay. We're going to start looking around."

"Be careful. That cab company has delivered a very fat little bundle of cash to the mainland. I think it's for you, $70,000."

"Is that all I'm worth? Even with the deflated dollar?"

"If that doesn't work, you'll probably be worth $100,000 soon."

"Hell, I'm worth that to a medicine show. Or a sports contract. How would that be if everything comes apart? A thirty-five-year old cornerback who retires at sixty? Chiun could play tackle. I bet he could. That would blow their minds. An eighty-year-old, ninety-pound tackle."

"Stop the foolishness."

"That's what I like about you, sweetheart. You're all joy."

"Goodbye," said Smith.

"Chiun. The ninety-pound Alex Karras."

Smith hung up and returned to the reports. They were all bad and getting worse. Perhaps his own fear of dying was now clouding his judgment. Perhaps CURE already had passed the point of compromise. Maybe he should have ordered Chiun back to Folcroft then and there.

From the safe on the left side of his desk, he withdrew a small air-sealed plastic bag. It held one pill. He put it in his vest and went back to the reports. Remo would contact again tomorrow.

The new reports were coming in again, this time with his razor. Remo's call line had been tapped and traced to Rye, New York. That information came from an assistant traffic manager of a telephone company in Boston.

Smith flicked the intercom to see if his secretary was in yet.

"Yes, Dr. Smith," came the voice over the intercom.

"Oh. Good morning. Please send a memo to the shipping department. We're almost certainly going to send an aluminum box of laboratory equipment to Parsippany, New Jersey, tomorrow. I'd like it routed through Pittsburgh and then flown in."

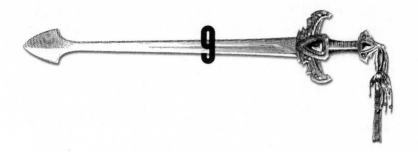

RICARDO deEstrana y Montaldo y Ruiz Guerner had told his visitor that $70,000 was not enough.

"Impossible," he said, strolling to his patio, his velvet slippered feet moving silently over the fieldstone. He walked to its edge and rested his breakfast champagne on the stone ledge separating him from his acres of rolling gardens that became forest, and beyond that, the Hudson River about to be enveloped in the glorious bright colors of fall.

"Just impossible," he said again, and breathed deeply the grape-scented breeze coming from his arbors nestling in the New York hills, good wine country because the vines must fight for survival among the rocks. How like life, that its quality was a reflection of its struggle. How true of his vineyards, which he personally supervised.

He was well into middle age, yet exercise and the good life left him remarkably trim and his continental manners and immaculate dress provided his bed with constant companionship. When he wanted. Which was always before and after, but never during the harvest.

Now, this grubby little woman with a purse full of money, obviously some sort of Communist affiliate, and more than likely just a messenger, wanted him to risk his life for $70,000.

"Impossible," he said for the third time and lifted the glass from the hard rock edge of his patio. He held it to the sun as a thank you and the tinted bubbling liquid glistened, as if honored to be chosen for an offering to the sun.

Ricardo deEstrana y Montaldo y Ruiz Guerner did not face his guest, to whom he did not offer champagne just as he had not offered her a seat. He had met her in his den, heard her proposition, and declined it. Yet she did not leave.

Now he heard her heavy shoes follow him, clomping out onto his patio.

"But $70,000 is more than twice what you get ordinarily."

"Madame," he said, his voice cold with contempt. "$70,000 is twice what I received in 1948. I have not been working since then."

"But this is an important assignment."

"For you perhaps. Not for me."

"Why won't you take it?"

"That is simply none of your concern, Madame."

"Have you lost your revolutionary fervor?"

"I have never had a revolutionary fervor."

"You must take this assignment."

He felt her breath behind him, the intense heat of a nervous sweaty woman. You could feel her presence in the pores of your skin. That was the curse of sensitivity, the sensitivity that made Ricardo deEstrana y Montaldo y Ruiz Guerner percisely Ricardo deEstrana y Montaldo y Ruiz Guerner. Once, at $35,000 a mission.

He sipped his champagne, allowing his mouth to surrender to its vibrancy. A good champagne, not a great one. And unfortunately, not even an interesting champagne although champagnes were notoriously uninteresting anyway. Dull. Like the woman.

"The masses have bled for the success which is imminent.

The victory of the proletariat over the oppressive, racist capitalist system. Now join us in victory or die in defeat."

"Oh, piffle. How old are you, Madame?"

"You mock my revolutionary ardor?"

"I am shocked at a grownup's addiction to it. Communism is
for people who never grow up. I take Disneyland more seriously."

"I cannot believe that you would say such a thing, you who
have fought the fascist beast."

He turned to examine the woman more closely. Her face was
lined with years of rage, her hair cast scraggly in many directions beneath a plain black hat that could use a cleaning. Her
eyes seemed tired and old. It was a face that had lived through a
lifetime of arguments about the absurdities of dialectical mate-
rialism and class consciousness, far from where human beings
lived their lives. She was about his age, he believed, yet appeared
old and worn as though beyond the reach of even a spark of life.

"Madame, I fought the fascist beast, and so, am qualified to
speak on it. It is identical to the communist beast. A beast is a
beast. And my revolutionary fervor died when I saw what was
supposed to replace the oppression of fascism. It was the oppression of such dullards as yourself. To me, Stalin, Hitler and
Mao Tse Tung are identical."

"You have changed, Ricardo."

"I should hope so, Madame. People do grow up, unless
stunted by some mass movement or other group sickness. I take
it you knew me before?"

"You do not remember me?" Her voice, for the first time,
wore some warmth.

"No, I do not."

"You do not remember the seige at Alcazar?"

"I remember that."

"You do not remember the battle at Teruel?"

"I remember that."

"And you do not remember me?"

"I do not."

"Maria Deloubier?"

The champagne glass shattered on the fieldstone terrace. Guerner's face paled.

"Maria," he gasped. "You?"

"Yes."

"Gentle, sweet Maria. No."

He looked at the haggard, cold face with the old eyes and he still could not see Maria, the young woman who believed and loved, who had reached out each morning for the sunshine as she reached out for a new world.

"Yes," said the old woman.

"Impossible," he said. "Time does not ravage like that, without leaving a trace."

"When you give your life to something, your life goes with it."

"No. Only if you give your life to something without life." Ricardo deEstrana y Montaldo y Ruiz Guerner gently placed his left hand on the woman's shoulder. He could feel the coarseness of the material, over the hardness of the bone.

"Come," he said. "We will eat. And we will talk."

"Will you do this thing for us, Ricardo? It is so important."

"We will talk, Maria. We have much to talk about."

Reluctantly, the woman agreed, and during the morning repast of fruit and wine and cheese, she answered questions about where she went after this cell collapsed, or that revolution succeeded, or this agitation failed or that one succeeded.

And Guerner discovered where Maria had fled, leaving only this passionless woman before him. Maria was the classic revolutionary, so involved with masses and power structures and political awareness that she forgot human beings. People became objects. Positive responses meant Communists, negative responses meant not Communist.

So it was easy for her to lump Nazis together with monarchists, democrats, republicans, capitalists. To her they were all alike. They were "them." He also found that she had never remained in a country where her revolutionary efforts were successful. Those who dream most of the promised land are the ones most afraid to cross its borders.

Maria had softened as she shared the wine. "And what of you, Ricardito?"

"I have my vines, my estate, my land."

"No man owns land."

"I own this land as much as any man owns anything. I have changed this land and these changes are mine. Its beauty is nature. Which I might add does very well without the help of a revolutionary committee."

"You no longer use your skill?"

"I use it in different ways. Now I create."

"When you left us, you worked for others also, no?"

"Sometimes."

"Against the revolution?"

"Of course."

"How could you?"

"Maria, I fought for the loyalists for the same reason many fought for the fascists. It was the only war around at the time."

"But you believed. I know you believed."

"I believed, my dear, because I was young. And then I grew up."

"I hope then that I never grow up."

"You have grown old without growing up."

"That is unkind. But I would expect that of someone who could pour a life into a hillside instead of giving it to mankind."

Guerner threw back his leonine head and laughed.

"Really. That is just too much. You ask me to kill a man for $70,000 and you call it serving mankind."

"It is. It is. They are a counter-revolutionary force that we have been unable to overcome."

"Does it not strike you as odd that they sent you to me with the money?"

"You once had a reputation."

"But why now?"

The woman cupped her harsh reddish hands around the goblet as she had done when she was young and soft and beautiful, when the wine was not that good.

"All right, Ricardito. We will follow your thinking because you are the only one capable of thinking. And everyone else, especially a committee, cannot match your wisdom."

"Your organization has many people who effectively eliminate others. True?"

"True."

"Then why after more than twenty years must they choose a mercenary? Do they think I would not speak if captured? Absurd. Or do they plan to kill me afterward? Why bother? They could get someone else, for much less than $70,000. Someone more politically reliable and less likely to need extermination. True?"

"True," said Maria, drinking more of the wine and feeling its warmth.

"They obviously chose me because they know they might not succeed with their own people. And how would they know this? Because they have tried before and failed. True?"

"True."

"How many times have they tried?"

"Once."

"And what happened?"

"We lost eight men."

"They seem to have forgotten my specialty is the assassination of one man. At the most, two."

"They are not forgetful."

"Why then do they expect me to attack a company?"

"They do not. It is a man. His name, as best as we can learn, is Remo."

"He killed eight men?"

"Yes."

"With what weapon? He must be very fast and select his range of fire brilliantly. And of course, he is accurate."

"He used his hands as near as we can tell."

Guerner put down his goblet. "His hands?"

"Yes."

He began to chuckle. "Maria, my dear. I would have done it for $35,000. He is perfect for my weapon. And easy."

Ricardo deEstrana y Montaldo y Ruiz Guerner threw back his head again and laughed. "With his hands," he said. "A toast to a man who is fool enough to use his hands." They toasted again but the woman took merely a formal sip.

"One more thing, Ricardo."

"Yes?"

"I must accompany you."

"Impossible."

"They wish to make sure that everything is done neatly. There is a Chinese girl who is not to be killed. Just the man and possibly his elderly companion."

She withdrew a picture from the purse she had kept on her arm all the while, even while eating.

"These are the men to die. The Caucasian definitely. And this girl is to live."

Guerner took the photograph between two fingers. It was obviously shot from above, with a telephoto lens. Because of the absence of depth of field and the obvious fluorescent lighting which would allow an f.4 opening, Guerner estimated the lens to be .200 millimeter.

The Oriental man was elderly, his wraithlike arms waving above him in gesture to the young girl. Behind him came the younger Occidental with the look of frustration. His eyes were deepset, his cheekbones slightly high, his lips thin and his nose strong but not large. Average build.

"The Oriental is not Korean?"

"No. She is Chinese."

"I mean the man."

"Let me see," said Maria, taking back the picture.

"I don't know," she said.

"No doubt they all look alike to you, my revolutionary friend."

"Why does it matter?"

"It would matter if he were a certain type of Korean. But that is doubtful. Keep the picture. I have it in my mind."

He whistled gently that afternoon as he removed a long tubular black leather case from the locked safe behind his family's coat of arms.

With a chamois cloth, he polished up the rich blackness of the leather, then folded the cloth and put it on the oak desk by the window. He placed the leather case beside the cloth. The afternoon sun made white flashes on the leather. Guerner placed a hand on either side of the case, and with a snap, it opened, revealing a Monte Carlo stock made of highly glossed walnut, and a black metal rifle barrel two feet long.

They rested on purple velvet, like machined jewels for the elegance of death.

"Hello, darling," whispered Guerner. "We work again. Do you wish to? Have you rested too long?"

He stroked the barrel with the tips of his right fingers.

"You are magnificent," he said. "You have never been readier."

"You still talk to your weapon?" Maria was laughing.

"Of course. Do you think a weapon is purely mechanical? Yes, you would. You think people are mechanical. But it is not. They are not."

"I only asked. It seemed . . . somehow . . . strange."

"It is stranger, my dear, that I have never missed. Never. Is that not strange?"

"It is training and skill."

Blood rushed to Guerner's aristocratic face, filling the cheeks like a child's coloring book.

"No," he said angrily. "It is feeling. One must feel his weapon and his bullet and his target. He must feel it is correct to shoot. And then the path of the bullet is correct. Those who miss do not feel their shots, do not carefully insert them into their target. I do not miss, because I feel my shots into my victim. Nothing else is important. The wind, the light, the distance. All are meaningless. You would more easily miss picking your cigarette up from the ashtray than I would miss my target."

Guerner then began his ritual, leaving the weapon unassembled in the case. He sat at the desk and rang for his butler by pulling a cloth cord that hung from the high beamed ceiling.

He hummed softly as he waited, not looking at Maria. She could never understand. She could not feel. And not feeling, she could not learn how to live.

The door opened and the butler entered.

"Thank you, Oswald. Please bring me my supplies." Only seconds later, the butler reentered bearing another black leather case, similar to a doctor's bag.

As he carefully emptied the bag onto the desk, Guerner spoke. "Those who buy ammunition and expect uniformity are incredibly foolish. They buy approximation and therefore attain approximation. The expert must know each bullet."

He picked up a dullish gray slug from the desk and rubbed it between his fingers, feeling his finger oil coat the projectile. He stared at the bullet, absorbing its feel and its shape and weight and temperature. He placed it before him at the right of the desk. He picked up dozens of slugs, one at a time, putting most of them back into the black leather bag, and finally choosing four more which he placed with the first.

From a small wooden box on the desk, he selected a cartridge casing, held it momentarily, then replaced it. He took another, held it, rolled it between his fingers, and smiled.

"Yes," he murmured, and placed it with the slugs. He continued until he had five. "Perfect," he said. "Created to be joined together. Like man and woman. Like life and death."

With a small silver spoon, he began to ladle a white powder carefully into each cartridge. It swished in silently, a few grains at a time, giving each shell its explosive charge. When he had finished, he delicately placed a slug into the open end of each shell, and then placed them one at a time into a chrome-plated device, which sealed them with a faint click.

"Now the cartridge, the bullet, the powder are one. Along with the maker. We will soon be ready."

Lifting the rifle barrel carefully from the case, he held it silently before him, peered through it, then put it down. He lifted out the stock, hefting it, holding it in firing position at his shoulder. With a soft murmur of approval, he placed the barrel on top of the stock and with a specially-tooled wrench began joining the two.

He stood up, extending his weapon from him in one hand. "We are done," he said, and inserted a bullet into the chamber, and pushed forward the bolt with a click.

"Only five bullets? Will that be enough for this job?"

"There are only two targets. Two bullets are enough for this job. The other three are for practice. My weapon and I have been inactive for so long. Get the binoculars. Behind you. On the shelf."

Guerner moved to the window, looking out over his valley, rolling lawns in front, the last blooming garden off to his right. The autumn sun was dying red over the Hudson beyond, bathing the valley in blood.

Maria picked up the 7×35 Zeiss Ikon binoculars from the shelf and noticed there was dust on the lenses. Strange. He worshipped that rifle as if a woman, and let a fine pair of binoculars gather dust. Well, he had once been very good.

She walked to the open window by him and felt the late afternoon chill. A bird sang harshly off in the distance. She wiped the binocular lenses clean on her sleeve and did not notice that this drew a glance of contempt from Guerner.

He looked forward out the window. "Two hundred yards from here," he said, pointing, "there is a small furry animal. I cannot see it too clearly."

She raised the binoculars to her eyes. "Where?"

"About ten yards to the left of the corner of the stone wall."

She focused on the wall and was surprised that through the lenses, the wall appeared better lit than to her naked eyes. She remembered this was characteristic of good binoculars.

"I can't see it," she said.

"It's moving. Now it's still."

Maria scanned the wall, and there perched on its hind legs, its forelegs tucked in front as though begging, was a chipmunk. She could barely make it out.

"I know what you're doing," she said, still looking. "You know little animals are always on that wall and when you shoot it will hide and you will say you shot it."

Maria felt the crack of the rifle at her left ear, just before she saw the chipmunk spin over as though slapped in the head with a paddle, a ball of orange fur bouncing backwards, rolling out of sight behind the wall, then rolling into sight again, the legs just as they had been, but without a head. The legs quivered. The white patch on the stomach still pulsated.

"That bird," said Guerner quietly and Maria again heard the painful crack of the rifle, and suddenly in a flock of dark birds far in the distance, perhaps 300 yards, one dropped. And she did not lift her binoculars because she knew its head was gone too.

"Another chipmunk," Guerner said, and the rifle cracked, and Maria saw nothing, partly because she had stopped looking.

"It is only possible if the target is alive," Guerner said. "That is the secret. One must sense the life of the target. One must feel it move into the orbit of your life. And then, there can be no miss."

He clutched his rifle to his chest, as though thanking the instrument.

"When do we perform against this fool, this Remo, who uses only his hands?" he asked.

"Tomorrow morning," Maria said.

"Good. My weapon can hardly wait." He squeezed it tenderly in his two large hands. "The target, the living target, gives itself to you. We want the living target to do it with. The secret is that you do it with the victim." His voice was smooth and deep and vibrant. As it had been 30 years before, Maria remembered, when they had made love.

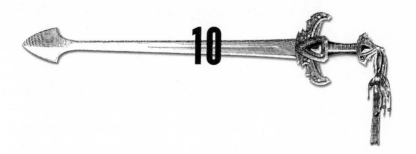

SEVENTY thousand dollars. How did they arrive at that price? Remo hung up the phone in the booth and walked out to Adams Street.

The sun made Boston alive, a very dead city from the time the first settler designed the dirty, gloomy metropolis, to this September noon when the air was warm with just a hint of growing coolness.

He had done his morning exercises behind the wheel of the rented automobile, driving all night from Montreal to the din of Chiun and the young Mrs. Liu. At one point, while he was reinforcing his breathing, Mrs. Liu surrendered to angry tears. Chiun leaned forward and whispered in Remo's ear: "They don't like that. Heh, heh."

"Chiun, will you cut that out now?" Remo said.

Chiun laughed and repeated the phrase in Chinese that had caused the anger.

"My government has sent me here to officially identify my husband," Mei Soong said in English. "They did not send me here to suffer abuse from this reactionary, meddlesome old man."

"I show you how old I am in bed, little girl. Heh, heh."

"You are gross, even for a Korean. Do you still remember your last erection?"

Chiun emitted a warlike shriek and then poured forth verbal Oriental abuse.

Remo pulled to the side of the road. "All right, Chiun. Up front with me."

Stilled instantly, Chiun moved into the front seat and adjusted himself angrily. "You are a white man," he said. "Like moldy dead grain. White."

"I thought you were mad at her, not me," Remo said, pulling back to the Thruway where cars were zipping by, most of them no longer under the control of their drivers. At 65 miles an hour in a soft-sprung comfort car, the operator was aiming, not driving.

"You embarrassed me in front of her."

"How?"

"By ordering me up front like a dog. You have no feeling for real people because you are not people. And in front of her."

"All white men are like that," said Mrs. Liu. "That's why they need running dogs like you to work for them."

"Shit," said Remo, summing up the situation.

He had lost two of the three cars following him by pulling off the roadway. But the last car still was on his tail. With one hand, Remo unwrapped the red cellophane covering from a pack of cough drops on the dashboard. He smoothed it out as best he could, then held it in front of his eyes, peering through it as he drove through the pre-dawn darkness.

He continued looking through the red filter for a full two minutes, as he began to push the car to its limits. Sixty-five. Seventy. Eighty. Ninety. As he came to the top of a rise with the pursuit car some 400 yards behind him, he saw what he was looking for. As soon as he cleared the rise, he turned off his lights and dropped the piece of red cellophane. His eyes, now functional in the dark, saw clearly the Boston exit, and without lights at

90 miles an hour, Remo whipped around the turn, then began slowing down without hitting the brake.

In his mirror, he could see the pursuit car—its driver blinded by darkness—plow ahead on the Thruway toward New York. Good-bye car number three.

"Barney Oldfield," Chiun said. "A regular Barney Oldfield. Did it ever occur to you that your life would be safer if you stopped and did combat, Mr. Barney Oldfield?"

"You can fasten your seat belt."

"I am my own seat belt. But that is because I can control my body the way civilized people are supposed to. Perhaps you should fasten your seat belt. Heh, heh."

"Reckless, inconsiderate driving," said Mrs. Liu. "Do you know that driving at these speeds consumes gasoline more rapidly than driving at lower speeds? Besides, I want to find my husband, wherever he is, not precede him to heaven."

"Shit," said Remo, and it was the last thing he said until they reached Boston. He wondered if he had been wise to shake the tail. But his mission called for finding General Liu, not endangering the general's wife. His followers would pick him up again, if they hadn't already, and he wanted the meeting on his terms, when his decisions would not be warped because of the danger to the girl.

Now, he was in Boston, it was just after noon, and it felt somewhat exhilarating to know that someone thought you were worth $70,000 to kill. But as he walked back to his hotel, a vague anger began to grow. Only $70,000?

A basketball player recently was sued for jumping a team, the team claiming he was worth $4 million. Four million for him and his life, and only $70,000 for Remo's death. Inside the hotel lobby, Remo felt concentration on him. It was not strong and his anger had almost dulled his senses. Collecting the extra room key, he noticed a scruffy woman in a black dress and hat reading a newspaper. But her eyes didn't move across the columns.

Maybe he should sell tickets? He thought momentarily of collecting fees from everyone following him, Chiun and the girl. Maybe go up to the woman and say, "Uh, look. We're the in thing this week. We're going to be at Fenway Park on Saturday and you can't tail us without a ticket that night. I recommend a good box seat so you can use a knife or even your hands if one of us should wander near the bullpen."

But Remo had been trained better than that. One never gave away the knowledge he was being tailed. One gives away nothing. As Chiun had said in the first weeks of training at Folcroft when Remo's wrists were still sore from the current of the electric chair:

"Fear is all right for you. But never induce it in your victim. Never exert your will on him. Never let him know you even exist. Give him nothing of you. Be like the strange wind that never blows."

It had sounded like any other of the many riddles Remo did not understand, and it took him years at his trade before he was able to perfect the skill of sensing people watching him. Some people experienced it occasionally, usually in crowded situations.

For Remo, it was everywhere, all the time. Like in the lobby of the Hotel Liberty. And the apparently harmless old lady putting the spot on Remo.

Remo strolled to the elevator. A crummy $70,000. The car stopped at the eleventh floor. A basketball player worth $4 million dollars.

The car door closed behind him. As the elevator started up, he went up in full jump, his chest stretched out to catch the nine-foot ceiling. And down he came again, dribbling an imaginary basketball, with a small cry of victory.

He had seen Lew Alcindor in a game once, and on that jump,

Remo would have gone over him. On most jumps, he would have, Remo thought. What Lew Alcindor did better than Remo was stand taller. And, of course, find a better job. One, not only with retirement benefits, but with retirement.

Remo wondered, when that last day came, if they would ever find a trace of his body. "That's the biz, sweetheart," he said to himself and unlocked the door to his room.

Chiun was sitting in the middle of the floor, his legs crossed, humming happily to himself, a tuneless, nameless song that he used to express happiness at a joyous event. Remo was immediately suspicious.

"Where's Mei Soong?" he asked.

Chiun looked up almost dreamily. He wore his white robes of joy, one of the fifteen changes he had brought with him. Remo had a valise, the girl brought everything in her coat pockets, and Chiun had a steamer trunk.

"She's fine," he said to Remo.

"Where is she fine?"

"In her bathroom."

"She's taking a shower?"

Chiun reverted to his humming.

"Is she taking a shower?"

"Ooowah, hummmmm, ooohwah . . . nee . . . shu . . . hmm-mmmm."

"Chiun, what did you do with her?" Remo demanded.

"As you suggested, I made sure she would not escape."

"You bastard," Remo said, dashing through the adjoining door. He had rented three rooms, the central one being Mrs. Liu's. The bathroom door was locked from the outside.

Remo opened it. And saw her.

She hung from the shower curtain rod, trussed like an animal being brought back to a village for a feast. Her wrists were bound with strips torn from sheets, and tied together over the chrome shower rod. Her feet were bound in the same fashion, over the shower rod, and her body made a "u" as she faced the ceiling, her mouth gagged, her thick black hair flowing toward the floor, her clothes laying in a pile by the tub. She was nude.

Her eyes were red with anger and fear, and she looked pleadingly at Remo as he threw the door open.

Remo quickly untied her feet and gently placed them on the rim of the white bathtub, then untied her hands. When her hands were free, she went for his throat, trying to dig her nails into the flesh. But Remo caught the hands with his left, and untied her gag with his right.

"Hold on," he said.

She screamed something in Chinese.

"Now wait a minute. Let's talk," he said.

"Talk, you fascist beast? You tied me up."

"I did not."

"Your running dog did."

"He lost his head. He won't do that again."

"Do not take me for a child, beast. I know the tricks. Your partner abuses me. You are friendly and then convince me of the virtues of capitalism. You do this because you have killed General Liu and now you wish me to join your capitalist clique and make a false report to the People's Republic of China."

"This is no hustle," Remo said. "I'm sorry."

"The word of a capitalist. How can I trust anyone without social consciousness?"

"I'm not lying." Remo could see her body untense and set itself in quiet hostility to him. He released her wrists. She dropped her hands, and appeared to be going for her clothes, when she moved for a sneak punch, which Remo dodged without even moving his feet or changing his expression.

"Bastard," she said, angrier now because she had missed. "I am leaving this country now and heading back for Canada and then home. You may stop me by killing me as you did my husband. But my disappearance will be the final proof my government needs of your country's perfidy."

Remo watched her step into her coarse white panties of material that would be unsuitable for any American or Japanese woman.

The mission was now a failure. He had been taken out of normal function, assigned as a bodyguard to prevent what had just happened—or something worse—and now he watched Mei Soong prepare to leave, with Dr. Smith's and the President's peace melted in the heat of her anger.

Since he was out of function already, he would step further out of function. It was a crazy ballgame and if the pitcher were suddenly assigned to play first base, then, dammit, he would do it the way he thought best.

While Mei Soong was hitching on her bra from behind, Remo stepped close to her and unhooked it. She tried to break free by kicking backwards toward his groin, but Remo spun her around and, laughing carried her into the bedroom and went down with her onto the tan bedspread, pressing her into the mattress, as her arms flailed wildly at his head.

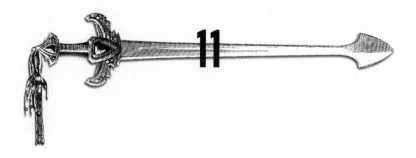

IN the other room, Chiun was amusing himself, reading a detailed analysis proving how little the *New York Times* understood of the turmoil inside China. The Page One article talked of militaristic elements anxious to stop the Premier's visit to America and of the desire among China's "more stable leadership"—Chiun snorted at that—to solidify relations with the United States.

In Washington, the President was still planning for the Premier's trip, the *Times* said, but there were rumors that he was fearful the Chinese would cancel it.

Chiun put the paper down. The press was slowly beginning to learn of the disappearance of General Liu. That could be serious.

But cancel the trip? Not if the Chinese thought there was any way of milking even one dollar from the fools who ran the United States.

His attention was distracted by noise from inside Mei Soong's room, and he cocked an ear to listen.

Inside, Remo had pinned her knees with his body and with his left hand manacled her wrists together above her head. Her soft, smooth face was twisted now, the teeth clenched tight, the lips drawn thin, the eyes narrowed, a mask of pure hate. "Beast, beast, beast," she yelled and Remo smiled down at her to let her see his calm and to understand it, to know that his need did not make him weak and that he was in full control.

Her body would be his instrument. Her hate and violent struggle would be used to his ends, not hers, because in fighting, she had surrendered her control and all he had to do was exploit it.

His right hand moved beneath her smooth buttocks, and neatly tore the coarse cloth panties. With his fingers, he began to work the muscles of her buttocks, while he kept his face impassive. His hand worked to the small of her back, and then down again to the other cheek, reinforcing the tension of the lower body.

He entertained the thought to kiss her on the lips, but that would be wrong now. He was not doing this for fun. Chiun had taken even that away from him. He had done the impossible. He had made sex boring.

It was on an early training session, this one a month's long regimen at Plensikoff's Gymnasium in Norfolk, Virginia, a small building off Granby Street that only a handful of people knew was not an abandoned warehouse.

It had started with the lectures, the dry riddles and Remo asking, "Okay, when do I get laid?"

Chiun had talked about the orgasm, which was a major requirement for a relationship only when nothing else held it together. Chiun was sitting on the gymnasium floor in a robin's egg blue kimono with yellow birds sewn on.

"When do I get laid?" Remo asked again.

"I see we have exceeded your usual attention span of two minutes. Could it hold your attention if a naked woman were to walk in here?"

"It might," Remo said. "But she's got to have big jugs."

"The American mind," said Chiun. "You should be distilled

and bottled as the American mind. Now. Imagine the woman standing here."

"I knew it was too good to be true," Remo said. The wooden gymnasium floor was hard and making his duff numb. He shifted his weight and saw Chiun cast a disapproving look at him. Afternoon sunlight came through the dust-lathered windows of the gymnasium and Remo could follow a fly in its light, until it disappeared between the windows, then reappeared again in light.

"Are you concentrating?"

"Yes," said Remo.

"You're lying," said Chiun.

"All right. All right. What do you want me to do?"

"See a woman standing naked before you. Create her outline. See her breasts. Her hips, the juncture of her legs. Do you see?"

Remo indulged the old man. "Yeah, I see her."

"You do," Chiun commanded.

Remo did.

"But you are looking wrong. What does her face look like?"

"I can't see her face."

"Ah, very good. You cannot see her face because that is the way you see women. Faceless. Now try to see her face. I will draw it for you. Simply. And I will tell you what she is feeling standing there undraped. What do you think she is feeling?"

"Cold."

"No. She is feeling exactly what she has been taught to feel since childhood. It could be embarrassment, or excitement, or fear. Maybe power. But her feelings about sex are social. And that is the key to awakening a woman's body. Through her social upbringing. You see, we must . . ."

Remo counted two more flies in a dogfight. The overhead lights were on, but they were weak, doing little but shining out the information that they were there.

Then he felt the slap across the face.

"This is important," said the old man.

"Shit," said Remo, his cheek stinging. He stayed with the lecture as long as the cheek stung, which was approximately a half hour, and he learned how to unleash the woman's senses, the proper time, control of himself, and how to use his body as a weapon against hers.

The next time he had sex, the woman was ecstatic and Remo less than pleased. He tried again with someone else. This time, it was like an exercise for him, albeit delirious enjoyment for his partner. One more try convinced him that Chiun had managed to rob him of his enjoyment of sex, and to transform it into just another weapon.

And now, in a Boston hotel room, he was using that weapon to assault the mind and body of a young Chinese woman with small but exquisitely symmetrical young breasts.

He allowed her to writhe beneath him until perspiration formed on her forehead and her breath came quickly, and all the while, he kneaded the base of her spine. When Remo felt her warm, lush body give less to each movement, accepting the fact that he was irresistibly atop her, accepting at least his presence because she could not fight it, the presence of an imperialist Caucasian about to commit rape, a man she hated, he stopped massaging the base of her spine and her cheeks, and slowly moved his fingertips down her right thigh to her kneecap, very slowly so she would not think it a deliberate move.

She stared up at him resignedly, dull eyes and set mouth, saying nothing, but all her muscles finally alive and warmed from use.

He stared into her eyes, and let his right hand rest on the kneecap as though it would not move again, as if they would stay like this for day upon tedious day. She smelled of freshness, something beyond bottling, the healthy fresh aliveness of youth. Her skin was golden and soft, her face eggshell round and smooth, her eyes deep black. And then Remo saw it in the eyes, that small slight desire that his hand move up again across her thigh.

And he did so, but hesitantly, and even slower than before. But coming down to the knee again, he brought it down faster and slightly harder, then to the inside of the thigh, steady smooth warm strokes always stopping short of her essence. The dark rims capping her golden mounds formed sharper edges and Remo lowered his mouth to their concentric circles, then drew a tongue line down to her navel, while never ceasing the slow rhythmic force on the tender inner thigh.

He saw her mouth relax. She would allow herself to be taken, even though she did not like it. This is what she would be telling herself. But she was lying to herself. She wanted him.

Remo still held her small wrists above her head. He had broken the pattern of taking her by force. If he let go she would be obliged by her upbringing to try to fight her way free. So he held them. But easily.

With his right hand, he worked her breasts, then her navel, her upper arms, her inner thighs before finally reaching her moistened essence. She was moaning, "You white bastard. You white bastard."

Then, the penetration, but not fully, holding out, waiting for her to demand. And she demanded. "Damn you, I want it," she groaned, her dark eyes almost disappearing beneath her upper lids.

He released her wrists now and with both hands began kneading her buttocks again, increasing pressure, increasing penetration, bringing maximum pressure on her sensory organ, willing her into orgasm, holding only for a bare moment of peak, then relaxing to the usual, ho-hum, hysterical shrieks of the woman.

"Ah," yelled Mei Soong, her eyes shut in ecstasy, "Fuck Mao. Fuck Mao," and Remo suddenly withdrew fully and stood up. Under different circumstances, he would have stayed, but now he needed her to follow him, to be unsure that he would ever want her again. So he left her exhausted on the couch, and zipped up his trousers, having performed fully clothed.

And then he saw Chiun standing in the doorway, shaking his head.

"Mechanical," he said.

"What the hell do you want?" Remo said, angrily. "You give me twenty-five exact steps to follow and then you call it mechanical."

"There is always room for artistry."

"Why not show me how it's done?"

Chiun ignored him. "Besides, I think to do it in front of another person is disgusting. But you Americans and Chinese are pigs anyway."

"You're some piece of work," said Remo who had enjoyed less passion in his sex than a man across the street intended to enjoy in Remo's death.

I MUST talk to you, Chiun," said Remo. He shut the door behind him, leaving Mei Soong still sprawled, exhausted and drained, across her bed.

Chiun sat down on the gray carpeted floor, his legs crossed before him in the lotus position. His face was passive.

Remo sat down before him. He could, if he wished, sit for hours now, having worked for years on his concentration and body control. He was taller than Chiun, but as they sat, their eyes were level.

"Chiun," said Remo. "You're going to have to return to Folcroft. I'm sorry, but you're just too much trouble."

And then Remo caught something, which he was sure he did not catch. He could not quite define it. Not in Chiun. In anyone else, he would have decided a preparation for attack or a decision to attack. But that was impossible in Chiun. For one, Remo knew Chiun had eliminated any telegraphing motions, at least as much as he was able, right down to the first flash of preparation which could sometimes be seen in the eyes but more often in the shift of the spinal column. Most people adept at the trade learned to give nothing from their eyes, but the shift in the spinal column was like hanging out a sign.

And Remo, if he did not know that Chiun did not give out signs, and if he did not know that Chiun had deep affection for him, would have sworn at that moment, in the hotel room in Boston, with the doors shut and the blinds drawn, that Chiun had just decided to kill him.

"Something troubles you," said Chiun.

"The truth is, Chiun, that you've become impossible. You're going to blow this mission with your nonsense about the Chinese. I've never before seen you less than perfect, and now you're acting like a child."

"Smith has ordered you to send me back?"

"Now don't get upset. This is just a professional decision."

"What I am asking is did Smith order my return?"

"And if I told you he did, would it make things easier for you?"

"I must know."

"No. Smith did not order it. I want it."

Chiun raised his right hand delicately, signalling that he wished to make a point and that Remo should listen with care.

"I will explain to you, my son, why I do things you do not understand. To understand actions, one must understand the person. I must tell you of me and my people. And you will know why I do what I do, and why I hate the Chinese.

"Many people would think of me as an evil man, a professional killer of people, a man who teaches other people to kill. So be it. But I am not an evil man. I am a good man. I do what I am supposed to do. It is our way of life in Sinanju, a way we needed for survival.

"You come from a rich country. Even the poorest countries of the west are rich compared to my home. I have told you some small things about my village of Sinanju. It is poor as you do not understand poor. The land can support only one-third of the families who live there. That is in the good years.

"Before we discovered a way to survive, we would destroy

half our girl babies at birth. We would drop them sadly into the bay, and say we were sending them home, to be reborn during better times. During famines, we would send the male children home the same way, waiting for another time more propitious to birth. I do not believe that by dropping them in the bay we send them home. And I do not believe that most of our people believe it. But it is an easier thing for a mother to say than that she gave her child to the crabs and sharks. It is a lie to make grief more endurable.

"Imagine China as the body and Korea as the arm. In the armpit is Sinanju, and to that village the lords of China and the lords of Korea would exile people. Royal princes who had betrayed their fathers, wise men, magicians who had done evil. One day, I believe in your year of 400 and our day of the nightingales, a man came to our poor village.

"He was as no man we had ever seen. He looked very different. He was from the island beyond the peninsula. From Japan. He was before ninjutsu, before karate, before all. He was, on his own island, accursed, having taken his mother as a woman. But he was innocent. He did not know she was his mother. But they punished him nevertheless, taking out his eyes with bamboo sticks."

Chiun's voice began to quiver as he imitated pomposity: " 'We cast you to the scum of this scum land,' the Japanese captain told the poor blind man. 'Death is too good for you.' And the blind man answered."

Chiun's voice now exuded integrity. His eyes lifted to the ceiling.

" 'Hark,' the man said. 'You who have eyes, do not see. You, who have hearts, know not mercy. You, who have ears, do not hear the waves lap upon your boat. You, who have hands, do not comfort.

" 'Woe be to you, when your hardheartedness returns and no doves mark its trail in peace. Because I see now a new people of Sinanju. I see a people who will settle your petty disputes. I see men of men. I see people of goodness, bringing their wrath to your foolish squabbles. From this day forth, when you approach Sinanju, bring money for the wars you cannot fight. That is the tax I place upon you and upon all those not from this village. To pay for the services you cannot do yourself, because you know not piety.' "

Chiun obviously was very happy with the story.

"Now, my son," he said to Remo. "Tell me what you think of this tale. With truth."

Remo paused.

"The truth," Chiun said.

"I think it's the same as the kids going home. I think the people of Sinanju became professional assassins because they had no other way to make a living. I think the story is just another way of making a shit deal more acceptable."

Chiun's face narrowed, the normal wrinkles becoming canyons, his hazel eyes burning. His lips were evil thin lines. He hissed: "What? Is that the truth? Will you not reconsider?"

"If I am to lose your affection, Little Father, because I tell the truth, then I will lose it. I do not want a lie between us because what we have dies with a lie. I think your story of Sinanju is a myth, made up to explain reality."

Chiun's face relaxed, and he smiled. "I think so too. Heh, heh. But you almost lied there because you did not wish to offend me. Heh, heh. It is a beautiful story, no?"

"It is beautiful."

"Well, back to business. In the year 1421, the Emperor Chu Ti hired our master, the man the village lives on."

"One man?" Remo asked.

"That is all that is needed. If the man is good enough, that is all that is needed to support the weak and the poor and the aged of the village, all those who cannot fend for themselves. And our master brought with him into China the sword of Sinanju, seven feet long and of the finest metal. It was his task to execute the architects and the builders of the T'ai-ho Tien, the throne room, because they had installed and knew the secret passageways."

Remo interrupted. "Why would he need a sword?"

"The hand is for attack. But the sword is for execution."

Remo nodded.

"He fulfilled his duties to the letter. On the afternoon of the completion of the T'ai-ho Tien, the Emperor called all the architects and builders to the secret passageway, where he had said they would receive their reward.

"But he was not there to reward them. Only the master. Whaa, the sword moved right. Whaa, the sword moved left. Whaa, the sword moved down, and scarcely a man there saw the blade or knew what was happening. Whaa."

Chiun two-handed a large, imaginary sword. It had to be imaginary because no seven-foot sword could move that quickly with that little effort.

"Whaa. And he left the sword there with the bodies, to return for it after he was paid. But before he was paid, the Emperor invited him to dinner. But the master said, 'I can not. My people are hungry. I must return with their sustenance.' This is the truth I speak, Remo.

"And the Emperor gave the master a poisoned fruit. And the master was helpless."

"Don't you people have a defense against poison?"

"There is only one. Not eating. Know your food. That is your weakness too, my son. Although no one need try to poison you because you poison yourself daily. Pizza, hot dogs, roast beef, mashed potatoes, the skin of poultry. Pheewww. Anyway, the master awoke in a field, because of his great strength, only numbed. On foot, weak, and without his powers, he returned to Sinanju. By the time he arrived, they were again sending the newborn home."

Chiun's head dropped. He stared at the floor.

"For me to fail is to send the children home. I cannot do that, even if you were the assignment. For today, I am the master."

"That's your tough shit, Chiun, not mine." Remo's voice was cold.

"You are right. It is my tough shit."

"What about the architects and builders? Why did they deserve death?"

"That is the price one must expect to pay for working for the Chinese."

"And Sinanju paid that price also," Remo said. He was beyond anger, in the whirlpool of frustration, unable to strike out at anything that would not hurt him more. He had always known that Chiun was professional and if need be Remo himself would be sacrificed. But he did not like to hear it.

"One always pays the price. Nothing is free," Chiun said. "You are paying it now. You are exposed, known, your greatest weapon, that of surprise, gone. You have no children whose lives depend on your service, no mothers to tell themselves lies because you failed. Your skills can give you the good life. Go. Escape."

The anguish Remo had felt left for a new pain, the hurt of telling a good friend something you did not tell even yourself. He leaned forward, hoping to avoid telling Chiun.

"What's the matter, Chiun? Don't you have it to kill me?"

"Do not be silly. Of course, I would kill you. Although death would be easier for me."

"I cannot abandon this assignment," Remo said.

"Why?"

"Because," Remo said, "I have children too. And they are being sent home, by heroin, by war, by crime, by people who think it a good thing to blow up buildings and shoot policemen and stretch the laws of our country until they protect no one. The children who are harmed by this are my children. And if we have a chance, that someday, we will not have wars, and our streets will be safe, and children are not poisoned by drugs and men robbed by other men, then, that day will I escape. Then, that day, will I put down my nation's sword. And until that day, I will do my job."

"You will do your job until you are killed."

"That's the biz, sweetheart."

"That's the biz," said Chiun.

And then they smiled, Chiun first, then Remo, because they felt that first little tinge that tells you someone is zoning in on you, and it would be good now to use their bodies again.

There was a knock on the door.

"Come in," said Remo, rising from the floor. It felt good to stretch his legs. The door opened, admitting the woman whom he had pointedly not noticed noticing him in the lobby. She was dressed now as a maid.

"Hello, sir," she said. "Your air conditioning is malfunctioning. We'll have to turn it off and open the window."

"By all means," Remo said sweetly.

The woman, giving more signals than the public address system at Grand Central Station, clopped into the room and pulled up the blinds. She did not look at either man, but was stiff and programmed and even perspiring.

Chiun made a face, indicating almost shock at the incompetence of the setup. Remo squelched a laugh.

The woman opened the window, and Chiun and Remo simultaneously spotted the sniper across the street, in a room one story higher than theirs. It was as easy as if the woman had shone a flashlight into the room across the street.

Remo grabbed her hands in his.

"Gee, I don't know how to thank you for this. I mean, it was getting stuffy in here."

"That's all right," said the woman, attempting to break free. Remo applied slight pressure behind her thumbs and stared into her eyes. She had been avoiding his, but could avoid them no longer.

"That's all right," she repeated. "I was glad to help." Her left foot began to tap nervously.

"I'd like to phone the desk and thank them for your help," Remo said.

"Oh, no. Don't do that. It's part of the service." The woman was so locked in her tension now that she had turned off her feelings, lest they explode. Remo let her go. She would not look back when she left the room, but would run where she must run.

Remo wanted them both, together. He did not want any corpses in his own room, or cluttering his hallway. But if he got them in their room, neat, done, then perhaps a small bite to eat. He had not eaten since the previous day.

She stumbled through the door, and it shut with a crack behind her and she was gone. Remo waited a moment, then said to Chiun:

"You know, I could go for seafood tonight."

"The sniper has been to Sinanju," said Chiun.

"Yeah, I thought so. You know, I felt him zoning in through the blinds." Remo held the doorknob.

"Incredibly effective," Chiun said, "except of course when it is incredibly ineffective. When the victim, not the shooter, is in control of the relationship. It was originally done with arrows, you know."

"You haven't taught me the firing yet."

"If you're alive in a few weeks, I will. I will keep him occupied," Chiun said, swaying slowly, as though dodging and teasing the end of a long, slow spear.

"Thanks," said Remo, opening the door.

"Wait," said Chiun.

"Yes?" said Remo.

"We had seafood yesterday."

"You can have vegetables. I'll have lobster."

"I'd like duck. Duck would be nice if cooked properly."

"I hate duck," Remo said.

"Learn to like it."

"See you later," said Remo.

"Think about duck," said Chiun.

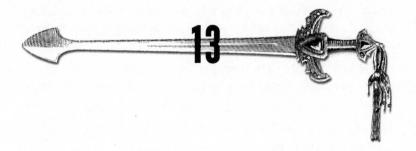

RICARDO deEstrana y Montaldo y Ruiz Guerner was a dead man. He had placed his beloved weapon on the soft bed behind him, and sat in the chair by the window, September giving chill to his bones, Boston hooting noisily at him from below.

And he stared at the smiling Korean who now sat still in the lotus position in the room across the street. Guerner had seen blinds open, had felt the presence of his victims even before they were open, saw them, then began to create the link between the bullet and the skull of the target. At first, it seemed easier than easy, because the vibrations were there, that feeling between him and what he was shooting at, and it was stronger than ever before.

The target was talking to Maria, and then Maria left, but a strong feeling from the Korean overpowered that from his primary victim and demanded that the Korean be killed first. And so, Guerner sighted, touching the imaginary spear which was his rifle to the yellow forehead, but just missing, and reaching again, and not quite able to keep the spear there, unable to get the correct shot, just moving the barrel back and forth. And then it was only a rifle in his hands, and for years, ever since Sinanju, he had not used a rifle merely as a rifle. He had been in North Korea as a consultant, and he had visited that village, and been outshot by a child, and they had apologized that the master was not there to show him some real shooting, and for a ridiculously small sum of money, they had taught him the technique.

He had thought then that they were foolish. But now, staring down the sights of his gun, he knew why the price was cheap. They had given him nothing, only a false confidence which would now be his death, now that he had met the master who had been missing that day years ago.

He tried to sight, like a normal shot, but the gun shook. He had not used it like that for years.

He concentrated on his bullet, the trajectory, blocking out the sight of the weaving Korean, and when all was set again, he put the imaginary spear to the victim's head, but the head was not there and Guerner's fingers trembled.

Shaking, he put the cold rifle on the bed. The elderly Korean, still in his lotus position, bowed, and smiled.

Guerner bowed his respects and folded his arms. His main target had disappeared from the room and would undoubtedly be at his door momentarily.

It had not been a bad life, although if he could have begun life with the vines, instead of entering this business, then perhaps it might have been better.

That was a lie, of course, he realized. He felt that he should pray now, but somehow it would not be right, and what did he really have to ask for. He had taken everything he wanted. He was satisfied with his life, he had planted his vines and harvested his grapes, so what more could he ask for.

So, Guerner silently addressed whatever deity might be out there and thanked the deity for the good things he had enjoyed. He crossed his legs, and then a request came to his mind.

"Lord, if you are there, grant me this. That there be no heaven and there be no hell. Just that it be all over."

The door opened and Maria entered puffing. Guerner did not turn around.

"You get him?" she asked.

"No," said Guerner.

"Why not?" asked Maria.

"Because he's going to get us. That's one of the risks of the business."

"What the hell are you talking about?"

"We lose, Maria."

"But it's only fifty yards."

"It could be the moon, my dear. The rifle's on the bed. Feel free to use it."

Guerner heard the door shut. "No need to shut the door, my dear. Doors won't stop these people."

Maria said, "I didn't shut the . . ." and then Guerner heard the crack of bone and a body bouncing onto the bed, then clumping into the wall near him. He looked to his left. Maria, her hair still scraggly, now was soaked with dark blood oozing from her broken skull. She could not have felt a thing, probably had not even seen the hands that performed the execution. Even in death, she looked so incredibly unkempt.

Guerner had another request of God, and asked that Maria be judged by her intentions, not her deeds.

"Hi there, fella, how's the sniper business?" came the voice from behind.

"Fine until you messed it up."

"That's the biz, sweetheart."

"If you don't mind, would you stop the small talk and get it over with?"

"Well, you don't have to be snotty about it."

"It's not that. It's just that I'm tired of dealing with peasants. Now, please, do what you must do."

"If you don't like dealing with peasants, why didn't you become a court chamberlain, shmuck?"

"I believe the job market was depressed at the time," Guerner said, still not turning toward the voice.

"First a couple of questions. Who hired you?"

"She did. The corpse."

"Who'd she work for?"

"Some Communist group or other. I'm not sure which."

"You can do better."

"Not really."

"Try."

"I did."

"Try harder."

Guerner felt a hand on his shoulder and then a vise, crushing nerve and bone, and incredible pain where his right side was and he groaned.

"Try harder."

"Aaaah. That's all I know. There's $70,000 in her purse."

"Okay. I believe you. Say, how's the roast duck in this town?"

"What?" said Guerner, starting to turn, but never finishing. Just a flash. Then nothing.

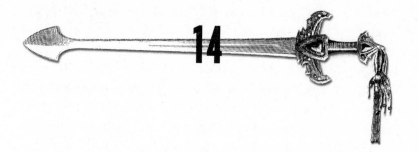

REMO drove off the New York Thruway on the same route General Liu's car had taken. It was a typical modern American highway junction with a confusion of signs stretched like meaningless miniature billboards 25 feet above the highway, so that to find a particular sign, one had to read them all.

It was a tribute to the thoughtlessness of highway planners that if Remo had not been the recipient of extensive training in mind and body control, he would have missed the turnoff.

The noon traffic seemed alive on the sunny fall day, perhaps a pre-lunch rush or just the normal clogging of an artery feeding a major city of the world.

Chiun had been making small, gasping sounds since the New York City air, a fume-laden, lung-corroding poison, had first seeped into the car's air conditioning.

"Slow death," Chiun said.

"Because of the insensitivity of the exploitative ruling class to the people's welfare. In China, we would not allow air like this."

"In China," Chiun said, "people do not have cars. They eat excrement."

"You allow your slave much freedom," Mei Soong said to Remo. The trio sat in the front seat, Mei Soong between the two men, and Chiun pressed as far against the passenger's door as he could get. Remo had not bothered to switch cars, and frankly hoped he was being followed. Time was getting short in the search for General Liu and he wanted contact made as soon as possible.

Remo did not like Chiun sitting near the window in his present mood, although for most of the trip Remo had been careful to avoid cars with peace emblems. Remo had been concentrating on Liu's disappearance, hoping for a flash of inspiration.

Then he had heard Chiun humming happily, and snapped to full consciousness, looking around carefully. Nothing wrong. Then he saw what unleashed the joy in Chiun's heart. A small foreign car with a peace emblem was passing on their right.

As the car moved by, Chiun, staring straight ahead, shot an arm through the open window, flicking at something. Remo caught sight of it in the rearview mirror. A clinketing sideview mirror going back up the road, shattering in shards of glass, bouncing as it disappeared out of sight.

It had happened so fast, of course, the driver of the other car never saw Chiun's wraithlike hand snap out, picking off the mirror. Up ahead, Remo had seen the driver look around in a little confusion and shake his head. Chiun hummed even louder, in joyous contentment.

So Remo had watched for the peace banner cars all the way back to New York. Once, he had tried to foil Chiun. He came close while passing a car with a peace sign, then turned away at the last moment, seeing how close he could come to fooling Chiun.

Remo wound up with a sideview mirror in his lap. Chiun loved that, especially when it bounced off Remo and landed on Mei Soong's hands.

"Heh, heh," Chiun had said, his victory complete.

"Bet you feel proud of yourself," Remo had said.

"Only feel proud when you defeat worthy opponent. Not proud at all. Heh, heh. Not proud at all."

This putdown had lasted Chiun all the way to the turnoff in New York City, with only an occasional "heh, heh, not proud at all."

Remo followed the route he knew General Liu had taken. Under the Jerome Avenue elevated train he drove, past the Mosholu Golf Course, to a crowded business district, shaded in the sunlight of day by the black grimy elevated traintracks, darkening the whole street. Hardware shops, delicatessens, supermarkets, more restaurants, two dry cleaners, laundries, candy and toy stores. Then Remo turned off the avenue two blocks beyond where General Liu had disappeared and prowled the neighborhood with the car. They were clean neat buildings, six stories high at the most, all brick, and all surprisingly quiet for New York City.

Yet Remo knew that New York City was not really one city but a geographical conglomeration of thousands of provincial neighborhoods, each as far away spiritually from the glamor of New York City as Sante Fe, New Mexico.

These neighborhoods—and sometimes just one apartment building consituted a neighborhood—enjoyed their own ethnic composition, Italian, Irish, Jewish, Polish; proof that the melting pot didn't really melt anything, but instead allowed the unmixed particles to go floating around happily in a common stew.

The houses on both sides of Jerome Avenue, between the Grand Concourse, the main thoroughfare of the Bronx, and the beginning of the elevated train, were the same. Neat, none more than six stories. All brick. Yet there were small differences.

"Chiun," Remo said, "do you know what I'm looking for?"

"Not sure."

"Do you see what I see?" Remo asked.

"No."

"What do you think?"

"This is an outskirt of a larger city."

"Notice anything different from one block to another?"

"No. This is one place all over the place. Heh, heh." Chiun knew when he created a phrase in English and would punctuate it with a laugh that was not a laugh.

"We'll see," Remo said.

Mei Soong piped up. "It is obvious that the middle level of your rulers lives here. Your secret police and army. Your nuclear bomber pilots."

"The lower proletariat," Remo said.

"A lie," she insisted. "I do not believe the masses live in buildings like these with street lights on corners and shops nearby under that train in the air."

Remo parked the car in front of a brown brick building with a tudor entrance and two rows of green hedges cut very thin, bordering the steps that led to the entrance. "Wait here," he told Mei Soong and motioned Chiun to follow.

"I'm pretty sure I know how General Liu disappeared," Remo whispered to Chiun as they walked away from the car.

"Who do you think you are, Charley Chan?" asked Chiun. "You are not trained in this sort of thing."

"Quiet," Remo said. "I want you to observe."

"Right on, Sherlock, heh, heh."

"Where'd you pick that up?"

"I watch television at Folcroft."

"Oh, I didn't know they had TV there."

"Yes," said Chiun. "My favorite shows are *Edge of Night* and *As the World Turns*. They are so beautiful and lovely."

On Jerome Avenue, it became clear to Chiun also. As they strolled through the busy shopping district, they drew curious glances from passersby, the fruit peddler, students with DeWitt Clinton High School jackets, a policeman collecting his weekly tithe from a bookie.

They stopped in front of a lot clustered with unmarked gravestones, and an incredibly ornate white marble angel, undoubtedly ordered by a family that had come to its senses too late after the first shock of loss.

The fresh smell of grass from the municipal golf course came as a blessed gift, telling them that grass was alive and well and living in some sections of New York City.

The afternoon heat, surprising for September, bore down heavily on the now gummy asphalt.

A train clattered overhead spraying metal sparks where its wheels met the tracks.

"Chiun, General Liu never left Jerome Avenue at this point. There were no reports on his being seen, but in this neighborhood there's no way that a couple of men, one of them an Oriental in uniform, could just walk away. He must have been plopped into another car a couple of blocks from here and taken somewhere."

Remo scanned the street. "And you don't make any turnoff up there," he said, nodding north, "without meaning to. Not from a caravan of cars. His driver must have turned off, General Liu realized it and shot him. And perhaps the other man too. But whoever they were working with got the General before the rest of the caravan could catch up."

"Maybe he forced his driver to turn off," Chiun said.

"No, he wouldn't have to. They were his own men. He's a general, you know."

"And you know as much about Chinese internal politics as a roach knows about nuclear engineering."

"I know a general's man is a general's man."

"Do you also know why a general in an armored car can shoot two of his own men, and then not fire a shot at somebody who forces him from the car?"

"Maybe it all happened too fast. Anyway, Chiun . . ." Remo stopped. "I've got it. That train overhead, you know where it goes? To Chinatown! That's it. They herded him on a train to Chinatown."

"Did no one notice the gang of men boarding the train? Did no one think it was odd to see a Chinese general struggling on a subway?"

Remo shrugged. "Just details."

"Everything seems clear to you because you do not know what you are doing, my son," said Chiun. "Perhaps General Liu is already dead."

"I don't think so. Why the big effort then to kill us?"

"A diversion."

Remo smiled. "Then they better up the price."

"They will," Chiun said. "Particularly now when the world learns that you are also a famous all-knowing detective."

"No more of your snot," Remo said. "You're just jealous because I figured it out and you couldn't. We're going to Chinatown. And find General Liu."

Chiun bowed from the waist. "As you desire, most worthy number one son."

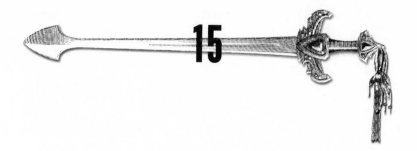

THERE was trouble in China. More rumors of Mao's death. Newsmen pontificating on the inner struggles in Peking. All of them pontificating, and none of them knowing that a Chinese war faction was spreading the word that America intended to sabotage the peace talks by murdering emissaries. After all, if they could put men on the moon, could they not protect emissaries?

So the reasoning went in China. So the whispers were whispered. And so, in a nation, where important decisions were discovered only after they had been implemented, people began to move before peace happened.

Remo commented on this, in a taxicab on his way to Chinatown. He had left his rented car at the midtown hotel they had checked into and had hailed a cab.

He was sure the answer was in Chinatown. He was sure General Liu's disappearance had something to do with the China turmoil. But he was no longer so confident of finding him. A needle in a haystack and only four days left before the Chinese cancelled the Premier's trip.

Remo was sure the Premier should, for safety sake, come to America now, without arrangements. A sudden trip announced only as he was in flight.

"Thank you, Mister Secretary of State," said Chiun.

"Do you think that the people of China will stand for one of their own beloved generals rotting in an American dungeon?" Mei Soong asked.

"The people in American prisons live better than you rice planters," commented Chiun to Mei Soong.

The cab driver knocked on the window. "This is it," he said.

Remo looked around. The streets were lit with merry lights and vendors sold pizza and hot sausages and little Italian pastries.

"This is Chinatown?" Remo asked.

"San Gennaro Festival. Little Italy spreads out during it."

Remo shrugged and paid the driver what seemed to be an excessive fare. He said nothing but he was disgusted. How was he going to find anyone—or be found—in this horde of Italians?

Now he pressed his way grimly down the middle of the street, squinting to close out the brightness of the overhead strings of lights. Mei Soong followed him, tossing insults back over her shoulder at Chiun, who shouted back at her. Their noise was deafening to Remo, not that anyone should have noticed. Hastily-erected plywood booths cluttering the already narrow streets drew crowds of Italians and the Oriental obscenities Chiun and Mei Soong shouted at each other sounded, in the din, only like warm greetings being exchanged by long-lost cousins from Castellamare.

None should have noticed the two shouting Orientals, but someone had. A young Chinese man, with long shiny hair, was ahead of them, leaning on the pole holding up the awning of an Italian zeppole booth, openly staring at them. He wore an olive drab Army-type jacket with a red star on each shoulder and a Mao-style fatigue hat, from under which hung a mass of long, sleek hair.

It was the third time they had passed him in the two-block

festival stretch of Pell Street. He waited until all three had passed him and then Remo heard him shout. "Wah Ching."

"Wah Ching."

The cry echoed down the street, then was picked up by more voices, and shouted back. "Wah Ching. Wah Ching. Wah Ching."

Remo slowed his pace and Mei Soong stalked roughly ahead, as Chiun came up alongside him.

"What does that mean?" Remo asked.

"What?"

"Whatever they're yelling."

"They shout Wah Ching. It means China Youth," Chiun said.

They had walked through the festival area and the street ahead of them turned abruptly dark. And then Remo saw four more young men step out of an alley 40 yards ahead of him. They wore the same costume as the man who had been trailing them, red-starred field jackets and fatigue caps.

They began to walk toward Remo, Chiun and Mei Soong, and Remo could sense the first youth drawing up on them from behind.

He took Mei Soong by the arm, and quickly but smoothly steered her around a corner into a narrow sidestreet. The street was brightly lighted but silent. Only the hum of air conditioners on the buff-colored three-story brick buildings that bordered the narrow street broke the silence, and the buildings served as a wall to seal out the shouting of the Italian hordes only a block away.

It had gone better than Remo had hoped. Perhaps they were going to find the fortune cookie among all that fettucini. But he had to keep the girl out of danger.

They stepped up onto the sidewalk and followed the twisting street, around the curve, when Remo drew up short. The street ended 100 feet ahead, passing through an unlit alley into the Bowery. Behind them, he heard footsteps approaching.

He pulled Mei Soong up short. "Come on," he said, "we're going to eat."

"Do you or the running dog have money? I have none."

"We'll bill it to the People's Rupublic."

The girl had still noticed nothing. She was used to being pulled around by Remo. Chiun, of course, would telegraph nothing, and Remo hoped that he had not, himself, given away their awareness that they were being followed.

As they walked casually up the stairs to the Imperial Garden restaurant, Remo said to the girl: "When the revolution comes and your gang takes over, pass a law putting all your resturants at street level. Around here, you're always walking up a flight or down a flight. It's like a city under a city."

"The exercise is good for the digestion," she said. Chiun snorted, but said nothing.

The restaurant was empty, and the waiter was sitting at a booth in the back, going over the racing form. Without waiting, Remo walked to a booth midway down the row on the left side. He slid Mei Soong into a seat, then motioned Chiun in alongside her. He squeezed in on the opposite side of the gray formica table. By turning his body sideways, he could watch both the front door and the doors leading to the kitchen in the rear of the restaurant.

Chiun was smiling.

"What's so funny?"

"A rare treat. A Chinese restaurant. Have you ever been starved to death in seven courses? But of course a people with no honor have no real need of sustenance."

Mei Soong's answer was cut short by the appearance of the waiter, at their side.

"Good evening," he said in precise English. "We have no liquor."

"That's all right," Remo said. "We've come to eat."

"Very good, sir," he said, nodding to Remo. He nodded also to Mei Soong, and turned his head slightly to acknowledge Chiun. Remo could see Chiun's eyes look up into the waiter's face, evaporating the smile that was there. The waiter turned back to Mei Soong and exploded in a babble of Chinese.

Mei Soong answered him softly. The waiter babbled something, but before Mei Soong could answer, Chiun interrupted their melodic dialogue. In a parody of their Chinese sing-song, he spoke to the waiter, whose face flushed, and he turned and walked rapidly to the kitchen in the rear.

Remo watched him push through the swinging doors, then turned to Chiun who was chuckling under his breath, wearing a smirk of self-satisfaction.

"What was that all about?" Remo asked.

Chiun said, "He asked this trollop what she was doing with a pig of a Korean."

"What did she say?"

"She said we were forcing her into a life of prostitution."

"What did he say?"

"He offered to call the police."

"What did you say?"

"Only the truth."

"Which is?"

"That no Chinese woman has to be forced into a life of prostitution. It comes naturally to them. Like stealing toilet paper. I told him too we would eat only vegetables, and he could return the dead cats to the icebox and sell them for pork tomorrow night. That seemed to upset him and he left. Some people cannot face up to the truth."

"Well, I'm just glad you handled it so pleasantly."

Chiun nodded an acknowledgement and folded his hands in front of him in an attitude of prayer, serene in the knowledge that no untrue or unkind word had passed his lips.

Remo watched the front door over Mei Soong's shoulder as he spoke to her. "Now remember. Keep your eyes open for any signal, anything that looks suspicious. If we're right, the people who have the General are around here somewhere, and they might like to add you to their collection. It gives us a chance of finding him. Maybe just a small chance. But a chance."

"Chairman Mao. He who does not look will not find."

"I was brought up believing that," Remo said.

She smiled, a small warm smile. "You must be careful, capitalist. The seeds of revolution may lie in you ready to sprout forth."

She reached forward with her leg, and touched her knee to Remo's under the table. He could feel her trembling. Since the hotel room in Boston, she had studiedly spent her time, signaling Remo with touches and rubbing. But Remo had reacted coldly to them. She had to be kept close and obedient, and the best way was to keep her waiting.

By the flicker of distaste in Chiun's eyes, Remo could tell the waiter was returning. Remo watched him in a mirror over the entrance way, walking angrily back down the floor toward them, three dinner plates extended up his arm.

He stopped alongside the table, and placed one in front of Remo. "For you, sir."

He placed the second in front of Mei Soong. "And for the lovely lady."

He dropped the third one on the table in front of Chiun, and it splashed small drops on the table top.

"If we were to return in one year," Chiun said, "these drippings would still be here. Chinese, you know, never wash tables. They wait for earthquake or flood to jar dirt loose. It is the same with their bodies."

The waiter walked away, back toward the kitchen.

Mei Soong squeezed Remo's leg between both of hers under the table. As women always do in such situations to disclaim ownership of the brazen legs, she began to chatter incongruously.

"It looks good," she said. "I wonder if it is Cantonese or Mandarin."

Chiun sniffed the plate containing the usual jellied mass of colorless vegetables. "Mandarin," he said, "because it smells like dog. Cantonese smells like bird droppings."

"A people who would eat raw fish should not cavil at civilization," she said, spooning vegetables into her mouth.

"Is it civilized to eat birds' nests?"

And they were off again.

But Remo paid no attention to them. In the overhead mirror, he could see back through the round door windows into the kitchen where the waiter stood, talking to the young man who had spotted them on the street. The man was gesturing, and as Remo watched, he snapped his fatigue cap off his head and slapped it across the waiter's face.

The waiter nodded and almost ran back through the swinging doors. As he passed their table, he mumbled under his breath.

"What did he say?" Remo asked Chiun.

Chiun was still playing with his spoon in the vegetables. "He called me pig."

As Remo watched, the waiter picked up the phone in front and dialed. Just three digits. A long one and two shorts. It was the emergency number of the New York City police.

But why the cops? Unless he had been told to try to separate the girl from Remo and Chiun? What better way than to have the police grab them and spirit the girl off in the shuffle? Remo couldn't hear the waiter's words whispered into the phone, but he leaned over and whispered to Chiun. "We're going to have to split up. You get the girl back to the hotel. Make sure you're not followed. Stay with her. No calls, no visitors and don't open the door for anyone but me."

Chiun nodded.

"Come on, we're going," Remo said to the girl, disengaging his leg from between hers.

"But I haven't finished."

"We'll get a dragon bag to take it home." The police might be helpful. It might set it up so that any contact with the girl would have to come through Remo.

They walked to the front counter, where the waiter was just hanging up the phone.

"But you haven't had your tea?" he said.

"We're not thirsty."

"But your cookies?"

Remo leaned across the counter and grabbed his arm, above the elbow. "You want to hear your fortune? If you try to stop us from going out that door, you'll have a busted rib. Can your in-scrutable mind fathom that?"

He reached into his pocket and tossed a ten dollar bill onto the glass counter. "Keep the change."

Remo led the way down the flight of stone stairs into the street. At their appearance, the five men in the field jackets, who had been lounging against the building across the street, started to walk toward them.

At the bottom of the stairs, Remo told Chiun, "You can go through that alley at the end of the street and grab a cab. I'll catch up to you later."

Remo stepped off the curb into the street, as Chiun took Mei Soong roughly by the arm and started walking off to the right, toward the Bowery. Remo had only to cover him long enough for him to reach the alley. There was no way anyone could catch up to Chiun in darkness, even with the girl as excess baggage.

Just then, the waiter stepped onto the top step and shouted, "Stop, thief!" The five men looked up at him, momentarily. Remo looked over his shoulder to his right. Chiun and the girl were gone. Vanished. As if the earth had opened and swallowed them.

The five young Chinese also saw that their target had vanished. They looked up and down the street, then dumbly at each other, then as if to take out their rage on something, they charged Remo.

Remo was careful not to hurt them. When the police arrived, he did not want the street cluttered with bodies. Too many complications. So he just moved in among them, dodging their punches and kicks. The waiter was still screaming at the top of the stairs.

Just then, a prowl car turned onto the narrow street. Its whirling red lamp shot slices of light along the buildings on either side of the street. The young Chinese saw it, and they took to their heels, toward the end of the street and the narrow alley where a car could not follow them.

The police car pulled up alongside Remo and stopped with a squeal of tires on the cobblestone street.

As the two policemen jumped out onto the street, the waiter shouted to them: "That's him. Hold him. Don't let him get away."

The two policemen stood alongside Remo. "What's it all about, mac?" one of them said. Remo looked at him. He was young and blond and still a little frightened. Remo knew the feeling; he had experienced it in those early days on the force. Back when he was alive.

"Damned if I know. I came out of the restaurant and five thugs jumped me. And now he's yelling like a lunatic."

The waiter had walked up alongside the three of them now, still careful to keep back from Remo. "He hit me," he said, "and ran off without paying the bill. Those young men heard me yelling and tried to stop him. I want to press charges."

"I guess we'll have to take you in," the second policeman said. He was older, a veteran with patches of gray hair at the temples under his cap.

Remo shrugged. The waiter smiled.

The older policeman steered Remo into the back seat of the squad car, while the younger officer helped the waiter close up.

They returned to the car and slid into the front seat, while the older cop sat in beside Remo. Remo noticed that he sat with his gun side away from Remo. Standard procedure, but it was good to know that there were still some professional policemen around.

The precinct house was only a few blocks away. Remo was marched in between the two policemen and stood in front of the long oak desk, reminiscent of all those he had stood in front of himself with prisoners in tow.

"Assault case, Sergeant," the older patrolman said to the bald-headed officer behind the desk. "We didn't see it. Do you have one of the squad around to handle it? We want to get back before that festival breaks up."

"Give them to Johnson in back. He's free," the sergeant said.

Remo wanted to hang around long enough to make sure the police had a record of his address. So he could be traced. Long ago, he had been given two authorized ways of dealing with an arrest.

He could do whatever physical had to be done. Of course, that was out of the question, since he was willingly going to leave his name and address, and he didn't need 30,000 cops looking for him at his hotel.

Or, the other way, he was allowed one phone call. He could call the number in Jersey City.

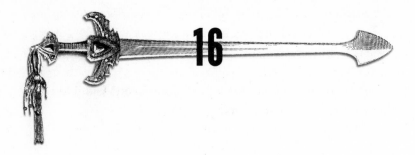

JEAN Boffer Esq., 34 years old and a millionaire twice over, sat on the brown plush sofa in his penthouse living room, looking across the 71 square yards of lime green carpeting that had been laid that afternoon.

He had taken off his purple knit jacket and carefully removed from its inside pocket the little electronic beeper that was to signal him whenever his private telephone line was ringing.

He had worn the beeper for seven years, and it had yet to beep.

But he was a millionaire twice over because he was willing to wear it all the time, and because, if the private telephone line ever rang, he would be ready to do whatever had to be done. Without knowing it, he was the private, personal counsel to a professional assassin.

Just then, as he held the beeper in his hand, it went off, and he realized that in seven years he had never heard the sound it would make. It was a staccato, high-pitched squeak, but it was muffled at that moment by the bell of his private telephone line which was also ringing.

He reached over, carefully, not quite knowing what to expect and picked up the white telephone without a dial. The beeper went silent.

"Hello," he said. "Boffer."

"You're a good lawyer, I hear," said a voice which was supposed to say "You're a good lawyer, I hear."

"Yes. I think the best," which was what Jean Boffer Esq. had been told to say.

Boffer sat up smartly on the couch and placed the book of forensic medicine carefully on his coffee table.

"What can I do for you?" he said casually.

"I've been arrested. Can you spring me?"

"Is there any bail set?"

"If I wanted to get out on bail, I'd pay it myself. What can you do about getting the whole thing dropped?"

"Tell me what happened."

"I was set up. A restaurant in Chinatown. The owner says I assaulted him but he's full of crap. I'm being booked now."

"What restaurant? Is the owner still there?"

"Yeah, he's here. His name's Wo Fat. The restaurant's the Imperial Garden on Doyers Street."

"Keep the owner there until I get there. Diddle around. Tell the cops you want to press counter-charges. I'll be there in twenty minutes." He paused. "By the way, what's your name?"

"My name is Remo."

They hung up simultaneously. Boffer looked over at his wife who was wearing large pilot earphones, listening to a private stereo concert and putting polish on her fingernails. He waved at her and she pulled off the earphones.

"Come on, we're going to get something to eat."

"What can I wear?" She was wearing a white pants suit with gold brocade trim. It would have been appropriate for the captain's dinner on a Bahama cruise.

"We'll stop and buy you a field jacket. Come on, let's go."

His car was waiting downstairs, and he slid behind the driver's wheel, and tooled the expensive car north on Kennedy Boulevard to the Holland Tunnel approach. They were in the tunnel before either of them spoke.

"It's a case, isn't it?" his wife said, easing imaginary wrinkles from the front of her white pants suit.

"Just an assault. But I thought it was an excuse for a meal."

He pulled out of the tunnel, smiling to himself as he always did when he saw the Port Authority's incredible overhead sign which looked like a bowl of spaghetti run amok.

He eased his car into Chinatown, its streets dark and empty now, littered with zeppole shreds and crusts of pizza.

He stopped in front of the darkened Imperial Gardens Restaurant.

"But this place is closed," his wife said.

"Just a minute." He walked up the steps to the second floor entrance of the Imperial Gardens. The restaurant was darkened with only the faint glow from a 7½ watt nightlight shining in the rear of the main dining area. He peered in through the glass, noting in the glow the location of the tables around the kitchen door.

With his left hand, he felt up the side of the door, trying to find the external casing of the hinges. There was none.

He went back down the steps, three at a time, and reentered the car. "We'll eat in fifteen minutes," he said to his wife, who was refreshing her lipstick.

The police precinct was only three blocks away, and he left his wife in the car as he went inside and walked up to the sergeant behind the 30-foot long oak desk.

"I've got a client here," he said. "Remo something."

"Oh yeah. He's in the detective's room. Him and some Chinaman are screaming at each other. Go right in, and look for Detective Johnson." He waved toward a room at the end of the large open room.

He walked in through the swinging wood door gate, to the open door. Inside he saw three men: one a Chinese; one sitting at the typewriter laboriously pecking out a report with two fingers was obviously Detective Johnson. The third man sat in the hard wooden chair, leaning back against a file cabinet.

Through the doorway, Boffer could see the skin slightly paler and tighter over his cheekbones, the mark of plastic surgery. The man's deep brown eyes looked up and burned into Boffer's for a moment. The eyes tipped off on everyone. But not on his new client. His eyes were deep brown and cold, as emotionless as his face.

Boffer rapped on the open frame of the door. The three men looked at him.

He stepped inside. "Detective Johnson, I'm this man's attorney. Can you fill me in?"

The detective came to the door. "Come on in, counsellor," he said, obviously amused by the striped purple suit. "Don't know why you're here? Nothing much to it. Wo Fat here says your client assaulted him. Your client is filing counter charges. They'll both have to wait until arraignment in the morning."

"If I could talk to Mr. Wo Fat for a minute, maybe I could clear the whole thing up. It's more of a misunderstanding than a criminal thing."

"Sure, go ahead. Wo Fat. This man wants to talk to you. He's a lawyer."

Wo Fat rose and Boffer took his elbow and steered him to the back of the room. He shook his hand.

"You run a fine restaurant, Mr. Fat."

"I've been in business too long to allow myself to be assaulted."

Boffer ignored him. "It's a shame we're going to have to close you down."

"What do you mean, close down?"

"There are very serious violations at your establishment, sir. The exterior doors, for instance, open inward. Very dangerous in the event of a fire. And very unlawful."

Wo Fat looked confused.

"And then of course, there's the seating plan. All those tables near the kitchen doors. Another violation. I know you run a fine establishment, sir, but in the interests of the public, my client and I will have to go into court with a formal complaint and bring about your closing as a health menace."

"Now, we should not be hasty," he said in his oiliest style.

"Yes, we should. We should withdraw the charges against my client immediately."

"He assaulted me."

"Yes sir, he probably did. In outrage at being caught in a restaurant which is an outright fire trap. It'll be a very interesting case. The publicity from the papers might hurt your business for a while, but I'm sure it will blow over. As will the stories about your assaulting a customer."

Wo Fat turned his hands up. "Whatever you want."

Detective Johnson had just reentered the room carrying two blue sheets used for booking.

"You won't need those, Detective," Boffer said. "Mr. Fat has decided to drop charges. It was just bad temper on both sides. And my client will drop them too."

"Suits me," the detective said. "Less paper work."

Remo had stood up and already had taken a few steps toward the door, in a smooth glide.

Boffer turned to Wo Fat. "That's correct, isn't it, sir?"

"Yes."

"And I've made no threats against you or any offers to induce you to take this action." He whispered, "Say no."

"No."

Boffer turned to the detective again. "And of course I stipulate the same for my client. Will that do?"

"Sure thing. Everyone can go."

Boffer turned to the door. Remo had gone. He was not outside in the main room of the precinct.

Out in front, his wife had her window rolled down. "Who was that lunatic?" she said.

"What lunatic?"

"Some man just ran out. He stuck his head in and kissed me. And said something stupid. And messed my lipstick."

"What did he say?"

"That's the biz, sweetheart. That's what he said."

REMO was not followed back to the hotel. When he went into his room, Chiun was sitting on a sofa, watching a late night talk show host who was trying to probe the hidden significance of a woman with a face like a footprint, who had raised yelling and shouting to an art form.

"Where's Mei Soong?" Remo asked.

Chiun pointed over his shoulder toward her room.

"Anybody follow you?"

"No."

"By the way, how'd you do that down at the restaurant? Disappear, I mean?"

Chiun smirked. "If I tell you, then you will go tell all your friends, and soon everyone will be able to do it."

"I'll ask the girl," Remo said, walking toward her room.

Chiun shrugged. "We ran up a flight of stairs and hid in a doorway. No one thought of looking up."

Remo snorted. "Big deal. Magic. Hah."

He walked into the next room and Mei Soong purred at him. She walked toward him, wearing only a thin dressing gown.

"Your Chinatown is very nice. We must go back."

"Sure, sure. Anything you want. Has anyone tried to contact you since you got back here?"

"Ask your running dog. He allows me no freedom or no privacy.

Can we go back to Chinatown tomorrow? I have heard that there is a marvelous school of karate that no visitor should miss."

"Sure, sure," Remo said. "Someone should try to contact you again. They'll probably be able to lead us to the general, so make sure I handle it."

"Of course."

Remo turned to go and she ran around to stand in front of him.

"You are angry? You do not like what you see?" She held her arms out and proudly thrust forth her young breasts.

"Some other time, kid."

"You look troubled. What are you thinking?"

"Mei Soong, I'm thinking that you are making it difficult for me to leave now," Remo said. Which was not what he was thinking. What he was thinking was that she had already been contacted because there was a new copy of Mao's Red Book on the end table near her bed, and she had not had a chance to buy one herself. Someone must have smuggled it to her. And suddenly, she was interested in going back to Chinatown, and seeing that wonderful karate school.

He said, "Let us sleep now, so we can go to Chinatown very early and look for the general."

"I am sure that tomorrow you will find him," she said happily, and threw her arms around Remo, burying her face against his chest.

Remo spent the night dozing in a chair against the door to her room, alert enough to detect any attempt by Mei Soong to leave. In the morning, he woke her roughly and said:

"Come on, we're going to buy you some clothes. You can't walk round this country in that damned greatcoat."

"It is a product of the People's Republic of China. It is a well-made greatcoat."

"But your beauty should not be hidden under it. You are depriving the masses of the sight of the new healthy China."

"Do you really think so?"

"Yes."

"But I do not wish to wear goods produced from the exploitation of suffering workers. The stitches made of their blood. The fabric made of their sweat. The buttons of their bones."

"Well, just some inexpensive clothes. A few garments. We're already too obvious to people as it is."

"All right. But just a few." Mei Soong held up a finger in lecture. "I will not profit from the capitalistic exploitation of slave labor."

"Okay," said Remo.

At Lord and Taylor's, Mei Soong discovered that Gucci workers were well paid. She adhered largely to Italian goods, because Italy had a large Communist party. This fealty to the working class became two print dresses, a gown, four pairs of shoes, six bras, six lacey panties, earrings because they were gold and thus undermined the monetary system of the west, Paris perfumes, and to show that China did not hate the people of America, just its government, a checkered coat that was made on 33rd Street.

The bill came to $875.25. Remo took nine $100 bills from his wallet.

"Cash?" said the sales girl.

"Yes. This is what it looks like. It's green."

She called the floor manager.

"Cash?" said the floor manager.

"Yeah. Money."

Mr. Pelfred, the floor manager, lifted one of the bills to the light, then signalled for another by holding out a hand. He lifted that one to the light also. Then he shrugged.

"What's the matter?" Mei Soong asked Remo.

"I'm paying for something in cash."

"Isn't that what you're supposed to pay in?"

"Well, most purchases are worked through credit cards. You buy whatever you want and they make an impression of your card and send you a bill at the end of the month."

"Oh, yes. Credit cards. The economical exploitation of people through subterfuge, giving them the illusion of purchasing power but making them merely wage slaves to the corporations that issue the cards." Her voice lifted to the ceiling of Lord and Taylor's. "Credit cards should be burned on a fire, along with the people who make them."

"Right on," came from a man in a double breasted suit. A policeman clapped. A woman draped in mink kissed Mei Soong on her cheeks. A businessman raised a clenched fist.

"Well, we'll take your money," said Mr. Pelfred.

"Cash," he yelled out.

"What's that," said one of the clerks.

"It's something they used to use all over. Like what you put in telephones on the street and things."

"Like for buying cigarettes, only more of it, right?"

"Yeah," said the clerk.

Mei Soong wore one of the pink print dresses and the department store packed her greatcoat, her sandals and her gray uniform. She clung to Remo's arm, leaning on him and resting a cheek against his strong shoulders. She watched the clerk fold the coat.

"This is a funny kind of coat. Where's it made?" asked the young girl with fried straw hair and a plastic label that read: "Miss P. Walsh."

"China," said Mei Soong.

"I thought they made nice things in China like silk and stuff."

"The People's Republic of China," said Mei Soong.

"Yeah. Chankee Check. The people's republic of China."

"If you are a servant, then be a servant," said Mei Soong. "Wrap the package and keep your tongue tethered to your mouth."

"You'll want a throne next," Remo whispered to her.

She turned to Remo looking up. "If we are living in a feudal system, then we who are doing secret work should appear to be part of it, correct?"

"I suppose."

Mei Soong smiled a smile of rectification. "Then why should I suffer insolence from a serf?"

"Listen," said Miss P. Walsh. "I don't have to take that crap from you or anyone. You want this package wrapped, then mind your manners. I've never been insulted like this before."

Mei Soong braced herself and in her most imperious manner, said to Miss P. Walsh: "You are a servant and you will serve."

"Listen, Dinko," said Miss P. Walsh. "We got a union around here and we don't have to take that kind of crap from anyone. Now you talk nice or you're getting this coat in your face."

Mr. Pelfred was telling his assistant manager about the cash purchases when he heard the commotion. Up running he came, hippity, hippity, his black shiny shoes pattering along the gray marble floors, his breath puffing from his fatty, shiny face, his hands atwitter.

"Will you please?" he said to Miss P. Walsh.

"Watcher mouth," yelled Miss P. Walsh. "Steward," she screamed. A gaunt hard woman in iron tweed stomped to the cluster around the packing of the greatcoat. "What's going on here?" she said.

"It's not a grievance, please," said Mr. Pelfred.

"I don't have to take this crap from customers or anyone. We got a union," said Miss P. Walsh.

"What's going on?" repeated the gaunt woman.

"There's been a minor disagreement," said Mr. Pelfred.

"I been crapped on by this customer," said Miss P. Walsh, pointing to Mei Soong who stood erect and serene, as if witnessing a squabble between her upstairs and downstairs maids.

"What happened, honey?" said the gaunt woman. "Exactly what happened?"

"I was wrapping this funny coat for her and then she told me to tie my tongue or something. She was real aristocratic and she crapped on me. Just plain crapped on me."

The gaunt woman stared hatefully at Mr. Pelfred. "We don't have to put up with this, Mr. Pelfred. She does not have to wait on this customer and if you order her to, this whole store is gonna shut down. Tight."

Mr. Pelfred's hands fluttered. "All right. All right. I'll do the wrapping myself."

"You can't," said the gaunt woman. "You're not in the union."

"Fascist pig," said Mei Soong coolly. "The masses have seen their exploitation and are breaking their chains of oppression."

"And you, lotus blossom," said the gaunt woman, "button your lip and get your friggin' coat out the friggin' door or you're going out the friggin' window, along with your sexy looking boyfriend. And if he doesn't like it, he's going out with you."

Remo raised his hands. "I'm a lover, not a fighter."

"You look like it, gigolo," the gaunt woman said.

Mei Soong slowly looked to Remo. "Are you going to allow these insults to be heaped upon me?"

"Yes," said Remo. Her golden face flushed pink and with great chill, she said: "All right. Let's go. Pick up the coat and dresses."

"You take half of them," said Remo.

"You take the coat."

"All right," said Remo. He looked mournfully at Miss P.

Walsh. "I wonder if you could do me a big favor. We have a long way to go and if you'd put the coat in a box of some sort, I'd really appreciate it. Anything would do."

"Oh, sure," said Miss P. Walsh. "Hey, look, it might rain. I'll double wrap it. We got a special kind of paper in the back room that's impregnate with chemicals. It'll keep it dry."

When the sales girl had left for the special paper wrapping and Pelfred had, as prissily as possible, marched back toward the elevator, and the gaunt woman had swaggered back to the stock room, Mei Soong said to Remo: "You need not have groveled before her."

And on their way back to the hotel, she added: "You are a nation without virtue." But she warmed in the lobby and by the time they had returned to their rooms where Chiun sat atop his luggage, she was bubbling over with enthusiasm about her upcoming visit to the karate school she had heard of and what great fun it would be.

Over her shoulder, Remo winked at Chiun, and told him, "Come on, we're going back to Chinatown. To see a karate demonstration."

Then Remo asked the girl, "Do you want to eat now?"

"No," she said quickly. "After the karate school, then I'll eat."

She did not say "we", Remo noticed. Perhaps she expected that he would not be around for dinner.

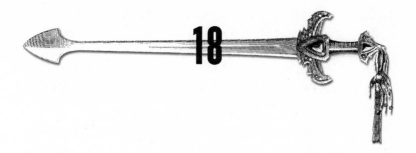

Sir, I must advise you that soon you may not place faith in our efforts concerning the matter."

Smith's voice had passed the stage of tension and chill and was now as calm as the Long Island Sound outside his window, a flat, placid sheet of glass, strangely undisturbed by its usual winds and waves.

It was over. Smith had made the decision which his character demanded, that character for which a dead president had chosen him for an assignment he did not want, that character begun in his youth, before memory, and which told Harold W. Smith that there are things you must do, regardless of your personal welfare.

So it was ending now with his own death. Remo would phone. Dr. Smith would order Remo to tell Chiun to return to Folcroft. Chiun would kill Remo and be returned to his village of Sinanju by the Central Intelligence Agency.

"You've got to stay with this longer," the President said.

"I cannot do that, sir. The three of them have collected a crowd around them. A line of ours was tapped, fortunately by the FBI. But if they knew for sure who we were, think of how they would be compromised. We are going through our prepared program before it will be too late. That is my decision."

"Would it be possible to leave that person still working?" The President's voice was wavering now.

"No."

"Is it possible that something will go wrong with your plans for destruct?"

"Yes."

"How possible?"

"Slight."

"Then if you fail, I still might be able to count on you. Would that be possible?"

"Yes, sir, but I doubt it."

"As President of the United States, I order you, Dr. Smith, not to destruct."

"Goodbye, sir, and good luck."

Smith hung up the special phone with the white dot. Oh, to hold his wife again, to say goodbye to his daughters, to play one more round of golf at the Westchester Country Club. He was so close to breaking 90. Why was golf so important now? Funny. But then why should golf be important in the first place?

Maybe it was good to leave now. No man knew the hour of his death, the Bible said. But Smith would know the exact second. He looked at his watch again. One minute to go. He took the container with the pill from his gray vest pocket. It would do the job.

The pill was white and oblong with beveled edges like a coffin. That was to let people know it was poison and not to be consumed. Smith had learned that when he was six. It was the sort of information that remained with a person. He had not, in his lifetime, ever had use for it.

With his mind now floating in the nether world of faces and words and feelings he had thought he had forgotten, Smith spun the coffin-like pill on the memo that would take the aluminum box to Parsippany, New Jersey.

The central phone rang. Smith picked it up and noticed his

hand was trembling and the phone slippery from the perspiration.

"I've got good news for you," came Remo's voice.

"Yes?" said Smith.

"I think I can latch on to our man. And I'm going to where he is."

"Very good," said Dr. Smith. "Nice going. By the way, you can tell Chiun to return to Folcroft."

"Nah," said Remo. "He's gonna work out fine. I know just how to use him."

"Well," said Smith. "He doesn't really fit into the picture now. You send him back."

"No way," said Remo. "I need him now. Don't worry. Everything is going to work out fine."

"Well, then," Smith's voice was calm in appearance, "just tell him that I asked for him to return, okay?"

"No good. I know what you're doing. I tell him that and he'll return, no matter what else I tell him. He's a pro like that."

"You be a pro like that. I want him back now."

"You'll get him tomorrow."

"Tell him today."

"No deal, sweetheart."

"Remo, this is an order. This is an important order."

There was silence at the other end of the phone, an open line to somewhere. Dr. Smith could not afford to give away what he had just given away and yet he had had to try strength.

It didn't work. "Hell, you're always worrying about something. I'll check with you tomorrow. Another day won't cripple you."

"Are you refusing an order?"

"Sue me," came the voice and Smith heard the click of a dead line.

Dr. Smith returned the receiver to the cradle, returned the pill to the little bottle, returned the bottle to his vest, and buzzed his secretary.

"Phone my wife. Tell her I'll be home late for dinner, then phone the club and get me a tee time."

"Yes, sir. About the memo on the shipment of the goods downstairs? Should I send it?"

"Not today," said Dr. Smith.

There was nothing he would be needed for until tomorrow at noon. The only function he had left was to die and take an organization with him. He could not do that until the first step—the death of Remo—was settled. And since he had no other decisions to make, he would go golfing. Of course, under all this pressure, he wouldn't break 80. If he could break 90, that would be an accomplishment under the circumstances of today. Breaking 90 today would be the equivalent of breaking 80 under other circumstances. Because of the seriousness of the day, Smith would allow himself a mulligan. No, two mulligans.

It was a peculiarity of Dr. Harold W. Smith that his honesty and integrity, steel bound unto death, would, when he put a white ball on a wooden tee, dissolve into marshmallow.

By the time he waggled himself into a solid stance at the first tee, Dr. Smith had given himself four strokes for his impending demise, winter rules because of his lower body temperature, and any putt within six feet of the pin. The last advantage still awaited a rationale, but Dr. Smith was sure he would have it by the first green.

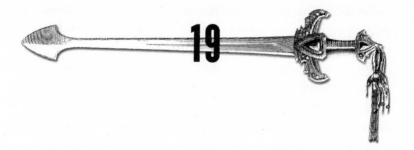

19

BERNOY Jackson packed a .357 Magnum revolver into his attache case, a pistol known as a cannon with a handle. He would have taken a real cannon, but it would not have fit, either into his attache case, or into the main floor of Bong Rhee's Karate Dojo.

He would have liked to have brought with him five button men from his own organization and perhaps, an enforcer or two from organizations in Brooklyn and the Bronx.

What he really wanted, and he knew this very well when he pulled his customized Fleetwood from the garage around the corner and clipped a hydrant on his way out, was to not be going to the school at all.

As the $14,000 gray vehicle with sun roof, stereo, bar, phone and color TV moved down 125th Street toward the East River Drive, he thought for a moment that if he turned north on the drive he could keep going. Of course, he would have to go back to his pad first, and remove cash from the hidden safe behind the third plant. What was that? $120,000. It was just a fraction of his worth, but he would be alive to spend it. Then he could start again, take his time, set up slowly. He had the bankroll for a good numbers operation and he knew how to run it.

The wheel was sweat-slippery in his hands as he passed under the Penn Central Railroad tracks. He was nine when he realized those tracks did not lead to all the faraway wonderful places in the world but just to upstate New York with Ossining on its way and an awful lot of towns that didn't want Nigger boys like Bernoy Jackson. His grandmother had been so wise: "The man ain't ever gonna do you right, boy."

And he believed it. And when he should have believed it most, eight years before, he didn't. And now, as befitting life in Harlem, having made the wrong decision, he was going to die for it.

Jackson turned the air conditioner to high, but found little comfort. He was simultaneously chilled and perspiring. He wiped his right hand against the soft dry material of the seat. His first Cadillac was lined with white fur, an incredibly silly venture, but one he had dreamed of. The fur wore too quickly and the car was vandalized five times in the first month, even in the garage.

Now his Fleetwood was gray with all the good things neatly hidden. He would be at the East River Drive soon. And when he turned right to go south, to go downtown, to go to his death, there would be no turning back. That was the big difference between Harlem and white America.

In white America, people could make a major mistake and recoup. In Harlem, your first big one was your last big one. It had seemed so easy eight years before when he should have remembered his grandmother's advice and taken counsel of his own beliefs. But the money was so good.

He was sipping a Big Apple special, three shots of scotch for the price of two, when another runner, they were all small time then, laid the word on him that a man wanted to see him.

He had purposely continued to sip his scotch slowly, showing no great concern. When he was finished, with great effort at being casual he left the Big Apple bar, out onto chilly Lenox Avenue, where a black man in a gray suit sat in a gray car and nodded to him.

"Sweet Shiv?" said the man, opening the door.

"Yeah," said Jackson, not moving closer, but keeping his hand in the right pocket of his jacket over the neat .25 caliber Beretta.

"I want to give you two numbers and one hundred dollars," the man said. "The first number you play tomorrow. The second number you phone tomorrow night. Play only ten dollars and don't play with your boss, Derellio."

He should have asked why he was the lucky recipient. He should have been more suspicious at the man knowing his nature so well, knowing that having been told to play a number with all the money, he would have played none of it. Having been just given a number he would have ignored it. But having been given $100 to play $10, he would risk the $10, just to make the phone call more interesting.

Jackson's first thought was that he was being set up to break a banker. But not on $10. Did the man in the car really want him to play the $100 and another $500 on top of that?

If so, why pick Sweet Shiv? Sweet Shiv wasn't going to put his own money into something he couldn't control. That was for little old ladies with their quarters and their dreams. That was what the numbers were in Harlem. The dream. If people really wanted to make money they would go to the Man's numbers, the stock market, where the odds were in your favor. But the Man's numbers were too real, it reminded you you didn't have nothing worth betting and you'd never make it out of the mud.

The numbers, however, they were pure sweet fantasy. You bought a day of dreaming of what you'd do with $5,400 for $10. And for a quarter, you got $135 worth of groceries, or rent, or a new suit, or a good taste if that was your pleasure. Or whatever your pleasure.

Nothing would ever replace the numbers in Harlem. Nothing would ever stop them, not unless someone came along with a new instant dream, payable the next day at the corner candy store.

Jackson bet the number and won. Then he phoned the other number.

"Now," came the voice, "bet eight fifty one and eight fifty seven, small. Play it with your boss, Derellio, and tell your players to play those numbers too. And phone back tomorrow night."

Eight fifty one paid off but the hit was not that big because Jackson's players did not trust him. Not that they thought he was untrustful, Jackson knew, but that they did not really have a handle on him.

When he phoned the number again, the voice said: "The number tomorrow is nine sixty two. Tell your people you have the strongest hunch ever. And tell them you can only take so much, they'll have to go to Derellio personally. And play the number straight."

The play the next day was heavy. Big. And when 962 appeared in the day's parimutuel handle on the next to the last page of the Daily News, Derellio was broken. He had been hit for $480,000 and had not laid off any of the bets.

The next night, the voice said: "Meet me on the ferry going toward Staten Island that leaves in an hour."

It was bitter cold on the ferry, but the man who had been in the car seemed not to mind the cold. He was well trussed in fur-lined coat and boots and fur-lined field cap. He gave Jackson an attache case.

"There's half a million in there. Pay off all Derellio's winners. And phone me again tomorrow night."

"What's your game?" asked Jackson.

"Would you believe," the man said, "that the more I learn of what I do, the less I know why I'm doing it."

"You don't talk like a brother."

"Ah, that's the problem of the black bourgeoisie, my friend. Good-bye."

"Wait a minute," said Jackson, hopping up and down on the deck of the ferry, beating his arms for warmth while trying to balance the attache case between his legs, "what if I take a walk with this bread, man?"

"Well," said the man wearily, "I sort of figure you're pretty smart. And you're not going to walk until you know who you're walking from. And the more you know, the less you're going to want to walk."

"You don't make sense, dude."

"I haven't made sense since I took this job. Just accuracy." The black man said good-bye again and walked away. So Jackson had paid off the players and taken over the bank. If they could give him a half million to throw away, they could give him a million for himself. Besides, then he would walk.

But he did not walk. He did not walk when he received his bankroll. He did not walk, even when he was told to stand on a street corner one night, only to be told by a white man an hour later, "You can go now." Derellio and two of his henchmen were discovered with their necks broken in a nearby store a half hour later, and Sweet Shiv Jackson suddenly had a reputation for having killed three men with his bare hands which vastly increased the honesty of his numbers runners. And all it cost was just a little favor every now and then for the weary-voiced black dude.

Just little favors. Usually information, and sometimes it was putting this device here or that there, or providing an absolutely unshakeable witness for a trial or making sure another witness had money to leave town. And within a year, his main job was running an information network that stretched from the Polo Grounds to Central Park.

Even his vacation in the Bahamas was not his own. He found himself in a classroom with an old white man with a Hungarian accent discussing in terms he had not used, things Jackson thought only the street knew. There were names for things like seals, links, cells, variables of accuracy. He had liked variables of accuracy. In street terms, it was "where he coming from?". It was cool.

And then his network one fine autumn day was suddenly very interested in Orientals. Nothing specific. Just anything about Orientals that might come up.

And then the dude reappeared and informed Sweet Shiv that now he would pay back in full for his good fortune. He would kill a man whose picture was in this envelope and he would kill him at the Bong Rhee karate dojo. The man had insisted that Sweet Shiv not open the envelope until he left.

And so for the second time, Sweet Shiv saw the face, the high cheekbones, the deep brown eyes, the thin lips. The first time had been when he stood on a corner he had been told to stand on at a certain time, and the man had come out of the shop where Derellios' body was found later and had said simply: "You can go now."

He was now going to see that face again, and this time Sweet Shiv was supposed to put a bullet in it. And Sweet Shiv knew as he turned south into Manhattan on the East River Drive that he was going to be wasted.

Somewhere a machine he had been part of was coming apart. And that machine belonged to the man. And the man had decided that one of its little black wheels was now going to be a piston. And if you lose a little black wheel trying to be a piston, well, what the hell, what's one Nigger more or less?

Sweet Shiv turned right on 14th Street, then made a U-turn in the middle of the block, got back on the East Side Highway and headed north.

He had $800 in his pocket. He would not stop at his home to pick up his cash, he would not even bother to seal his car when he reached Rochester. He would leave nothing by which anyone could trace him.

Let them have the money. Let some stranger take the car. Let them have everything. He was going to live.

"Baby," he said to himself, "they really had you going."

He felt somewhat happy that he was going to live another day. He felt this way until just before the Major Deegan Highway leading to the New York Thruway and upstate. A black family was sitting by their stalled 1957 Chevrolet, a paintworn, chipped, banged-up leftover of a car which had apparently surrendered its ghost for the last time. But Jackson figured he could make it run again.

He pulled it over, the wide soft wheels with their magnificent springs and shocks, taking the curb like a twig. He stopped on the grass which rose to a fence which separated the Bronx from the Major Deegan a few miles south of Yankee Stadium, the Black and Puerto Rican Bronx with dying buildings teeming with life.

He opened the door and got out into the stale-smelling air and looked at the family. Four youngsters had been playing with a can, four youngsters in clothes so casual they looked as if they had been rejected by the Salvation Army. These four youngsters, one of whom might have been Sweet Shiv Jackson 15 years before, stopped playing to look at him.

The father sat by the front left fender, his back to the flat bald tire, his face cemented in resignation. A woman, old as flesh and weary as millstones, snored in the front seat.

"How you doin', brother?"

"Fine," said the man looking up. "You got a tire that will fit?"

"I got a whole car that will fit."

"Who I got to kill?"

"Nobody."

"Sounds fine, but . . ."

"But what?"

"But I wouldn't make it to your wheels, man. You got company."

Sweet Shiv, maintaining his cool, slowly scanned behind him. A simple black sedan had pulled up behind his Fleetwood. From the near window, a black face stared at him. It was the dude, the man on the ferry, the man who had given him the numbers and the methods, and the orders.

Jackson's stomach dissolved into strings. His arms hung leaden as though enervated by electricity.

The man stared directly into his eyes and shook his head. All Bernoy (Sweet Shiv) Jackson could do was nod. "Yowsah," he said, and the man in the car smiled.

Jackson turned to the man on the grass and carefully peeled from a roll of bills in his pocket all but $20.

The man eyed him suspiciously.

"Take it," said Jackson.

The man did not move.

"You got more smarts than I got, brother. Take it. I won't need it. I'm a dead man."

Still no movement.

So Sweet Shiv Jackson dropped the money in the front seat of the remnant of a 1957 Chevrolet and returned to his Fleetwood which still had one payment on it outstanding. The life of Bernoy (Sweet Shiv) Jackson.

20

REMO Williams spotted the man with the .357 Magnum first. Then the man with the very big bulge in his Oscar de la Renta suit spotted Remo. Then the man smiled weakly.

Remo smiled too.

The man stood before the Bong Rhee karate school, a walk-up entrance with a painted sign telling people to walk up one flight and that when they traversed the stairs they would be in one of the leading schools of self-defense in the Western Hemisphere.

Remo said, "What's your name?"

"Bernoy Jackson."

"How do you want to die, Bernoy?"

"No way, man," said Bernoy honestly.

"Then tell me who sent you."

Bernoy recounted the story. His black boss. The numbers that hit. Then standing on the corner near where three men were killed. And the information.

"That corner. That's where I saw you."

"That's right," Remo said. "I probably should kill you now."

Sweet Shiv went for the gun. Remo snapped out his knuckles into the man's wrist. Jackson grimaced in pain and clutched his wrist. His pain brought sweat to his large forehead. "All I gotta say, honkie, is you a bunch of mean bastards. You the meanest, toughest bastards on this planet earf."

"I hope so," Remo said. "Now beat it."

Sweet Shiv turned and walked away and Remo watched him go, quietly sympathizing with the man who was obviously a CURE agent and did not know it. Remo had been framed. Bernoy Jackson had been bought. But they were brothers under the skin somehow, and so Jackson lived.

What hurt was that Remo had been marked for death. And now he could trust no one. But why had they sent that Jackson? CURE must be compromised beyond saving. Then why go through with the search for Liu? What else was there to do?

Remo went into the door of the karate school. He felt Chiun follow him up the creaky wood steps in the narrow stairway, boxed in by grease-coated, dust-catching green paint. A lightbulb at the top of the stairs illuminated a red painted arrow. The paint was fresh. Mei Soong followed Chiun.

"Oh how wonderful it is to work with you, Remo," Chiun said.

"Drop dead."

"Not only are you a detective and secretary of state but now you are becoming socially aware. Why did you let that man walk away?"

"Swallow your spit."

"He recognized you. And you let him go."

"Suck cyanide."

Remo paused at the top of the stairs, Chiun and Mei Soong waiting behind him.

"Are you contemplating the stairwell or a new cause of social justice?" Chiun's face was serene.

It would be Chiun. Remo had always known it, but did not want to believe it. Who else could do it? Not that Jackson. Yet Chiun had not terminated him.

That Chiun had not been able to was out of the question.

The thought momentarily arose in Remo's mind that Chiun might have refrained because of affection for Remo. The thought was as fleeting as it was absurd. If Remo had to go, Chiun would do it. Just another job.

Then it was the message that had failed. It had not reached Chiun. Remo thought of the phone call to Smith, and his insistence that Remo tell Chiun to return to Folcroft. Of course that was the signal—and Remo had not transmitted it.

The course for Remo now was clear. Just throw a shot to the frail yellow throat in the hallway, now while they were pressed together. Stun him. Kill him. And then run. And keep running.

That was his only hope.

Chiun looked up at him quizzically.

"Well," he said, "are we to reside here forever to become an element of the scenery?"

"No," said Remo with heaviness in his voice. "We're going inside.

"You will find it a most attractive and rewarding experience to witness the martial arts," Mei Soong said.

Chiun smiled. Mei Soong pushed past them and opened the door. Chiun and Remo followed, into the large low-ceilinged white room with sunlight coming in over the backs of large pictures in the front windows of what had once been a loft. Off to the right were the usual paraphernalia of karate schools, sandbags, and roofing tiles, and a large box filled with beans, used for toughening the fingertips.

Mei Soong confidently walked over to a small glass-windowed office with a bare desk upon which sat a young Oriental man in white floppy karate suit tied with a red belt. His head was shaven almost clean, his features smooth, his expression calm with the kind of calmness that comes with years of training and years of discipline.

Chiun whispered to Remo: "He is very good. One of only eight true red belts. A very young man in his early forties."

"He looks twenty."

"He is very, very good. And would give you an interesting exercise, if you choose to allow it to be interesting. His father, however, would give you more than an interesting exercise."

"Danger?"

"You are an insulting young man. How dare you think that someone I trained these many years would be in danger of such a red belt? What insulting stupidity. I have given you years of my life and you dare to say that." Chiun's voice lowered slightly. "You are a very stupid man and also forgetful. You fail to remember that anyone taught pure attack can defeat karate, even a man in a wheelchair. Karate is an art. A minimal art. Its weakness is that it is a killing art only at time, a small slice of the circle. We approach the circle. They do not."

Remo watched Mei Soong, her back to him. The Oriental in the red belt listened closely. Then he looked up, seeing Remo but concentrating on Chiun. He left his office, still peering at Chiun and when he was five feet away, his mouth opened and blood appeared to drain from his face.

"No," he said. "No."

"I see, Mr. Kyoto, that you have earned young your red belt. Your father must be very proud. Your family has always loved dancing. I am honored to be in your presence and extend utmost cordialities to your honorable father." Chiun bowed slightly.

Kyoto did not move. Then, recollecting his functions, he bowed extremely deeply in a smooth graceful motion, then backed away quickly until he bumped into Mei Soong.

From the wall farthest from the window, where a sign read dressing room, a file of men emerged through a door, seven black men in phalanx, all wearing black belts. They moved with grace and silence, their white karate uniforms blurring against each other, creating a mass which made definition more difficult.

"Go back, go back," yelled Kyoto. But they kept coming until they had surrounded Chiun and Remo.

"It is all right, Mr. Kyoto," said Chiun. "I am just an innocent observer. I give you my word I will not get involved."

Kyoto glanced back at him. Chiun nodded politely, smiling.

One of the black men spoke. He was tall, six-feet four, 245 pounds and no flab. His face looked carved of ebony. He was grinning.

"We of the third world has nothin' against a brother of the third world. We wants the honkey."

Remo glanced at Mei Soong. Her face was frozen, her lips clamped thin. She was undoubtedly going through more emotional tension than Remo who was just going to do what he was trained to do. A woman in love betraying her lover was an airport of signals.

"Learned master of all arts, am I to understand you will not intrude yourself?" asked Kyoto.

"I will stand aside to witness the spectacle of all these people attacking one poor white man. For I can see that is what they are prepared to do," Chiun said this almost as a sermon, then pointing a shaking forefinger at Mei Soong, he added: "And you, faithless woman, luring this unsuspecting young man into this den of death. For shame."

"Hey, old man. Don't feel sorry for no honkey. He our enemy," said the man of the ebony face.

Remo listened to the interchange, yawned. Chiun's dramatics did not impress him. He had seen Chiun play humbled before. Now Chiun was setting them up for him, although from their swaggering they appeared not to need setting up.

"Move over," said the leader to Chiun, "or we'll move on over you."

"I beg a boon," implored Chiun. "I know this poor man who is about to die. I wish to say goodbye to him."

"Don't let him, he'll pass him a gun or something," yelled one of the blacks.

"I have no weapon. I am a man of peace and solitude, a frail flower cast upon the harsh rocky soil of conflict."

"Hey, what he talk?" came the voice of the man with the largest Afro, a spray of coiled black weeds exploding in all directions from his tan head.

"He say he ain't carrying," said the leader.

"He look funny for a gook."

"Don't say gook. He third world," said the leader. "Yes, old man. Say goodbye to the honkey. The revolution is here."

Remo watched the crowd raise their fists to the ceiling of fluorescent lights and wondered how much he would reduce New York City's welfare bill. Unless, of course, they were somewhat competent in which case he would reduce the crime rate.

The group was now giving each other fancy handshakes, saying "Pass the power, brother."

Remo looked at Chiun and shrugged. Chiun beckoned Remo's head to lower. "You do not know how important this is. It is very important. I know personally Kyoto's father. You have some bad habits which inhibit grace when you become excited. I have not corrected them because they will work themselves out and to change them now would inhibit your attack. But what you must avoid at all costs is a full energy attack, because these habits will surely show, and Kyoto's father will hear about your lack of grace. A companion of mine lacking grace."

"Gosh, you have problems," Remo said.

"Do not joke. This is important to me. Perhaps you do not

have pride in yourself, but I have pride in myself. I do not wish to be embarrassed. It is not like white or black men were watching but a yellow man of red belt whose father knows me personally."

"And it's not like I'm going against Amos and Andy," Remo whispered. "These guys look tough."

Chiun peered briefly around Remo's shoulder at the group, some of whom were taking off their shirts to show their muscles, for Mei Soong's benefit.

"Amos and Andy," Chiun said, "whoever they are. Now please, I ask this favor of you now."

"Will you give me a favor in return?"

"All right. All right. But remember. The most important thing is not to embarrass my instructional methods."

Chiun bowed and even pretended to brush away a tear. He stepped back, signalling Mei Soong and Kyoto to join him. One of the men who had removed his shirt showed fine round muscled shoulders and a good rippling stomach stacked with rows of muscles like a washboard. A weight lifter, thought Remo. Nothing.

The man swaggered to Chiun, Kyoto and Mei Soong, signalling they should go no further.

"He is my pupil of a few days," Chiun confided openly to Kyoto, while pointing to Remo.

"You stay where you is. All of you," said the well-muscled man. "Ah don't wants to hurt no brother of the third world."

Remo heard Kyoto snort laughter.

"I take it," Chiun said, "that these are the students of your honorable house."

"They have walked in," came Kyoto's voice.

"Walk in?" Remo heard the guard behind him say. "We been working out here for years."

"Thank you," said Chiun. "Now we will see what years of Kyoto instruction does in comparison with just a few humble words from the house of Sinanju. Begin if you will."

Remo heard Kyoto groan. "Why must my ancestors be forced to witness this?"

"Don't worry," came the black guard's voice. "We'll do you up proud. Real proud. Black power proud."

"My heart trembles before your black power," said Chiun, "and my respect for the House of Kyoto knows no bounds. Woe is me and my friend."

The seven black men moved wide for the kill. Remo set for the attack, his weight centered for instant movement in any direction.

It was funny. Here Chiun was warning him about performance, and Remo needed no warning. It was the first time Chiun would see his pupil in action and Remo wanted, as he wanted few things, to win praise from the Little Father.

One should not concern oneself with appearances but results. That is how Remo's training differed from karate, but now he was worried about appearances. And that could be deadly.

THERE were seven and Remo prepared to work right, slant in left, pick up two, then come back across, pick up one, and work it from there. It wasn't necessary.

The biggest one, with the ebony face, stepped into the circle. His Afro was manicured like a well-tended hedge, and he stood with his forearms held forward, wrists limp. One of the blacks behind him, who did not practice the Preying Mantis attack of the school of Kung Fu, laughed.

Large, strong men rarely used the Praying Mantis. It was an attack small men used to compensate. If the big man with the flaming Afro should slip past Remo's attack, Remo would be dead with one blow.

"Hey, Piggy," said the black who had laughed. "You look faggy."

Piggy moved fast for a big man, extending one leg, then moving a stroke towards Remo's head. Remo was under the stroke, driving fingers into the solar plexus, then back up to catch the sirloin roll neck with a down stroke, knee up to smash the face and set it up for a follow-through with the fingers extended into the temple. The body hit the mat almost silently, the face still surprised. The left hand remained curved.

Then there were six, six stunned black faces, eyes widening. Then someone had the correct idea to attack en masse. It looked like a race riot in martial arts robes. "Get the honkey bastard. Kill whitey. Get whitey."

Their screams echoed in the hall. Remo glanced to Chiun to see if there was approval. Mistake. A black hand came into his face and he saw darkness and stars, but as he felt himself going down, he saw the white of the mat, and saw the arms and legs and black hands with lighter palms, and felt a foot come up toward his groin.

He brought one hand up behind the kneecap, and using his fall flipped the body attached to the knee over his head. He brought a foot up into a groin and rolled. As he did so, he moved to his feet, caught an Afro and cracked down into it, smashing a skull.

A voiceless body hit the mat. A black belt launched an attack with a foot shot. Remo grabbed the ankle and kept it going behind his head and brought his thumb up sharply into the man's back, damaging a kidney and flinging him to the side, shrieking in pain. Now there were four, and they weren't as anxious to get whitey. One was downright brotherly as he nursed his broken knee. Three black belts surrounded Remo in a semi-circle.

"All at once. Attack. On three," said one, making sense. He was very dark, black as night and his beard was scraggly. His eyes had no whites, just black fires of hate. Perspiration beaded his forehead. By showing his hate so openly, he had blown his cool.

"Ain't like the movie, Shaft, is it, Sambo?" said Remo. And he laughed.

"Mother," said the black belt to Remo's left.

"Is that a plea? Or half a word?" Remo asked.

"One," called out the man with hate.

"Two," called out the man with hate.

"Three," called out the man with hate, and he went with a foot, the other two with straight ahead punches.

Remo was down beneath them, slipping behind the man who hated. He spun around, snatched his foot and kept spinning him to the bean box where students and instructors toughened their fingertips by ramming them into eight inches of beans. Remo rammed his hand into the box very quickly, but it did not reach the bottom.

It did not reach the bottom of the box because under his hand was the hate-filled face. It no longer hated because jammed into the box at that speed, it was no longer a face. It was a pulp. Beans had been driven into the eyes. From above, it looked as if the black belt who had weakened to hate under the pressure of fear was drinking from the box deeply, the beans covering his head. Blood seeped up through the beans, swelling them.

Remo did a waltz skip to a pile of tiles with the other two black belts swinging about his head and toward his back. He scooped up two curved gray tiles from the pile and began to whistle, and as he dodged blows and kicks, he began clacking the curved bricks in rhythm to the melody.

He spun around one blow and brought the two bricks, one in each hand, together, with an Afro between them. Directly in the middle of the Afro was a head. The two bricks made valiant effort to meet. But they cracked. So did the head in the Afro between them.

The Afro with the open-mouthed head went to the mat. The remnants of the tiles went into the air. The last black standing threw an elbow that missed and then said, eloquently:

"Sheeit."

He stood there, his arms hanging, his forehead perspiring. "Ah don't know what you got, man, but Ah can't take it."

"Yeah," said Remo. "Sorry."

"Up yours, honkey," said the man, breathing heavily.

"That's the business, sweetheart," said Remo and as the man

made one last desperate lunge, Remo shattered his throat with a back slash.

He untied the black belts as the corpse staggered by and walked over to the man with the broken knee who was trying to crawl to the door. He dangled the belt in front of his face.

"Want to win another one fast?"

"No man, I don't want nuthin'."

"Don't you want to wipe out whitey?"

"No, man," cried the crawling black belt.

"Ah, c'mon. Don't tell me you're one of those who save his militancy for deserted subways and classrooms?"

"Man, Ah don't want no trouble. Ah ain't done nuthin'. You brutalizing."

"You mean when you mug someone, that's revolution. But when you get mugged, that's brutality."

"No, man." The black covered his head awaiting some sort of blow. Remo shrugged.

"Give him the black belt of the dojo of Kyoto," sang out Chiun. Remo saw anger flood the face of Kyoto, but it was quickly controlled.

"Unless, of course," Chiun said sweetly to Kyoto, "you of years of experience would care to teach the martial arts to my humble student of just a few moments?"

"That is not a humble student," said Kyoto. "And you did not teach him art, but the methods of Sinanju."

"All the house of Sinanju had to work with was a white man. But in our small way, we attempt to do the best we can with whatever is given us." The black belt with the broken knee was now scurrying into a dressing room out a side door, which slammed shut behind him. Kyoto's eyes followed the sound and Chiun said, "That man has the instincts of a champion. I will tell your honorable father how successful you are in teaching track and field. He will be happy that you have deserted dangerous sports."

Remo folded the black belt in his hands carefully, walked over and flipped it to Kyoto. "Maybe you can sell it to somebody else."

The dojo looked as if it had just surfaced from a whirlpool that had struck in the middle of a class. Chiun looked happy, but he said: "Pitiful. Your left hand still fails to extend properly."

Mei Soong was ashen-faced.

"I thought . . . I thought . . . Americans were soft."

"They are," snickered Chiun.

"Thanks for bringing me here," Remo said. "Any other places you wish to visit?"

Mei Soong paused. "Yes," she finally said. "I'm hungry."

In the long march, there had been nothing like it. In the days of hiding in the caves of Yenan there had been nothing like it. And there was no answer in the thoughts of Mao tse Tung. Even in the spirit of Mao, there was no answer.

General Liu forced himself to accept with politeness the news from the messenger. In the decadent monarchist regimes of the past, the evil of the news would have fallen on the head of its bearer. But this was a new age, and General Liu simply said: "You may go and thank you, comrade."

There had been nothing like it before. He watched the messenger salute and depart, shutting the door behind him, leaving General Liu in the windowless room which smelled of oil on metal and had but one chair and a bed, and very poor ventilation.

Other generals might live in splendor, but a people's general could never aggrandize himself. Other generals might live in palace houses like warlords, but not him. Not a real people's general who had buried his brothers in mountains and left a sister in a winter's snow, who had at 13 been requisitioned for service in the Mandarin's fields, just as his sister had been requisitioned for service in the Mandarin's bed.

General Liu was a great general of the people, not in his pride but in his experience. He could smell the quality of a division ten miles away. He had seen armies rape and pillage, and he had seen armies build towns and schoolhouses. He had seen a lone man annihilate a platoon. But he had never seen what he was seeing now. And in comfort-loving America, of all places.

He looked down again at the note in his hands, as he had looked at other notes during the three days he had been in hiding.

First, there were the hired gangsters in Puerto Rico. Not revolutionaries, but competent. And they had failed.

Then there was Ricardo de Estrana y Montaldo y Ruiz Guerner, of personal experience a man who had never failed. And he had failed.

And there was the Wah Ching street gang. And it had failed.

And when guns and gangs had failed, there were the great hands of the karate black belt.

He looked down at the note in his hands. And now that too had failed. They had all failed in both their missions: to eliminate those who were trying to find the general and to bring to him his bride of only one year.

And if General Liu and his men continued to fail, his people would cast themselves at the feet of the peacemakers in Peking, ready to forget the years of hardship and to end the revolution before it was complete.

Did they not know that Mao was just a man? A great man, but just a man and men grow old and weary and wish to die in peace?

Did they not see that this step backward, making peace with imperialism, was a retreat, just when the battle was being won? With victory in their mouths, would they now succumb to the son of a mandarin, the Premier, and sit at the same table with the dying beast of capitalism?

Not if General Liu could stop it. General Liu would not have peace. The Premier had misjudged his cunning, misjudged even his motives.

He had been careful not to let himself be seen in China as a leader of the war faction. He was just a people's general, until chosen by the Premier to arrange safe journey for his trip to see the swine American President. He had quietly arranged for the deaths on the transport plane, and when that did not halt plans for the Premier's visit, he volunteered to go to America himself. And then after changing to western garb, he had shot his own guards and slipped alone, unnoticed onto the train which had brought him here.

It should have been easy to stay hidden during the seven days of grace the Premier had given the Americans. But this impossible American could not be denied, and even now was probably closing in on General Liu. When his followers heard of the escape from the karate dojo, they would lose heart. They must be firmed up.

General Liu sat down on his hard cot. He would go through his plans three times, thinking over the details from three angles. Then he would speak to his people.

And then, when he was ready, he would act with thoroughness, and when the plan proved successful, he would hold in his arms once more Mei Soong, the beautiful flower, the only pleasure of his life outside duty.

This plan must not fail. Not even before this impossible American who had once again revived the ancient fairy tales of an ancient China. Yes. He must first discredit the fairy tales.

General Liu rose from his cot and banged on the heavy steel door. A man in drab army type clothing opened it. "I will meet with the leaders immediately," General Liu said. Then he shut the door with a clang and heard the lock fall into place.

Within minutes, all had gathered, standing in the little airless room. The early arrivals were fidgeting for want of fresh air. Some perspired and General Liu noticed how fat some faces were, how flaccid, how pale. They were not like the people of the long march. They were like the people of Chiang Kai Shek and his soft running dogs.

Well, General Liu had often led unfit men into combat. He talked now to them . . . of the long struggle and of the dark hours and how these had been overcome. He talked of hunger and cold and how these had been overcome. He spoke to the pride in the hearts of the people before him and when they no longer suffered from the heat or the air but were overcome by revolutionary fervor, he hit his target where he wished to hit his target.

"Comrades," he said in the outlawed Cantonese dialect, looking around the room and meeting their eyes, "we who have accomplished so much, how can we now fall prey to a child's fairy tale? Was not the winter in the caves of Yenan fiercer than a fairy tale? Were not the armies of Chiang and his running dogs fiercer than a fairy tale? Are not the armaments of modern times fiercer than a fairy tale?"

"Yes, yes," came the voices. "True. How true."

"Then why," asked General Liu, "should we fear the fairy tales of Sinanju?"

One young man said triumphantly: "Never fear suffering. Never fear death. Never fear, least of all, fairy tales."

But an old man, in what were once the clothes of the mainland, said: "He kills like the night tigers of Sinanju. This he does."

"I fear this man," General Liu said, stunning his audience. "But I fear him as a man, not as a fairy tale. He is a formidable man, but we have defeated formidable men before. But he is no night tiger from Sinanju, because there is no such thing. It is just a village in the People's Republic of Korea. You, comrade Chen. You have been there. Tell us of Sinanju."

A middle aged man in a dark, single breasted business suit, with a face of steel and a haircut that looked an accident of shrub shears, came forward to stand by General Liu. He faced the men crowded into the stuffy room.

"I have been to Sinanju. I have spoken to the people of Sinanju. They were poor and exploited before the glorious revolution. Now they are beginning to enjoy the fruits of freedom and . . ."

"The legend," interrupted General Liu. "Tell them of the legend."

"Yes," said the man. "I sought out the Master of Sinanju. What master, the people asked me. The master of the night tigers, I said to them. There is no such thing, they said. If there were, would we be so poor? And I left. And even the Spaniard who once worked for us said he could not find the Master of Sinanju. So why should we believe there is such a one?"

"Did you put money in the pockets of the people of Sinanju?" asked the old man who had spoken before.

"I did not," the man responded angrily. "I represented the revolution, not the New York Stock Exchange."

"The people of Sinanju are money worshippers," the old man said. "If you had offered money and they had still said no, I would be more heartened."

General Liu spoke up. "The American we are talking about is a man whose face is pale as dough. Would the master of Sinanju make of a pale face a night tiger? Even in the legend, only people of the village of Sinanju become night tigers."

"You are wrong, comrade general. The legend says that there will someday be a master so enamored of money that for great wealth he will teach a pale face who has died all the secrets of

Sinanju. He will make of him a night tiger, but the most awesome of night tigers. He will make him kin to the gods of India,
kin to Shiva, the destroyer."

There was silence in the room. And no one moved.

"And within an hour," said General Liu, "this Destroyer, this
dead man, will be lying on this cot. And I will give you the privilege of executing his legendary body. Unless, of course, our revolution must be cancelled because of a fairy tale."

This broke the tension, and everyone laughed. Everyone but
the old man.

He said, "The white man has been seen with an elderly Korean."

"His interpreter."

"He could be the Master of Sinanju."

"Nonsense," General Liu said. "He is a frail flower ready for
interment." To save the old man the great hurt of losing face,
General Liu bowed to him in the old way. "Come, comrade. You
have done too much for the revolution, not to join with us now
in our moment of glory." He signalled for the man to stay. The
others chattered with confidence as they filed through the narrow steel door. They were a unit again.

General Liu went to the door and closed it and motioned the
old man to sit on his cot. He placed himself on the single chair
in the room and said: "This Sinanju. I have heard the legend too,
but I do not believe it."

The old man nodded. His eyes were old as shale, his face as
stiffening leather.

"But I have been confronted by other things I find hard to believe," Liu continued. "Supposing this fairy tale, this Shiva the
Destroyer, exists. Does the legend tell of a weakness?"

"Yes," said the old man. "He is influenced by the moon of
justice."

Liu lashed his anger to the controlling rod, withholding the storm inside him. How often he had been forced to deal gently with the archaic poetry of thought that chained his people to poverty and superstition. He forced himself to speak gently.

"Are there any other weaknesses?"

"Yes."

"How can he be overcome?"

The old man said quickly and simply, "Poison." But he added cautiously: "One must not trust poison. His body is strange and may recover from the poison in time. Poison to weaken him, and then a knife or gun."

"Poison, you say?"

"Yes."

"Then, poison it shall be."

"You have a way to deliver this poison to his system?"

They were interrupted by a knock at the door. A messenger entered and handed Liu a note.

He read it and beamed expansively at the old man: "Yes, comrade. A lovely, charming delicate way to deliver this poison. She has just arrived upstairs."

23

IT was the best beef in oyster sauce Remo had ever tasted. A special dark flavor that raised the senses to the thin strips of beef bathing in brown syrup. Remo speared another dark sliver with the stainless steel fork and twirled it in the oyster sauce, then lifted it, dripping, to his mouth, where he let it rest, tingling, vibrant and delicious.

"I have never enjoyed any dish like this before," he told Mei Soong.

Mei Soong sat across the white table cloth from him, at last silent. She had denied everything of course. She had not received any messages from Liu's captors. She didn't know where the little red book in her room had come from. She denied being told to lure Remo to the karate school.

She denied this while walking to the restaurant. She denied it while on her way to the ladies' room in the restaurant, where she received her instructions from an old Chinese woman. She denied all this even as she placed her order for beef in oyster sauce, and she denied it as she suddenly lost her appetite and let Remo eat the entire dish.

Remo kept eating, just waiting for whatever would come out of the walls. They had gone through four major assaults and now, whoever held General Liu captive, must strike openly. The poor old bastard. Probably in a dungeon someplace, and now betrayed by his wife. Perhaps it was his age that had turned the girl against him. Or perhaps, it as Chiun had said:

"Treachery is the basic nature of a woman."

Remo's answer had been typically thoughtful. "You're full of crap. What about mothers? Many women aren't treacherous."

"And there are cobras that will not bite. I will tell you why women are treacherous. They are of the same species as men. Heh, heh."

He had chuckled the way he had just chuckled when leaving the table for the kitchen to make sure his food did not contain cats, dogs, Chinese and other vermin.

"The beef in oyster sauce is especially nice, isn't it?" Mei Soong said, as Remo finished up the last morsel.

A sense of warmth overcame him, then a deep feeling of well being and an extreme relaxation of his muscles. The air bloomed with cool smells and Mei Soong's delicate beauty entranced his entire body. The imitation leather seats became pillows of air, and the dark green walls with white pictures became dancing lights, and all was well with the world because Remo had been poisoned.

Before it became too dark, Remo reached out to say good-bye to Mei Soong, a little gesture like putting his left forefinger into her eyesocket to take her with him. He was not sure that he reached her however, because suddenly he was going into a very deep and dark place which spun people around and never let them go. And the oyster sauce was rising back up through his throat into his mouth. That delicious oyster sauce. He would have to get the recipe some day.

The cook, of course, was giving Chiun lip. Answering back heatedly about the quality of his food until he was made reasonable and responsible and polite, by a pan of hot grease which had, by some mysterious force, sent hot steaming droplets at the cook's arrogant face.

But no one responded to investigate the cook's frenzied yelling. Chiun decided to investigate this. Where was everyone?

He moved from the kitchen, testing the hinges on the swinging doors by seeing how fast the doors could give way to a tray-laden waiter going through them. They gave way very fast, and Chiun pretended to be even more aged than he was when he stepped over the pile of broken dishes out into the main dining hall of the Imperial Gardens. Remo and Mei Soong were gone.

Would Remo leave him like this?

Of course, he would. The child liked to do things like this and often did inexplicable things. Then again, he might have received a message which he knew would be Chiun's signal to terminate him. What fools the white men. To have Chiun terminate what was undoubtedly the finest Caucasian on the earth. Would they ask him to terminate Adrian Kantrowitz or Cardinal Cook or Billy Graham or Leontyne Price? People of no value at all?

No. They would ask him to terminate Remo. The fools. But that was the nature of white men. Why, in just thirty or forty years, Remo probably could come close to Chiun, and if he discovered some locked-up hidden power, might even surpass him.

But would the white man wait thirty years? Oh, no. Thirty years was forever to a white man.

A waiter walked up and stood between Chiun and Remo's table. Chiun removed the waiter from his vision, by putting him in a seat. With a broken shoulder. Then Chiun saw the brownish spit on the side of the tablecloth where Remo had been sitting. He asked the waiter where Remo had gone. The waiter said he did not know.

In the mirrors over the front entrance door, Chiun saw a group of men in Chinese waiters' garb spill out of a side door into the main dining area, heading for him.

They did not come to offer assistance. They came to make people uncomfortable. Two of them immediately stopped making Chiun uncomfortable, because they had to attend to their lungs. Their lungs needed attention because they had been punctured by their ribs.

Patrons screamed and huddled against the formica walls of dining booths, as one man came racing at Chiun waving a cleaver over his head. He kept going. So did the cleaver. So did his head. His head rolled. His body gushed blood all the way to the crowd that suddenly was not a crowd. The cleaver landed onto a table next to a tureen of won ton soup. The head rolled to a stop at the feet of the vice president of the Mamaroneck Hadassah.

And into the din, beyond all voices, spoke Chiun:

"I am the Master of Sinanju, fools. How dare you?"

"No," screamed the waiter and huddled fearfully into a corner of the booth.

"Where is my child that you have taken from me?"

"What child, oh, Master of Sinanju?" said the cowering waiter.

"The white man."

"He is dead of fatal essences."

"Fool. Do you think his body would entertain them? Where is he?"

With his good arm, the waiter pointed to a wall with a large relief of the city of Canton.

"Wait here and speak to no one," Chiun ordered. "You are my slave."

"Yes, Master of Sinanju."

To the bas relief went Chiun, and through its interlocking mechanism went the terrible swift hand, ignited in all the fury of its art. But there was no one left in the restaurant to see him. Only the terrified slave who sobbed in a corner. And he, of course would wait for his master. The Master of Sinanju.

General Liu saw his loved one coming down the passageway in the dank hallway with the rest of the group, the old Chinese man and two waiters bearing the impossible one.

He had been waiting, hearing the minute by minute reports of the message given, the poison served, the poison eaten, and then an eternity before the impossible one passed out.

Now it was all worth it. He was captured and would soon be dead. And she was here. The delicate, fragrant blossom. The one sweet joy of his hard and bitter life.

"Mei Soong," he said, and brushed past the scurrying water waiters and past the old man. "It's been so long, darling."

Her lips were moist with American lip paste, her dress was of frail material which clung more luxuriously to her young vibrant body. General Liu clutched her to his chest and whispered, "Come with me. It has been so long."

The old Chinese man, seeing the general trundle off with his wife, called out: "What shall we do with this one, comrade general?" and rubbed his hands nervously. The air was very hot in the passageway. He could scarcely breathe.

"He's half dead already. Finish him off." And the general disappeared into his little room, tugging Mei Soong along behind him.

Then the old Chinese man was in the hall way with the white man held up by the two waiters. He nodded to an adjacent door, and drew from his pocket a ring of many keys. Finding one special key, he inserted it in the lock of the wooden door.

It opened easily, revealing a small chamber and an altar lit by flickering candles. A pale porcelain Buddha sat content at the apex of the altar. The room smelled of incense, burned in the memory of years of incense and daily devotions.

"On the floor," said the old man. "Put him on the floor. And say nothing of this room to anyone. Do you understand? Say nothing."

When the waiters had left, shutting the door tightly behind them, the old man went to the altar and bowed once.

There were always new philosophies in China but always there was China, and if the new regime looked scornfully upon devotions to gods other than material dialectics, still it would accept the other gods one day, just as all the new regimes eventually accepted all the old gods of China.

Mao was China today. But so was Buddha. And so were the ancestors of the old man.

From his suit pocket, he removed a small dagger and returned to where the white man lay. Perhaps the night tigers of Sinanju were of gods no more, and the master gone with them, and Shiva, the white Destroyer, come and gone where all had gone before.

It was a fine knife, of steel from the black forests of Germany, sold by a German major for many times its worth in jade when the Germans and the Americans and the Russians and the British and the Japanese buried their differences to press the face of China further into the mud.

The major had given the knife. Now, the old man would return it to the white race blade first. The black wooden handle was wet in his palm as the old man pressed the point to the white throat. He would plunge it straight in, then rip to one side, then rip to the other, and then step away to watch the blood flow.

The face seemed strangely strong in its sleep, the eyes deep behind their closed lids, the lips thin and well-defined. Was this the face of Shiva?

Of course not. He was about to die.

"Father and grandfather, and for your fathers and their fathers before them," the old man intoned. "For the indignities upon indignities suffered from these barbarians."

The old man knelt so that he would bring the full force of his shoulder behind the blade. The floor was hard and cold. But the face of the white man was growing pink, then red, as though filled with blood before blood was spilled. A brownish line formed between the thin lips. The old man looked closer. Was it his imagination? He seemed to feel the heat of the body about to die. The line became a dark brown dot on the lower lip, then an elongated puddle that flowed to the sides, then a stream, and then a gush as the face turned red and the body heaved, and out, coming out on the floor, out of the body's system was the oyster sauce and the beef and with it, the poison essences, mixed with the body's fluid and smelling like oysters and vinegar. The man should have been dead. He should have been dead. But his body was rejecting the poison.

"Aiee," screamed the old man, "it is Shiva the destroyer."

With a last desperate effort, he raised the knife for the most forceful plunge he could effect. A last chance was better than none at all. But at the knife's apex, a voice filled the basement in thunder.

"I am the Master of Sinanju, fools. How dare you? Where is my child whom I have made with my heart and with my mind and with my will? I have come for my child. How will you die? Now you shall fear death because it is the death brought by the Master of Sinanju."

Outside the door to the little room, servants were screaming directions. "There, there. He is in there."

The old man did not wait.

The dagger came down swiftly and hard, with all his strength. But it did not plunge straight down. Instead, it created an arc to his own heart. It was pain and hot and shocking to his essence. But it was true to its mark and of all his pain, all the pain would not be so bad as punishment from the Master of Sinanju. He tried to twist the knife further into his own heart as his body trembled. But he could not. And it was not necessary. He saw the cold stone floor coming toward him and he prepared to greet his ancestors.

Remo came to with a bony knee in his back. He was facing the floor. Someone had vomited on the floor. Someone had also bled on the floor. A hand was slapping his neck sharply. He attempted to spin, cracking the slapper in the groin to render him harmless. When he was unable to do this, he knew it was Chiun slapping him.

"Eat, eat. Gobble like a pig. You should have died, it would have taught you a most lasting lesson."

"Where am I?" said Remo.

Slap. Slap. "Why should one who eats like a white man care?" Slap. Slap.

"I am a white man."

Slap. Slap. "Do not remind me, fool. I have already been made painfully aware of that. Do not eat slowly. Do not taste your food. Gobble. Gobble like a buzzard. Stick your long beak into the food and inhale." Slap. Slap.

"I'm okay now."

Slap. Slap. "I give you the best years of my life and what do you do?"

Remo had raised himself to his knees. Momentarily, during the pounding on his neck, he thought he could perhaps get a sidehand crack at Chiun's jaw, but abandoned the notion. So he let Chiun slap away until Chiun was satisfied that Remo was breathing properly again.

"And what do you do? After all my careful teaching? Hah. You eat like a white man."

"It was really great beef in oyster sauce."

"Pig. Pig. Pig." The word came with the slaps. "Eat like a pig. Die like a dog."

Remo saw the old man lying face down in a layer of blood, that was already darkening about the edges.

"You do the old man?" he asked.

"No. He was smart."

"He looks it," Remo said.

"He understood what would happen. And chose the wise course."

"Nobody as smart as you Orientals."

With a last ringing slap, Chiun finished his work. "Stand up," he ordered. Remo rose, feeling like the pavement during the Indianapolis 500. He blinked his eyes, breathed deeply a few times. And felt quite fine.

"Ecch," he said, noticing the stains of vomit on his shirt. "They must have had knockout drops in the food."

"It is lucky for you," lied Chiun, "that it was not a deadly poison. For if you thought you could survive poison, you would never end your foolish eating ways."

"It was deadly poison, then," Remo said smiling.

"It was not," Chiun insisted.

Remo smiled broadly, straightened his tie, and glanced around the room. "This the basement of the restaurant?"

"Why? Are you hungry?"

"We've got to find Mei Soong. If she's with the general, she might be trying to kill him right now. She's one of them, remember. And the general's in danger."

Chiun gave an abrupt snort, opened the door, and stepped over the two bodies lying outside in a hallway that smelled of musk. Remo noticed that the wooden door had been splintered away from its lock.

Chiun moved like silence in the dark, and Remo followed as he had been taught, in sideways steps along the corridor, in perfect rhythm with the old man before him.

Remo stopped when Chiun stopped. In electric fast movement, Chiun's hand snapped against a door which flung open, momentarily blinding Remo with the light from within. On a plain cot, the hard, yellow, muscled back of a man was on the rise. Two young legs wrapped around his waist. His black hair was crossed with white. Remo saw the soles of Mei Soong's feet.

"Quick, Chiun," he said. "Think of something philosophical."

The man's head spun around in shock. It was General Liu.

"Uh, hello," Remo said.

Chiun spoke, "Have you no shame? Get dressed."

General Liu unplugged with speed and lunged for a .45 caliber automatic on the plain wooden chair. Remo was at the chair in a flash, catching General Liu's arm at the wrist and righting him so he would not fall.

"We're friends," Remo said. "That woman has betrayed you. She is in league with those who captured you and held you prisoner."

Mei Soong rose on her arms, a look of surprise, then of terror on her face. "Untrue," she screamed.

Remo turned to her, and since the movement of the .45 automatic was not to him, he did not respond with automatic movement, but then heard the crack as he saw the top of her head blasted into the stone wall, splattering blood and gray matter, leaving her brain like a coddled egg about to be eaten from the shell of her skull.

He snatched the gun from General Liu.

"She betrayed me," said General Liu, trembling. Then he fell down and sobbed.

It would not be until he strolled a Peking street that Remo would realize that the general's tears were from relieved tension, and that indeed, Remo had been a very poor detective. He watched Liu fall to his knees and bring his hands to his face, heaving, sobbing.

"Poor bastard. All this and then his wife betraying him too," Remo whispered to Chiun.

Chiun responded with a phrase carrying a very special meaning. "Gonsa shmuck," he said.

"What?" said Remo, not really hearing.

"In English, that means very much a shmuck."

"Poor bastard," said Remo.

"Shmuck," said Chiun.

THE President's heart was lighter as he watched the newscast. His closest advisor watched also, twisting an index finger through his kinky blond hair.

They sat in the office in deep leather chairs. The President's shoes were off and he twiddled his toes on the hassock. To the right of his left big toe was the advisor's face on the television screen, saying that he would make a trip to Peking and accompany the Premier back to the United States.

"The trip is carefully planned and thorough. Everything will be routine," the voice intoned on TV.

"A routine bit of incredible luck," the President interjected.

A reporter asked the TV face a question. "Will events in China now influence the trip?" he said.

"The Premier's journey is proceeding according to schedule and plans. What is happening in China now influences it in no way."

The President framed his advisor's face between his two big toes. "Now that General Liu is returning with you."

The advisor smiled and turned to the President: "Sir, just how did we find General Liu? The FBI, the CIA, Treasury, everyone says they had nothing to do with it. The CIA wants to guard him now."

"No," the President said. "They will all be busy trying to track down those two men who kidnapped the general. The General will go back to Peking with you. He will be with two men. They will take the rear of your plane."

"I take it you have some special agents I know nothing about."

"Professor. Once I could have answered that question. Today, I'm not even sure. And that's all I can say." The President glanced at his watch. "It's almost eight o'clock. Please go now."

"Yes, Mr. President," said the aide, arising with his briefcase. They shook hands and smiled. Perhaps peace, a realistic peace, might yet be achieved by man. Wishing or running rampant in parks with peace symbols would not bring it, however. It would come if one worked and schemed and plotted for peace, just as one did for victory in war.

"It looks good, Mr. President," the aide said.

"It looks good. Good night."

"Good night, sir," said the aide and left. The white door shut behind him. And the President listened as various people spoke of Phase Two of his economic policy. There were five people with five different opinions. It sounded like a meeting of his economic advisors. Well, it was a great country and no President could do it much harm.

The second hand on his watch circled the six and headed up past the seven and nine and eleven, then met the twelve, and there was no ring. God Bless you, Smith, wherever you are, thought the President.

Then the special line rang, like a symphony of bells, and the President hopped from his chair and soft-footed it to his desk. He picked up the receiver on the special phone.

"Yes," he said.

"In answer to your question of two days ago, sir," came the lemony voice, "we will continue but under different circumstances. Something didn't work. I will not tell you what, but it did not work. So in the future, do not even bother to ask for the use of that person."

"Is there some way we can let him know of his nation's gratitude."

"No. As a matter of fact, he is incredibly lucky to be alive."

"I have seen pictures of him from agents tailing Mei Soong. One of them was killed in a karate school. Your man was seen."

"It will not matter. He will not look like that any longer after he returns."

"I do wish there was some recognition, some reward we could give him."

"He's alive, Mr. President. Is there anything else you wish to discuss?"

"No, no. Just tell him thank you from me. And thank you for letting him deliver the general safely to his destination."

"Good-bye, Mr. President."

The President hung up the phone. And he chose to believe, because he wanted to believe, that America still had men like Smith and the man who worked for Smith. The Nation produced men like that. And it would survive.

25

REMO was uncomfortable.

Peking was making him edgy. Everywhere he and Chiun went with their escorts, people noticed them, and stared. Now it was not the noticing that made him uncomfortable, not that. Their eyes were telling him something, even in the crowded shopping areas, the broad pin-neat streets. But he didn't know what.

And something else was bothering him. They had delivered General Liu and received thanks. Two Chinese generals of Liu's Army had looked at Remo very closely and mumbled with Liu. And one of them had said, in obviously mistaken English, "Destroyer . . . Shiva," which was probably a Navy captain or something.

And that afternoon, they would formally be shown the Working People's Palace of Culture, in the Forbidden City, as a special honor.

Chiun was unimpressed with the honor. He had been noticeably cool ever since Remo had expressed heartfelt hurt that Chiun would kill him. Chiun was emotionally distressed that Remo would take it that way.

It had come to a head after Remo had telephoned Smith to tell him the mission was successful. Smith had been silent for a long moment, and then had ordered Remo to tell Chiun his blue butterflies had arrived.

"Can't you think of a better signal than that?" Remo had asked.

"It's for your own good. Inform Chiun of that."

So that afternoon in their hotel room, Remo thought he would bite the bullet once and for all, and see what happened. He was not totally unprepared to take on Chiun, given, of course, that nothing he had been taught would be new to Chiun and that Chiun's attack would be based on that. But Remo had a secret weapon, one the old man might not expect. A right cross to the jaw, as taught in the CYO boxing team of Newark, New Jersey. Not a perfect weapon, but it might have a chance.

He readied himself in the middle of the room to make Chiun come to him. Then he said softly, "Chiun, Smith says your blue butterflies have arrived."

Chiun was sitting in the lotus position watching the television set, absorbed in whether a young doctor should tell the mother of a leukemia victim that her daughter had leukemia, an especially difficult task because the doctor had once had an affair with the woman and was not sure if it was his daughter or the daughter of Bruce Barlow who owned the town in which they all lived, and who had just contracted a venereal disease, possibly from Constance Lance whom the doctor's stepfather was engaged to, and who had a weak heart which any shock might destroy. Besides, Barlow, as Remo had gathered from two days of that pap, was considering a gift to the hospital to buy a kidney machine which Dolores Baines Caldwell needed desperately if she were to live to finish her study of cancer before her laboratory was repossessed by an as-yet-to-be-introduced Davis Marshall whom the leukemia victim had met on a holiday in Duluth, Minnesota.

"Chiun," Remo repeated, ready to see the last of the world in a sterile hotel with air like ice and bed spreads of drab white ruffles, "Smith says your blue butterflies have arrived."

"Yes, good," Chiun said without looking up from the set.

Remo waited for the show to end but Chiun still did not move. Did he want to catch Remo in his sleep?

"Chiun," Remo said as Vance Masterson pondered with James Gregory, district attorney, the fate of Lucille Grey and her father, Peter Fenwick Grey, "your butterflies are in."

"Yes, yes," Chiun said. "You've said that three times. Quiet."

"Isn't that the signal for you to kill me?"

"No, it's the signal for me not to kill you. Quiet."

"So you would have killed me."

"I will kill you now with pleasure if you do not silence your mouth."

Remo walked over to the television set and with the edge of his hand cracked the back of the tube and Chiun sat horrified as the picture sucked itself into a dot of light, then disappeared. Remo dashed out of the room and down the long hallway. On a straightaway, he could beat Chiun. He scrambled down a flight of stairs, along a hallway, and stopped near an open window and laughed until he cried. He sneaked back to the room that evening, and Chiun was sitting in the same position.

"You are a man without heart or soul," Chiun said. "Or intelligence. Angered by the truth of what you know should be true, you foolishly take vengeance on someone who would do something that would be more painful to him than his own death. And neglectful, because I am left to guard the general in the next room and you should be doing that."

"You mean you would rather die than kill me?" Remo asked.

"And that makes you feel better? I do not understand you," Chiun had said. And he had been cold and distant all the way to Peking.

Now, on a Peking street, Remo realized what was bothering him about the peoples' stares. "Chiun," he said. "Stay here and watch me. Tell the guards to stay with you."

Remo did not wait. He hitched his casual blue woolen sweater down over his light tan slacks and walked casually into the main thoroughfare with its occasional cars, its shop windows, under giant posters with Chinese characters, past the rows of Mao pictures, then walked directly back to Chiun and the two guides. One of the guides was on the pavement, his hands to his groin. The other was smiling politely and desperately.

"He said you couldn't be allowed to go alone," Chiun said, nodding at the man in pain on the ground.

"Were you watching?" Remo asked.

"I saw you."

"Did you watch the people?"

"If you mean, did I realize that your theory of General Liu's disappearance in the Bronx was ridiculous, correct. No two men took him anyplace. They would have been seen. He disappeared alone. And like you, just now, aroused no interest at all."

"Then if he disappeared alone . . . ?"

"Of course," Chiun said. "Didn't you know that? I knew it immediately."

"Why didn't you tell me?"

"Interfere with Chief Ironsides, Perry Mason, Martin Luther King, William Rogers and Freud?"

So, thought Remo, Liu had not been kidnaped. He had ordered the drivers off at Jerome Avenue. Then shot them. Then walked away from the car, caught the train and met his cohorts in Chinatown. He had sent people after Remo because Remo had represented the one threat to his plan to sabotage the President's trip. And he had killed Mei Soong, who had known about it, before she could spill what she knew. And now he was back in Peking, a bigger hero and a bigger threat than ever.

"The question is, Chiun, what do we do?"

"If you wish my advice, it is this: mind your own business and let the world of fools hack themselves to death."

"I expected that from you," Remo said. Maybe he could tell someone with the American mission. But no one on the mission knew him. All they knew was that he had return tickets for two to Kennedy Airport and was not to be bothered.

Perhaps call Smith? How? He had enough trouble trying to call him from New York City.

Leave it for the Chinese to settle. But it galled him, right to the gut, it galled him. The son of a bitch shot his wife, and didn't care that millions might die in another war. He wanted this. That was bad. But worse was that he dared to do it. That he thought he had a right to do it, and that bothered Remo deep into his soul.

He looked around the wide clean street with drably dressed people scurrying to their trivia of the moment. He looked at the clear China sky, unshrouded by air pollution because the people had not yet advanced enough to pollute the air, and thought that if Liu had his way, they never would be granted the gift of dirty air.

Chiun was right of course. But because he was right did not make it right. It was wrong.

"You're right," Remo said.

"But you do not feel that way in your soul, do you?"

Remo didn't answer. He looked at his watch. It was almost time to return for their grand tour of the Working People's Palace of Culture.

General Liu's aide, a colonel, had stressed what an honor it was. The Premier himself would be there to meet the rescuers of the people's general, the colonel had said.

Chiun's advice on that subject was "watch your wallet."

The Forbidden City was truly a splendor. Remo and Chiun and their two guards walked past the stone lion guarding the

Gate of Heavenly Peace, for 500 years the main entrance to the city which had once housed emperors and their courts.

They walked across the vast cobblestone plaza toward the yellow pagoda roofed building which now housed the main museum but which had been a throne room. In a section of the plaza off to their left, Remo saw young and old men exercising in the highly disciplined moves of T'ai Chi Ch'uan, the Chinese version of karate.

The building was beautiful. Even Chiun, for once, had nothing slanderous to say. But its contents reminded Remo of one of those New York auction houses that seem to be devoted exclusively to large and ugly porcelain figures. He did not listen to the rambling explanations of dynasties or thrones or vases or clumsy looking objects, all of which showed that China had discovered this or that or something else way back when Remo was still painting himself blue.

By the time they reached the central vault where General Liu and the Premier waited for them, Remo had been verbally painted blue with enough coats to lather a Celtic army.

Standing in the central vault under the fifty foot high ceiling, the Premier looked like a display porcelain. He was more frail than his pictures. He wore a plain gray Mao suit, buttoned to his neck, but while the suit was plain, the tailoring was immaculate.

He smiled and offered a hand to Remo: "I have heard much about you. It is a privilege to meet you."

Remo refused the hand. "To shake hands," he said, "is to show that I have no weapons. To shake hands therefore would be a lie." The hell with him. Let him and Liu play their goddam war games with the President's staff; they got paid to deal with these devious bastards.

"Perhaps someday, no one will have to bear a weapon," said the Premier.

"In that case, it will no longer be necessary to shake hands to show you have no weapon," Remo said.

The Premier laughed. General Liu smiled. He looked younger in his uniform, but then, that was the reason for uniforms. To make the nasty business of killing impersonal and institutional, something separate from men and pain and all the other hassles of day to day life.

"With the Premier's permission," said General Liu, "I would like to show our guests a most interesting exhibit. I hope you two gentlemen do not mind that we have soldiers present but the Premier must be protected at all costs."

Remo noticed on a narrow step a few feet away were eight soldiers, all of them seeming rather old for the privates' uniforms they were wearing. They had their guns trained on Remo and Chiun. Well, sweetheart, Remo thought, that's the biz.

General Liu nodded with stiff politeness and walked to a glass case, containing a stone-encrusted sword. His leather shoes made clacking sounds on the marble floor and his holster slapped against his side as he walked. The room itself was chilly and badly lighted, blocking out the sunlight and its joy.

"Gentlemen," said General Liu. "The sword of Sinanju."

Remo looked at Chiun. His face had no expression, just an eternal calm that hid wells deeper than Remo's reasoning.

It must have been a ceremonial sword of some sort, Remo thought, because not even a Watusi could wield a sword seven feet long, and flaring out to become as wide as a face, before it came abruptly to a point. The handle was encrusted with red and green stones. It appeared as unwieldly as a wet sofa. If a man's hands were tied to that weapon, you could spit him to death, Remo thought.

"Do you gentlemen know the legend of Sinanju?" General Liu asked. Remo could feel the Premier's eyes upon them.

Remo shrugged. "It's a poor village, I know that. Life is hard there. And you people never treated them very fairly." Remo knew Chiun would love that.

"Truth," said Chiun.

"But do you know the legend? Of the Master of Sinanju?"

"I know," said Chiun, "that he was not paid."

"This sword," said General Liu, "is the sword of the Master of Sinanju. There was a time when China, weak under the monarchistic system, hired mercenaries."

"And did not pay them," said Chiun.

"There was one master of Sinanju who left this sword after slaughtering slaves and then a favorite concubine of the Emperor Chu Ti."

Out of the side of his mouth, Remo whispered to Chiun: "You didn't tell me about the nookie."

"He was assigned the concubine and was not paid," Chiun said aloud.

General Liu went on. "The emperor, realizing how foreign mercenaries were destructive to the Chinese people, banished the Master of Sinanju."

"Without paying him," said Chiun.

"Since then we have prided ourselves in never asking for the services of the Master of Sinanju or his night tigers. But imperialists will hire any scum. Even create the destroyer for their evil designs."

Remo saw the smile disappear from the Premier's face as he looked at General Liu with questioning.

"In a society where the newspapers function as an arm of the government, word of mouth becomes the believable truth," said General Liu. "Many people believe that the Master of Sinanju is here, brought by the Imperialist Americans. Many believe he has brought Shiva, the Destroyer, with him. Many people believe that the American imperialists do not seek peace but war. That is why they have sent the Master of Sinanju and his creation to kill our beloved Premier."

Remo noticed Chiun look to the Premier. There was a slight shake of Chiun's head. The Premier remained cool.

"But we will kill the paper tigers of Sinanju who have killed our Premier," General Liu said, raising a hand. The riflemen on the balconies aimed their weapons. Remo looked for a display case to dive under.

Chiun said, looking at the Premier: "The last Master of Sinanju to stand in this palace of emperors was not paid. I will collect for him. Fifteen dollars American."

The Premier nodded. General Liu, still holding one hand in the air, took his pistol from its holster with the other.

Chiun laughed then, a resounding, shrieking laugh.

"Rice farmers and wall builders, hear you now. The Master of Sinanju will teach you death." The words echoed through the high-ceilinged chamber, bouncing hollowly off the walls and corners and coming back, until it seemed as if the voice came from everywhere.

Suddenly, Chiun became a blurred line, his white robes swirling about him as he moved toward the Premier, then left across General Liu's line of fire. And then the glass case was shattered and the sword seemed to fly into the air with Chiun attached.

The sword swished and blurred with Chiun, whose voice rose maniacally in ancient, high-pitched chants. Remo was about to dart up to the step to go after one of the riflemen and work from there, when he noticed the guns were no longer pointing at him or at the Premier or at Chiun.

Two men clung loosely to their weapons, one whose pants showed a dark wide blotch, growing wider. The other just trembled, his face whitening. Another was vomiting. Four had run.

Only one still aimed his rifle but the butt was pressed firmly to a shoulder that had no neck, just a round, dark gushing wound where a head had been. Remo spotted the head, one eye still squinting, rolling to the base of a cabinet where it stopped rolling and stopped squinting. And the sword, now dripping blood, spun faster and faster in Chiun's hands.

The Premier's face was impassive as he stood, his hands folded in front of him. General Liu squeezed off two shots which chipped into the marble floor then bounced into walls with dull thumps, sounding through the museum. Then he stopped squeezing shots, because where his trigger finger had been, there was only a red stump.

And then the hand itself and the pistol were gone as the sword continued to whistle through the air with Chiun seeming to dance under it.

And then, with a shriek, Chiun was without the giant sword. He stood motionless, his arms at his sides, and Remo heard the sword whirring above him, toward the ceiling. Remo looked up. The sword seemed hung in history just a breath from the ceiling, and then it descended, the giant blade turning slowly, until in one last graceful turn, it came down into Liu's looking up face.

With a whunk, it split the face and drove straight down through the body, stopping only a foot from the hilt. The clean tip of the blade nicked marble, and then began to gather blood from above. It looked as if General Liu had swallowed too completely the seven foot sword of Sinanju.

In awesome silence, he tottered, then backward fell, skewered on a sword, creating small flowing lakes of blood around him on the gray marble floors. The hilt seemed to grow from his face.

"Fifteen dollars American," said the Master of Sinanju to the Premier of the latest China. "And no checks."

The Premier nodded. So he was not part of the plot. He was one of the peacemakers. In blood was peace sometimes baptized.

"Sometimes, according to Mao," said the Premier, "it is necessary to pick up the gun to put down the gun."

"I'll believe it when I see it," said Remo.

"About us?" asked the Premier.

"About anyone," Remo said.

They escorted the Premier to a car outside and Chiun anxiously whispered to Remo:

"Was my wrist straight?"

Remo, who had barely seen Chiun, let alone his wrist, answered, "Sloppy as hell, Little Father. You embarrassed me no end, especially in front of the Premier of China."

And Remo felt good.

THE DESTROYER
Slave Safari

AUTHORS' INTRODUCTION

ANY resemblance between the African nation of Busati in this book and the actual country of Uganda is purely, maliciously intentional.

In the early seventies when *Slave Safari* was written, the common wisdom was that the new leaders who were taking over the countries of Africa had to make some drastic changes to free their nations from the burden of colonialism. There was nothing basically wrong with these leaders. Oh, no. How could there be? Didn't most of them rename their countries the People's Republic of something or somebody's Socialist Democracy? And didn't they all hate the United States? How could there be anything wrong with them?

So, with their apologists cheering from the sidelines, these leaders redelivered Africa to the dark ages. Countries that had fed themselves for centuries suddenly, under centralized farm planning, faced starvation and were reduced to the status of the world's beggars. The only thing that grew were the numbered Swiss bank accounts, swollen with money stolen from aid and relief programs.

Civil liberties vanished, the free press vanished, and anyone foolhardy enough to speak up in opposition vanished, too. In countries where some of the people were forbidden to vote, equality was introduced: Everybody was forbidden to vote and anybody who didn't like it might wind up as granola for croco-diles.

The awful thing is that the tragedy that is Africa continues to unfold, even today. It's only in books like this one that occasion-ally a story ends happily.

—DICK SAPIR *and* WARREN MURPHY
August 1985

A WORD OF AGREEMENT

OF course this book has a happy ending. Every one of these so-called *Destroyers* has a happy ending because at last the abysmal thing is finally over.

In this deplorable excuse for a book, the two scribblers write words in what they claim is Swahili. Do not be deceived. This is not the elegant formal Swahili language spoken by cultured people of many lands. Instead, it is a gruesome type of gutter slang that is an affront to the ear.

But why expect good Swahili from these two when even good English is so obviously beyond them? You read junk.

—CHIUN, MASTER OF SINANJU

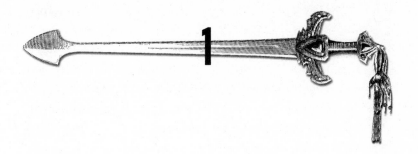

WHILE Europe was a collection of warring tribes and Rome merely another city-state on the Tiber and the people of Israel shepherds in the Judean hills, a little girl could carry a sack of diamonds across the Loni Empire in East Africa and never fear even one being taken from her. If she suffered an injured eye, here alone in all the world were men who could repair it. In any village she could receive a parchment for her jewels, take it to any other village, then collect gems of exactly identical weight and purity. Waters from the great Busati River were stored in artificial lakes and channeled into the plains during the dry season, long before the Germanic and Celtic tribes that later became the Dutch ever heard of dikes or canals. Here alone, in all the world, a man could set his head on pillow without fear of attack in the night or hunger in the morning.

Historians do not know when the Loni ceased to care for their canals and dams, but by the time of the Arab slavers, the Loni were no more than a small tribe, hiding in the hills to escape mass slaughter. The plains were death dry; the Busati River flooded at will; and one in ten were blind for life. The land was ruled by the Hausa tribe, whose only governmental policy was to track down and to kill the remaining Loni.

Some of the Loni could not successfully hide, but instead of being killed, they were often taken to a spot on the river and traded for food and a drink called rum. Sometimes the person who took them went the way of his merchandise. Whole villages disappeared in chains to serve the plantations of the Caribbean Islands, South America and the United States. The Loni were very valuable indeed because, by this time, it had begun to be written that the men were strong and the women were beautiful and the race lacked the courage to resist.

In the year one thousand, nine hundred and fifty-two, dated from the birth of a god worshipped in Europe, the Americas and small parts of Africa and Asia, the colony called Loniland became independent. In a stronger wave of nationalism in the 1960's the colony became Busati, and in a yet stronger wave in the 1970's, it expelled the Asians who had come with the British to open stores, when the lands along the Busati River had been called Loniland.

When the Asians fled under the policy called "Busatinization," the last people capable of mending an eye left the land of the Loni. Little girls dared not venture into the streets. No one carried valuables for fear of the soldiers. And high in the hills, the scattered remnants of the Loni Empire hid, waiting for a promised redeemer who would restore them to the glory that once was theirs.

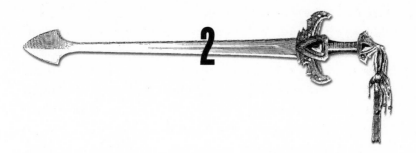

JAMES Forsythe Lippincott yelled for his boy who was somewhere in the Busati Hotel, which still used towels labeled Victoria Hotel and still had the ornate V's inscribed, embossed and sewn all over halls, drapes, busboys' uniforms and water faucets.

There had been no hot water since the British left, and now with the last planeload of Asians having taken off from Busati Airport the day before, there was no cold water either.

"Boy," yelled Lippincott, who, back in Baltimore, would not even call a nine-year-old black child "boy." Here, he was yelling for his porter. According to the new Busati tradition, published the day before in the last edition of the *Busati Times*, any foreigner, most especially a white, who called a Busatian "boy" could be fined up to a thousand dollars, thrown in jail for ninety days and beaten with sticks.

But if you paid your fine in advance to the Minister of Public Safety and to the great conquering leader, Dada "Big Daddy" Obode, who that very morning had successfully defended Busati against an air invasion by America, Britain, Israel, Russia and South Africa, using—according to Radio Busati—the very latest in atomic planes, you would not have to pay your fine in court.

This process in Busati was called pre-guilt payment, a revolutionary system of justice.

In Baltimore the same process was called graft.

"Boy, get in here," yelled Lippincott. "There's no water."

"Yes, Bwana," came the voice from the hallway followed by a black, perspiring man in loose white shirt, loose white pants and a pair of cracked plastic shoes—which made him one of the richer men of his village ten miles up the Busati. "Walla here to serve you, Bwana."

"Get me some fucking water, nigger," said Lippincott, snapping a towel in Walla's face.

"Yes, Bwana," said Walla, scurrying from the room.

When Lippincott had come to Busati, he fully intended to respect the proud African traditions and search for old forgotten ones. But he found quickly that this politeness earned him only derision, and besides, as the Minister of Public Safety had said:

"Bush niggers need beatings, Mr. Lippincott. Not like you and me. I know it's against our laws for a white to hit a black nowadays, but between civilized men like you and me, the only way to treat a bush native is to thrash him. They're not like us Hausa. They're not even Loni, God help them. Just poor mongrels."

It was then that James Forsythe Lippincott learned of pre-guilt payments and, as he handed over two hundred-dollar bills to the Minister of Public Safety, was promised, "If any of these boys give you trouble, just let me know their names. You won't see them around anymore."

In Baltimore, James Forsythe Lippincott was careful to call the maids by their marital title and last name, and to promote blacks to executive positions in the family company he ran, but in Busati he did as the Busatians. It was the only way to get things done, he told himself, and he did not even suspect how much he truly liked this method of beatings and brutality, in preference to the enlightened Baltimore way where every problem was solved by holding another seminar in race relations.

This was Busati, and if he did not follow the Busati system of beating bush niggers, well, then, would that not be a subtle form of racism, thinking his American way was superior to the Busati way?

James Lippincott examined his stubble of a beard. He had to shave it. Couldn't let it go another day or he might be mistaken for one of the hippies who regularly never returned from Busati. In Busati, a man with a clean shave and wearing a suit got some respect. Those seeking truth, beauty and a communion with man and nature, just never showed up again.

Walla rushed into the room with a soup tureen of water.

"Why did you bring that in?" asked Lippincott.

"No more pots, Bwana."

"What happened to the pots?"

"Liberated yesterday by the army, Bwana. So that imperialist aggressors won't get them. Atomic planes come to steal our pots, but our great conquering leader destroyed the attackers."

"Right," said Lippincott. "A great attack by imperialistic nations." He dipped a finger into the soup tureen of water and became angry.

"This is cold, Walla."

"Yes, Bwana, no more hot water."

"You brought up boiling water from the kitchen yesterday."

"No more gas for the stove, Bwana."

"Well, how about firewood? They can certainly burn firewood. You don't need Asians to show you how to make a fire, do you?"

"Got to go upriver for wood, Bwana."

"All right," said Lippincott, annoyed. "But for every cut I get from using cold water, you get two cuts. Understand?"

"Yes, Bwana," said Walla.

Lippincott counted three cuts on his face when he turned from the mirror and took the blade out of his safety razor.

"That's six for you, Walla."

"Bwana, I got something better for you than cutting."

"Six cuts," said Lippincott who had intentionally given himself the last two in anticipation of taking revenge for his discomfort on Walla.

"Bwana, I know where you can get woman. You need woman, Bwana, don't cut poor Walla."

"I don't want some little black ape, Walla. Now you have cuts coming to you and you know you deserve them."

"Bwana, you look. You want woman. You don't want Walla."

It was then that James Forsythe Lippincott realized his body was indeed calling out for a woman.

"White women, you do whatever you want. White women, Bwana."

"There are no white women available in Busati, Walla. That will be another cut for lying."

"White women. Oh, yes. White women. I know."

"Why haven't I heard of them before?"

"Not allowed. Not allowed. Secret. White women at the big house with the iron gate."

"A whorehouse, Walla?"

"Yes, Bwana. White women in the whorehouse. Don't cut Walla. You can do anything to them you want if you got money. Anything. You can cut white women if you got enough money."

"That's outrageous, Walla. If you're lying, I'll give you twenty cuts. Do you hear me?"

"I hear, Bwana."

When Lippincott drove up to the large white house with the iron gate, he saw to his delight that the windows held air-conditioning units. Iron bars held the gray units in place. If he had looked closer, he would have seen that there were bars also on windows that had no air conditioners. But he did not look closer, nor did he wonder why Walla did not accompany him, even though the servant knew he would be punished for just disappearing the way he had.

Lippincott was pleasantly surprised to see that the buzzer button on the gate worked. He tried it only after he found that the gate did not open to his pushing.

"Identify yourself," came a voice from a black box over the mother-of-pearl button.

"I was told I could find entertainment here."

"Identify yourself."

"I'm James Forsythe Lippincott, a close personal friend of the Minister of Public Safety."

"Then he sent you?"

If Lippincott had lived a life that exposed him to any sort of danger, he might have taken cautioned notice of the fact that in a country where brass doorknobs were stolen regularly, no one had pried loose the little mother-of-pearl buzzer from that front door. But James Lippincott was discovering himself, and in the excitement of finding that he truly loved to inflict pain, he neither worried nor cautioned.

"Yes, the Minister of Public Safety sent me and said everything would be okay," Lippincott lied. So what? Instead of a pre-guilt payment, there would be an after-guilt payment.

"All right," said the voice in the hollow raspiness of a speaker system. Lippincott could not place the accent, but it sounded faintly British.

"The car can't get through the gate," said Lippincott. "Will you send a boy out to watch it?"

"No one will touch a car in front of this gate," came the voice. The gate clicked open and such was Lippincott's anticipation that he did not wonder what might protect a car in front of this house, when ordinarily Busatians stripped a parked car like piranha working over a crippled cow.

The path to the door of the mansion was inlaid stone and the door handles shiny brass. The door of oak was polished to a gleam and the bell knob was the crafted head of a lion—not African lion but British. Lippincott knocked. The door opened and a man in Busati Army whites, with sergeant's stripes on his sleeves, stood in the entrance.

"A bit early, what?" he said in a British accent, that seemed even colder coming from his anthracite face.

"Yes. Early," said Lippincott, assuming that was what he should say.

The sergeant ushered him into a living room with ornate Victorian furniture, chairs stuffed to discomfort, bric-a-brac filling crannies, large portraits in gold frames of African chiefs. It was not British, but almost British. Not the almost-British of Busati, but the almost-British of another colony. Lippincott could not place it.

The sergeant motioned Lippincott to a seat and clapped his hands.

"A drink?" he said, lowering himself into a stuffed sofa.

"No, no, thank you. We can begin now," he said.

"You must have a drink first and relax," said the sergeant, grinning. An old wizened black woman came into the room silently.

"We'll have two of your special mint juleps," the sergeant said.

Mint juleps. That was it. This home was furnished the pre–Civil War South, *American South,* thought Lippincott. Like a pre–Civil War whorehouse, perhaps in Charleston, South Carolina.

Lippincott made a show of looking at his watch.

"Don't rush yourself, the girls will wait," said the sergeant. The man was exasperating, thought Lippincott.

"Tell me, Lippincott, what brings you to Busati?"

Lippincott resented the over-familiar use of the last name, but answered, "I'm an amateur archaeologist. I'm looking for the causes of the breakdown of the great Loni Empire and the assumption of power by the Hausa tribe. Look. I'm not really thirsty and I'd like to get on with, well, with the business at hand."

"I'm sorry for the inconvenience," said the sergeant, "but you are not on the approved list to use this house, so I'll have to find out more about you before you may begin. Terribly sorry, old boy."

"All right, what do you want to know?"

"Must you make it seem like an interrogation, old boy?" the sergeant said. "Interrogations are so crass."

"When crass is faster, crass is nicer."

"All right, if you must be barbaric, who told you of this place?"

"The Minister of Public Safety," lied Lippincott.

"Did he tell you the rules?"

"No."

"The rules are these. You don't ask the girls their names. You tell no one of this house. No one. And, old boy, you don't just drive up to the gate. You phone in advance. Make an appointment. Understand?"

"Yeah. Yeah. C'mon. How much?"

"It depends upon what you want to do."

Lippincott did not feel comfortable talking about it. He had never done this before, not what he wanted to do, and before coming to Busati had never even suspected that he had such desires. He fumbled with the words, stepping into the area of his longings, then skirting them, then approaching them from another angle.

"Whips and chains, you mean," said the sergeant.

Lippincott nodded silently.

"That's not so unusual. Two hundred dollars. If you kill her, that's $12,000. Severe damage is prorated. These girls are valuable."

"All right, all right. Where do I go?"

"Cash in advance."

Lippincott paid, and after insolently recounting the money, the sergeant led him upstairs to a long broad hallway. They stopped in front of a polished steel door. From a tall chest next to the door, the sergeant took a cardboard box, and handed it to Lippincott.

"Your whips and chains are in here. Hooks are on the wall. If the girl gives you any trouble, just ring the buzzer in the room. If she refuses you anything, threaten to ring the buzzer. She shouldn't be any trouble though. Been here three months. Only the really new ones give trouble. Haven't been educated, so to speak."

The sergeant took a key from a ring on his belt and unlocked the door. Lippincott gripped the paper box tightly under his arm and went into the room like a schoolboy discovering an abandoned pastry shop.

He slammed the door behind him, and in his rush into the room, almost stumbled over a wide metal cot. On it lay a nude woman, her legs drawn up to her stomach, her arms shielding her head, her red hair a dirty tangle on the mattress, which was speckled with dried bloodstains.

The room smelled of camphor and Lippincott assumed it must be from the ointment that glistened on the girl's flanks over fresh and precisely drawn lash marks. Lippincott suddenly felt compassion for the creature and was tempted to leave the room, perhaps even buy her freedom, when she peered from beneath her folded arms and seeing a man with a box, rose slowly from the cot. When he saw her young breasts flecked with dried blood as she rose from the cot, a driving rage enveloped him, and when she dutifully walked to the dirty, blood-spattered wall and raised her hands above her head to an iron ring, Lippincott was trembling. He fumbled the chains around her wrists, then pounced on the whip as if someone might snatch it from him.

As he readied himself for the stroke, the girl asked, "Do you want screaming?" She was American.

"Yes, screaming. Lot of screaming. If you don't scream, I'll whip harder and harder."

Lippincott whipped and the girl screamed with each cutting crack. Back came the whip, then forward, crack, and the polished snakelike cord glistened with blood, back and forward, back and forward, faster until the screams and the whip and the cracking became a single sound of anguish and then it was over. James Forsythe Lippincott was spent and with the sudden quenching of his strange and sudden thirst, his powers of reasoning assumed command and he was suddenly afraid.

He realized now the girl had screamed almost as a duty despite the great pain. She was probably drugged. Her back looked like raw meat.

What if someone had taken pictures of him? He could deny them. It would be his word against some bush nigger's. What if the Minister of Public Safety found out he used his name improperly? Well, three, maybe four hundred dollars would take care of that.

What if the girl died? Twelve thousand dollars. He gave more than that each year to the Brotherhood Union for Human Dignity.

So why be afraid?

"Are you through, Lippy?" the redheaded girl asked dully, her voice heavy with drugs. "If you are, you're supposed to take the chains off."

"How do you know my name? That's only used in my social circle."

"Lippy, this is Busati. Are you through?"

"Uh, yes," he said, going to the wall to get a better look at her face in the dimly lit room. She was about twenty-five, the fine, lean nose had been broken days before and was swollen and blue now. There was a gash in the lower lip that had crusted around the edges.

"Who are you?"

"Don't ask. Just let me die, Lippy. We're all going to be dead."

"I know you, don't I? You're . . . you're," and he saw the features, now mangled, that had once graced Chesapeake Bay society, one of the Forsythe girls, a second cousin.

"What are you doing here, Cynthia?" he said, and then, in horror, remembered and said, "We just buried you in Baltimore."

"Save yourself, Lippy," she groaned.

In his panic, that was just what Lippincott intended to do. He envisioned Cynthia Forsythe somehow getting back to Baltimore and disclosing his terrible secret. Lippincott grabbed the end of the whip and wrapped it around the girl's neck.

"You're a fool, Lippy, you always were," she said and James

Forsythe Lippincott tightened the whip and kept pulling the ends until the red swollen face of the girl disclosed a tongue and the eyes bulged and he kept pulling.

The sergeant downstairs understood why James Forsythe Lippincott did not wish to write out a personal check, and yes, he would trust him to return to his hotel and make arrangements with the National Bank of Busati to get cash. "We do not worry," the sergeant said. "Where would you go?"

Lippincott nodded, although he was not sure what the sergeant meant. He understood only that he would be allowed to pay for what happened upstairs, and that was all he wanted to hear.

When Lippincott returned to his hotel, Walla was still missing. He called for him several times, then vowed that when he saw Walla again, the busboy would get a beating to carry on his back for the rest of his life.

The vice-president of the bank offered to supply guards to Lippincott because walking around Busati with $12,000 was not the wisest of courses. "This is not New York City," the banker explained, apologetically and inaccurately.

Lippincott refused. He was sorry three blocks later. One of the many military patrols stopped him and as he reached into his pocket to show his identification and a ten-dollar bill, he must have disclosed the bulk of his cash, for the officer reached into his pocket and took out the envelope of one hundred and twenty hundred-dollar bills.

"That belongs to the house with the iron gate," said Lippincott hoping the power the house seemed to have would extend to the officer. Apparently it didn't, because the officer simply double-checked Lippincott's identification, asked him again if he were indeed James Forsythe Lippincott, then shoved him into the Land Rover and personally drove the vehicle away.

Out of the capital they drove, and along the great Busati River they drove. Darkness fell over the Busati and still they drove on, alone, the rest of the patrol having been ordered to stay back in the city. They drove so far that when they stopped Lippincott swore the stars seemed close, as close and as clear as they must have been when man first descended from the trees.

The officer told Lippincott to get out.

"Look, I can give you twice that amount of money. You don't have to kill me," said Lippincott.

"Get out," said the officer.

"I'm a personal friend of the Minister of Public Safety," said Lippincott.

"You'll find him over there behind that wide tree," said the officer. "Go."

So Lippincott, finding the Africa night chilly and his heart even chillier, went to the wide tree that rose like a little prickly mountain from the Busati plain.

"Hello?" he said but no one answered. His elbow brushed up against something on the tree. He looked around. It was a boot. A leg was in the boot and on top of the leg was a body. The dangling hands were black. The body did not move and it smelled of the last release of the bowels. The body was in an officer's uniform. Lippincott stepped back to escape the smell and to try for a better look at the face. Suddenly a flashlight illuminated the body's features. It was the Minister of Public Safety. A large spike protruded from his head. He had been nailed to the tree.

"Hello, Lippy," said an American voice.

"What?" gasped Lippincott.

"Hello, Lippy. Squat down on your haunches. No, not your butt on the ground. On your haunches, like a slave waiting for his master. On the haunches. That's right. Now, Lippy, before you die, if you're very nice, you may ask me a question."

The flashlight had gone off and now the voice came out of the African dark, and try as he might, Lippincott could not see the speaker.

"Look," he said, "I don't know who you are, but I can make you a rich man. Congratulations on successfully scaring the crap out of me, Now, how much?"

"I've got what I want, Lippy."

"Who are you?"

"Is that your one question?"

"No, my one question is what do you want?"

"All right, Lippy, I'll answer that. I want to revenge my people. I want to be accepted in my father's house."

"I'll buy your father's house. How much?"

"Ah, Lippy, Lippy, Lippy. You poor fool."

"Look. I want to live," said Lippincott, straining to keep his backside just off his raised heels. "I'm humbling myself. Now what can I give you for my life?"

"Nothing. And I don't care about your humbling yourself. I'm not some Harlem shine who calls himself Abdulla Bulbul Amir. Humbling doesn't do anybody any good."

"You're white? I can't see."

"I'm black, Lippy. African. Does that surprise you?"

"No. Some of the most brilliant men in the world are black."

"If you had any chance at all, you just blew it with that lie," the voice said. "I know better. I know every one of you Lippincotts and Forsythes. There isn't one of you who isn't a racist."

"What do you want?" asked Lippincott. "What do you want?" The man was obviously keeping him alive for something. There was silence. Far off, a hyena howled. There would be no lions near here, not with vehicles and men having been around the area.

"I can get you recognition from America," said Lippincott. "My family can do that."

"Who is America to recognize or not to recognize?"

"What do you want?"

"Some information."

"If you kill me, you won't get it."

"First I'll get it and then I'll kill you. There are many ways to die and some aren't so bad."

Lippincott believed the man and like many people who find death too strong to face, he told himself a little lie. He told himself he would be spared if he told the man the truth.

"The Minister of Public Safety didn't tell you about the house, did he?"

"No, he didn't," Lippincott said, remembering again the gruesome corpse hanging from the tree near his head. "My boy Walla did."

"Never mind, the Minister had to die anyway," the voice said. "Unlike most members of this government, he would not see things my way. Now, you've done research on slave ships and the original slave trade into the States. There was a Butler plantation on which you still have the records, isn't that so?"

"Yes. I can show them to you. They're at my Chesapeake Bay estate."

"In the basement storage or the library?"

"I forget. But I can show you."

"No matter. We'll get them, now that we know which of your homes they're in. That's all I needed. Anything I can give you besides your life?"

"Nothing," said Lippincott on the hope that if only his life would do for a favor, his life he might get.

"Don't you want to know the answer to your research about the breakup of the great Loni Empire?"

"I want my life."

The voice ignored him. "The Loni Empire," it said, "broke up because it put its faith in outsiders. It hired people to do what it should have done itself. And they grew soft and weak, and finally the Hausa just pushed them over, as if they were soft, fat children."

Despite his predicament, Lippincott was interested. "That's too simple," he said. "To build a great empire takes character. The Loni must have had it. They would not just roll over and play dead."

"No, you're right," the voice said. "They would have fought. But something got in the way. Your family's accursed slave trade. So the best of the Loni wound up shipped away to grow cotton for you. But I'll tell you a story. The Loni are going to return to power again. I hope that makes you feel better."

"It doesn't," Lippincott said, "but suppose you tell me how. Right now, the whole Loni tribe couldn't build a shoebox."

"Simple," the voice said. "I'm going to lead them back to power." He paused. "Really horrible thing you did to that girl. Not that it matters, Lippy. Not that she matters or that you matter. You'd have to pay a long time before the Lippincotts and the Forsythes ever got even. It doesn't matter. What matters is in the mountains."

Lippincott heard the hyena sounds and smelled the death smells of the Minister of Public Safety and felt a sudden great shock to his back, that came out his chest, and he fell forward on a spear that was through his body. When his head hit the Busati plain, he was dead, another small piece of fertilization, no more than an ancient Loni emperor or an ancient Loni child. Africa took him as one of its own, the earth as ever being the only truly equal opportunity employer in the history of man.

Walla, being more intelligent than either the Minister of Public Safety or Lippincott, was safely up the Busati River in his village.

He had something to sell of far greater value than the last pieces of silver engraved with the old English "V" at the Busati Hotel. He had information; information was always salable.

Hadn't the clerk from the Ministry of Justice sold a copy of the files of the Busati secret police for gold—real gold—coins you could roll in your hands and buy fifty wives with or twenty cattle or shoes and plows and shirts and maybe even a radio for private use, instead of sharing it with the whole village?

So Walla told his brothers he was leaving the village and that his eldest brother should meet him over the border in Lagos, Nigeria, in a month.

"You are selling tales, Walla?" asked the elder brother.

"It is best you do not know what I do," said Walla wisely. "Governments do terrible things to people who know things."

"I have often wondered why we have governments. Tribal chiefs never did terrible things to people who knew things."

"It is the white man's way."

"If the white man is not here anymore, and if, as the radio says, we are getting rid of everything white, why cannot we get rid of white governments?"

"Because the Hausa downriver are fools," Walla said. "They want to get rid of the white man so they can *be* white men."

"The Hausa have always been fools," said the elder brother.

In jeeps with massive supplies, the journey to Lagos would have taken a Busati army patrol a month. Walla, carrying a knife and no food, made the journey on foot in sixteen days.

Walla found a neighbor from his village and asked him for a good place to sell information.

"Not here," said the neighbor who was an assistant gardener at the Russian Embassy. "They were paying good last year but this year is terrible. The Americans are best again."

"The Chinese, are they good?" asked Walla.

"Sometimes they are good, but often they think it is enough to tell you funny stories in exchange for your information."

Walla nodded his head. He had heard these things of the yellow men back in Busati, how they would give a button or a book and think of that as payment, and then be surprised and angry when told that was not nearly enough.

"Americans are the best again," said the gardener, "but take only gold. Their paper is worth less each day."

"I will take gold and I will return here and see you. Your information has been of value."

"See the cook at the American Embassy. He will tell you the price to ask."

The cook at the American Embassy promptly fed Walla and listened to his story, asking questions so that Walla would be well prepared to negotiate.

"This Lippincott disappearing is a good thing. Quite valuable. But the nature of the house is even more valuable possibly. Who are these white women?"

Walla shrugged. "I do not know."

"Who frequents the house?" the cook asked.

"I was told of it by a soldier. He said that Busati soldiers who do good things are given leave to go to the house and do terrible things to the women."

"Does President Obode run the house?" the cook asked.

"I do not know. I think not. I was told that the sergeant who is at the house is a Loni."

"A Loni? Are you sure he is not a Hausa? Hausa do those sort of things."

"I know Hausa from Loni," said Walla. "He is a Loni."

"A Loni who is a sergeant. That is very important," the cook said.

"It is worth gold?" Walla asked.

The cook shook his head. "The Americans do not know Loni from Hausa and could not care less that a Loni has reached a sergeant's rank in Busati's army. Do you have anything on the women in the house?"

"They never come out alive."

The cook shrugged a so-what shrug.

"I know a name. It was told to me by a fellow of our village who worked at the airport. I remember it because it was like Lippincott's name."

"Her name was Lippincott?" the cook asked.

"No. Forsythe. Lippincott had a Forsythe in his name. My friend said he saw her being taken from a plane to a car. She screamed who she was, and then was dragged into the car. She said she was Cynthia Forsythe of Baltimore."

"What did she look like?"

"White," Walla said.

"Yes, but what kind of white? All whites do not look alike."

"I know that," said Walla. "Our friend said she had hair of flame."

The cook thought about this and did not respond immediately. Instead he began chopping vegetables for dinner. When he had finished shredding long green leaves, he snapped his fingers.

"Eighteen thousand dollars. Gold," he said.

"Eighteen thousand dollars?" asked Walla, astounded.

The cook nodded. "That is what we ask for. We settle for fifteen." And he told Walla to withhold the name of the girl until he got the money, but to mention Lippincott's name quickly to make sure he got the money. He explained that the man he would introduce Walla to was J. Gordon Dalton, who was some kind of a spy. He would offer Walla ten dollars or twenty dollars, whereupon Walla should get up to leave, and then Dalton would pay the fifteen thousand.

"I knew a man who had a hundred dollars once," said Walla. "A very rich man."

"You will be rich too," said the cook.

"I will have to be. I can no longer return to Busati."

By nightfall, Walla was the richest man in the history of his village and J. Gordon Dalton was sending frantic codes to Washington. A top level officer unscrambled the message:

JAMES FORSYTHE LIPPINCOTT, BALTIMORE, MISSING. BELIEVED DEAD IN BUSATI BUSH. FOUL PLAY SUSPECTED. CYNTHIA FORSYTHE, BALTIMORE, HELD HOSTAGE. AWAIT INSTRUCTIONS. INVESTIGATING.

Since Lippincott was part of the famous Lippincott family which numbered governors, diplomats, senators and most important, bankers, the message went to several department heads at 4:00 A.M. There was one problem with Dalton's message. Cynthia Forsythe could not be a hostage in Busati. She had been killed in an auto accident three months earlier. It had made the papers because she was related to the Lippincotts.

It was decided quietly to check out the dead girl's body. By noon, from dental work and a thumb print, the body was identified as not, *definitely not,* the body of Cynthia Forsythe.

"Who is it then?" asked the State Department man.

"Who cares?" said the FBI man. "It's not the Forsythe girl. That means she probably is a hostage in Busati."

"Well, we're going to have to tell the White House," said State. "God help anyone who runs afoul of the Lippincotts. Especially the bankers."

Five reports on the case were made in the White House, four of which went to various Lippincotts. The fifth was hand-delivered to an office in the Agriculture Department in Washington, where it was coded and sent by scrambler to what the sender believed was an office in Kansas City. But the line went to a sanitarium in Rye, New York, and in that sanitarium a decision was made that unknowingly fulfilled an ancient prediction made soon after the Loni tribe had lost its empire:

"Terror from the East shall join with terror from the West, and woe to the enslavers of the Loni when the destroyer of worlds walks along the Busati."

HIS name was Remo and his life was being made miserable by a television programming decision.

"Because of our coverage of the Senate investigation into Watergate, *As the Planet Revolves* and *Dr. Lawrence Walters, Psychiatrist-at-Large* will not be shown today," the announcer had said.

When Remo heard that, he uttered his first prayer since childhood. "Lord, have mercy on us all."

The wisp of an Oriental who had sat placid in his golden kimono before the color television set, let out a sound Remo had heard him use but once before, and then only in his sleep.

"Yaaawk," said Chiun, the Master of Sinanju, his wisp of a white beard shaking in disbelief. It was as if someone had hit the old man a body blow—that is, if there was a man who walked the earth who could do that, which Remo doubted very much.

"Why is this? Why is this?" demanded Chiun.

"Not me, Little Father. Not me. I didn't do it."

"Your government did it."

"No, no. The television people did it. They thought that more people would want to watch the Senate investigation than the soap operas."

Chiun pointed a long bony finger at the set. The long fingernail seemed to quiver.

"Who would want to watch those ugly white men when they can see the beauty and the rhythm and the grace of true drama?"

"Well, they have polls, Chiun. And they question people about what they like and don't like and I guess they figured more people would want to watch the investigations than your serials."

"They did not ask me," said Chiun. "No one asked me. Who asked me? If they asked me, I would say let the beauty of the drama remain. Beauty is rare but investigations you have with you always. Where is this person who does the questioning? I would speak with him for surely he would be interested in my opinion also."

"You're not going to kill a pollster, Little Father," said Remo.

"Kill?" said Chiun, as if Remo had broached the subject to a Carmelite nun, instead of the most deadly assassin in existence.

"Those things do tend to happen, Chiun, when someone gets in the way of your daytime shows. Or are you forgetting Washington and those FBI men, or New York and all those Mafiosi? You remember. They turned off your programs. Chicago and the union thugs. Remember? Remember who had to get rid of the bodies? Do you forget those little things, Little Father?"

"I remember beauty being interrupted and an old man, who has given the best years of all his skills to an ingrate, being reprimanded for attempting to enjoy a moment of beauty."

"You have a very selective memory."

"In a country that fails to appreciate beauty, a memory which forgets ugliness is a necessity."

And that had begun the renewed personal supervision of Remo's training by the Master of Sinanju. No longer could Remo do his exercises alone. Deprived of his daytime TV shows,

Chiun had to supervise the basics and Remo could do nothing right.

Sitting by Lake Patusick in the Massachusetts Berkshires where they rented a cottage for the spring, Remo heard Chiun tell him he breathed like a wrestler. During the water movements, Chiun screamed that Remo moved like a duck, and when Remo was doing the stomach flips—an exercise in which Remo lay flat on his stomach and then used his abdominal muscles to flip himself over onto his back—Chiun said Remo moved like a baby. "You should have a nurse, not the Master of Sinanju. That was slow and clumsy."

Remo assumed the position again, the spring grass near the cool Berkshire lake tickling his cheeks, the smell of the fresh muddy rebirth of life in his nostrils, the morning sun on his bare back, illuminating but not warming. He waited for Chiun's click of fingers to signal the flip. It was a simple exercise, trained into his reflexes more than a decade before, as he began the training that changed a man the public thought had been electrocuted into the killer arm of a secret organization that was designed to fight crime.

Remo waited for the snap of the fingers but it did not come. Chiun was having him wait. Better to wait, he thought, than have to find a place to put the body of the man who was responsible for taking *As the Planet Revolves* off the air. He felt a slight pressure on his back, probably a leaf falling.

He heard the snap of Chiun's fingers and his stomach muscles slapped the ground like springs released from restraint, but his body did not spin around as Remo expected. The instant pressure of two feet on his back sent his body flat down in the wet spring mud. Remo spit the mud out of his mouth. It was not a leaf he had felt fall on his back, but the Master of

Sinanju alighting, weightlessly on him. Remo heard the chuckles above him.

"Do you need help, little baby?"

To the untrained eye, it would appear that a thirtyish man of moderate build with extra thick wrists and dark hair had attempted a pushup and failed because an old Oriental was standing on his back. Actually, the force expended by both men could shatter slate.

This simple little accident was viewed by three men who had walked around from the front of the cottage and now stood watching the pair—the young white man face in mud, the aged Oriental giggling.

The three men wore dark business suits. The shortest carried a briefcase, the others .25 caliber Berettas that they believed were hidden under their jackets.

"I'm looking for a Remo Mueller," said the man with the briefcase. Remo lifted his head from the mud and felt Chiun alight from his back. He wanted to send a razor sharp hand into the old man's giggling face, but he knew the cutting edge of the hand would be jelly before it ever touched the face. Perhaps in ten years, his mind and body would equal Chiun's and then maybe Chiun would not use Remo as a punching bag for his frustrations.

Remo saw by the way the two taller men stood that they were carrying weapons. There is a reaction of the body to a weapon it carries, a certain heaviness of the body around the weapon. The two men stood with heaviness.

"Remo Mueller?" asked the man with the briefcase.

"Yes. That's me," said Remo, spitting out mud. He had been given the name Mueller several weeks before. This was the first time he'd heard anyone use it, and he wondered if it should be pronounced Muell-er as in fuel or Muell-er as in full. This man pronounced it as in full.

"The name's pronounced Mueller . . . as in fuel," Remo said, deciding that Chiun had no corner on perversity this day.

"I'd like to talk to you about a magazine article you wrote for the *National Forum of Human Relations.*"

Magazine article. Magazine article, thought Remo. Sometimes upstairs planted an article under his byline when they wanted to give him a cover as a magazine reporter, but he did not remember being informed of any article by upstairs recently. He had been told to rest.

Remo stared blankly at the man. What could he say? "Let me see the article I was supposed to have written." Upstairs moved in peculiar ways, right from the first day when former Newark policeman Remo Williams discovered that upstairs had been responsible for the frameup that put him in the electric chair, and equally responsible for getting him out alive, the man who did not exist for the agency which did not exist.

The explanation was simple, as most of upstairs' explanations were. The Constitution no longer worked; the country could no longer withstand the onslaught of crime. The answer was an organization that functioned outside the Constitution, doing whatever it had to do to equalize the odds.

"And I'm the guy who's going to do the dirty work?" Remo had asked.

"You're elected," he was told. Thus began a decade of training under Chiun, the Master of Sinanju, a decade in which Remo had lost count of the number of people he had killed, just remembered the moves.

"Would you care to talk inside?" Remo asked the three men.

The gentlemen said they would be happy to do so.

"Ask them if they know the vile pollsters of Washington," said Chiun.

"I think this is business," said Remo, hoping that Chiun

would choose to get lost. Only three men knew that the secret crime-fighting organization called CURE existed, and Chiun was not one of them. But as the Master of Sinanju, there was only one thing he needed to know of an employer. Did he pay on time and did his payments reach Sinanju, the little Korean village that Chiun and his ancestors had supported through the centuries by renting out their deadly assassin's skills? This question being answered affirmatively, Chiun would not have cared if his employer were the Girl Scouts of America.

"Business, business, business," said Chiun. "You are a nation of businessmen."

"Your servant?" asked the man with the briefcase.

"Not exactly," said Remo.

"Do you men know the vile pollsters of Washington?" asked Chiun.

"We might," said the man with the briefcase.

"Chiun, I think this is work. Please," said Remo.

"We can be of help in many ways," said the man with the briefcase.

"He doesn't need your help. Inside if you please," said Remo, but Chiun, hearing that there might be some way of restoring his daytime soap operas to the screen, followed the gathering into the cottage. He sat cross-legged on the floor watching the men on couches and chairs.

"This is confidential," said the man with the briefcase. He had the quiet authority of one backed by much wealth.

"Ignore him," Remo said of Chiun.

"Your magazine article proved of great interest to my employer. I saw your surprise when I mentioned it. I can understand your wondering how we saw the article when it won't even be published until next week."

Remo nodded as if he knew what the article was about.

"I have a question for you," the man said. "Just what are your contacts with Busati?"

"I'm afraid that all my sources are confidential," said Remo who did not know who or what or where a Busati was.

"I admire your integrity. Mr. Mueller, let me be frank. We might want you for something."

"Like what?" asked Remo, noticing the edge of a manuscript poke from the man's briefcase.

"We'd like to hire you as a consultant for our offices in Busati."

"Is that my story you have in there?" Remo said.

"Yes. I wanted to discuss it with you."

Remo reached out a hand for the manuscript. "Just want to review it myself," he said.

Even under an assumed name, Remo felt embarrassed by the story. Busati, he quickly surmised, was a country. According to what he was supposed to have written, Busati was forging new forms of socialism after throwing off colonialist chains, under the guidance of President General Dada "Big Daddy" Obode. Any report of tribal friction was an invention of the neo-colonialistic fascist imperialistic powers who feared the enlightened progressive leadership of the Saviour of Busati, General Obode, who brought electricity to the villages, ended crime in the capital and had made the first major inroads against poverty in Busati since the white man had first enslaved the little nation. Why this capitalist fear of Obode? Because his brilliance threatened to undermine the substructure of racist oppressive Western government and all Western nations quaked before the glory of his brilliance.

The article was called "An Unbiased View of Busati." Remo returned the manuscript.

"You're rather an interesting fellow, Mr. Mueller," the man

said. "We looked into your background and, frankly, we found nothing at all. Not a thing. Not even fingerprints. Now a traveler of your stature should have prints in someone's file. Do you mind telling us why not."

"Yes," said Remo. He turned to Chiun. "What's for dinner?"

"I have not decided," said Chiun.

"Of course, your background is your business," said the man with the briefcase. "We just wish to employ you at great profit to yourself. Very great."

"Duck would be good," said Remo, "if you cooked it right."

"We had duck last night," said Chiun.

"I'm here to make you an offer you can't refuse," said the man with the briefcase, smiling a wide row of very even white teeth.

"What?" said Remo.

"An offer you can't refuse."

"I'm refusing it," said Remo.

"Can you refuse $2,000 a week?"

"Sure," said Remo.

"Are you willing to see your stories turned down by every magazine in the country? It would not be hard for you to get a reputation as an unreliable nut, and then who would print your stories?"

"Who cares?" Remo said. He thought of the article he was supposed to have written. If that was sanity, he wondered what magazines thought insanity was.

"Come now, Mr. Mueller. I represent the Lippincott Foundation. Surely you've heard of us. A year's contract with us for one hundred thousand dollars could *make* an ambitious young man like you. You'd have the Lippincott family behind you forever."

Remo looked at the man and thought deeply for a moment.

"So what's wrong with duck two days in a row?" he asked Chiun.

"Nothing is wrong with duck two days in a row. There is just nothing very right with it two days in a row," said Chiun.

"Mr. Mueller, I'm talking to you."

"I know," said Remo. "Why don't you stop?"

"Mr. Mueller, if that's who you are, we have vital interests in Busati. We want only an introduction to the leadership of that country. We cannot use formal diplomatic channels because all whites and Asians have been expelled from the country. Just an introduction, that's all we want from you. It might take you only a day, or just a few hours. For that, you would be a wealthy man. For not doing that, you will be a ruined man. Now what is your answer?"

"Right or wrong, duck," said Remo.

"I'm sorry it has to be this way, Mr. Mueller. I'm going outside. I will be back in five minutes or whenever I hear the word 'yes' yelled at the top of your lungs. If you still have lungs."

The man with the briefcase rose somberly and walked to the front door. He left it open and Remo could see him light a cigarette in the front yard. The two men with the concealed weapons rose and approached Remo.

"Stay out of this, old man, and you won't be hurt," one said to Chiun. The Master of Sinanju smiled sweetly. "Oh, thank you so much for sparing a frail old man."

Remo shot him a dirty look. He didn't like it like this, not with Chiun watching. There would be non-stop bitching later on about Remo's technique. Well, Remo would be very simple and stick to basics. He was not in the mood for a harangue.

"We would rather be easy on you," said the man nearest Remo. He grabbed Remo's wrist and twisted ever so slightly. It was a move of either kung fu or karate, but Remo did not remember. Chiun liked to catalog these foolishnesses, but Remo did not want to be bothered. All of them were incomplete tools, even at their most advanced levels where they became workable for actual use. This man was being "the clinging vine" or something. He twisted.

Remo saw Chiun watch his elbow. Damn. Well, whatever. Remo brought his gripped hand back, taking the man with him and caught the chestbone with his right thumb. A single timed move that enabled him to step over the falling breathless body to the man facing Chiun, who now realized what Remo was doing. Remo tried to put the second man between him and Chiun so that Chiun would not witness the stroke.

The man guarding the old Oriental saw his parchment bearded face, saw him suddenly dart into a crouching position and look around the man's waist. The man looked down behind him, but saw nothing. Suddenly everything was black.

"Your stroke was rushed on the second man. I could not see the first because of the falling body," Chiun said.

"You couldn't see the second either, Little Father."

"I saw it."

"You cannot see through flesh."

"I saw the stroke of your hand in the heel of that foot," said, Chiun, pointing to the man on the floor. "It was rushed."

One of the men twitched.

"Well, the stroke worked," Remo said glumly.

"A child playing by the beach builds castles that work also, but they are not enough to live in and certainly not enough for the storm. You must build a house for the storm, not for the sunny afternoon. Your stroke was for a sunny afternoon."

"These guys were a sunny afternoon."

"I cannot reason with you," said Chiun and lapsed into a stream of Korean with such recognizable terms—to Remo—as the inability of even the Master of Sinanju to make a banquet from rice husks or diamonds from mud.

The man with the briefcase returned to the cottage with an order: "Don't you two guys hurt him too much. We need him," he said and then he saw his two guys.

"Oh," he said.

"They faw down, go boom," Remo said. "Now I'd like to ask you a question or two in all fairness and honesty."

To assure fairness and honesty, Remo placed a hand very quickly on the back of the man's neck, and as he pinched a nerve just so, the man too felt fairness and honesty were the only way to answer questions.

He worked for the Lippincott Foundation. His direct boss was Laurence Butler Lippincott. Another Lippincott, James Forsythe, had disappeared in the Busati bush. The government was working on it, but Laurence Butler Lippincott thought he could do better. Remo Mueller was wanted because he obviously was friends with General Obode. The Lippincotts would use him to get to Obode, to get his help in finding James Forsythe Lippincott. Laurence Lippincott himself had ordered that Remo be approached.

Remo released the pinch on the nerve.

"Your friends will come to in a moment or so," he said. "Where can I find Laurence Butler Lilliput?"

"Lippincott," the man said. "No one finds Mr. Lippincott. You see him by appointment only, if you're lucky."

Remo decided to rephrase the question and there must have been something in the manner of his voice because he got an immediate response. Laurence Butler Lippincott was at the headquarters of the International Bank of New York City, 88th floor, the Lippincott Suite.

He appeared promptly each morning at 11:30 A.M. and

worked through till 4:30 P.M. Non-stop. He was the responsible Lippincott. Remo released the man's neck again.

"No one gives Mr. Lippincott orders," said the briefcase man. "Maybe you stopped me, but there'll be more. No one can stand up against vast money. No one. Not governments. Not you. No one. All you can do is serve and hope you'll be rewarded."

"You will personally see your vast money in little soggy lumps," Remo said.

"Have you learned nothing?" shrieked Chiun. "Boasting? A boast is more fatal than a rushed stroke. A boast is a gift to an enemy. Have you learned nothing?"

"We'll see," said Remo. "Do you want to come along?"

"No," said Chiun. "A boast is bad enough but a successful boast is worse because it encourages other boasts, and they surely will cost in price. Nothing in this world is without payment."

Payment was a good word and Remo thought about it as the briefcase man drove him to New York City. Every so often, the two bodyguards would wake up and Remo would put them back to sleep. This went on until the Taconic Parkway when the two men finally got the general idea that they were no longer expected to overpower Remo.

Laurence Butler Lippincott did not have his offices in the huge tower his banks were famous for financing. They were instead in a tall, aluminum, looming building just off Wall Street, a narrow side street made wider by a large open entranceway with modern sculpture, which the briefcase man told Remo cost the Lippincotts more than two million in lost office space. Most people were amazed that Lippincott had spent $70,000 for the sculpture, but never considered that it cost so much more just to give it space. If Remo would think about reality, he too would appreciate what working for Lippincott meant. Remo did not appreciate reality.

He pushed the two bodyguards and the briefcase man ahead of him and managed to compress them all in a revolving door with the breaking of only one bone, the briefcase man's left arm which didn't quite fit. He screamed appropriately.

They had to take two elevators to the Lippincott floor. The first went only up to the 60th floor where three guards and a manager questioned Remo and his party.

Remo was polite and he was honest. He told the three guards and the manager that he was going to see Mr. Lippincott and would be delighted if they would accompany him. This, three of them did, with happy hearts. They were happy because they were not the fourth man who lay on the carpeting of the 60th floor foyer with his ribs and nose broken. The happy throng burst out into the 88th floor with exuberance, two guards going across the magnificent mahogany desk of Lippincott's private secretary, driving her back into a Picasso original. The office was like an art gallery, except that few galleries could afford this collection of Picassos, Matisses, Renoirs and Chagalls. Remo grabbed a blue picture with many dots off the wall and led his group to see Mr. Lippincott himself. A guard protested, so Remo left him behind—with his head in a bookcase.

The office of Laurence Butler Lippincott had no door. None was needed, Remo realized. The door was really back down at the 60th floor.

Lippincott looked up from a typewritten page he was reading. He was a graying elderly man, with taut skin and the placid confidence of the very rich in his face.

"Yes?" he said, apparently undisturbed by the commotion.

"My name is Remo and I say no."

"Mr. Lippincott," the briefcase man tried to explain while clinging to a splintered arm, but he did not have a chance to finish because he was flying over his employer's head. Lippincott scarcely noticed.

"Really, Mr. Mueller, must you? The man is injured."

So Remo threw the 60th floor manager at Lippincott.

"If something is on your mind, say it," said Lippincott. "No need to hurt innocent people."

Remo placed one of the bodyguards on Lippincott's desk, which surprisingly looked very ordinary, right down to the pictures of family. Remo knocked the air out of the bodyguard. Lippincott merely removed the typewritten sheet from beneath him.

Remo placed the second bodyguard, who had suddenly tried to break for the door, on top of the first. He too suddenly lost his breath.

"You're trying to tell me something," Lippincott suggested.

"Yes," said Remo.

"You're trying to tell me that all my employees and all my money won't do me any good with you."

"Yes," said Remo.

"Are you also threatening me with physical violence if I should attempt to send others?"

"Yes," said Remo.

"Sounds reasonable," said Lippincott. "Would you care for something to drink?"

"No thanks," said Remo.

"Cigar?"

"No thanks," said Remo.

"A fifteenth of Venezuela?"

"No thanks," said Remo.

"Is there anything I can give you?"

"Leave me alone."

"You're sure we can't make some sort of deal?"

"Right."

"That sounds impossible," Lippincott said. "Everyone wants something. What do you want?"

"None of your business."

"Sounds reasonable although I don't understand it. If you should ever want anything of me, please let me know because I want your help and somehow I think I'll figure out a way to get it."

Remo heard a scream from outside and he saw Lippincott switch on an intercom.

"It's all right, Miss Watkins. No cause for alarm."

"There's a madman in your office, Mr. Lippincott."

"It's all right. First clear-talking man I've met since grandfather died."

"I'll get the police."

"Nonsense. Get a doctor. We have wounded men in here. We don't need the police." He switched off the intercom. "A pleasure meeting you, Mr. Mueller."

"Same here," said Remo.

"If only these clowns knew how to talk to people. That's the trouble with having so much money. Everybody thinks they know what you want and they don't bother to find out what you really want. They do all sorts of horrid things in your name. I take it you're all right."

"I'm fine," said Remo.

"You weren't going to destroy that Seurat, were you?"

"I was," said Remo, returning the painting with dots.

"To prove that money meant nothing to you, I suppose."

"Yes," said Remo.

"I'll buy it back."

"No need," said Remo. "It wasn't mine to begin with." And he left Lippincott's office feeling that if only people made their positions clear, half the problems in the world could be solved by reasonable men, reasoning together.

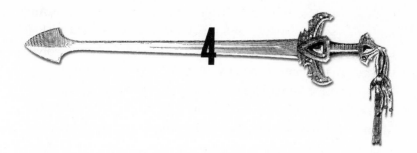

WHEN Remo returned to the Berkshires, upstairs had left a message. Chiun, who did not follow telephone codes, recognized the words "Aunt Mildred."

"Aunt Mildred what, Chiun?" asked Remo.

"Aunt Mildred. I do not play your little word games. If Dr. Smith wishes to see you, why doesn't he just say, 'I wish to see you?' Instead, Aunt Mildred is very sorry she cannot come or Aunt Mildred will have dinner ready or Aunt Mildred will refurnish the blue room."

"Do you remember which one?"

"I do not," said Chiun imperiously, as if Remo had overstepped his bounds by asking.

"I only ask because one of the things you mentioned means we should run for our lives and another means that everything is hunky dory."

"Running for one's life is the surest way to lose it."

"That's not the point, Chiun. It's that they mean different things."

"They mean nothing to me."

"But they mean something to me."

"Then you should be here to answer the telephone instead of fulfilling boasts," answered Chiun, thus closing the conversation to his satisfaction.

Remo waited until early dawn for the phone to ring again, but it did not, and he was about to nap when he heard a car pull up to the driveway. Just by the slow, careful and neat way it parked, by the careful opening of the door so as not to wear the hinges unduly, Remo knew that it was upstairs, Dr. Harold W. Smith, director of CURE. The message must have been Aunt Mildred will have dinner ready. That meant stay where you are. Will contact in person.

"I see Chiun got the message correct," said Smith, not bothering to thank Remo for opening the door or even acknowledging his greeting. "You really shouldn't complain that he can't relay codes. He did very well this time. You're here."

Smith wore a dark suit and a white shirt and striped tie. With the crispness of a mail clerk he walked onto the sun porch. The sun was sending little red cracks into the gray early morning sky over Lake Patusick.

"I don't suppose you have any coffee," asked Smith.

"Right. We don't have coffee. Want some cold duck?"

"Alcohol this early?"

"No alcohol. Leftover duck from last night's dinner."

"Sounds awful," Smith said.

"Tastes worse."

Remo eyed Smith and the small bulge in his left jacket pocket that looked like an overstuffed envelope. He wondered how many people played small unknowing roles in collecting what went into that envelope . . . a secretary who made an extra income by adding a file in a magazine office that said Remo Mueller was a writer who could be counted on for Africa stories . . . a banker who a month before had quietly opened a bank account and a line of credit for a man he had never seen, but whose name was Remo Mueller and who came highly recommended by friends. CURE was in that envelope, hundreds of people doing little jobs and not knowing the overall picture.

"I see you're interested in the envelope. Your tickets to Busati and your passports are in here along with an article under your byline. You should read it. You wrote it."

"I read it," said Remo.

"It hasn't been published yet."

"Some clown who works for Lippincott showed it to me. They offered to hire me."

"Excellent. Beyond my fondest hopes. Perfect. We had planned to get you into Busati as a journalist, let the blame fall on the magazine. But working for Lippincott is even better. For the first time, Remo, I see operations proceeding even better than planned, which is unusual for you."

"I won't be working for Lippincott," Remo said. "I sort of explained to him that I couldn't."

"You met Laurence Butler Lippincott?" asked Smith, with a tinge of reverence in his voice that Remo resented.

"Yeah. I met Lippincott. I threw a few of his employees at him."

"You what?"

"I told him I didn't want to work for him."

"But he'd make an excellent cover. We need someone to take the heat if you get messy in Busati."

Remo shrugged.

"You haven't even been committed yet," Smith groused, "and you've already created your first foul-up."

"So, don't commit me," said Remo and left the sunporch for the refrigerator where he grabbed the carcass of a cold duck and a bowl of cold rice and, against previous warnings by Chiun, ate even though his mind was not at peace. Smith had followed him into the kitchen.

Remo tore off a greasy drumstick and began to chew the mouthful into liquid. The problem, Smith explained was not just that James Forsythe Lippincott was missing in the Africa bush. Those things happened. CURE wouldn't bother to get involved for that, not even for a Lippincott. No, a dangerous pattern was emerging. Very dangerous.

Remo took a little ball of rice between his fingertips and placed it into his mouth. How he would love a hamburger, he thought.

"A pattern that could undermine the American people's faith in the ability of its government to protect them," Smith said.

Perhaps if he mixed the rice and duck together in his mouth, thought Remo, it might taste better.

"The basis of any government is the protection it gives its citizens," Smith said.

Remo tried mixing a sliver of duck with a few grains of rice.

"We don't have final proof, but we believe that someone is raiding America for slaves."

Perhaps if Remo washed down the duck and the rice with warm water. Maybe that would improve it.

"In the last year, several wealthy young girls from branches of the Lippincott family have met violent deaths. Or at least we thought they had. But now we have found out that the girls did not really die. In their coffins there were other bodies. We believe someone is somehow smuggling these girls out of the country to Africa, as slaves. Sort of a reverse slavery."

Remo turned the water faucet on hot and filled a glass. He sipped it and that didn't help either.

"Reverse slavery?" he asked.

"Yes," Smith said. "Blacks taking whites."

"Doesn't sound reverse to me," said Remo. "It's slavery."

"Correct," Smith said. "It's just that historically, whites took blacks."

"Only an idiot lives in history," said Remo repeating something Chiun had once told him and which he had never understood.

"Right," Smith said. "It's really a rather simple sort of operation. Get into Busati, find out what happened to the missing Lippincott, free the girls, and get out."

"Why not do it through the government?"

"We can't," Smith said. "Our sources indicate that General Obode, the President of Busati, is somehow behind this. If we try to approach him directly, he'll just kill the girls. No. We've got to get them freed first. Then our government can deal with Obode, and he can't lie his way out."

"Can I kill Obode?"

Smith shook his head. "Too risky. He's a nut, but he's our nut. Killing him might cause us real problems in that part of the world."

"You say your sources say that Obode's in it. How good are your sources?" Remo said.

"Impeccable," Smith said. "CIA type sources."

"Do your sources know where the girls are?"

"No. All we've heard is that there's a white house with an iron gate in the capital city of Busati."

"You don't know though, right?"

"Correct."

"And you don't know how the girls are being kidnaped, right?"

"Correct."

"And you were trying to get me fixed up with Lippincott, but you didn't tell me you were doing it, right?"

"Right," said Smith.

Remo returned the duck and the rice to the refrigerator. Nothing would improve its taste.

"You know, Smitty," he said, "nothing works right in America anymore. Nothing."

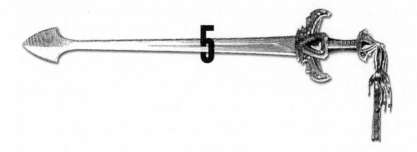

PRESIDENT General Dada "Big Daddy" Obode would see no one that morning. The stars were wrong. Hadn't a jackal made its way into the palace grounds the night before and howled three times, yet no one saw the jackal? Where was the jackal? This he demanded out loud on the balcony of his sitting room, once the sitting room of the former British governor—whom Big Daddy had served as a sergeant major in Her Majesty's Kenya Rifles.

"Where is the jackal?" he yelled. And had not the elephants at the Busati Army compound been seen wandering, even before the dry season? Why were they wandering? Who were they looking for? And what of the Minister of Public Safety who had been found nailed to a tree?

General Obode asked these questions of himself and there was no answer. His wise men were not wise, his generals were not courageous, his counselors lacked counsel.

He walked before a large ornate mirror, and looked at his massive frame and his thick dark features. A Hausa among Hausa he was.

"Dada, I ask you to search your heart with honesty and truth," he said to his image in the mirror. "Is it possible that you are the cause of your own problems? Be honest now, because I will brook no deceit, especially from you, you . . . sergeant major."

General Obode furrowed his brows and thought. He thought a very long time. He looked at his gold watch. Fifteen seconds. Enough thought. He had the answer.

"It is not your fault, General Obode. You are a good leader. It is the fault of your enemies. Destroy your enemies and you will destroy he who was responsible for the jackal."

With that he clapped his hands for his clothes, changed his mind and decided he would hold his morning audience. There was a full schedule today. The Ambassador from Libya—that was important because of the money; the representative of the Third World Liberation Organization—that was unimportant because all they did was talk and there were a lot of yellow men. He did not trust yellow men any more than he trusted Indians or white men, at least those white men who were not English officers.

He liked English officers. English officers never bothered anyone, especially during operations when they knew they would muck things up and so left the business in the hands of sergeants major who knew how to get things done. He thought another ten seconds and decided he did not like Arabs either, even though he had been a Moslem from birth.

"Who do you like—honestly, General Obode?" he asked himself.

"I like you, big fella," he said. "You're all right." With that he laughed a booming laugh and laughed, while servants put on his boots and white uniform pants and shirts with the medals and general's pips on the shoulders.

When he was ready for the day, he called for Colonel William Forsythe Butler, who had been insisting that the general see a magazine writer named Remo Mueller, because Remo Mueller had written a nice story about General Obode and nice stories were rare nowadays.

"Nice story today, bad story tomorrow, to hell with him,"

General Obode had told his American-born chief of staff, who had all sorts of mixed blood mucking up his veins and who called himself black. He was a clever one though, this Colonel William Forsythe Butler. A good man to have around. He was not a Hausa, so he would not be jealous of General Obode's magnificence; he was not a Loni, so he would not hate General Obode for no reason at all. He was, he once had explained, "just an American nigger, but I'm working on that."

A good man. General Obode would humor him. Today, he would try to see this pipsqueak writer with the funny name of Remo.

Colonel William Forsythe Butler was the first to enter. He appeared thin, but General Obode knew him to be a most powerful man, the only one in Busati to have wrestled him to a draw one afternoon, after Obode threw two generals and three sergeants simultaneously before the cheers of his troops. He had been a football player, this Colonel Butler, Morgan State, and then the New York Mammoths—or was it the New York Giants? These names Americans had were all peculiar.

"Good morning, Colonel," said General Obode, sitting down in the ornate high-backed governor's chair which was now the president's chair. "Did you hear the jackal last night?"

"I did, Mr. President."

"And what would you make of a jackal in America if it howled at night? Three times?"

"We don't have jackals in America."

"Aha," said General Obode, clapping his hands. "And we do not have jackals in the palace grounds, either. Then what would you make of a jackal in your New York City?"

"I would think it strange, Mr. President."

"And so do I. I will teach you another lesson in governing that even your CIA didn't teach you."

"It would be an honor to learn, Mr. President."

General Obode clapped his hands and in marched eight men in neat Western suits and neat Western shirts and neat Western ties. When they talked, they talked in neat British accents. They were Obode's civilian council of state to whom he gave no power at all, preferring to surround himself in important jobs with military men. Six of the civilian council were Hausa, the other two were Loni, appointed reluctantly by Obode at Butler's urging. Butler had told him that the Western world would recognize this as an act of greatness, assimilating into his government the members of a once hated and hunted enemy tribe.

"A jackal howled three times last night," announced Obode. "Now to you Oxford and Cambridge people, it is nothing. And I'm sure it is nothing at some fancy United Nations office where all they have to do is worry about the air conditioning staying on. But this American here, this Butler, who has come home to his rightful land, he thinks it is something and he is CIA formerly. Now all of you have heard of the Central Intelligence Agency. It is not Oxford. It is not Cambridge. It is not the United Nations."

"It is a vicious, dangerous organization, Mr. President," said the chairman of the council who was a Hausa. "It will stop at nothing to achieve its ends."

"Right," said General Obode. "Therefore we can have some respect for it. And this former CIA man tells me a jackal howling at night is something strange. What do you think?"

While Obode spoke, Butler looked down at the floor, his left fingers twisting a ring he wore on his right hand, a ring fashioned of miniature golden chain links.

It was the consensus of the council that the howling jackal was definitely strange. The strangest thing they had ever heard of.

"Not the strangest thing," said General Obode angrily. "A strange thing. We will investigate CIA-style."

He dismissed the council with a wave of his hand. Seven of them, while leaving, caught Colonel Butler's eye with a conspiratorial look, the look one gives a partner one trusts when there is really nothing to talk about.

Obode summoned the captain of the palace guard who was a Hausa, and whose hatred of Butler fairly oozed as he entered the president's quarters and saw the American there. The captain had also heard the jackal last night, and he had arrested a lieutenant for imitating the animal, just to intimidate the president.

"From the Loni," said the captain, looking at Butler. "This lieutenant was a Loni and he was the jackal."

"Let us see this jackal," said General Obode. When the captain of the guard left, Obode explained his logic to Butler. Jackals did not live in the palace. Soldiers did. Therefore the jackal was a soldier.

"I don't think so," said Colonel Butler.

"What is your rank, Butler?"

"Colonel, Mr. President."

"And what is my rank?"

"General, Mr. President."

"Did they teach you discipline in your CIA?"

"They did."

"Then you know that when a colonel disagrees with a general, a general is right." Big Daddy clapped his hands gleefully.

"No, Mr. President, they taught me that the general gets his way. But any man can be right."

Obode frowned, a deep dark frown. He summoned Butler's ear forward with a finger.

"When I want logic, Butler, I'll ask for it," he said.

262 • WARREN MURPHY AND RICHARD SAPIR

"The lieutenant is innocent, though," whispered Butler, hearing the captain again approach the door.

"Maybe he is, maybe he isn't. He could be the jackal."

"He's not," Butler said. "I am the jackal."

Obode leaned back and stared at Butler. "You want to die, Colonel?"

"No, Mr. President, I want your life saved. I brought the jackal into the palace last night to root out your enemies. If I put the jackal there, whoever says he found a man to be the jackal is a liar. The captain of your guard is a liar. He knows that you want to bring the Loni into the government, and so he is trying to destroy your plan by accusing the Loni lieutenant of a crime he did not commit. You see your enemy? He is as far away as the captain."

Obode did not look up at the captain who was now approaching the President's chair. Intrigue was afoot.

Butler looked at the captain, who returned his look with loathing. Butler winked. The captain had been one of the few men close to Obode who did not agree with Butler that Obode was a lunatic whose continued rule would make Busati a worldwide joke. Because the captain did not agree with Butler, the captain was dangerous to Butler. But now he had overplayed his hand.

The captain stood in front of Obode with a hand on the shoulder of a thin man, wearing the tattered remnants of a lieutenant's uniform. The man's legs and wrists were in heavy gray irons. His mouth was a blotch of blood. A tooth stuck out through his lower lip.

"He has confessed that he is the jackal, General," said the captain.

"A confession is a confession," said Obode. "That is logic and the CIA style of investigation is logic, so the man is guilty. But I will ask him myself."

Obode looked up at the lieutenant, who had to be continually jerked upright by the captain of the guards.

"Are you the jackal?"

Drops of dark red blood fell to the clean marble floor at the man's feet, building a puddle, splattering faint rays of red around it as each drop hit. The man, his eyes swollen almost shut, nodded and the puddle became bigger.

Butler twisted the gold chain ring on his right hand.

"Guilty," said Obode. The captain smiled.

"Set up a firing squad," said Obode. "I will personally administer the execution." He clapped his hands, the man was led away, and servants rushed in with rags and water to clean the blood off the palace floor.

Big Daddy took care of the Libyan Ambassador in three minutes. He confided to the Ambassador that Israel was planning a raid on the Busati plain and he needed $85 million more in gold reserves to repel it. When the Libyan Ambassador appeared somewhat dubious, Big Daddy wistfully remembered the fine training he had personally received from the Israeli paratroopers and how he longed to wear again the wings he had earned at such a high personal cost. He also reminded the Ambassador that he was the only leader of a nation to publicly say to the foreign press that Hitler had been right. That was worth at least $85 million right there. The Libyan Ambassador timidly suggested that Big Daddy had been paid for that already, but finally agreed to ask his glorious revolutionary leader, Colonel Quadaffi, for the funds.

"Don't ask—tell," said Obode and that took care of the Libyan Ambassador.

"We'll get $25 million," Obode told Butler when the Ambassador had left. "Better than nothing. I can't wait for their oil to dry up. They smell funny. Who's next?"

"The journalist, Remo Mueller, from America. The one who wrote the favorable piece about you," said Butler.

"I'll see him tomorrow."

"You've been saying that for three days."

"I'll say that for three days more. We have an execution for me to administer. But first I wish to see the jackal you say you brought into the grounds."

"Will you still execute the lieutenant?"

"I said there would be an execution. I cannot go back on my word," said Obode.

The salutes along the corridors by the guards were crisp and rigid, a perfection of discipline that could only be imposed by the best of British sergeants major.

As they walked down steps to a small cell beneath the palace, Obode asked Butler how things were at the white house with the iron gate.

"Just fine, Mr. President. Your soldiers who use it bless your name continuously. You should pay it a visit yourself."

Obode sneered and shook his head.

"You don't like white women, General?"

"You don't have to put them in chains to bang them. I will tell you, Colonel, that before you came I had white women. I had yellow women. I had Hausa women and Loni women. I had old women and young women, fat women and skinny women, women who smelled of perfume and women who smelled of dung. Colonel Butler," said Obode, pausing before an iron door to which Butler had the key, "there isn't a spit's difference between any of them. And your adventures to get young rich American girls cost too much, and may yet get us into trouble with your American government."

"But, General, isn't it fitting that the greatest soldiers of the great leader of a great country get the very best?"

"Best of what? Queen Elizabeth or the lowest bush tribe whore. Same thing."

"You have had Queen Elizabeth?"

"No. But if a man eats one hundred hogs, does he have to eat another to know what it will taste like?"

"I'm sorry, General, I thought you approved of what I was doing for your men." Butler twisted the gold ring on his right hand.

Obode shrugged his massive shoulders. "You wanted to have your house and your games so I let you. I like you, Butler. You are the only man on my staff who has not loyalty to one tribe or another, but is loyal just to me. Even if you *are* soft on the Loni. So, I let you have your house. Now let me see your jackal."

Butler turned the key and opened the door on an empty cell. Obode walked in and sniffed the air. Before the stunned Butler could move, Obode snapped the Colonel's revolver from his holster as if disarming a recalcitrant enlisted man.

"I put the jackal here myself. I tied it right to that wall. I wanted to show you there were liars in your guard. The jackal was here, General. What reason would I have to lie to you?"

"Outside, Butler," said Obode.

The palace courtyard was hot in the morning African sun, baking hot with dust in the very grass itself. The captain of the guard grinned broadly when he saw the Loni-loving American Colonel go before the General with his hands up and holster empty. He winked broadly at Butler, and then turned and motioned his firing squad to kneel.

"Against the wall," said General Obode.

At the wall, Butler spun around beside the Loni officer who was chained against the wall in a standing position, but whose body hung heavy from his wrist manacles.

"You're a damned idiot, General," Butler yelled. "When you

shoot me, you shoot the best officer you have. I just want you to know that, you dumb bastard."

"You call me a dumb bastard," yelled back Obode, "but you're the one who's got his hands up against the wall."

At that, Butler laughed.

"You're right, you fat bastard, but you're still shooting the best officer you ever had."

"That's where you're wrong, skinny little man. I am going to shoot the officer who lied to me about the jackal."

The captain of the guard smiled. The firing squad behind him waited for a signal. It did not get one. There was the crack of a pistol and the captain of the palace guard was no longer smiling. There was a very dumb look on his face and a very wide dark red hole between his eyes, although few people saw it because the head was jerked back by the force of the shot. The body followed. It hit the burned grass with a whoomph and moved no more.

"So much for people who lie to me about jackals. And now for those who call me a fat bastard," said General Obode. He extended the pistol at arm's length and walked up to Colonel Butler's face.

"Don't do it again," he said to Butler and spun the pistol around, Western style, offering it handle first.

"How do you know I won't shoot you now, you . . ." said Butler, stopping as the pistol spun once more in Obode's hand so that now Butler was again looking down the barrel.

". . . glorious leader," smiled Butler, finishing the sentence.

"You and you," Obode yelled to two soldiers still kneeling, waiting for an execution order. "Take that man down from the wall. And treat him carefully. He is your new captain of the palace guard."

"He is a Loni," Butler said, taking the pistol from Obode and returning it to his holster.

"The other one was a Hausa, and he lied to me. How much worse could a Loni be?"

As he and Butler walked from the courtyard, Obode said, "You looked funny when that cell was empty. Did you look funny! Did you really think, though, that anyone could hide a jackal smell from me? Especially when the Hausa custom is that the chief must protect himself when the jackal howls at night?"

"I have a nose too, General. I smelled nothing but disinfectant in that call."

"Right," said Obode. "And who would wash a cell with disinfectant unless he was trying to hide a smell? The captain obviously found your jackal and disposed of it. I tell you, if more generals were sergeant majors, the world would be a better place." He paused and said, "I wonder if that captain was responsible for killing the Minister of Public Safety."

Butler shrugged. "Maybe," he said. "And maybe we'll never know. Anyway, now that we know the jackal wasn't magic, General, perhaps we can get on to other things."

Obode shook his head slowly, as he turned and led Butler down a graveled path leading into the heavily-treed palace grounds.

"You think because one thing I believe in is disproven, I should not believe in anything I know to be true? Wrong. Because one of America's missiles doesn't work, do they stop building missiles? No. Because they know the majority of missiles are good. These are strange times in Busati, Butler. We are not rich and advanced like in Kenya or Zaire. But there are things one does not learn in universities. These things I know."

"I do not understand," said Butler. He saw a lizard scurry under a bush. For that lizard to brave the noonday African sun meant there must be a predator about, probably a rodent of some sort. This Butler had learned from Obode.

"Why do you think I have expelled all the Asians?" Obode asked. "Why do you think I expelled all the whites? The whole world thinks, here goes Big Daddy being cruel to whites and Asians he needs for his economy. Oh, what a crazy man is this Dada Obode. That is what they think. I know that. I am not a fool. Why do you think I did those things?"

"I don't know, General."

Big Daddy paused by a large wide mango tree, like the one Colonel Butler had nailed the Minister of Public Safety to, like the one Butler had killed James Forsythe Lippincott under, like the ones which stood before the hills where the Loni hid. Butler looked absent-mindedly for the predator to follow the lizard into the bush. But he saw no predator.

"It is all connected, Butler. All of it. And there is a reason for all the things I do."

Butler nodded, still wondering where the predator was. He saw the lizard's tail sticking out from under the bush, motionless.

"You do not know the Loni," Obode said. "Today, they are just a weak collection of spineless mountain bands, but once they were powerful. Once they ruled the Hausa as we now rule them. But there is a legend that says the Loni will again come to power. The legend says that when East and West are like father and son near the Busati River, then a force that no man can stop will come to shed blood in the river and in the mountains."

Butler nodded.

"You nod, but I do not think you understand, Colonel. The legend says that the Loni children will come home. It says a man from the East will purify the Loni and make them again worthy to rule. And it says a man from the West, a man who walks in the shoes of death, will rid the Loni of a man who would enslave them."

"And you're the man who would enslave the Loni?" Butler asked.

Obode shrugged his shoulders. "Who else could the legend mean but the Hausa man who is the leader of the country? You wonder why I have listened to you and put Loni men into my government? I have done it because I want to be free of the title of 'man who would enslave them.' But still I fear. I do not think that one can outsmart a legend."

"I see." Butler watched the lizard's tail poke out of the bush. When General Obode went into one of his prophecy raves, the best thing to do was to nod.

"Perhaps you are beginning to see," Obode said.

"The legend says a man from the East and a man from the West. Yellow and white. To serve the Loni. And if that happens, the Hausa are through and I am dead. That is why I got rid of our Asians. That is why I got rid of our whites. I do not want yellow men and white men joining, lest they become this force to free the Loni. You see?"

Butler, who had his own very good ideas on what the legend meant and how it was soon to be fulfilled, simply nodded at Obode's explanation. Where was the predator? Why was that lizard's tail still sticking out of that bush?

"Butler," said Obode. "I think there are times when there are some things you not only fail to understand, but you refuse to try understanding."

"I'm only a colonel," Butler said.

"All right. Now you're a general. You must understand everything now. Understand this, General. I take no chances with the Loni legend. I do not want Westerners in Busati. I do not want this Remo Mueller. I do not want any more of your white women from America."

"As one general to another, Big Daddy, let me say I've got to have one more."

"Get one from China."

"No. It's got to be America. It's got to be a certain one."

"No more," said Obode.

"This one is the most important one. I've got to get her. If you say no, I'll resign."

"Over a white woman?"

"A special one."

Obode thought deeply for a few seconds. He cupped his chin in his ham-wide, cave-black hands. "All right. But this is the last."

"After her, General, I will want no more. She makes it all perfect."

"And you say I am hard to understand," said Obode. "One last thing, General Butler. Do not think the legends are all lies or that General Obode is a fool."

He put a heavy hand on Butler's shoulder. "Come, I will show you something you do not think I know. You have been watching that tail under the bush, you think there is no predator around because you do not see one. You think the lizard ran into the sun for no reason, right?"

"Well, yes, I guess that's what I was thinking," said Butler, surprised that Obode had seen his interest in the bush.

"Good. Good to show you a point. Even if you cannot see something, it does not mean that it does not exist. There is a predator around."

"I saw no rats or birds. I still see the tail."

Obode smiled. "Yes, you see the tail. But come quickly or you will not see it."

When they reached the bush, Obode drew aside the green foliage. "Look," he said, smiling.

Butler looked. He had seen a tail all right, but that was all that was left of the lizard, sticking from the full mouth of a very fat frog.

"Sometimes when you run from danger, you run to it," said Obode, but he forgot the lesson very quickly that afternoon when he again not only refused to see the writer, Remo Mueller, but ordered him evicted from Busati. Immediately.

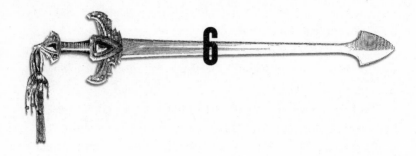

THE Busati Hotel had air-conditioning that did not work, faucets that gave no water, and elegant carpeting with inlaid old food. The rooms were like furnaces, the hallways smelled like sewers and the only remnant of its former grandeur was a clean brochure with Victoria Hotel scratched out and Busati Hotel penciled in.

"Spacious, air-conditioned and elegant, the Busati Hotel offers the finest conveniences and the most gracious service in all East Africa," read Remo.

Chiun sat on the floor, his white robe flowing and motionless behind him. Remo sat on the edge of the bed with the high brass posters.

"I've heard of untruth in advertising," said Remo, "but this is a bit much."

Chiun did not answer.

"I said this is a bit much."

Chiun remained a silent statue.

"Little Father, there is no television set before you. You're not watching your shows. So why don't you answer me?"

"But I am watching my shows," said Chiun. "I am remembering them."

Remo was surprised that he shared a bit of Chiun's anguish at the master's loss of the daytime soap operas. They had been a constant nettle to Remo through the years, but now that they were gone, he felt sorry for the Master of Sinanju.

"That Watergate thing will not last, Chiun. All your shows will return."

"I know that," said Chiun.

"So you don't really have to sit staring at a wall."

"I am not staring at a wall. I am remembering. He who can remember the good things as though they were present can live his happiness forever."

"Well, let me know when you stop remembering, so we can talk."

Remo looked at his wristwatch. At home, Chiun's soap operas went off at 3:30. He would time Chiun and see how close he came to judging the time.

At 3:27 by Remo's watch, Chiun toward turned him.

"You missed, Chiun."

"Missed? What stupidity are you pursuing now?"

"The shows go off at 3:30. And it's only 3:27 and you were done," Remo said triumphantly. "Three minutes off. A child could have a better sense of time than that. Three minutes is a long time."

"Three minutes is not very long in the life of one who has dedicated every minute to foolishness," Chiun said.

"Meaning?"

"Meaning, you forgot the moments of selling. I do not watch them. I do not use soap powder."

Chagrined because he had indeed forgotten the three minutes of commercials at the end of the day's stories, Remo said, "Yeah, well, anyway, I was talking about the brochure."

"It may not be a lie," Chiun said.

"Look around you, it's not a lie?"

"I look around and I see that perhaps at one time it was the truth. I see elegance in decay. So if these things were said about this palace when they were true, then the advertisement is true."

"Are you telling me, Little Father, that to say this is a stinkhole is a lie?"

"I am telling you that truth is a matter of time. Even in this very land there are people who were once great and who now hide in the hills like frightened calves."

"Well, I don't need that drivel now, Chiun. I need advice. I'm supposed to see the top man in this country to find out about that white house, without letting him know that I know. But he won't see me."

Chiun nodded. "Then my advice to you is to forget all your training and run head first like a crazed dog into what you, in your lack of perception, think is the center of things. There, thrash about like a drunken white man, and then, at the moment of maximum danger, remember just a brief part of the magnificent training of Sinanju, and save your worthless life. At the end of this disgrace, you might by good fortune have killed the right man. This then is the advice of the Master of Sinanju."

Remo blinked. He stood up from the bed.

"That's utterly stupid, Chiun."

"I just wanted for once to give you advice I am sure you would follow. But since I have invested such wealth of knowledge with you, I shall increase this investment. You think because the emperor appears to be the center of things, he is the center of things."

"It's president, not emperor."

"Whatever name you wish to give to an emperor is your pleasure, my son, but emperors do not change in nature. And what I am saying to you is that you must know the center of this thing before you can attack it. You are not an army that goes blindly wandering through bush and hill and can by sheer weight of numbers accidentally accomplish what it wants. You are skill, a single skill that is designed to crush one point, not ten thousand. Therefore you must know that point."

"How can I find that point waiting around here in this crummy hotel?"

"A man sitting sees many sides very well. A man running sees only ahead."

"I see many sides when I run. You taught me that."

"When you run with your feet," said Chiun, and was silent. Remo left the room to see if he could find something to read, someone to talk to, or even a vagrant breeze to get into the middle of. He was unsuccessful. But at the stately doors of the hotel, he saw a busboy run desperately past him with fear in his eyes. The manager of the hotel hid the books. The doorman snapped to attention.

And then Remo saw it. Coming up the main street of the capital city of Busati, an army convoy, machine guns bristling from jeeps. Leading it was the man who had extended the invitation that writer Remo Mueller see General Obode.

When the lead jeep of the convoy arrived at the doors of the Hotel Busati, it stopped in a screech of dust off the unpaved street. Soldiers jumped off their jeeps all along the line before their vehicles braked.

"Ah, Remo, glad to see you," said now-General William Forsythe Butler, quickly climbing the once-white front steps of the hotel. "I've got a bit of bad news for you. The bit is you're returning to America this afternoon. But I've got some good news for you too."

Remo smiled perfunctorily.

"The good news is I'll be going with you and I'd be happy to answer every question you have. As a matter of fact, Busati feels it owes you a favor which it hopes to repay."

"By kicking me out of the country?"

"President Obode has had some very disappointing experiences with white journalists."

"Then why'd you say I could get to see him?"

"I thought I could prevail upon him but I couldn't." Butler shrugged, a big muscular shrug of his shoulders. "We'll talk about it some more on the way to the airport."

Frankly, Butler was relieved that this Remo Mueller would be leaving the country since the fewer Americans there were nosing around, the less chance of the white house being discovered. That relief only grew when he got his first look at Remo Mueller's traveling companion, an aged Oriental who padded silently out of the Busati Hotel behind Remo, acknowledged Butler's lukewarm greeting with a silent stare, and sat like stone in the back seat of the jeep.

What was it Obode had said? "When East and West are like father and son near the Busati River, then a force that no man can stop will come to shed blood in the river and on the mountains."

East and West. The aged Oriental and the young white American.

Butler could do without Remo and the Oriental. He had his own interpretations of the legend . . . an interpretation that he knew would carry him to the Busatian presidential palace, and power over all the people of all the tribes.

He thought about this in silence as the jeep convoy rolled toward the airport, and then realized he was being a bad host.

It was where the road banked in along the Busati River, that he turned toward the back seat to see how his passengers were doing.

They were gone.

"What the hell?" said Butler. "Stop the damned convoy."

He looked at his driver, then looked back to the rear seats. They were indeed empty.

"Did you see them jump out?" asked Butler, almost as a reprimand.

"No, General," said the driver. "I didn't know they were gone. We were doing forty-five miles an hour, General."

The long convoy bunched up into tightly packed jeeps as it stopped on Busati's Route One and Only, which ran from the capital city to the airport. Butler could see for a half-mile in each direction. There was no sign of them.

"Their bodies must be up the road no more than a hundred meters or so, General."

Butler stood up in the jeep signaling to the vehicle cramped in tight behind him.

"Sergeant, did you see our passengers?"

"Sir?" called out the sergeant.

"The white man and the Oriental. Did you see them jump from the jeep?"

The sergeant threw the snappy kind of British salute Butler hated so much. He used the word "sir" to punctuate his reply.

"Sir, no sir. No passengers observed leaving your vehicle sir."

"Form search parties and scour the road. Fan out. Find them. They do not know this earth."

"Sir, very good, sir," said the sergeant.

But Remo and Chiun were not found, although it came to be believed that at least five men might have stumbled on them or on something, because the necks of the five were broken and they lay peacefully in search formation, the safeties off their rifles and their fingers on the feather-light triggers, as though a breeze of death had gently put them to sleep.

Three other men were missing, one of them a captain, but General Butler would not wait. He would not have waited if the gates of hell opened before him. He was going to catch a plane for America to settle the last payment on a three-hundred-year-old debt, and when that had been collected, the world might see greatness as it had not for thousands of years.

At the airport, Butler told his personal Army detachment to continue the search for the Oriental and the American and to hold them in custody until he got back. "I shall be back in two days," he said, and with that walked quickly to the loading ramp of the Air Busati 707, with British pilots and navigators.

Three years before, in an advertisement for Air Busati, two Hausas posed in pilots' uniforms for photographs and the planes emptied of passengers in less than a minute, most of the passengers being Hausas too.

This Butler remembered as he entered the plane on which he would be the only passenger and headed for the lounge in the back to change from his military uniform. Butler remembered the advertisement well. It did not appear in any African newspaper for fear of losing Air Busati the few passengers it had, but it made quite a hit in *The New York Times* where one militant several days later had called on the Busati Air Force to launch an immediate strike against South Africa.

The militant had held up the advertisement as he said: "Why don't these black pilots spearhead an attack on racist South Africa? I will tell you why. Because capitalism forces them to fly commercial airliners."

Butler had almost cried when he saw the news story about the militant, and when he thought that black men did indeed fly fighter aircraft—in America.

As the 707 jet rose sharply into the darkening Busati sky for the first leg of its journey to Kennedy Airport in New York City

William Forsythe Butler leaned back in a reclining seat, aware that he was making his last trip west to a land to which centuries before his ancestors had been transported, shackled in the holds of ships built for carrying cattle.

Those trips had taken months. Many had died and many had thrown themselves overboard when they had a chance. They had come from many tribes—Loni, Hausa, Ashanti, Dahomey—and they would surrender this heritage to become a new people called "nigger." Few would ever find their way home.

William Forsythe Butler had found his way home. In the depths of his bitterness, he had found his home and his tribe and his people, and a curious legend that told him what he must do. Although, in truth, he had always been the kind of boy—then man—who seemed to know what he would do and how he would do it.

When he was eleven years old in Paterson, New Jersey, he suddenly realized he was very fast afoot, as fast as the wind. He was reading when this realization overcame him. He told his sister.

"Get outa here, Billie, you're a fat chubkins," she had said.

"I know, sis, I know. But I'm fast. I mean, I got the speed in me."

"I can outrun you, fatty," said his sister.

"Today, yeah. But not next month. And the month after that you won't even see me."

"Ain't nobody gonna move that flab fast, fatty," said his older sister.

But Billie Butler knew. All he would have to do would be to find that speed in himself. And he did. In football, he became high school All-American, and did the same at Morgan State.

His performance there was good enough to get him an offer

from the Philadelphia Browns which, at the time had an interesting way of judging football talent. They could have done it with a light meter. If you were black and fast and didn't come from a Big Ten school, you were a cornerback. And if your name was William Forsythe Butler, you became Willie Butler. Not Bill, not Billie, but Willie.

"I don't want to play defense," Butler had told them. "I want to play offense. I know I can play offense." But the Browns already had one black halfback. Butler became a cornerback.

He swallowed his pride and tried to look straight ahead. He read about the black reawakening, which seemed to center around kids calling press conferences to announce imminent rebellions, which featured every sort of cuckoo in the black community being exalted by the white press as a black leader; and featured very few of his own people, the people who had sweat blood and tears and pain to wrest even the ownership of a home from a hostile land.

Just as he had known as a child that he had speed within him, he knew now what would happen in this still-hostile land of America.

He tried to explain to one militant he met on a plane.

"Look, if you're going to have a damned revolution, it might help not to announce your plans in *The New York Times*," he had said.

"Revolution is communication with the masses," the militant had said. "They must first be conscious that power comes from the barrel of a gun."

"Did it ever occur to you that the whites have most of the guns?"

"Whitey soft. He through. He dead, man."

"God help you if you ever back him into a corner," Butler told the youth, who responded that Butler was an Uncle Tom of a dead generation. Butler saw the name of the militant again one month later when the newspapers reported the youth had been arrested for holding up a drugstore.

Some of Butler's friends said this was a sign that the youth was really arrested for his political beliefs.

"Bullshit," said Butler. "If you know anything about how anything operates, that kid is just what you want for an enemy. He wasn't doing any harm to the government. He was really helping it."

"He was raising the consciousness of his people," said Butler's sister.

"Every time that kid opened his mouth, ten thousand whites moved to the right."

"That's a twisted way of thinking," said his sister. "I don't know about you, but I'm tired of tomming."

"And I'm tired of losing. We're cutting off all our support in the north, and in the south, forget it."

"We got the Third World. We outnumber Whitey."

"Numbers don't count any more," Butler had said. "An army is made up of people who can work together and, most important, be in the right place at the right time. If I were running a black revolution in this country, I'd give the kids watches, not rifles."

"They really got to your head, didn't they, Mister not-allowed-to-carry-the-ball cornerback. And don't give me Whitey's talk about being wiped out. We been wiped out every century. And here we are."

"No," said Butler sadly, "I don't think we're going to be wiped out, because I don't think we can get up a good enough revolution right now to get wiped out. We're gonna be smothered in our own stupidity."

His sister's response was that Butler was too impressed with

Whitey. Butler's answer was that Whitey wasn't all that good and pretty stupid himself, but that his sister made even the worst white cracker look like an intellectual giant.

Butler's despair deepened with almost every daily newspaper story about non-negotiable demands, the unity of the Third World and the talk of bullets. When departments of African studies were introduced across the land, William Forsythe Butler was at the point of tears. "The engineering schools, you dumb bastards," he would yell in the privacy of his apartment. "The engineering schools. That's survival."

Few of his friends spoke to him anymore, naturally, since he was an Uncle Tom without courage. Butler took it out on the gridiron. He was a cornerback with a vengeance, and he had a plan. One day, it all worked and Butler had a new team, the New York Giants, and a promise that he would be given a real shot at running back.

Opening day, he started the season at cornerback. He ended the season there.

It was then that William Forsythe Butler began to wonder if just maybe his sister weren't right.

The black consciousness movement was taking hold now in football and Butler became its spokesman. He did a statistical survey of the league that showed that more blacks than whites were jolted out of positions and put onto defensive teams.

He demanded to know why blacks got paid less for playing the same position as whites. Twentieth century slavery, he called it. He said that racism was the reason there wasn't a black quarterback, and announced that he would try out for that position the next year with his team.

These were the things Willie Butler talked about, but no answers came from organized football. Soon the sports pages froze him out of space, not wanting to do anything to damage the all-American spirit of the game.

And then one day, the back page of the *New York Daily News* bannered a headline that triggered in Butler a violent response and made him vow never to forget the slavery that had brought his forebears to the country. The headline read:

WILLIE BUTLER SOLD

Butler first heard of it reading the paper, and rather than be sold anywhere by anyone, he retired from football.

He was still a young man, so he drifted into the Peace Corps, where he was shipped to Busati to try to develop an irrigation project that might raise a small parcel of the nation's land to its fertility level of two thousand years before. While working there, happy to be away from America, he was approached by the CIA man assigned to the Busati Peace Corps. The CIA man was going home; he had seen Butler at work and realized he was a true American; how would he like to work for the CIA?

For the extra money, Butler said *sure,* determined to screw up the intelligence apparatus by sending in ridiculous reports of non-occurring events and by predictions that bordered on the sublime.

In Busati's heat, the predictions all seemed to come true. Butler was put on full $36,000 salary by the CIA, assigned to help then-Colonel Obode, who was pro-West at the time, seize power.

About that time, William Forsythe Butler made a journey to the mountains of the Loni. As soon as he stepped into the first village, he knew he was home.

And he was ashamed of his home. The Loni were divided into small bands who hid in the hills; the men were timid little root-grubbers who spent their lives looking over their shoulders for the approach of the Hausa, or for oncoming elephants, or for anything larger than a lizard. The Loni Empire, probably because of the cowardice of its men, had turned into a matriarchy, the three major packs being led by three princess sisters. Butler met one sister and told her he knew he was a Loni.

How do we know you are not making up a story, he was asked.

And in his frustration, Butler made a hissing clicking sound in the back of his mouth as he had always done since childhood. The princess suddenly embraced Butler and welcomed him home.

Butler was confused.

The Princess explained that Loni men, when angered, always had made that hissing sound in their throats. She had not heard it in a long time.

Butler forgot about Obode and about his CIA assignment. He spent two weeks in the village where, for the first time, he heard the Loni legend. He had been brought up in a society which did not believe in legends, but even he thought there was enough in the legend that pertained to him.

The Loni children coming home. Well, wasn't he a Loni child who had come home?

And the man of the West, who was dead, killing the man who would enslave the Loni. Well, wasn't Butler from the West? And couldn't you call him dead, in a sense, because he had given up his former life to come live with the Loni? And the man who would enslave the Loni? Who else but Obode?

He did not understand anything about the Oriental who would redeem the Loni in the ritual flames, but who said legends had to be letter-perfect?

It was close enough to him to count. And to show his brotherhood in blackness to the Loni people by repaying those who had taken them in slavery, and also to indulge himself a little bit, Butler decided to add something to the legend . . . the man who collected payment for a centuries-old sin.

He opened the briefcase on the seat next to him in the 707 jet and stared at the brown-cornered parchment, a ship's manifest, a load of slaves from East Africa. Another old parchment was a bill of sale. There was a yellowed fragment of paper from a plantation. Another fragment showed a family tree. And woven through all the documents were the names of the Lippincotts, the Butlers, the Forsythes: the three American families whose fortunes had been made in the slave trade.

From a small envelope he took a stack of newspaper clippings. The last one was a pretty little piece in the *Norfolk Pilot* about a Hillary Butler's engagement to a Harding Demster III. He hoped Harding Demster III would not be upset about waiting at the altar.

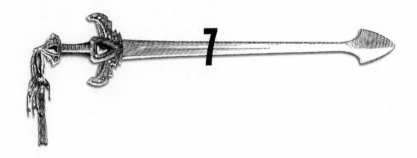

THERE had been trouble at the Busati Airport. According to the army detachment continuously assigned to Air Busati, largely to prevent the planes' tires and wheels from being stolen, seven large lacquered trunks were missing from the baggage terminal, and fourteen soldiers were unaccounted for.

The periodicals' stall had also been ransacked. It was believed that a riot had occurred in the stall because of the extensive damage, yet there were not enough people at the airport to cause such a riot. In fact, the only people there who were not Busatians were a white American and an aged Oriental, who had vanished along with the soldiers and the lacquered trunks.

"Do you think it is true?" asked General Obode of his personal valet, a fellow Hausa.

"About the riot?"

"About everything."

"You mean the East and the West, father and son?"

"Yes," said Obode.

The valet shook his head. "The Loni are in their mountains and there they shall stay. We should have no fear of a heartless mountain band. Especially now that you have begun to give them positions in the government. They shall not rise again. Fear not."

General Obode thought a minute. "Draw another $10,000

from the Ministry of the Treasury and deposit in my Swiss bank account," he said.

Meanwhile, across the Busati plains, a caravan plodded toward the mountains. Seven trunks on the shoulders of fourteen soldiers bobbed along the line, the sun glinting off their lacquered exteriors.

In front of this line marched the Master of Sinanju and Remo. Remo was furious.

"You're a damned two-faced sonuvabitch," he said.

"A contract is a contract," said Chiun. "A preceding unfilled contract always takes precedence over a more recent one. It is only fair."

"You're talking about a contract over two thousand years old. The House of Sinanju didn't even exist then, damned two-faced sonuvabitch."

"Name-calling no more obviates a contract than a few years here or there."

"This thing dates back before Christ. A few years. A few years, Little Father?"

"It is you who choose to date things from the time of Christ, not the House of Sinanju. We have an unfilled contract, paid for, mind you, paid in full. It was from the year of the ram. Or was it the year of the rat?"

"Probably from the year of the two-faced sonuvabitch."

"No matter. It was before the year of your 1950s or was it 1960s when the House of Sinanju agreed to train something dragged in off the streets, as a stopgap measure in lieu of a real assassin."

"May your autographed picture of Rad Rex be burned," said Remo.

Chiun looked back at the trunks and said something to one of the soldiers in what Chiun had explained was a Loni dialect.

By the tone of the voice, Remo could tell Chiun was reminding the soldiers that the trunks contained valuables, probably that the first trunk contained the picture of Rad Rex, the star of *As the Planet Revolves,* and in case of emergency, it should be saved first.

It had shocked Remo when he had first heard Chiun speak this Loni tongue. He had thought the Master of Sinanju knew only Mandarin, Chinese, Japanese, Korean and some English.

But at the airport where he and Chiun had headed by foot after leaving General Butler in the jeep, Chiun had silenced him while moving to the airport gate. When they had gotten out of Butler's jeep, Remo had wanted to go right back to town to get on with the job of looking for the white house behind the iron gate. But Chiun had demanded they go to the airport and pick up Chiun's luggage. He would not negotiate or compromise. He wanted his luggage, he told Remo.

They did not know it but they reached the airport only minutes after Butler's airplane had taken off, and the permanent military detail at the airport was lounging around in the terminal when the two entered.

"I will speak to them in the language of the Loni Empire," Chiun said, "to find where our luggage is."

"The Loni? That's a tribe, Chiun."

"No, it is a great kingdom of great virtue," Chiun had said, which Remo took to mean that when they hired assassins they paid their bills on time.

"Well, let's get your luggage and get back to the capital. I've got work to do."

Chiun raised a long bony finger. The nail reflected the overhead light like a sliver of diamond. Chuin called to one of the guards in what sounded to Remo like the Swahili spoken as the main language of Busati.

"They're not going to talk to you, Chiun. We're foreigners."

"Speak for yourself, white man," had said the Master of Sinanju.

Remo crossed his arms and waited confidently for Chiun to get a rifle pointed at him by one of the guards. Let him fight his own way out, thought Remo. Perhaps there would even be a flaw in a stroke. That would be good to watch, even though Remo wasn't going to hold his breath waiting to see it.

Chiun spoke first in Loni dialect, then translated for Remo.

"I am the Master of Sinanju and this is Remo who is white but close to me. I tell them close, Remo, because they would not understand your natural disrespect and lack of appreciation. I would see your king for a debt I owe as a Master of Sinanju. Remo, they will know this, for it must be spoken of widely in their villages and temples that there is a debt owed by the Master of Sinanju."

The two guards conversed heatedly between themselves. Remo smiled.

"You mean to tell me, Little Father, that two African soldiers are going to remember a centuries-old contract by a foreign hit-man."

"Try as you might, Remo, you will not understand the nature of Sinanju. The Loni know how to appreciate the services of the Masters of Sinanju, not like the Chinese emperors or the vile Americans."

Remo shook his head. When Chiun began on the glories of Sinanju, there was no reasoning with him. Perhaps five people in all the world had heard of the House of Sinanju—four of them must be in intelligence agencies and the fifth an obscure dust-covered historian. But to hear Chuin tell it, Sinanju was more important than the Roman Empire.

Chiun babbled on and the soldiers looked confused. They motioned for Remo and Chiun to follow them.

"You will see how a true people of dignity treat a Master of

Sinanju," Chiun whispered proudly to Remo. "There are those with enough culture in the world to see a true assassin as more than a hitman as you call him. You will see."

"Chiun, you don't even know if these soldiers are Loni. They're probably going to shake us down."

"You have them confused with Americans," Chiun said.

The soldiers led Chiun and Remo to an officer where Chiun again explained something, hands moving unusually rapidly for just the telling of a story. Remo tried to discern from the officer's face what the reaction was, but the officer's night face was as changeless as space.

The officer pointed to a newstand inside the airport.

Chiun nodded and beckoned to Remo.

"You'll see. You'll see what true respect is," he said. "Follow me."

Remo shrugged. The air terminal—slightly smaller than the one in Dayton, Ohio—was five times too big for the passenger use. Remo waited with Chiun at a periodical stand which had mostly English language publications.

"We'll store your luggage, Chiun, making sure your picture of Rad Rex is safe, and tonight I'll check out the white house with the iron gate."

"No," said Chiun. "We must wait for that officer. To leave now would be disrespectful to the Loni."

"How come, Chiun, these Loni have your respect?"

"Because, unlike some people, they have earned it."

"Chiun, I don't want to hurt your feelings, but really now. Every Master of Sinanju has been taught Loni dialect for centuries, because you still owe them a contract?"

"Correct."

"I kind of think that little debt might have been forgotten by now. Just how many languages do you know well?"

"Really well?"

"Yeah."

"One. My own. The rest I use."

Remo noticed an imported copy of *The New York Times* selling for $2.50. Under the fold of the front page, there was a story about the television networks adjusting their Watergate coverage to allow the showing of soap operas.

"*As the Planet Revolves* is back on the air in the states," said Remo, mildly.

"What?" demanded Chiun.

"Your shows. They're back on."

Chiun's mouth began to work as he tried to speak, but nothing came out. Finally he said, "I left America under the condition that I was leaving a void. America has lied to me. How could they have returned the programs just like that after taking them off just like that?"

"I don't know, Little Father. But I think now we can get about our business so we can get back to the States faster, right? You can pay your respects to the Loni some other time. If they've waited a couple of thousand years, they can certainly wait another one or two."

For the first time, Remo saw Chiun in conflict.

Just then, the Army captain they had spoken to walked up to them, and said, in British-tinged English: "My men and I have been delighted, sir, by your telling of that silly Loni fairy tale. To show our pleasure, we will be glad to retrieve your luggage for only one hundred dollars American."

Remo put his hand up over his mouth to stifle a laugh.

Chiun resolved his internal conflicts. The frail Oriental went whirring into the newspapers, shredding them. The stand went into a wall rack and the wall rack went into the vendor who went into the lighting fixtures along with the rack, stand and little shredded bits of white papers that slowly settled like a soft snowfall in the Busati Air Terminal.

"Just so it should not pass, this perfidy, in calmness," said Chiun. The captain who had tried to shake them down had begun to back away, when a word from Chiun stopped him.

This time, Chiun did not translate for Remo as he spoke with the captain. Finally, Chiun beckoned for Remo to follow him. As they walked behind the captain, Chiun said softly to Remo, "They are not Loni, these people."

"Good. Then let's go to the city and finish what we came to do."

"First I must finish what I came to do," Chiun said.

Several hours later, as they trudged across the Busati plain, Remo was still picking little bits of newsprint out of his jacket pockets and bitching at Chiun for deceiving him into thinking they were going back to the capital city.

"I told you," Chiun said. "An older contract takes precedence."

"That doesn't answer my problem, Little Father."

"To a fool, nothing is an answer."

"You and I are paid by the same employer. We have a job to do and we are not serving him."

"You may leave if you wish," Chiun said.

"How?" said Remo looking around the plain. "I don't even know where I am."

"When did you ever?" said Chiun and marched on happily toward the mountains in the distance. For a full day they walked and Remo complained about the assignment being missed, the Loni who would undoubtedly rob them when the two got to their village and the awesome dryness of the plain which Chiun kept referring to as the lush gardens before the mountains, for they had once, he explained, been the most beautiful gardens in the world.

"The Loni must have paid your ancestors pretty good," said Remo.

"They recognized true worth."

"They're gonna jump us as soon as we get to enough of them."

"The Loni are fair and just and decent."

"They must have really paid," said Remo. He felt clammy and dusty and grimy, not having changed clothes in two days. Chiun, naturally, had seven trunks full of changes.

As they climbed into the mountains, night descended in its awesome majesty upon the old continent. Remo noticed immediately that these were not simple paths, but stairways cut of rock worn by centuries of feet.

They continued marching into the night, pushing onward and upward. Remo was amazed at the ability of the soldiers to keep going under the burden of Chiun's baggage.

Around one bend a fire shone from a high wall.

Chiun cupped his hands to his face and yelled the Loni dialect of Swahili.

"I told them I was here," he said to Remo.

"Now we get it," said Remo, prepared to slash his way back down the mountain.

From arches in the wall came men bearing torches and spears, just a few men at first who hung back and waited until their numbers grew, and then moved forward, their torches illuminating the night with fire as though they were high beam lamps.

There were too many with too many spears to escape unscathed. Remo decided to take a route through the center, prepare his body to take some wounds, and then to keep going. Retreat was impossible. Behind him he heard Chiun's trunks striking the ground, and the scuffling feet of the Hausa soldiers as they turned and fled down the mountainside.

Oddly enough the Loni tribesmen did not pursue them. Instead, when they got within striking distance, they fell to their knees and a cry of praise rose from their throats in powerful unison.

"Sinanju. Sinanju. Sinanju."

Then, up over their heads on the mountaintop, Remo could see in the flame light, a tall black woman wearing a short white gown. She carried in her hands a shiny metal brazier from which a fire burned. Remo and Chiun moved closer, and the crowd which chanted "Sinanju" stopped, upon one word from her.

She spoke. Chiun translated for Remo.

"Welcome, Master of Sinanju. Our ambitions have been awaiting the return of your awesome magnificence. Oh, Awesome Magnificence, the Gods of the Loni greet you in fire. Our hopes await the glory of thy majestic presence. Oh, Awesome Magnificence, the throne of the Loni once again will be secure because you have deigned to come among us."

"They really saying those things about you, Chiun?" said Remo from the side of his mouth.

"That is how civilized people greet the Master of Sinanju," said Chiun, the latest Master of Sinanju.

"Shit," said Remo Williams, ex-Newark cop.

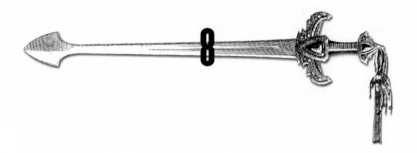

GENERAL William Forsythe Butler rented a car at the Washington, D.C. airport when his plane landed there, and drove out in the quiet night toward Norfolk, Virginia.

The air was sweet with the hot smells of spring and he rode with the air-conditioning turned off and the windows open, listening to the land, feeling its beauty around him.

How long ago had those first slaves set foot on this land? Had they perhaps traveled this same road? Of course, it would not have been much more than a cart path then. Perhaps the rich dirt got between their toes and warmed and welcomed them and they thought the way Butler once had: that the land was rich and good. After a trip of unrelieved brutality, perhaps they felt that they had chanced into something good—a growing, fertile land where they could build a full and rewarding life. The Loni princes would have thought that way. And instead of happiness and fulfillment, they found only the chain and the whip and the sun-hammered days of backbreaking labor in the fields, labor unrelieved by the release of humor, by the circle of family; by the slow, lazy forgetfulness of happiness.

The Loni had once been prideful people. How many of them had tried to change their lot, first by reasoning with the white-eye brutes, then by fleeing, then by rebellion?

Butler thought of them and then of what the Loni, subjugated and beaten, had become even in their native land.

He trod heavier on the gas pedal. In Norfolk, he drove to the city's bustling waterfront and parked his car in a now unsupervised parking lot near a small amusement arcade. Before he even left the car, the watery feel and smell of salt and brack coated everything. He could feel it working its way into the soft silk fibers of his light blue suit, as he stepped along the riverfront street.

He stopped near the piers and looked up and down the street, blinking and bright with neon lights for a half-mile in each direction. His man would be in one of three places.

The first bar was air-conditioned cold, and he felt the sweat on his body dry almost immediately as he stepped inside the door. It was a sailor's bar. A *white* sailor's bar. The tavern was filled with seamen, their clothes, their tattoos, the leathery but still untanned look of their faces and hands giving away their occupation. Heads turned toward him as he stood in the doorway, realizing he had made a mistake and this was not the bar he was looking for, but determined to brazen it out as a free man, first looking along the bar, then toward the tables, scanning faces.

"Hey, you," the bartender called. "This is a private bar."

"Yassuh," Butler said. "Jes' looking for somebody, boss."

"Well, you won't find him in here."

"Not a him, boss. A her. You see her, maybe? Big blond woman with big titties. Wearing a little, short, red dress, way up high around the nice, fine, warm ass." He grinned, showing teeth.

The bartender sputtered.

Butler said, "Never mind, boss. She ain't here. But if she come in, you tell her to get her white ass home, 'cause her man gonna whomp her good iffen she don't. You tell her, she don't get right home, and she ain't getting no more of this good stuff right here," Butler said, stroking the groin of his trousers.

There were a few muzzled mumbles. The bartender's mouth still worked, getting ready to talk, but before he could speak, Butler turned and walked out into the street, letting the heavy wood and glass door swing shut behind him.

He stopped here on the sidewalk and laughed, a full, roaring laugh that only a trained, intelligent linguist's ear could tell was punctuated by the Loni throat click of anger.

Then Butler turned and walked away down the block. It didn't feel so oppressively hot anymore. The heat felt good on his skin.

The second tavern was uneventful, but empty and he found his man in the third saloon he entered. The man sat in the back, his face *café au lait* light against the dark blue of his crisp tailored gabardine uniform. Despite the heat, he wore his braided jacket and his braided duck-billed cap, with the gold stringwork across the crown and bill.

The bar was noisy with black sailors and no one looked up when Butler came in or paid any especial attention to the black dude in the light blue suit. He was twice offered drinks by sailors as he walked the length of the bar and turned them down with what he hoped was a gracious shake of his head, and finally reached the table where the ship's officer sat, drinking alone, a bottle of Cutty Sark scotch in front of him.

The officer looked up as Butler eased into the seat.

"Hello, Captain," Butler said.

"Why, Colonel Butler," the man said. "What a pleasure to see you." His tongue was a little thick in his mouth; he had been drinking too much, Butler realized with distaste. "It's been a long while."

"Yes," Butler said, "but now I have need of your services."

The ship's officer smiled softly as he filled his old-fashioned glass to the brim with Cutty Sark. He sniffed the smoky scotch, lifted it to his mouth, and then began to swallow it smoothly, slowly.

He stopped when the glass was half empty. "Why, of course," he said. "Same arrangement?"

Butler nodded.

The same arrangement meant $5,000 in cash for the captain of the Liberian-registered tanker. At least that was the polite fiction that Butler and the ship's captain maintained. The full truth was that the "same arrangement" meant that the captain's wife and mother and children who lived in Busati would continue to live there and not turn up dead in a ditch. This point had been made clear at Butler's first meeting with the captain ten months before; it had never been raised again since there was no need for it. The captain remembered.

"However," Butler added, "there will be a slight difference this time." He looked around the room to be sure no one was watching or listening. The small bar reverberated with the soul-screeching of the jukebox. Reassured, Butler said, "Two women."

"Two?" the captain said.

Butler smiled. "Two. But one will not complete the trip."

The captain sipped his drink, then smiled again. "I see," he said. "I see." But he did not see why he should carry two women for the same price he was paid for carrying one. Yet, neither did he see how he could raise the subject to Butler without risking serious trouble. Again, he said, "I see."

"Good," said Butler. "When do you sail?"

The captain glanced down at his watch. "Five o'clock," he said. "Just before dawn."

"I'll be there," Butler said. He rose from the table.

"Join me in a drink, Colonel?" the captain asked.

"Sorry, no. I never drink."

"Too bad. I should think you would. It makes life so much easier."

Butler put his big hand on the table and leaned forward to the officer. "You don't understand, Captain. Nothing could be easier than my life is now. Or more pleasurable."

The captain nodded. Butler paused a moment, almost challenging a comment, but when none came, he pushed away from the table, turned and left.

Butler's next stop was a motel on the outskirts of the city, where he rented a room under the name of F. B. Williams, producing identification in that name, paying cash and rebuffing efforts by the motel clerk to engage him in conversation.

Butler checked the room. The door locks satisfied him. He tossed his small traveling bag on the bed and returned to the car.

For an hour, he cruised the streets of Norfolk, looking for a person. It had to be a special kind of person.

Finally, he found her. She was a tall willowy blonde with ashen hair. She stood on a corner near a traffic light in the time-honored fashion of whores everywhere—ready to cross the street if a police car came along, but willing to stand there forever if the fuzz didn't come, or at least until the right kind of man came along in the right kind of car.

Butler saw her, quickly drove the rented Buick around the block, then timed it so that he rolled up in front of her as the traffic light turned red.

The girl looked at him through the windshield and Butler pressed the button that unlocked the car doors. The heavy, clicking sound was another universal signal. The girl came over, leaned on the door and stuck her head inside the open window, carefully glancing into the back seat first. She was just about the right size and age, Butler guessed. The coloration looked about right also.

"Want to party?" she said.

"Sure," Butler said.

"Go down for fifteen dollars, straight for twenty-five."

"You go all night?" Butler asked. He thought it odd that the words and phrases of the street came back to him so easily, almost as if they had never left his mind.

"Naah," the girl said. "All night's a bummer."

"Three hundred dollars make it more pleasant?" Butler asked, knowing that the figure was outrageous and could have hired the best efforts of any three girls on the block.

"You got three hundred?"

Butler nodded.

"Let's see it."

"Get in and I'll show you."

The girl opened the door and slid into the front seat next to Butler. The light was green and he turned the corner and pulled up into a spot near an all-night bookstand.

Butler reached his wallet from his pocket and took out three one-hundred-dollar bills, making sure that the girl got a look at the remaining fat wad of bills in the wallet. He held the three up in front of the girl.

"Payment in advance," she said warily.

"Two hundred now," he said. "You can stash it. The other hundred after."

"How come you're so eager?" she said.

"Look. I'm no freak. No whips, none of that shit. I just like white women. If you're good to me, there's another hundred in it that nobody has to know about."

She looked at Butler's face again, hard this time, obviously trying to fit him into one of her danger categories of fuzz, freaks and fighters, but he didn't match. "Okay," she said, "wait here. I'm going to drop off the two hundred and I'll be right back."

Butler nodded. He wouldn't trust a prostitute out of sight for any reason but money, so he had made a point of showing her all the cash in his wallet and her little brain already was working overtime, he knew, trying to figure out how to get more out of him than the four hundred dollars already promised. She would be back as soon as she gave the two hundred to her pimp.

Three minutes later she returned and as she slid into the front seat she grabbed him.

"My name's Thelma," she said. "What's yours?"

"Simon," he said. "I've already got a room." He snapped the door locks shut and drove off.

Ten minutes later, they were in Butler's motel room. Twenty minutes later, she was tied, gagged, drugged and lying on the floor behind the bed, not visible from the window and out of reach of the telephone. The last was an unnecessary precaution because she would be out for the rest of the night.

Butler looked at her one more time before leaving the room and he was satisfied. The size was right; the hair coloring about right. It wouldn't be perfect; it certainly might not fool anyone for too long, but it should do. It would buy enough time.

He whistled as he drove out through the hot city into the rolling fox-hunting hills of rich-bitch Virginia.

He drove the road three times before he found the cutoff to the long winding drive that led to the Butler estate. With his headlights out, and after sitting in the dark for a moment, he could see the main house high up on a hill, two hundred yards from the road. He decided not to drive up; the roadway was probably hooked up to an alarm. He cruised slowly down the highway for another hundred yards, found a deep shoulder off the road covered by an overhang of trees, and drove in.

He closed the car up, checked his pockets to make sure he had his materials and then set across the razorcut lawns of the

Butler estate toward the big house on the hill, keeping close to the line of trees at the property's northern end.

As he loped, he glanced at the luminous dial of his wristwatch. Cutting it close, but still enough time.

The grass oozed up a damp coolness that enveloped him as he moved, and he imagined himself in an earlier day, trudging barefooted along these hills, dressed perhaps in a monkey suit, bringing drinks to Massa on the patio. When had it happened? When had he come to hate so?

He moved in a rhythmic trot, his giant athlete's body swinging free and easy, the way he used to on the grass-covered fields of football, when he performed in the big open-air cage for the whites lucky enough to have a friend who could help them get season tickets.

No matter when he started to hate. He hated. That was enough of an answer, but then he remembered. King Kong was why he hated.

Butler had had a particularly bitter argument with his sister, had gone out into the New York night, and somehow had wound up listening to a free lecture on racism at the New School for Social Research.

The lecturer was one of that roving band of nonteaching teachers who make a headline with one interesting, if erroneous, statement and then milk it for lecture fees at campuses for the next twenty years. The lecturer began to talk about racism in the films, drawing unsupported conclusions from unsubstantiated data, to the growing applause of the two hundred people, mostly white, in the audience.

Then the house lights dimmed and film clips from the old King Kong classic began to be shown on the screen. There were five minutes of the giant ape terrorizing Fay Wray in the jungle, then climbing the Empire State Building with her in his giant hand, then standing there atop the building until he was gunned down by the fighter planes.

The speaker seemed to want to match the auditorium darkness with the lack of light in his own analysis.

King Kong, he said, was just a thinly veiled attack by white filmmakers on black sexuality, a pandering to the redneck's fear of the potent black man. The leering expressions of King Kong as he lifted the white girl up in his giant black hand; his mindless, headlong, unswerving search for her which typified the mythical lust of black men for white women; and the cheaply symbolic end where King Kong was shot down while hanging on to the building's phallic symbol of a tower, thus signifying that the black man would be done in by his erect phallus—all these were cited as proofs by the speaker.

Butler looked around the auditorium at the heads nodding up and down in agreement.

And these were the liberals, he thought, the best hope of blacks in America—and not one of them questioned, for even a moment, their own willingness to equate a giant movie monkey with a black man. Didn't they teach anthropology in the schools any more? Didn't they teach anything? The ape was hairy, and blacks were hairless. Blacks had thick lips, but apes had no lips at all. And yet these looney-tunes could believe that people would find blacks and apes interchangeable. Why could they believe that of others, if they didn't really know it of themselves?

And *they* were supposed to be the best America had to offer.

Butler had left the auditorium convinced by the speaker of just one thing: his sister had been right and he had been wrong. *It would take confrontation and possibly violence to get what the black man deserved in America.*

Butler tried. Then came that visit to the Loni village, when William Forsythe Butler had known that he had come home.

He heard the legend of the Loni and knew that he—he alone—could be the redeemer of that legend, that he could use the Loni to take over power in Busati and show what a black man could do with a government if given half a chance.

He was at the house now. It was dark and silent. He was glad there were no dogs. Willie Butler was afraid of dogs.

He paused close to the wall of the house, looking around him, remembering the floor plan that had been outlined to him by a researcher, who had found it in the Library of Congress, under Historical Homes of Virginia. The girl's room would be second floor front right.

He looked up. Latticework, buried under vines, covered the front of the big building. He hoped the thin wood would hold his weight.

Butler tested it by reaching up, grabbing a piece of wood with his right hand, and lifting his feet off the ground.

He hung there suspended by his right hand momentarily; the wood was anchored and strong. He grunted softly to himself and then began climbing the latticework like a ladder. The window to the second floor bedroom was unlocked and open slightly at the top. Inside he could hear the faint whirring of central air-conditioning breathing coolness into the room.

The night was black as a railroad tunnel at midnight, and the inside of the bedroom seemed to be brightly lighted by the small lamp built into the light switch near the door.

In the bed, under a shiny sheet, he could make out a woman's form. That should be Hillary Butler.

Holding onto the latticework with one hand, Butler inched the bottom window up until it was fully opened. Then he carefully stepped into the room, his shoes sinking deeply into the plush velvet carpet that covered the floor. He paused, sipping his breath carefully through his nose, trying to make no sound, then moved toward the bed, the foot, around the side. He could see the girl's face now. It was Hillary Butler, sleeping the dreamy sleep of the peaceful-with-the-world. That she slept in this air-conditioned room under that satin sheet because her ancestors had carted men and women and babies across an ocean in the hold of a stinking rat-infested ship, did not seem to intrude on her sleep at all. Butler hated her.

He stepped back and from his pocket took a small foil-wrapped packet. Carefully he pinched the top to break the air-tight seal.

The characteristic smell of chloroform rose from the package into his nostrils. From the packet, he pulled out a heavy gauze pad soaked with the drug, and carefully put the foil back into his jacket.

Quickly he moved forward. He stood alongside the girl and transferred the chloroform pad to his right hand. Then he reached down and covered the girl's nose and mouth with the pad. Hillary Butler bolted upright in bed, and the big man dropped his body on hers to hold her still. She thrashed for a few seconds, her eyes wide open and shocked, trying to see her attacker, but only able to see the glint of light reflecting off a golden chain-link ring on the hand that covered her face. Her thrashing slowed down. Finally, she was still.

Butler stood up and looked down at the unconscious girl. He left the pad on her face and methodically began to search the room.

He carefully went through a clothes closet that ran the length of one wall, looking at dresses and rejecting them until he found one, a blue and white jersey shift with a hand-made label from an exclusive New York City couturier. He made sure the other garments were hanging neatly before he closed the closet. On a dressing table, he saw a polished ebony wood jewelry box. He reached inside and grabbed a handful of jewelry, carried it to the room's little night light, and inspected it. He took an engraved golden charm bracelet and a pair of gem earrings. The rest he returned to the box.

Butler rolled up the blue and white dress and stuck it under the belt of his trousers. The jewelry went into an inside jacket pocket.

At the bed, he pulled the chloroform pad off the girl's face, put it back in his pocket, then lifted the girl up in one muscled arm, carrying her under his arm like a rolled up set of blueprints and went back to the window.

With ease that surprised him, he carried the girl down. Still holding her under one arm, he moved toward the line of trees and headed back for the roadway where his car waited.

He dumped the little rich girl on the floor in the back of the car, covered her with a blanket and then drove off quickly. He didn't want to be stopped by any policemen wondering what a black in a rented car was doing in this section of the county at almost three o'clock in the morning.

After parking in the motel lot in front of his room, Butler placed a fresh chloroform pad near Hillary Butler's face, then went inside his room where the prostitute was still unconscious.

He dressed her in Hillary Butler's blue and white dress, then put on the stolen jewelry. The charm bracelet engraved on the back. "To Hillary Butler from Uncle Laurie." Earrings. They were made for pierced ears. The whore's ears were not pierced. Butler swore under his breath. Damn, just like a white bitch, not to have holes where you wanted her to. He rammed the point of one earring through the fleshy lobe of the unconscious girl who did not even stir, even though drops of blood ran down her ear from the small hole. He clipped the earring in back with the small squeeze lock attachment, then fastened the other earring in the same way.

Butler untied the girl's ropes and stashed them in his small suitcase. From a back compartment of the bag, he pulled out two heavy brown-colored plastic bags, shaped like army duffle bags.

He stuffed the prostitute into one of them. The bag locked at the top with metal snaps but there was enough gap in the closure for air to get in. General William Forsythe Butler took the other bag out into the parking lot. There was no one in sight. Only three cars were parked in the lot, and those rooms were darkened, their occupants probably asleep. Butler opened the back door of the Buick, reached in and began to feed Hillary Butler into the bag. He handled her without tenderness, breaking the strap of her light nylon nightgown. The gown slid down, revealing a creamy white well-formed breast. Butler laid his black hand on her breast, feeling its warmth, looking in the dim light at the contrast between her skin and his. He tweaked the end of the breast viciously, and the girl flinched in her stupor. He grimaced to himself as he released her. Get used to it, honey, he thought. There's gonna be more where that came from. Your family's got a three-hundred-year-old bill to pay, and payment's gonna come right out of your fine white hide.

Butler closed the bag with the snaps, then again glancing around the lot, slipped back into his room, picked up the bag containing the street girl, and carried that back to the car. He tossed her into the back seat on top of Hillary Butler.

Then he cleaned everything out of the room and left, wiping all the doorknobs free of prints, and leaving the key in the door of the room.

Fifteen minutes later, his rented car was parked in a black unlit street, a scant hundred yards from the pier where the Liberian freighter was now coming to life, preparing to sail.

Butler locked the doors of his car and went looking for the captain. He found him on the bridge of the ship and whispered a few words to him.

The captain called a sailor to him and talked to him softly. "Your keys," the captain asked Butler. Butler gave them to the sailor who turned away.

Ten minutes later, he was down on dockside below the ship with a big steamer trunk on a forklift.

"Carry that trunk to my cabin," the captain told another sailor, who scurried down the gangplank and helped the other lug the heavy trunk aboard.

Butler waited a few minutes, then went to the captain's cabin.

The trunk was neatly in the middle of the floor. Butler opened it and roughly yanked the plastic bag out of the trunk. He opened the clips on top, glanced in and saw the prostitute wearing Hillary Butler's blue and white dress. Carefully, he pulled the plastic bag down until the girl's face and shoulders were free.

Butler looked around the cabin. On a small table near the captain's big bed was a fourteen-inch-long bronze statuette. Butler hefted it in his hand. It was heavy enough.

He walked back and knelt alongside the unconscious whore. How peaceful she looked, he thought, as he raised the heavy statuette over his head and slammed it down with the force of a hammer into the girl's face.

Butler was thorough. He shattered her teeth, broke her facial bones, and for good measure broke one of the bones in her left arm.

He stood up, puffing slightly from the exertion. The carpet on the floor was spattered with gore, and with a towel from the captain's private bathroom, he mopped it up as best he could, then washed the statuette clean. He noted what looked like specks of blood imbedded in the link design of his gold ring, and carefully washed it out under running water.

Butler snapped the dead girl back into the bag but left it on the rug in the middle of the floor. Before leaving the room, he checked to make sure Hillary Butler was still alive in her plastic cage, then slammed the lid of the heavy trunk shut.

Back on the bridge, Butler called the captain to one side. From his inside jacket pocket, he took an envelope containing $5,000 in hundreds.

"Here," he said. "Your fee."

The captain pocketed it and then looked again at Butler with a bland open face.

"What do I do this time to earn it?"

"There is a bag on the floor of your cabin," Butler said. "When your ship is underway ten minutes and it is still dark, dump its contents overboard. It would be best if you were to do it yourself. Your crew should not know."

The captain nodded.

"And there is a trunk in your room. Inside there is another bag with another set of contents. You will follow our usual procedure with that, turning the trunk over to my man who will meet you at your next port. He will fly it to Busati."

"I see," the captain said.

Butler reached into his pocket and withdrew a half dozen of the foil packages of chloroform pads. "Take these," he said. "They may be helpful in keeping your cargo . . . let us say, pliable."

The captain stuck the packs in his pocket. "Thank you. By the way," he said, with a small smile at the corners of his mouth, "May I make use of this cargo?"

The Busati chief of staff thought a moment, thought of Hillary Butler, thought of her warm white breast, thought of her next home in the house behind the pearl door button, and shook his head. "Not this time, Captain," he said. Hillary Butler was the last one, and random rape simply would not do. There just was not enough terror in it, at least not for one whose ancestors had given his ancestors their slave name. Nothing but gang rape under his own personal supervision would suffice. For a starter.

"Sorry," he said.

The captain shrugged.

"Now don't forget with the other bag," Butler said. "Ten minutes out to sea, dump her. The current should run her ashore sometime tomorrow."

"It shall be as you say, Colonel."

"Oh, by the way, it's General now. I've been promoted."

"I'm sure you're worthy."

"I try to be," Butler said.

He took his car keys, trotted lightly down the gangplank and returned to his car. For the first time since he'd reached America, he turned his air-conditioner up high.

Two hours later, he was back in the 707 jet, on his way home to Busati.

The last name on his list, he thought. The legend was coming true.

For a moment, a random thought of that American Remo and the elderly Oriental intruded on his mind, but he rejected it. By now, they would either be out of Busati or in the custody of the troops, in which case he would see that they were exiled from the country for good. The Loni legend was to be his alone to fulfill.

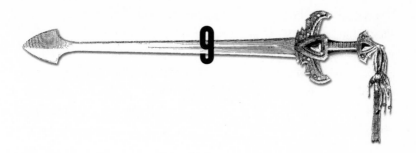

9

ONCE we lived in palaces. Our buildings stretched to the clouds. Our land was rich and we were at peace."

The girl turned away from Remo who lay on his back on a hillock, chewing a piece of grass. "And now, this is our world," she said bitterly, waving her arm across the field of her view. "A land of thatched huts and poverty, of ignorance and disease. A land in which we are hunted by the Hausa like game animals. We are a people from whose men the courage has been bred out, like milk-giving is bred into a cow."

Remo rolled on his left side to look at the girl. She was tall and lithe, and silhouetted against the white daylight sky of Africa, she seemed blacker than was her dark skin. She wore only a short white robe in the fashion of a Grecian toga, but its outlines, too, looked dark against the hot white sky. Her back was toward Remo, and out in front of her, down at the bottom of the hill, he could see the grubby little camp which now represented the once-great Empire.

"Could be worse," Remo said.

"How?" The girl turned and came to Remo, and in a smooth graceful motion slid down to the grass alongside him. "How could it be worse for my Loni people?"

"Take my word for it," Remo said. "You complain that civilization has kind of passed your people by. Well, you haven't missed a thing. I come from what they call civilization, and I prefer it here. At least, if you stay out of the Hausas' way, you've got some kind of peace."

He reached forward and took her left hand in his. She recoiled involuntarily from him, then tried to relax, but Remo released her hand. Princesses of the Loni Empire were virgins till they were wed; they knew not of men and no man entered into them until it was by ceremony and custom ordained. His was probably the first male hand which had ever touched the beautiful artist's hand of Princess Saffah of the Loni Empire.

"Do not release me," she said. "It feels warming, your hand. And you are right, it *is* peaceful here. But peacefulness is like rain. It is nice, but always to have it pressed upon you is quite another thing."

She took Remo's hand up in hers, silent for a moment as if shocked by her own boldness. "You, for instance," she said. "You lie here now, sucking grass like a cow, and talking of how lovely peace is, and you know that as soon as you can you will go back to this world you hate."

Remo said nothing; she was right. When he found and freed the slave girls and discovered what had happened to James Forsythe Lippincott, he would leave.

"Could I stay if I wanted?" he finally said.

"I do not know. The legend is silent."

"Oh, yeah. The legend."

Since he and Chiun first had arrived two days before, they had heard of little else but the legend. Chiun had been installed, seven steamer trunks and all, in the finest thatched hut the Loni had to offer. Princess Saffah, who ruled this camp as her two younger princess sisters ruled the other two Loni encampments in the nearby hills, had moved out to make room for Chiun.

"Dammit, Chiun, that's not right," Remo had said. "Move into some other place instead of moving people around."

"Not right?" Chiun said. "What is not right? That the people of the Loni should not honor a man who has come thousands of miles across the seas to repay a debt centuries old and to put them back into power? They should not give up a hut to a man who will give them palaces?"

"Yeah, but moving their princess?"

"Princess? Suddenly you are a royalist. Remember this then. Princesses and princes and kings and queens come and go. But there is only one Master of Sinanju."

"Talk about the world being lucky," Remo said sarcastically.

"Yes, the world is lucky to have such a one. But even luckier are you who have been permitted to bask in the warmth of the Master's magnificence."

And so Chiun had moved into the hut of Princess Saffah.

In quiet protest, however, Remo refused. He insisted upon moving into one of the smaller huts of the village. The first night he was cold. The second night he was wet. The morning of the third day, he walked into Chiun's hut with his blanket in his hand.

"I thought you might be lonely," Remo said, "so I decided to move in to keep you company."

"I am happy you think so much of me," Chiun said. "But please, I would not want you to do anything against your principles."

"No, that's all right, Chiun. I've made my mind up. I'll stay."

"No," Chiun said. "I insist."

"Sorry, Chiun, I'm not leaving. I'm going to stay here and keep you company whether you like it or not."

"You are leaving this instant," Chiun said, and then called the entire Loni village to remove Remo by force if necessary. As

Remo slunk away back to his own little mud hut, he could hear Chiun explaining behind him: "Sometimes the child forgets himself and must be reminded of his place. But he is young and will yet learn."

Remo had wandered up the hill and Princess Saffah had followed him. She had come to console him.

"Yeah, the legend," Remo repeated. "Look, you're a smart girl. Do you really believe the Loni are going to return to power because Chiun is here?"

"Not just the Little Father," she said. "You are here too and you are part of the legend." She opened the palm of his hand and pretended to examine it. "Tell me, when did you die?" She laughed as she felt Remo's hand tense momentarily. "You see," she said laughing. "The legend speaks only truth."

"You'd better tell me of this legend," Remo said. He was happy that she still clung to his hand.

"Once," she began, "many years ago there was a Master from across the sea. And because he stood with the Loni, the Loni were a great and just people. They lived in peace; they inflicted injustice upon no man. In the ancient days, by your calendar, the great libraries of the world were said to be at Alexandria in the land of Egypt. But the greatest of all was at Timbuktu and it was the library of the Loni. This is true, what I am telling you, Remo, you could look it up. And it was the Loni Empire that gave to the world the gift of iron. That, too, is true. We had men who could repair damaged eyes; we had physicians who could heal those with twisted brains; all these things, the Loni had and did and we were a great people, blessed of God.

"It was said of the Master that the Loni had given him their courage for safekeeping, while they used their heads for science and their hands for art. And then this Master from across the sea went away and the Loni who had relied on him were overwhelmed by an inferior people and our empire was lost. Our best men and women were sold into slavery. We were hunted and tracked like animals until we retreated, three small bands all that was left, into these hills where you now find us and where we hide from our enemies.

"But this Master sent word across the years and across the seas and across the mountains that one day he would return. He would bring with him a man who walked in the shoes of death, a man whose earlier life had ended, and this man would face in mortal combat an evil man who would keep the Loni in chains. That is you, Remo, and this is truth I tell you."

Remo looked up and saw that Princess Saffah's dark eyes were tinged with sadness.

"Does the legend say whether I win or lose the fight?" Remo asked.

"No," she said. "The legend is silent. But it tells what must happen. The Loni children must come home. And if you are victorious, the Lonis will again rule the land and children will be able to walk the streets and the blind again can be made to see."

"It sounds like I'm doing all the work," Remo said. "What does the legend say of Chiun? Does he do anything except lay in your hut down there like Henry the Eighth?"

Princess Saffah laughed, and the smile brought beauty back to her finely chiseled face. "You must not speak unkindly of the Little Father. Centuries of hardship have changed the Loni people. Where once we were kind, we are now vindictive. Where once we had charity, we now have malice; where love, now hate; where courage, now cowardice. It is written that the Master will purify the Loni people in the ritual of the sacred fire. In that fire, he will restore to the Lonis the goodness that once was theirs, so that they may again be fit to rule this land. The Little Father may perish in this task, which is why we revere him so."

Remo rolled over and searched Saffah's deep eyes. "Perish?"

"Yes. So it is written. The flames may consume him. He is a very great man to come back to us, knowing that here he may hear the clock strike the hour of his death."

"Chiun knows this?"

"Of course," Saffah said. "He is the Master, is he not? Did you not hear his words when first he arrived? No, of course not, you would not understand because he spoke the tongue of the Loni. But he said, 'I have traveled these ages from the land of Sinanju to stand here again with my brothers, the Loni, and to place my body on the sacred coals to purify their lives with my life.'"

"He didn't tell me," Remo said. "He didn't say anything about any ritual fire."

"He loves you very much," the Princess said. "He would not worry you."

"What about you, Saffah? You believe the legend?"

"I must, Remo. I am first in the line of succession to the crown of the Loni Empire. My faith sustains my people's faith. Yes. I believe. I have always believed. I have believed in the past when others have come to us and we thought, perhaps *here,* perhaps *this* is the redeemer of the legend. But when they failed, it was just their failure, not the failure of the legend. Not long ago, another came and we believed that he might be the one but now, now that you and the Little Father have arrived, we know that he was not the one. You are."

"We who are about to die salute you," Remo said.

She leaned forward and said closely to his face. "Do you believe in sin, Remo?"

"I don't think anything is wrong between two consenting orangutans."

"I do not understand." Her face assumed a look of quizzicality which softened when she saw Remo smile. "You jest," she accused. "You jest. Someday you must tell me of your jesting and what it means."

"I will someday," he said. "No, I don't believe too much in sin. I think sin is not being able to do your job. Not much else."

"I am glad you have said that, because it is said to be a sin for a Princess of the Loni to know a man before she is wed. And yet, Remo, I want to know you and I want you to enter into me."

"Best offer I've had today," Remo said lightly, "but I think you ought to think about it some more."

Princess Saffah leaned forward, pressed her lips against Remo's and kissed him hard. She pulled her head back triumphantly. "There," she said. "I have already committed the sin of touching a man. Now when your time comes, you will have no reason not to take me."

"When I'm sure you're ready," Remo said, "no reason could stop me. But first duty calls."

Duty for Remo meant two things: freeing the girls in the white house behind the iron gate and finding out what had happened to Lippincott.

But Princess Saffah could give him no answers to either of those problems, although she suggested that if evil was involved, it was probably the work of General Obode.

"We have a friend," she said, "in Obode's camp. Perhaps he will be able to help you."

"What's his name?" Remo asked.

"He is a countryman of yours," Saffah said. "His name is Butler."

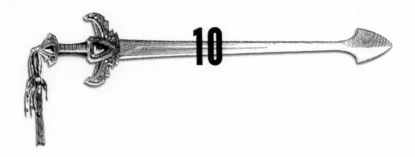

In the American circles that concerned themselves with the activities of the Four Hundred, it was well known that the Forsythes and the Butlers talked only to their cousins, the Lippincotts, and that the Lippincotts talked only to God or to whomever else could match His credentials.

So when the body washed onto the beach a few miles from Norfolk, Virginia, pummeled and battered by the stones near the shore, it became a big story because the body was identified as that of Hillary Butler. The identification was made through her blue-and-white dress and from engraved jewelry the corpse wore.

The Butler family bit its lip, as such families do, and refused to indulge in speculation for the press as to how their daughter, soon to be married, had managed to wind up dead and drowned in the ocean.

The family detested the whole idea, but part of the routine in such accidental deaths was an autopsy.

Clyde Butler was called by the county medical examiner that afternoon.

"Mr. Butler, I have to see you," the doctor said.

Resentfully, Butler agreed and made an appointment to see the examiner at his private medical office, where Butler's arrival would not draw attention, as it certainly would have at the county administration building.

Despite the unseasonable spring heat, Butler wore a heavy dark pin-striped suit as he sat in the doctor's office, facing him across a tan-painted metallic desk.

"I suppose it's about my poor daughter," Butler said. "Really, haven't we gone through enough without . . . ?"

"That's just it, sir," the doctor said. "That body was not your daughter's."

Butler could not speak. Finally, he said, "Repeat that."

"Certainly. The dead girl who washed ashore was not your daughter."

"You're sure of this?"

"Yes, sir. In making the autopsy, I discovered that the girl whose body was found had syphilis. Discreetly, I obtained your family's records from your physician and dentist. It was very difficult because of the mutilation, but I can now say without a twinge of doubt that some other young woman is on the slab at the morgue right now."

Butler grimaced at what he considered unnecessarily explicit phrasing by the doctor.

He thought momentarily, then said: "Have you told anyone else?"

"No one at all. I wanted to talk to you first. Frankly, I did not know if your daughter might have known this other girl, or if your daughter's disappearance might be tied in somehow with this girl's death, or precisely what. It's only fair to tell you that the dead girl wasn't drowned. She was dead before she entered the water. I thought before I announced anything I would give you a chance to explain."

"You've done very well," Butler said, "and I appreciate your thoughtfulness. I would like you to do something else for me, if you would."

"If I can."

"Give me an hour and then I will be back here. Then we can decide what to do and what to say."

"Of course, Mr. Butler. Just so long as we both understand that I must fulfill the requirements of my office."

"Naturally I understand that, Doctor. Just an hour."

Butler left the doctor's office. In the middle of the next block was a bank in which the Butler family was the controlling stockholder. Butler went in, spoke briefly to the bank president, and in five minutes was ensconced, as he had asked to be, in a private office with a private telephone and a guarantee of no interruptions.

It was a sticky problem, Butler realized. At first blush, he would immediately think kidnaping and ransom. But why then would the kidnapers have gone to the trouble of dressing someone in Hillary's clothes and jewelry and trying to make it appear as if his daughter were dead? No. Kidnaping was out. Therefore, the next step might be that Hillary herself was somehow involved in this. He had no idea how to handle a thing like that, no knowledge of police processes. And hanging over it all was the publicity problem because of the Butler family's relationship with the Lippincotts.

Children with a problem go to their fathers. Butler went to the head of the Lippincott family and all its branches, Laurence Butler Lippincott.

Succinctly, calmly, he told Lippincott over the phone what had happened. Lippincott, with no trace of emotion in his voice, got Butler's number and told him to stay put; he would call him back.

From Laurence Butler Lippincott, a call went to the Senate Office Building. From there, a call went to the White House. From the White House, a special call went to Folcroft Sanitarium in Rye, New York. Problems were discussed, options were considered, decisions were reached.

The links in the chain were then reversed, and finally, the telephone rang in the air-conditioned bank office where Butler sat.

"Yes," he said.

"This is Laurie. Please listen very carefully. We believe your daughter is alive, but that she is no longer in this country. The very highest agencies in our government are now attempting to rescue her. This rescue effort, however, is guaranteed to fail if the people involved suspect that we know anything except what they wanted us to think. Therefore this is what we will do."

Butler listened as Laurie Lippincott spoke. Finally he said, "What of Martha?" thinking of his wife who was in a state of near collapse.

"She's already done the worst of her suffering," Lippincott said. "Tell her nothing."

"Nothing? But she ought to know."

"Why? So she can worry? Become hysterical? Perhaps drop a word here or there that could mean Hillary's death? Please. The very best thing is to let her think Hillary is dead. If we can get Hillary back, Martha can rejoice. And if we fail, well, one can only grieve once."

"What are the chances, Laurie?"

"I won't lie to you. They're less than fifty-fifty. But we're pulling out every stop. The best we have is on it."

"We? You mean the family?"

"No. I mean the United States of America," Lippincott said.

Butler sighed. "Okay, Laurie. Whatever you say. But I'm worried about the doctor. He's a snotty young bastard. He may give me flak."

Laurence Butler Lippincott took the name of the doctor, while allowing himself a small chuckle. "He shouldn't be too difficult," he said. "Not if his tax return is like most doctors'."

So it was that ten minutes later, Butler was back in the office of the doctor, explaining that the doctor must remain silent, must permit the funeral to go ahead as if the dead body were really that of Hillary Butler.

"Never," the doctor said angrily. "I don't know what your game is, but I'm not playing it."

His intercom rang. The doctor picked up the phone and said sharply, "I said I wasn't to be . . . oh . . . oh, I see. Yes, of course."

He pressed a blinking lit button on the telephone receiver. Warily, he said, "This is he." He said nothing else for a full sixty seconds. Finally, he said, "Of course, Senator. Yes. Senator, I understand. Of course. No problem. Be glad to, Senator. Yes, I understand." When he hung up the phone, beads of perspiration dotted his forehead.

He looked at Butler and nodded. "I won't say a thing," he said.

"Good," Butler said. "Sometime in the near future, I hope to be able to explain all this to your satisfaction," he added, wondering if he were not making too big a concession to a social inferior.

The doctor raised a hand. "No need of that. Whatever you want."

"Then, good day," Butler said. "I must go to the funeral home and console my wife."

In Rye, New York, Dr. Harold W. Smith leafed through a pile of reports and tried not to think of the Butler girl or of Remo and Chiun, five thousand miles away in Busati.

He had done the best he could and assigned his top weapons to the project. There was nothing more he could do, so there was no point in worrying.

Right? Wrong. Unless the matter were cleared up satisfactorily there might be substantial problems coming from the direction of the Lippincott family. And if they leaned into the President, the President might just fall over on top of Smith, Remo, Chiun and the whole CURE operation.

And the Lippincotts wouldn't give a damn that Smith had been considering America's best interests when he told Remo he could not kill General Obode.

Unless Remo moved pretty quickly, the whole mess might be beyond unscrambling.

He wished Remo would phone, but he knew it was not likely. It took forever for CURE's Busati source to reach them by telephone, and he was a high official of the government. Smith thought of the CURE contact, ex-CIA man William Forsythe Butler. Perhaps if Remo were not successful in getting this squared away quickly, Smith might contact Butler for his advice and help.

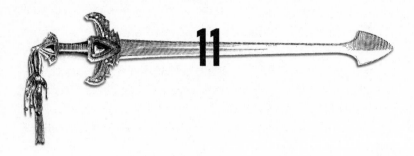

THE man trotting up the hill wore immaculate white gabardines cut in the style of a British khaki bush uniform.

As he walked into the village, he called aloud a few words of the guttural Loni tongue. The village at first seemed deserted, but slowly people came out of huts and greeted him.

General William Forsythe Butler stood in the center court of all the huts, talking to Loni tribesmen, scanning the village, looking for a glimpse of Princess Saffah.

She came around a corner and his face lit when he saw her.

"Oh, Butleh," she said, "we are glad you have returned to visit your people."

He reached for her, then withdrew his hands. He wanted to tell her of Hillary Butler, but held back. Perhaps she would not share his view that the act of revenge had helped even more to cast him in the mold of the Lonis' redeemer.

"I am glad to be here," he said.

"We have great news." To his raised eyebrow, she said, "Yes. The legend. It is being fulfilled."

She knew, Butler thought, but how had she guessed? It didn't matter. It was enough that Saffah and the rest of the Loni knew the legend was being fulfilled in his person. He smiled to her, the warm knowing smile that one smiled to another with whom he shared a secret.

He would have preferred it another way. It would have been better if he and Saffah had been able to discuss it first and then announce it to the Loni in the proper fashion. But if this was the way it was to be, well, who was he to argue? One must seize the moment of history; time is not always tidy.

Graciousness would probably be the right approach, so he smiled at Saffah, a smile of acceptance that said there would always be between them a special bond of friendship.

She smiled back, the smile a teacher gives a student who has not thrown up on his desk that day, then turned and extended an arm toward the hut Butler knew was hers.

The entrance to the hut was empty, and then framed in the doorway, wearing a yellow robe stood the small Oriental of the hotel and the airport.

He stood there benignly, his arms folded in front of him.

"Sinanju," the villagers cried as if in one voice.

"Sinanju."

The old man smiled and raised his arms for silence, with all the sincerity of Jack Paar trying to quiet the opening applause.

Saffah turned back to Butler. "He is the Master for whom we have waited. He has come these many miles across the seas. The legend comes true."

"But . . . but . . . but what of the man who gave up his life?" Butler asked.

Just then, Chiun stepped aside and Remo came out of the hut. He saw Butler, nodded a greeting, and then snapped his fingers.

"I got it now," he said. "Willie. Willie Butler. I saw you against the Packers one day at the Stadium. I've been trying to place you since the first time I met you. Well, I'll be . . . old Willie Butler." He advanced toward Butler as if to shake his hand, but General William Forsythe Butler turned on his heel and walked away, trying to put distance between himself and the memory of the Willie Butler who once was an entertainer of white men.

By dinnertime, Butler had regained his composure and begun to make his plans. When his men had told him they had found no trace of the American and the Oriental, he had thought they had left the country. But they were here now, and so a new plan had to be set up. There had been fulfillments of the legend before, and they had turned out false. And so it would be again. When Remo and Chiun were dead, the Loni would recognize that only in Butler was the legend come to life.

Butler ate with Saffah, Chiun and Remo in the large hut which Chiun had taken over. They sat on reed mats around a rock slab table that reflected the scarceness of hardwood in their barren hilly empire, and ate the flesh of fowl.

"You have come from Sinanju?" Butler asked.

Chiun nodded.

"Why?"

"Because there is a debt owed to the people of the Loni. A debt unpaid is an affront to my ancestors."

"So you will restore the Loni to power? How?"

"As it is written. In the purifying rites of the fire." Chiun ate delicately, then wiped his mouth with a silken cloth from one of his steamer trunks.

"And you?" Butler said to Remo.

"Me? I'm the man who accompanied Chiun to Loniland. Just a second banana. Tell me, you ever hear of a white house behind an iron gate?"

Butler hesitated. Of course. A U.S. agent, come to solve the mystery of the girls.

"Why?" he asked.

"Because I understand there's something there I ought to see."

"There is such a house," Butler said. "But it is under the personal protection of General Obode," he added, repeating the lie he had told to his CURE contact.

"His house?" Remo asked.

Butler nodded. "He is a man of curious tastes." A plan was beginning to form in his mind.

"I want to see it," Remo said.

"I can tell you where it is, but I cannot take you there," Butler said. "Being discovered would put an end to my career with Obode and I need that career to help my Loni people."

"You a Loni?" Remo asked. "A Loni from Morgan State? You're probably the only guy in the tribe who ever played cornerback. Old Willie Butler."

"The location of the house is in the capital city of Busati," Butler said coldly. "From my sources, I know that it is guarded. It will be very dangerous."

He gave Remo the location of the building. "We'll be careful," Remo said.

Butler nodded. "One can never be too careful in this land."

It was agreed Remo and Chiun would visit the house before dawn. Butler left the camp shortly after dinner, on the pretext that important business awaited his return to Busati.

But the only business on his mind was the warning he wanted to give General Obode about the two imperialist American agents who were planning to assassinate him, but who would be vulnerable tonight because Butler had enticed them into visiting his house of many pleasures.

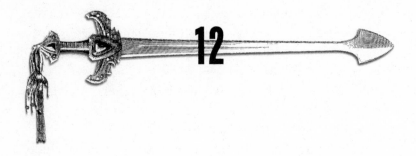

12

IN an American city, it would have been a ghetto, a slum, the final demonstration that capitalism could not work unless it allowed the hog robber-baron rich to step on the poor man's neck and grind his face into the dirt.

But in Busati, it was one of the better streets. And the whorehouse behind the iron gate was definitely one of the better buildings.

It had once belonged to a British general who had come to the country planning to teach the heathen savages a thing or two, and who had instantly developed a letch for black women of all sizes and shapes. He had had his throat slit one night by a woman whom he thought loved him for his obviously superior soul.

She took his wallet and the seventy-three British pound notes it contained and returned to her native village where she was as venerated as Marjorie Meriwether Post.

The house meanwhile was recaptured by the Busati government for non-payment of the four-dollar annual real estate tax—Busati facing its own urban crisis at the time, the necessity to buy another four push-brooms for the one-man street cleaning force who was charged with keeping the city immaculate.

The house had since that time belonged to the Busati government, remaining vacant until now-General William Forsythe Butler took it over and decided to use it for his own purposes.

"Look. In the tree," Chiun said. "Have you ever seen such foolishness?"

In the dark, Remo's eyes made out the figure of a soldier with a gun, notched in the fork of the tree across the street from the white house.

"And in the window of that building over there," Remo said softly, gesturing with his eyes toward the window where he had just seen a glint of light that could come only from a rifle barrel. "It looks as if General Obode is expecting company tonight."

Remo and Chiun stood in the shadows, half a block away from the large white house behind the metal gate.

"And look," Chiun said, "there are two . . . no, three more behind that motor vehicle over there."

"I guess no one told them that the Master of Sinanju was coming," Remo said. "They're not properly impressed."

"We must do our best to remind them of their good manners," the old man said.

Before Remo could say a word in answer, Chiun was up at the large stone wall. His fingers bought a hold in the wall and he smoothly clambered up it, paused momentarily on the top and then vanished into the grounds behind the fourteen-foot-high barrier.

Remo moved close to the wall and heard Chiun say, "Shall I send a litter bearer for you, my son?"

"Up yours, my Father," Remo said, but too softly for Chiun to hear. Then Remo, too, was up and over the stone wall.

He stood alongside Chiun. "Better be careful," he said. "There are probably more soldiers in here."

"Oh, thank you, Remo," Chiun said.

"For what?"

"For alerting me to danger. For helping to prevent me from falling asleep and into the hand of these terrible dangerous men.

Oh me, oh my." This was Chiun's new phrase which he had picked up from Rad Rex on the last installment he had seen of *As the Planet Revolves,* the one show, Remo swore, in all of television history in which nothing not only never happened, but in which nothing even threatened to happen.

"Buck up, Chiun," Remo hissed. "The only thing we have to fear is fear itself. I'll protect you."

"My heart soars like the eagle."

They moved through the darkness toward the house. "Are you sure," Chiun said, "that this is what you want to do?"

"It's what I was supposed to do before you tricked me into playing Prince Charming for that gang on the mountain," Remo said.

"Please not to embarrass me," Chiun said. "The Loni might hear of any foolishnesses of yours and this would lower me in their eyes." Chiun led the way up one of the stone walls of the house and into an open second-floor window. The room they entered was empty; they moved out into a broad dimly-lit hallway, built like a balcony, from which they could see the main door of the house below.

Behind the door were a half-dozen soldiers wearing Busati whites and carrying American Army grease guns. One of the soldiers was a sergeant. He looked at his watch.

"Very soon now," he said. "Very soon we will have our company and we will put them to sleep."

"Good," one of the privates said. "I hope they come quickly so we have time to sample the merchandise."

"By all means," the sergeant said. "This merchandise is to be sampled as often as possible, as vigorously as necessary. *Mi casa es su casa.*"

"What does that mean?" the first soldier asked.

"That means screw your brains out," another soldier said. "Use up that white ass."

"I can hardly wait," the first soldier said. "Where are those bastards anyway?"

"Right here," Remo said. He stood on the balcony looking down toward the main entrance. At his side stood the tiny Chiun, wearing not his customary robe, but a black Ninja costume which he wore only at night.

"I said, right here, you stupid gorilla bastard," Remo said, louder this time.

Chiun shook his head. "Always on display," he said. "Do you never learn?"

"I don't know, Chiun. Something about him there just pisses me off."

"Hey, you, get down out of there." The sergeant spoke.

"Come and get us," Remo said. "Use the stairs. They work both ways."

"You come down from there or, by God, we're gonna plug you."

"You're all under arrest," Remo said, seeing himself as Cary Grant in the temple of the thugs.

Chiun leaned against the railing, shaking his head in disgust.

The sergeant started for the stairs, followed by the other five soldiers. They moved slowly and Remo wondered why.

"Oh, oh," Remo said. "I just thought. If they fire their guns, the guys outside'll hear it and come in," Remo whispered to Chiun.

"I doubt much that you 'just thought' of anything," Chiun said, "since you seem incapable of thought. But if that worries you, don't let them fire guns," Chiun said as if that answered everything.

"Of course," Remo said. "Why didn't I think of that? Don't let those six men fire their guns."

"Not six. Ten," a voice said from behind Remo. He turned.

Standing in an open doorway was another soldier in Busati whites. He carried an automatic. Behind him in the dimness, Remo could see three more men. He realized now why the sergeant had been very slow about leading his men upstairs; he was waiting for the other half of the trap to close.

"I surrender," Remo said, raising his hands.

"A wise decision, friend," the soldier with the automatic said. He nodded to the other three men who poured out of the room and joined the six men coming up the stairs. They put their guns away, slinging them back over their chests, as they surrounded Remo and the small Korean.

After all, ten against two did not require weapons, did they?

Of course not.

The sergeant, who was the house doorman, as much as told them that before he felt himself being lifted up by the small Oriental, and then being spun around as if he were a long stick and used as a battering ram against the other men.

The soldier who had been in the doorway reached for his automatic again to free it from the holster.

But the holster was gone, ripped away from his side by the young American. "This yours?" Remo said. Stupidly, the soldier nodded. Remo gave them back. Holster, automatic and ammunition right through the soldier's face into his throat. Deep.

Behind him, Remo heard the thwack, thwack, thwack, the machinelike periodicity that meant Chiun was at work.

"Chiun, keep one of them alive," Remo yelled, before two soldiers were on him. Then he violated his own injunction, dropping them heavily onto the body of the soldier whose face had sprouted a gun.

Then there were no more sounds. Remo turned to Chiun who was releasing the feet of the sergeant he had used as a battering ram. The soldier slipped shapelessly onto a pile of bodies.

"Chiun, dammit, I said . . ."

Chiun raised a hand. "This one breathes," he said. "Therefore present your lectures to someone who needs them. Perhaps you might talk to yourself."

The sergeant groaned and Remo reached down and yanked him roughly to his feet.

"The girls," Remo said. "Where are they?"

The sergeant shook his head to clear it. "All this for women?"

"Where are they?" Remo said.

"The room at the end of the hall."

"Show us."

Remo shoved the sergeant who led the way down the wide oak-planked hallway, staggering slightly from side to side. A head wound dripped blood onto his white uniform. His right arm hung limply; a shoulder separation, Remo thought. He grabbed the sergeant's right wrist and yanked, then choked off the sergeant's scream by tossing his hand around the soldier's mouth.

"Just a reminder," Remo growled, "that we ain't your friendly neighborhood team of United Nations advisors. No tricks."

The sergeant, his eyes wide with fright and pain, nodded quickly, almost frantically.

He walked faster, then stopped outside a large oak door at the end of the hall. "In there," he said.

"You first."

The sergeant unlocked the door with a key from a ring on his belt, pushed open the door and stepped inside.

The room was just beginning to be lit by the first dim blush of the morning sun. Remo forced the pupils of his eyes to widen, and in the darkness, he could see four bunks. Each was occupied.

The four women in the beds were naked. They were tied

with ropes, their arms up over their heads lashed to the bed posts. Their legs pulled wide apart and their ankles tied to the posts at the foot of the beds. Cloth gags were in their mouths.

In the faint glints of light from the window and from the hallway, their eyes sparkled as they watched Remo. They looked like animals peering from the dark ring around a campfire.

The room smelled of excrement and sweat. Remo brushed past the sergeant and entered the room. The sergeant looked around but Chiun stood in the doorway behind him, blocking escape.

Remo took the gag from the girl in the nearest bunk and as he did leaned forward close enough to see her clearly. Her face was scarred and broken. One eye had been deformed from a badly healed beating. Her mouth was toothless.

Whip marks covered her naked front from her face to her ankles. Hard black cankers dotted her body where it had been used as an ashtray.

Remo released the gag and said, "Don't worry. We're friends. You're going to be all right now."

"Be all right," she repeated dully. She smiled suddenly, the toothless grimace of an old hag. Her eyes sparkled. "Treat you nice, mister. You like to whip me? I do everything if you whip me. Hard. You like hard? I like hard. Make me bleed, I treat you nice, mister. You like kiss me?" She puckered up her mouth and scroontched an imaginary kiss toward Remo.

He shook his head and backed away from her.

"Hee, hee, hee," the vision cackled. "I got money. I treat you right if you whip me hard. My family is rich. I pay. Just hit me, soldier boy."

Remo turned away. He went to two more girls. They were the same. Lamed, twisted, mindless husks that once were people. None of them could have been much over twenty, but they spoke with the grim sadness of ancient wizened women who sit on corners and whose eyes suddenly light up as they remember something nice that once happened to them. Nice was, for these girls, the whip, the chain, the knife, the extinguished cigarette.

The fourth girl began to cry when Remo removed her gag. "Thank God," she said, "Thank God for somebody."

"Who are you?" Remo asked.

Through her tears and sobbing, she said, "I'm Hillary Butler. They kidnaped me. I've been here two days."

"Kinda rough, kid, huh?"

"Please," she said. Remo began to free her.

Behind him, he heard the sergeant start to speak. "I have nothing to do with it, man," but his words were cut off as he oomphed, Chiun putting a hard hand into his back.

"Who are these others?" Remo asked, as he tore the knots from Hillary Butler's ropes.

"I don't know," she said. "Americans too, the sergeant said. But there's nothing much left of them. They're on heroin."

"You too?" Remo asked.

"Just twice," the girl said. "Last night was the first time, and then this morning."

"You may be all right then," Remo said. "It doesn't work that way."

"I know." The girl stood up and then suddenly put her bare arms around Remo and began to sob heavily. "I know," she blubbered. "I've been praying. And I knew when I stopped praying that it would be all over. I'd be just like them."

"It's okay now," Remo said. "We got here in time. At least for you." He led her to a closet where robes hung and covered her uncut naked body with one. "Can you walk?" he asked.

"Just bruised but unbroken," she said.

Remo's voice grew hard and cold. "Chiun, take Miss Butler downstairs and wait for me. You," he said to the sergeant. "Get in here."

Reluctantly, the sergeant entered the room. Remo closed the door behind him, after watching Chiun lead Hillary Butler down the hallway.

"How long have these girls been here?" Remo asked.

"Different times," the sergeant said. "Three months. Seven months."

"You give them the narcotics?"

The sergeant looked toward the closed door. He looked toward the window where the sky was brightening with the pre-dawn sun rays.

"Answer me," Remo said.

"Yes, boss. I give them. They die now without them."

"There was a man named Lippincott who came here. Where is he?"

"Dead. He killed one of the girls. She recognized him, probably. So he got killed too."

"Why all the soldiers here tonight?"

"General Obode put the guard here. He expected someone to break in. Must have meant you. Look, I got some money. If you let me go, it's yours."

Remo shook his head.

The sergeant's eyes brightened. "You like the girls, mister? They take good care of you. I housebreak them well. Anything you want, they do." His voice came faster now. It pleaded even though the words themselves were not a plea. Not yet.

Remo shook his head.

"You going to kill me, man?"

"Yes."

The sergeant lunged at Remo. Remo waited; he let the sergeant grab his arm; he allowed the sergeant to hit him with a punch. He wanted to put meaning into what he was about to do, and the best way was to remind himself that this was a man. Let him touch, let him feel, let him understand what was coming.

Remo waited, then jammed his left fingertips forward into the sergeant's separated right shoulder. The sergeant stopped as if suddenly simonized in place.

Remo hit again in the same spot with his left fingertips, then with his right, then with his left again, hammering shot after shot into precisely the same place. The sergeant swooned and fell to the floor. Remo kneeled down over him, grabbed a handful of neck and twisted. The sergeant came awake, his eyes staring at Remo in horror and fright, glinting, Remo realized suddenly, like the eyes from the beds, watching the tableau.

"Awake now?" Remo said. "Good."

He lunged forward again into the injured shoulder. Beneath his fingertips he could feel the once strong and stringy muscles and fibers turning into soft mush. Still his fingertips pounded. The softer the target became, the harder Remo struck. The sergeant was unconscious now, long past reviving. Remo wished he could think of something more painful. The cloth around the sergeant's shoulder was ripped now and pummeled into powder. Remo kept hitting. Blood and ooze and chips of bone came out under his fingertips. The skin had long since given way.

Remo reared back and came forward one last time. His right fingertips went through where once there had been cloth and skin and muscle and flesh and bone. The fingertips came to rest on the wooden floor.

His anger spent, Remo stood. He kicked the sergeant's right arm away. It rolled awkwardly like an imperfect log, finally coming to rest under the bed Hillary Butler had vacated. Then Remo came down on the sergeant's face with both feet, feeling the crunch and crack beneath him. He stood, looking down at the sergeant, realizing that he had taken out of him a payment in advance for what Remo still must do. The three women, still tied in their beds, looked at Remo wordlessly.

He moved to them one after another, sitting on the edges of their beds. To each one he whispered, "Dream happy dreams," and then as gently and painlessly as he could, he did what he had to do.

Finally he was done. He untied the hands and feet of the three dead girls and covered their bodies with robes from the closet. Then he walked out into the hallway and closed the door behind him.

The instructions from Smith had been to keep Obode alive. Well, Smith could take his instructions and shove them. If Obode got anywhere in Remo's way, if he got within his line of vision, if he came anywhere within reach, Obode would know pain such as he had never even guessed existed. When Remo was done with him, he would consider the sergeant in the girls' room blessed.

Chiun waited at the foot of the steps with Hillary Butler. She looked at Remo. "The others?" she said.

Remo shook his head with finality. "Let's go," he said evenly.

Already, Smith would go berserk because Remo had not freed the other three girls. But Smith had not been there, had not seen them. Remo *had* freed them, the only way they could be freed. It had been his decision and he had made it. Smith had nothing to say about it, just as he no longer had anything to say about what Remo would do to Obode if the chance presented itself.

Only two soldiers guarded the back of the building through which Chiun and Remo exited.

"I'll take them," Remo said.

"No, my son," Chiun answered. "Your anger breeds danger for you. Protect the child."

The sun was almost rising. Remo saw Chiun and then in a flash, saw him no longer as the little man in the black costume of the Ninja night devils slid away into what was left of the darkness.

From his position inside the back doorway of the house, Remo could see the soldiers clearly, twenty-five feet away at the base of a tree. But he never saw Chiun. Then he saw the two soldiers, still there, but suddenly their bodies were twisted, useless. Two corpses. Remo strained his eyes. Still no sign of Chiun. Then, Chiun was in front of him.

"We go."

Two blocks from the house, an Army jeep was parked at the curb with a soldier behind the wheel.

Remo came up behind him. "Taxi," he said.

"This is no taxi," the soldier said, wheeling and staring angrily at Remo.

Remo extended his bloodied hands toward the soldier.

"Too bad, Charley, cause that was your only chance."

Remo left the soldier's body lying in the street and helped Hillary Butler into the back where Chiun sat alongside her.

Remo started the motor and peeled rubber, burning off down the pockholed dirt street, heading for the hills over which the sun was now rising in its daily ritual of the affirmation of life.

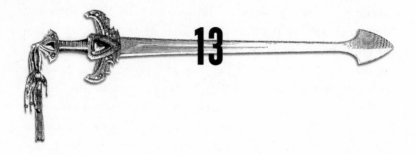

How many are dead?" Obode's question was an elephantine trumpet.

"Thirteen," General William Forsythe Butler said.

"You said there were only two men coming."

"That's all there were."

"They must be very special men," Obode said.

"They are, Mr. President. One comes from the East; the other is an American. Already, the Loni talk that they are the fulfillment of the legend."

Obode slumped down in his velvet-backed chair in the big Presidential office.

"So they come to restore the Loni to power by grinding into dust the man of evil."

"That's what the legend says," Butler said.

"I have tolerated the Loni and their legend long enough. I was wrong, Butler, to listen to you, to try to bring the Loni into the government. Now, Dada is going to do what he should have done before. I am going to wipe out that accursed tribe."

Butler lowered his eyes so that Obode would not see the exultation there. Let him think Butler looked away to hide his disagreement. But now that the cursed Oriental and American had escaped the trap, this was best. Let Obode chase them; let

Obode kill them; and then Butler would take care of Obode. Men loyal to him were now in positions of power throughout the government; they would flock to Butler's support. The Loni would acclaim him as the man who embodied the legend, and with a united country, Butler could return Busati to the power and dignity it held centuries before.

"Shall I mobilize the Army?" Butler asked.

"The Army? For the Loni? And for two men?"

"Those two men just killed thirteen," Butler protested.

"Yes. But they did not face Big Daddy. And they did not face you, Butler. One company and us. That will be enough to take care of both the Loni and the legend, once and for all."

"You have tried before to eliminate the Loni," Butler reminded him.

"Yes. Back before you arrived here. And always they scurried, like bugs before heat. And then I stopped because I listened to you. But this time, I will not stop and I do not think the Loni will run." He grinned a broad faceful of mirth. "After all, are not the redeemers of the legend there among them?"

Butler nodded. "So it is said."

"Well, we shall see, Butler."

Butler saluted, turned and walked toward the door. His hand was on the knob when he was halted by Obode's voice.

"General, your report lacked one item."

Butler turned. "Oh?"

"Your women. What happened to them?"

"Dead," Butler said. "All of them."

"Good," Obode said. "Because if they lived they might speak. And if they spoke, it might be necessary for me to make an object lesson of you. We are not yet ready to defy the American government."

He meant it, Butler knew, which was why he had lied in the first place. Soon enough, Obode would be dead and the kidnapings could be blamed on him.

"Dead," Butler repeated the lie. "All dead."

"Don't take it so hard," Obode said. "When we are done with these accursed Loni, I will buy you a new whorehouse."

Obode smiled, then thought again of the thirteen soldiers dead at the hands of the American and the Oriental. "Better yet, Butler. Make that two companies of soldiers."

Princess Saffah came from the hut wiping her hands on a small cloth.

"She sleeps now," she told Remo.

"Good."

"She has been ill-treated. Her body has been used badly."

"I know."

"Who?" Saffah asked.

"General Obode."

Saffah spat on the ground. "The Hausa swine. I am glad that you and Little Father are here because soon we will be free of this evil yoke."

"How?" Remo asked. "We sit up here in the mountains. He sits down there in his capital. When are the twain going to meet?"

"Ask the Little Father. He carries in him the seed of all knowledge." She heard a slight moan behind her from inside the hut and without another word, turned and went inside to minister to her patient.

Remo walked off through the village. Chiun was not in his hut, which was built against the protection of a large stone formation, but Remo found him in the square in the center of the encampment.

Chiun wore a blue robe which Remo recognized as ceremonial, and the old man watched as Loni tribesmen stacked wood and twigs into a pit. The pit which had been dug that morning was twenty feet long and five feet wide. Its one-foot depth had been filled to the brim with wood, but in between the branches and twigs, Remo could see that the pit was filled with smooth white stones, the size of goose eggs.

As he watched, one of the tribesmen set the wood in the pit afire and the flames quickly spread until the entire pit was ablaze.

Chiun watched for a few moments, then said: "Adequate. But remember to keep the fire fed. It must not be allowed to dwindle."

He turned to Remo and waited for him to speak.

"Chiun, I've got to talk to you."

"I am writing my remembrances? I am watching my beautiful stories? Speak."

"The legend of the Loni," Remo said. "Does it say I get the shot at the baddie?"

"It says the man from the West who once died will grind into dust the man who would enslave the Loni. Is that an accurate English translation of what you have said?"

"All right," Remo said. "I just wanted to make it clear between us that I get the shot at Obode."

"Why is it so important to you now?" Chiun said. "After all, the House of Sinanju owes this debt. Not you."

"It's important to me because I want Obode. You didn't see what he did to those girls. He's mine, Chiun. I kill him."

"And what makes you think the legend has anything to do with your General Obode?" Chiun asked, and walked slowly away. Remo knew it would be useless to follow and ask just what he meant by that last statement; Chiun would speak only when the urge to speak came upon him.

Remo looked back toward the pit of fire. The dried wood had already passed the peak of its blaze and now the flames were lowering. The Loni tribesmen were busy feeding more wood into the fire, and over the sound they made, Remo could hear the stones in the pit cracking and splitting from the intense heat. An errant puff of wind blew across the pit toward Remo and the surge of heat sucked the breath from his lungs.

His inspection was interrupted by a shout from the hill that loomed over the small village. Remo turned and looked up.

"*Tembo, tembo, tembo, tembo,*" the guard kept shouting. He was hollering and pointing out across the tree-speckled flatlands in the direction of the capital city of Busati.

Remo moved toward the edge of the plateau, hopped up onto a rock and looked in the direction the guard was pointing.

A big dust trail moved, perhaps ten miles away, across the plain. He forced his eyes to work harder.

Then he could pick out figures. There were jeeps with soldiers in them, and keeping up with the slowly moving vehicles were three elephants, soldiers on their backs, moving along in the stiff-legged elephant gait.

Remo sensed someone at his side. He looked down, saw Princess Saffah and extended a hand to help her up onto the stone. The guard was still shouting, "*Tembo, tembo.*"

"What's he getting all worked up for?" Remo said.

"*Tembo* means elephant. In the Loni religion, they are considered animals of the devil."

"No sweat," Remo said. "A peanut or two, and keep the mice away."

"The Loni long ago sought a meaning for good and evil in the world," Saffah said. "Because it was so long ago and they had not yet science, they thought that animals embodied not only the good in the world but the bad. And because there was so much bad, they decided that only *tembo*—the elephant—was large enough to hold all that evil. He is a feared beast among the Loni. I did not believe Obode was smart enough to think himself of bringing elephants."

"This is Obode?" said Remo, suddenly interested.

"It can be no one else. The time draws near. Little Father has begun the fire of purification."

"Well, don't expect too much from the Little Father," Remo said. "Obode belongs to me."

"It shall be as Little Father wishes," Saffah said.

She hopped down and walked away and behind her back, Remo mumbled to himself, "As Little Father wishes. No, Little Father—Yes, Little Father—in your hat, Little Father. Obode's mine."

And then, he thought, his job would be over. Get the girl back to America; report to Smith what had happened, that the missing Lippincott was dead; and then forget this whole God-forsaken country.

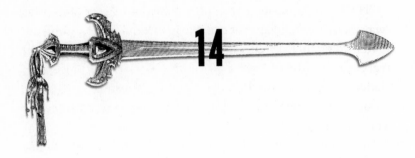

OBODE and his soldiers camped at the base of the hills in which the Loni camp sat, and throughout the day, tension built in the small mountainside village.

Remo sat with Chiun in his hut, trying to make conversation.

"These people got about as much backbone as a worm," he said.

Chiun hummed, his eyes fixed intently on the fire pit which shimmered heat and smoke at the other end of the village square.

"The men are wetting their pants just because Obode's got a couple of elephants. They're all ready to run away."

Chiun stared and hummed softly to himself but said nothing.

"I don't know how the House of Sinanju ever got into such a crap deal, taking care of these Loni. They're not worth it."

Chiun did not speak, and exasperatedly Remo said, "And another thing, I don't like this business about the fire ritual. I'm not letting you take any crazy chances of getting hurt."

Slowly, Chiun turned and confronted Remo. "There is a proverb of the Loni," he said. *"Jogoo likiwika lisiwike, kutakucha."*

"Which means?"

"Whether the cock crows or not, it will dawn."

"In other words, whether I like it or not, you're going to do what you're going to do?"

"How quickly you learn," Chiun said and smilingly turned away to stare again at the fire.

Remo left the hut and wandered the village. All he heard, everywhere he went, was *"tembo, tembo, tembo."* The entire population was in a snit about a couple of elephants. Worry instead about Obode's soldiers and their guns. Pfooey. The Loni weren't worth saving.

He was annoyed and only later realized that he might be taking out his anger at Obode in annoyance against the Loni. The more he thought about it, the surer he was, and late that night, stripped naked, Remo slipped past the guards and out of the village. It was well after midnight when he returned. He moved silently, unseen, past the guards who capped the nearby rocks, stepped into his hut and immediately sensed the presence of someone else there.

His eyes scanned the bare hut and then saw the outline of a form on the raised grass mat which served as his bed.

He moved closer and the form turned. In the faint flicker from the flames in the ceremonial pit, he could make out Princess Saffah.

"You have been away," she said.

"I got tired of hearing everybody yelling *tembo*. I decided to do something about it."

"Good," she said. "You are a brave man." She lifted her hands toward him and he could feel and see the warmth of her smile. "Come to me, Remo," she said.

Remo lay down alongside her on the mat and she wrapped her arms around him. "When the sun is high tomorrow, you face your challenge," she said. "I want you now."

"Why now? Why not later?"

"What we have between us, Remo, may not survive a later. I have this feeling that all may be changed after tomorrow."

"You think I might lose?" Remo asked. Along the length of his warm flushed body, he felt the black coolness of her ebony skin.

"One can always lose, Remo," she said. "So one must take victories where one can. This now will be our victory. And then, no matter what happens on the morrow, we will always have this victory to remember."

"To victory," Remo said.

"To us," Saffah said, and with surprisingly strong arms moved Remo over her. "I was conceived a Loni and born a princess. Now make me a woman."

She placed Remo's hands on her breasts. "God made you a woman," he said.

"No. God made me a female. Only a man can make me a woman. Only you, Remo. Only this way."

And Remo did go into her and did know her and it could be truly written that on that hour she did become a well-made woman. And when both had done and the first rays of the sun were beginning to pink the sky, they slept, side by side, man and woman, God's team, by God's design.

And while they slept, General Obode arose.

It was barely dawn when he pushed aside the flaps of his umbrella tent and, scratching his stomach, walked out into the pre-sun mist and did not like it at all.

His sergeant major's eyes scanned the camp quickly. The campfire had burned out. The guards who had been posted at the corners of the small campsite were not at their stations. There was too much stillness in the camp. Things bring stillnesses, the wrong things. There was sleep on duty and that was one kind of stillness but that was not this kind. And there was death, and this was that kind of stillness, which hung heavy in the air like a mist.

Obode stepped forward and with his toe kicked the ashes of

the campfire. Not even an ember remained, not even a glow. Farther from his tent now, he looked around the camp. Next to him was General Butler's tent, its flaps still closed. All over the clearing lay the sleeping bags of the soldiers who had accompanied them, but the bags were empty.

He heard a sound ahead of him and looked up. The elephants had been chained to scrub trees up ahead, and they were hidden from his view by bushes. Despite his feeling of foreboding, Obode smiled. The elephants had been a good idea; the Loni fear of them was strong and traditional.

They must have seen them marching with Obode's soldiers and that must have terrified them. Today, Obode and his soldiers would storm the main Loni camp, and the Loni would look upon the slaughter that followed as inevitable, resign themselves to it as a historical fact. It had been a good idea. The great conquerors had used elephants. Hannibal and . . . Well, Hannibal anyway, thought Obode. Hannibal and Obode. It was enough to make a case.

The invincible elephant; the sign of the conqueror.

He thought for a moment to wake up Butler, but decided to let him sleep. This was a military matter for a military man, not a football player no matter how brave or loyal he was. He pushed his way through the bushes. Up ahead, forty yards away, he saw the vague gray forms of the elephants but there was something wrong with that too. Their outlines seemed somehow blunt and muted. And what was that before them on the ground? Slowly now, apprehensively, Obode moved forward through the thinning brush. Thirty yards now. Then twenty. And then he saw things clearly and his fingers rose to his lips in the Moslem supplication of mercy.

The elephants' outlines had been softened because their tusks were gone.

Like a moth pursuing a flame, despite himself, he went closer. The tusks of the three elephants had been hacked off near their bases. Only stumps of ivory remained, broken, chipped, craggy, like a memorable bad teeth that demanded the ministrations of tongue.

And the lumps on the ground. They were his men, his soldiers, and he did not have to look hard to be sure they were dead. Bodies lay there twisted, limbs askew, and through the chests of six of them, impaling them, spiking them to the ground were the six elephant tusks.

Obode, horrified, moved yet closer, impelled by some instinct of duty, some disremembered tradition that told the sergeant major he must be sure of his facts to be able to give a thorough report to the commander.

On the ground near the foot of one of the soldiers, he saw a piece of paper. He picked it up and looked at it.

It was a note penciled on the back of a printed military order that must have come from one of the soldiers.

The note read:

"Obode."

"I wait for you in the village of the Loni."

That was all. No name. No signature.

Obode looked around him. There had been two companies of soldiers here. Some must still be around, because these corpses sure weren't two companies worth.

"Sergeant," he bellowed. The sound of his voice rolled across the fields, across the land. He could almost hear it grow weaker as it traveled, unanswered, across the miles of Busati plain.

"Lieutenant," he shouted. It was as if he were shouting into a bottomless well in which sound reverberated but did not echo.

There was no sound and no sign of his soldiers.

Two whole companies?

Obode looked at the note in his hand again, thought deeply for a full ten seconds, dropped the paper, turned and ran. "Butler," he shouted as he neared the other tent. "Butler."

General William Forsythe Butler came from the tent, sleepy, rubbing his heavied eyes. "Yes, Mr. President?"

"Come on, man, we getting out of here."

Butler shook his head, trying to get a grasp on the morning's events. Obode flew past him into Obode's own tent. Butler looked around the camp. Nothing really unusual there. Except . . . except there weren't any soldiers to be seen. He followed Obode into his tent.

Obode was wrestling his white shirt on.

"What's wrong, Mr. President?" Butler asked.

"I'll tell you what's wrong. We leaving this place."

"Where are the guards?"

"The guards are dead or deserted. All of them," Obode said. "And the elephants. Their ivory been removed. We leaving. We leaving now 'cause I ain't gonna have nothing to do with nobody who can kill my soldiers and cripple my elephants in the night, without a sound, without a trace. Man, we getting out of here."

Obode brushed past Butler before his subordinate had a chance to speak. When Butler got back outside, the sun was beginning its climb into the sky and Obode was behind the wheel of one of the jeeps. He turned the ignition key to start position but nothing happened. He tried again, then with a curse jumped heavily down from the jeep and went to another vehicle.

That one would not start either.

Butler came to the jeep and opened the hood. The insides of the engine compartment had been destroyed. The battery had been broken in half, wires were ripped and wrenched apart, the distributor had been crushed into broken black powder and chips.

Butler inspected the other four jeeps in the clearing. They were all the same.

He shook his head at Obode, sitting disconsolately on the seat in the driver's seat of one of the vehicles.

"Sorry, General," Butler said, although he was not sure he was sorry at all. "If we go anywhere, we walk."

Obode looked up at Butler. "In this land we haven't a chance. Even the Loni could pick us off like flies."

"Then what do we do, Mr. President?"

Obode slammed a ham-sized fist down into the steering wheel of the jeep, cracking the wheel and sending the vehicle rocking back and forth on its wheels.

"Dammit," Obode shouted, "we do what armies should always do. We charge."

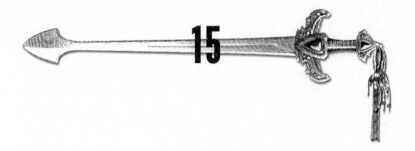

WHILE Remo slept, Princess Saffah slipped out of his hut and went back to the hut where Hillary Butler slept.

Saffah could not recognize the feeling that gripped her on this day. All her life, she had waited for the legend to come true; now the men of the legend were here; soon the people of the Loni tribe would be restored to power; and yet, she felt a vague feeling of unease.

Legends were never simple. There were many ways for one to come true. Had they not, for instance, thought that Butler might be the Master of the legend? He had given up his former life in America to become the Loni's friend, so one might call him a dead man. And his returning to the Loni might fulfill the prophecy of the Loni children coming home. So she had thought, but that was wrong.

Might not other things be wrong? You are being a fool, child. What of Obode? Do you doubt that he is the evil man of the story? And that Remo must face him today? Yes, yes. And what of the Little Father? Doubt you that he will purify the Loni? No, no, but how? How?

Saffah ducked into the hut where the young American girl slept. She slid down smoothly onto her heels at the side of the small raised cot. The white girl breathed smoothly and evenly, and the faint trace of a smile played at the corners of her mouth.

She would be well, Saffah knew, for one who could dream could live.

She put her ebony hand out and rested it on Hillary's pale white arm and looked down at the contrast. Hillary did not stir. Why was it so important, all this concern with color? Skin was skin, black or white or yellow as the Little Father's. What counted only was what was under the skin; the spirit, the heart, the soul. She looked at Hillary Butler and thought, might it not also be thus with tribes? Could hatred between Loni and Hausa end if they could only consider each other as people, good and bad, but each different?

She squeezed Hillary Butler's arm gently, reassuringly.

Chiun was up early and Remo found him at the pit of fire. The fire had been stoked and allowed to smolder during the night and now dry weeds and twigs were being thrown upon it.

As Chiun directed, four Loni tribesmen began to cover the unburned wood in the pit with leafy green branches of trees which dripped water, and sizzled and hissed on the white hot stones in the pit. Steam rose and smoke poured out from under the corners of the branches in lazy coils like drunken sated snakes.

"We going to have a cookout?" Remo asked. "Do you need a duck? I'll run to the store for hamburger rolls if you want."

"Need you go out of your way to appear gross?" Chiun asked. "For certainly, you need no assistance, no more than the duck needs help in quacking."

They were interrupted by a roar behind them. Along the trail, around the corner of the huts, striding into the village square came Obode and Butler, Obode leading the way, bellowing like a bull moose taunted by flies and gnats.

"Cowards and washwomen of the Loni tribe, General Obode is here. Come out, fly swatters and mosquito killers."

The village square was deserted as the few Loni men in it seemed to slip away. At one end of the square, near the fire pit, stood Remo and Chiun; at the other end, seventy-five feet away, stood Butler and Obode. The four men stood looking at each other.

Out of a hut halfway between the two pairs came Princess Saffah. She stood black and tall, silent and majestic, wearing her almost-Grecian short robe, staring imperiously at Obode who continued to challenge the Loni men to combat, one at a time or all at once.

"Silence your mouth, braying beast," Saffah said finally.

"Who are you?" Obode shouted, after a moment's pause in which, Remo saw, he was stunned by Saffah's beauty.

"I am Saffah, first princess of the Loni Empire, and I order your silence."

"You order? *You* order? I am General Dada Obode, President of Busati, commander of all this land, and I am the one who orders."

"Perhaps in your brothels and in your pig sty of a capital, but here you can be silent. We are glad you came, General."

"When I am done," Obode said, "Perhaps you will not be so glad."

Saffah clapped her hands, three times, sharply. Slowly, obviously reluctantly, the Loni began to come from their huts, first women and children, and then men.

"We are glad you came nevertheless," she said smiling, as Loni men drew near Obode and Butler. "And you, Butler," she added, "you have done well to get the gross beast into our camp."

Butler gave a slight bow and Obode's head snapped toward him as if on a rubber band. Suddenly, so many things made sense. Butler was his traitor. Obode roared and lunged with both hands for Butler's throat. Butler was surprised by the attack and fell back before Obode's weight until Obode, at a signal from Saffah, was pulled away and restrained by six Loni tribesmen.

Chiun and Remo walked slowly down the length of the plaza toward Obode who still glared at Butler.

"Coward, traitor, Loni dog," Obode spat.

"Welcome to my people, fat pig," Butler said.

"You have not even the courage of the assassin," Obode said. "For you feared to take my life by yourself as you could have many times because I trusted you. Instead, you waited until you could deliver me into the hands of this flock of sheep."

"Discretion, General, discretion."

"Cowardice," Obode roared. "The armies I have known would have shot you like the dog you are."

Into the chaos, above the voices, rose the command of Chiun: "Silence. The Master of Sinanju says stop your tongues of women."

Obode turned toward Chiun who now stood directly in front of him and looked him over, as if he had just noticed him for the first time. The Busati President towered over the aged Korean by a foot and a half. His weight was three times Chiun's.

"And you are the Master of the Loni legend?"

Chiun nodded.

Obode laughed, tipping his head back to offer his laughter to the sky. "Mosquito, stay out of Dada's way before I swat you."

Chiun folded his arms and stared at Obode. Behind Chiun, the square was now packed with people and they were hushed as if listening through thin walls to a family arguing next door.

Remo stood next to Chiun, peering coldly at Obode. Finally, the President's eyes met his.

Contemptuously, he asked: "And you? Another of the fortune-telling fairies?"

"No," Remo said. "I'm the chief elephant trainer and jeep repairman around here. Have a nice walk?"

Obode began to speak, then stopped, as if realizing for the first time that he was the prisoner of an overwhelmingly large number of enemies. Not as lowest recruit, not as British sergeant major, not as commander in chief of the Busati; but now, for the first time in his long career, he realized that death might be a real possibility.

"Kill him," Butler said. "Let us kill him and end this ancient curse on the Loni."

"Old ant," Obode said to Chiun, "since this is your party, I ask that when you kill me you do it like a man."

"Do you deserve the death of a man?"

"Yes," Obode said. "Because I have always given a man a man's death and I have tried to be fair. In my day, I wrestled regiments and no man feared to try to beat me because of my rank or station."

"Wrestling is very good for the teaching of humility," Chiun said. "It is the weakness of you Hausa that the most developed muscle in your body is your tongue. Come. I will teach you humility."

He walked back into the center of the open plaza, then turned to face Obode again. Remo came up alongside Chiun. "Chiun, he's mine. We agreed."

"Silence," Chiun ordered. "Do you think I would deprive you of your pleasure? It is written in the legend what you must do. You will do that; you will do no more."

He called to the Loni holding Obode:

"Release him."

Chiun wore his white *ge*, the shin-length pants and white jacket known in America as a karate uniform. The jacket was tied with a white belt, which Remo recognized as an act of humility on Chiun's part. In the Westernization of the Oriental combat arts, the white belt was the lowest grading. Black belts were highest and there were various degrees of them. And then, beyond the black belt, beyond the knowledge of simple experts, there was the red belt, awarded to a handful of men of great courage, wisdom and distinction. The Master of Sinanju, foremost among the men of the world, was entitled to wear such a belt. Chiun instead had chosen beginner's white, and, as a beginner would, he wore it tied tightly around his waist.

He stood now in front of the fire pit where the continually dampened leaves and branches still steamed and smoldered, and beckoned to Obode.

"Come, one of the great mouth."

His arms free suddenly, Obode lunged forward, then slowed down and stopped. "This isn't right," he said to Chiun. "I'm too big. How about your friend? I wrestle him."

"He has no more humility than you. The Master must teach you," Chiun said grandly. "Come. If you can."

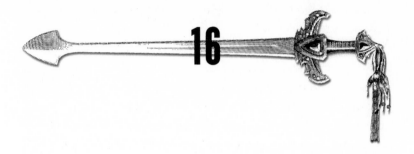

OBODE moved forward slowly, almost unwillingly, his heavy booted shoes kicking up little puffs of tan dust as he came.

He put a hand up in front of him, gesturing peace to Chiun. Chiun shook his head. "It is said the Hausa are brave and courageous. Are you the exception to that rule? Come. I will make the contest more even."

From under his sash, Chiun pulled a square of white silk, no more than eighteen inches on a side. He carefully placed it on the ground in front of him and stepped onto it, his body so light that his bare feet seemed not even to crinkle the cloth. "Come, loud one," he said.

Obode shrugged, a big heavy moving of his massive shoulders, and then he unbuttoned and stripped off his white uniform shirt. The sight of his shoulder muscle rippling black and sleek, almost purple under the hot African sun, drew a murmur from the crowd. And against him was arrayed only poor pathetic old Chiun, eighty years old, never having seen one hundred pounds, but standing, facing Obode, impassive, arms folded, his eyes like fiery hazel coals burning into the big man's face.

Obode tossed his shirt to the ground and Remo picked it up and moved past Obode to the rear of the square where General William Forsythe Butler stood. Obode kicked off his shoes; he wore no socks.

Remo turned to Butler. "Two bucks on the little guy, Willie," he said.

Butler refused to answer.

"I'll take it easy on you, old man."

Obode said that and lunged toward Chiun, his powerful arms spread wide. Chiun stood still, unmoving on his square of silk and let Obode engulf him in the black coils of muscles. Obode locked his hands behind Chiun's back, then arched his own back to lift Chiun off the ground, snapping as he would if lifting a heavy garbage pail. But Chiun's feet remained planted on the ground. Obode lurched again and almost fell backward as Chiun remained rooted to the spot.

Then Chiun unfolded his arms, with delicate, slow majesty. He reached forward with both hands and touched two spots on the underside of Obode's arms. As if torched by electricity, Obode's arms released Chiun and flew wide apart.

He shook his head to clear it from the sudden jolt of nerve pain, then moved forward again toward Chiun, his left hand assorting air in front of him, seeking the classic wrestler's finger lock.

Chiun let Obode's hand approach his shoulder and then the President was flying through the air. Chiun had not seemed to move. His hands had not touched Obode, but the shift of Obode's weight was across Chiun's standing line of force, and Obode went somersaulting through the air to land with a thud on his back behind Chiun.

"Ooooof," he exploded.

Chiun turned slowly on the silken square until he was facing the fallen Obode. Ripples of laughter went through the Loni men, standing around, as Obode raised himself to a kneeling position.

"Silence! Silence!" Chiun demanded. "Unless there is one among you who would take his place."

The noise subsided. Remo whispered to Butler, "Willie, you saved yourself two bucks." Privately, Remo was just a tinge surprised at how easily Chiun was handling Obode. Not that Obode represented any real danger. But Chiun was an assassin and how often had he told Remo that an assassin who could not, for some reason, enter combat prepared to kill his opponent was even more defenseless than the average man because the focus of his energy was dissipated and some of it must turn back upon himself. Yet, Chiun was obviously keeping Obode alive, and it did not seem to pose any special danger for Chiun. Oh well, Remo thought, that is why there is only one Master of Sinanju.

Obode was now on his feet. He turned toward Chiun, a questioning look on his face, and then lurched forward toward him. The old man stood in place, but when Obode neared him, Chiun shot out a silent swift hand. It planted itself near Obode's collarbone and Obode dropped as if he were a ball rolling off the end of a table. Except a ball bounces. The President of Busati didn't. He lay there in a dust-covered crumpled heap.

Chiun stepped back, retrieved his silk handkerchief, dusted it, folded it neatly and tucked it back in under his waistband.

"Take him," he said to no one in particular. "Tie him to that post."

Four Loni tribesmen dropped their spears and came out into the arena. They grabbed Obode by his hands and feet and tugged him, sliding along the ground, past the ceremonial fire pit which was still steaming and smoking, and to an eight-foot stake planted in the ground at the far end. Two of them propped the unconscious Obode up, while two more lifted his arms high and tied them with a rope through the large iron ring at the top of the eight-foot post.

Obode hung there, slowly regaining consciousness, hanging

by his wrists. Chiun meanwhile had turned from him and looked to Saffah.

From the ground behind her, she lifted a golden brazier, shaped like a Japanese hibachi, and carried it by its handles toward Chiun. Heat waves shimmered off the bowl and the red glow of the burning coals it contained cast an aura around the golden dish. She placed it at the feet of Chiun.

Chiun looked down at the burning coals.

The silence of the moment was interrupted by a call from a sentry posted on the north side of the hill over the small encampment.

"Loni! Loni! Loni!" he called, obviously in great agitation. Remo turned and looked up toward him. He was waving an arm toward the hills to the north.

Remo moved to the edge of the camp and looked north. Coming up the hillsides, toward the encampment, were other natives, and Remo placed them instantly as Loni. The men were tall and lean and strong-looking; the women lithe and beautiful . . . two of them in particular.

The long chain of people was now only a hundred yards from the camp and the two women led the band of Loni men and women and children as if they were generals reviewing a parade. They were tall—black as night, their faces impassive and strong-boned, and Remo knew immediately these were the two younger sisters of Saffah, crown princess of the Loni.

Remo glanced back at Chiun. Chiun had sat in the center of the small square, his legs twisted into a full lotus, his fingertips in front of him in praying position. His eyes were closed and his face leaned forward toward the brazier of hot coals on the ground before him.

Remo looked at Chiun hard, but there was no way to tell what he was thinking or doing. The whole thing had confused

Remo. Remo was to kill the evil man, but why had Chiun insisted upon playing with Obode first? Why not just give him to
Remo? And what was this ritual purification by fire that Chiun
was to do? And this nonsense about Chiun perhaps sacrificing
his life? If it was anything dangerous, Remo would not let him
do it. That was that case closed. No crap about it either.

And then the Loni were streaming into the village. There
were hundreds of them, led by the two beautiful black women.
As they came into camp, their impassiveness melted as they saw
Saffah and each ran forward to be embraced by her.

It took fifteen minutes before the procession had ended; the
square was now filled with all three existing Loni bands. Remo
looked around. From what was once the greatest empire in all
the history of Africa, this was left. Five hundred men, women
and children. Hardly enough to fill a Newark tenement, much
less create a new empire.

And still Chiun sat. The Loni looked at him silently as they
crowded in around the village square, enclosing the pit of fire
and an area the size of a large boxing ring. They buzzed to
themselves as they saw General Obode tied to the post at the far
end of the pit of fire.

Obode was now awake, clearly wondering what was happening. His face darted from side to side, looking for an explanation, seeking a friendly face. He saw General William Forsythe
Butler at the far end of the field and spat viciously onto the
ground near his feet.

Inside a hut outside the square of people, Hillary Butler
stirred. There was so much noise and it was so hot. But it was a
nice hot; the kind of hot that makes your muscles work and
your bones swing loose and easy. For the first time since she had
entered the Loni village, Hillary Butler decided she would get
up and walk outside and see what kind of place she was in.

But first she would nap just a few minutes more.

Saffah walked forward now to Chiun and stood in front of him, looking down at him across the heat waves rising from the brazier of coals.

"It is a great moment, Little Father. The legend has begun. The Loni children are home."

Chiun rose to his feet in one smooth fluid movement and opened his eyes. He turned and looked at the Loni men who continued to water down the leafy branches covering the fire pit, and nodded. They put down their containers of water and almost instantly the smoke from the pit grew heavier.

Chiun turned then and folded his hands in front of him.

"The legend is the truth," he intoned. "The Loni children are coming home.

"But wait! Are the Loni home? Are the Loni I see today the Loni that my ancestor served many years ago? Are these Loni, these Hausa-hating, elephant-fearing cowards who run like children in the night from noises they cannot see? Are these the Loni, whose bravest souls are their women?

"Are these the Loni that brought light and justice and knowledge to a dark world so many years ago?"

Chiun stopped and looked slowly, silently around the vast crowd, seeming to stop at each and every face, as if seeking an answer.

No one spoke and Chiun went on.

"The legend says that the Loni children will come home. And then the man who walks in the shoes of death must destroy the man who would enslave the Loni. And then the Master of Sinanju must purify the Loni people in the rites of fire.

"But this Master looks and wonders if these Loni can be redeemed."

Remo and Butler stood side by side, watching Chiun with

equal intensity, thinking vastly different thoughts. He's going to renege, Remo thought. Did the House of Sinanju give refunds? Butler was exploring the depths of his satisfaction. Nothing had gone exactly as he had planned, but no matter. It seemed clear that before the day's events were over, Obode would be dead. The Loni would support the leadership of Butler; so would most of Obode's cabinet and most of the Army leaders. It would be a fine day for William Forsythe Butler, next President of Busati.

"Where is the nobility that once filled the hearts of the Loni people?" Chiun was saying.

"Gone like the fire goes," Chiun said, and as the crowd gasped, he reached his hands down into the golden brazier and brought out two handfuls of coals. Slowly, not even seeming to feel the heat, he scattered the coals around the ground. "Together, coals are a fire, but singly, they are but coals and soon die. It is thus with people; their greatness comes because each shares in the tradition of their greatness." He dropped again to his haunches, and began scattering with his hands the coals from the brazier.

Behind him, the leaves and twigs still smoldered, the heat waves rising from the pit like steam from a subway grating.

Inside the hut, Hillary Butler could no longer sleep. She got to her feet, happily surprised that she wore so sparkling clean a blue robe. She knew now that she was going to be all right. That evil house; the man on the ship; it was all behind her now. She would soon be home; she would be married as she had planned; somehow she knew that everything would be all right.

She moved toward the entrance to the hut, her steps weak and slightly shaky.

Outside the hut, Remo stood next to General Butler. "Willie," Remo said, putting his arm conspiratorially around the other man's shoulder, "you were a good one. But that was a good team you played for. Tell me something I always wanted to know. Did you guys shave the point spread? I remember, you guys were always like five-point favorites and you always wound up winning by three. You cost me a lot of bucks, Willie. I never could figure why you guys would shave. I mean, you were making the big dough already; it just wouldn't seem to be worth the risk. You know, it's not like you were slaves or anything, Willie."

Hillary Butler stepped out of the hut and blinked in the bright sunshine. Just ahead of her, she saw Remo and she smiled. He had been so nice. His arm was around that black man in the white uniform and they were talking.

"Get out of here, for Christ's sake, will you?" William Forsythe Butler said to Remo. He raised his right hand to Remo's shoulder and pushed. Something on his hand glinted in the sun. It was a ring. A gold ring. A gold ring formed in the links of a small chain.

Hillary Butler had seen that ring before. Just once, when the heavy black hand holding the chloroform pad had lowered over her face.

Hillary Butler screamed.

Remo turned, as silence descended over the entire village. The white girl stood there in the entrance to the hut, her mouth open, her finger slowly raising to point. Remo came to her side.

"Oh, Remo," she said. "You've got him."

"Got him? Oh yeah, right. Obode," Remo said. "He's tied up down there."

"No, no, not Obode. That one," she said, pointing to Butler. "He was the one who took me from my house. He kidnaped me."

"Him?" Remo said, pointing to Butler.

She nodded and shuddered.

"Old Willie?" Remo asked.

"That one," she said pointing.

Suddenly everything had come undone for William Forsythe Butler, but perhaps there was still a chance. He broke through the crowd, pulling the pistol from his holster, running toward Obode. He might yet manage it. Kill Obode, then say he took the girl under Obode's orders.

He raised the gun to fire. Then the gun was gone from his hand, thudding softly, sending up a little puff of dust where it hit the ground and Chiun stood alongside him.

Butler stopped in his tracks.

"You have done evil to the Loni people," Chiun said. "Did you hope someday to be king of this land? To one day enslave not only Hausa but Loni too?" Chiun's voice rose in pitch.

Butler slowly backed away from him. "You have disgraced the Loni people. You are not fit to live."

Butler turned to try to run, but there was no break in the crowd. He turned. Then Chiun turned his back on him and was walking away.

Remo moved out into the clearing.

"It was you, Willie?"

"Yes," Butler hissed, the Loni click in his throat chattering his anger. "I would repay in kind what the whites did to me. What they did to the Loni people."

"Sorry, Willie," Remo said, remembering the girls he had been forced to kill. "You were a good cornerback but you know how it is: you can't argue with a legend."

He moved toward Butler, who drew himself up to his full height. He was bigger than Remo, heavier, probably stronger. The white bastard had never been able to forget for one minute that he had been Willie Butler. All right. So be it. Now he would show him what Willie Butler could do if he had wanted to play the white man's game.

He crouched down and from deep in his throat growled at Remo: "Your ball, honkey."

"I'm going to flood your zone with receivers," Remo said. "That always confused you goons."

Remo began trotting toward Butler who went widelegged into a tackling stance. When Remo was within reach, he sprang, leaving his feet, rolling on his side toward Remo. Remo skipped lightly over him and Butler quickly rolled up onto his feet.

"First and ten," Remo said.

He came back toward Butler who assumed the same stance, but this time as Remo drew near, Butler straightened up, leaped into the air and let fly a kick at Remo's face. Remo caught the heel of the foot in both hands and continued pushing it upward, tumbling Butler back over onto his back.

"Unsportsmanlike conduct, Willie. That'll cost you fifteen yards."

Butler got up again and charged now in a rage at Remo, who dodged away. "Tell me, Willie, what was it you were trying to prove? What'd you need the girls for?"

"How could you know? That accursed family . . . the Butlers, the Forsythes, the Lippincotts . . . they bought my family as slaves. I was collecting a debt."

"And you think that poor little girl over there had something to do with it?"

"Blood of blood," Butler grunted, as he wrapped his arms around Remo's waist. "The bad seed has to be uprooted, no matter how big it's grown." He slid off Remo to the ground as Remo skipped away.

"It's people like you, Willie, that give racism a bad name."

Butler had edged around, slowly facing Remo, moving in a circle. He widened the circle gradually until his back was against the line of Lonis who were quietly watching this contest, so unlike anything they had ever seen.

Without warning, Butler reached behind him, grabbed a spear from one of the Loni men and jumped back into the squared arena.

"At last, your true colors come out," Remo said. "You're just another dirty player."

Butler moved toward him with the spear, holding it like a javelin, his hand on its middle, its weight poised over his right shoulder, ready to throw.

"Now you tell me something, white man. The legend says a dead man comes with the Master. How are you a dead man?"

"Sorry, Willie, it's true. I died ten years ago. Now you can worry about the legend."

"Well, dying didn't seem to take. So I think you ought to try it again."

Butler was only six feet from Remo now and he reared back with the spear and let it fly. Its point flew straight at Remo's chest and Remo collapsed backward out of its way and as the spear passed over his head, Remo's hand flashed out and cracked the center of the shaft. The spear snapped in two, both halves clattering across the ground toward Chiun, who stood quietly watching.

Remo slowly regained his feet. "Sorry, Willie, you just lost the ball on downs."

And then Remo moved toward him with a leap.

"This one's for the Gipper," Remo said.

Butler rammed a forearm toward the bridge of Remo's nose but the arm struck only air and then Willie Butler felt a biting pain in his chest that turned to fire and the fire was flashing red and pure and it burned worse than all the fires he'd ever seen and in that last flash of flame, he thought back, and his mind said, it's me, Sis, it's Billie, I really can run fast because I know it, and someday I'm gonna be a big man and his sister was saying no tomming swamp nigger ever gonna amount to anything, but Sis, you were wrong, I was wrong, hate and violence isn't the way, it just doesn't work, but his sister didn't answer and suddenly Willie Butler didn't care anymore because he was dead.

Remo stood up and rolled Butler over with his foot so his face was buried in the dust.

"That's the biz, sweetheart," he said.

The Loni were still silently watching. Chiun moved toward Remo, put his hand on Remo's arm and said loudly: "Two parts of the legend are now completed."

He looked slowly around the circle of Loni, confused and staring, then at Obode who had regained his dignity and stood erect, his arms yanked high up over his head, determined to die like a British soldier.

"The evil in the world is not always Hausa evil," Chiun said. "The Loni curse has not been the Hausa, but the Loni people who have no heart. We must give you back your heart."

Chuin released Remo's arm and turned toward the fire pit. Almost as if by signal, the last of the water evaporated, and the pit went aflame with a searing whoosh that seemed to swallow the oxygen in the arena and that moved Obode back, cringing slightly.

From a bowl alongside the pit, Chiun took salt and began sprinkling it at the end of the pit, seemingly oblivious to the heat. While Chiun's ritual went on, Saffah and her two sisters moved forward behind Chiun.

The flames died quickly as the dried-out wood almost exploded into fire and Chiun motioned to the two Loni men who stood near the rear corners of the pit. Using long staves, they began to spread the fire, shaking the twigs and embers loose, and exposing through the fire the giant ostrich egg-sized rocks, now glistening white hot from their two-day baking.

Remo came up alongside Chiun.

"What the hell are you up to?" he demanded.

"One does not worry about the Master. One only observes and learns." Chiun looked at Remo, seemed to understand his concern and said, "No matter what happens you must promise not to interfere. No matter what."

"Chiun, I won't let you do anything foolish."

"You will do as I say. You will not interfere. My House's debt to the Loni has been a family disgrace. You dishonor me if you stop me from discharging that debt. Do nothing."

Remo searched Chiun's eyes for any weakness, any hint, but there was none.

"I don't like it," Remo said glumly, even as he started moving back.

"Your preferences are of little interest to my ancestors. They like what I do."

The entire pit had now been raked until it was an evil mix of white hot stones and red hot embers.

Chiun looked around him at the Loni people. "The Lonis must again be taught of bravery."

He nodded to Princess Saffah and her sisters and they slowly walked forward in a single line toward the pit. Remo stood alongside and watched them, a procession of three proud and beautiful women. He could understand why once this land had great kings and queens. Saffah and her sisters were royalty in any land in any day. Traditional royalty was a gift of governments or an accident of heritage, but real royalty came from the soul. The sisters had soul.

Saffah stepped into the ritual bed of salt Chiun had prepared, then folding her arms, without hesitation, she placed her right foot into the bed of hot coals and began to walk into the pit of fire. The Loni gasped. Remo stood stunned. Obode appeared in a state of shock.

But oblivious to all their feelings was Saffah, who was now walking, resolute step after resolute step, down the center line of the pit. Her feet kicked up little clouds of sparks and heat shimmered around her bare ankles. When she was halfway across, the next sister stepped through the salt pit and out into the coals. And a few moments later, the third sister followed.

Remo watched their faces carefully; not a sign of pain or concern showed. It was some kind of trick. Cheapie old Chiun had done some finagling with the fire. Unworthy, Remo decided. Definitely unworthy of a Master of Sinanju. He would have to tell him.

The three sisters now stood in a row near Obode at the far end of the fire pit.

"Your princesses have shown you that the Loni can still breed courage," Chiun said, "but that is not enough to purify you."

Chiun stepped his bare wrinkled yellow feet into the small salt bed and then he too stepped out into the field of flame and fire and heat.

As he walked, he intoned a chant softly to himself. *"Kufa tutakufa wote."* Remo had never heard it before but recognized it as part of the Loni tongue.

Carefully, yet decisively, Chiun walked straight along the length of the fire bed.

And then in the middle he stopped.

Good trick, Remo thought. A real show-stopper, Chiun.

Chiun stood there, feet not moving, arms folded, face impassive as ever, still mouthing his chant *"Kufa tutakufa wote."*

"What's that mean?" Remo said to a Loni standing behind him.

"It means, As for dying, we shall all die."

The Loni watched Chiun and their small buzzings turned to silence as the seconds ticked on and Chiun stood still in the middle of the fiery pit, the heat waves rising around him, making his body seem to shimmer and shake even though he did not move.

Then a small wisp of smoke began to curl up the side of Chiun's leg. Remo could see that Chiun's shin-length white pants had singed at the bottom. A little speck turned brown, then black, then broadened, and now gave out thin trails of smoke. An orange dot appeared at the edge of one leg as the overheated fabric neared its flash point. A tiny lick of flame puffed up.

The Loni gasped. Remo took a step forward, then stopped, indecisive, not knowing what to do.

And over the gasping and the whispers roared the voice of General Obode.

"Will no one help that man?"

The roar was an anguished cry.

Yet no one moved.

"Help him," Obode demanded at the top of his voice.

Still no one moved.

With a bellow of rage and anger, Obode wrenched at the eight-foot post to which he was tied.

The force of his huge body tore the iron ring from its mounting and his hands came loose, still tied together with the ring now suspended on the rope connecting his wrists.

Chiun's *ge* was breaking into flame at the shins, at the waist.

Without hesitation, Obode raced forward the two steps separating him from the fire pit, seemed to pause momentarily, and then, barefooted, ran through the pit to the place Chiun stood. Each step he took, he screamed. Yet he ran on. When he reached Chiun, he scooped with both hands together and lifted Chiun in his giant arms like a baby, then ran the short distance across the pit to exit at the side. He put Chiun down gently and with his hands began to beat out the flames of Chiun's uniform. Only when they were out, did he roll onto his back and begin to try wiping away the glowing bits of wood and rock that still stuck to his burned-black feet. He was still screaming in pain.

The Loni watched quietly as Chiun sat unconcerned and Obode ministered to his feet.

And then, a full-throated cheer went up from the watching crowd. Hands clapped in the peculiar unrhythmic African manner. Women shouted approval. Children whistled. The Loni princesses left their places and came running toward Obode and Chiun. Saffah snapped her fingers and shouted some words. In a seeming split second, women were back with leaves and buckets that appeared filled with mud and Saffah began making a poultice for Obode's feet.

Remo came over and as he moved in front of Chiun, he saw with astonishment that Chiun's feet were unmarked and so were his legs and hands. His uniform was singed and scorched, in places crisped away into hard flecks of black charcoal, but Chiun was unhurt.

As Remo stood there, Chiun moved to his feet and stood over the figures of the three princesses ministering to General Obode.

"People of the Loni, hear me now and hear me well because I have traveled many miles to bring you these words." He waved a hand toward Obode, writhing on the ground in pain.

"You have learned through this man today that the Hausa may have courage. It is the beginning of wisdom. You have applauded his courage, and that is the beginning of self-worth. The Loni did not lose an empire because of the Hausa. They lost it because they were not fit to hold it. Today, your people have regained their fitness. The legend has been redeemed. The debt of the House of Sinanju has been paid."

One voice piped out of the crowd. "But our return to power. What of that?" Several voices mumbled in concert with him.

Chiun raised his hands for silence. "No man bestows power, not even the Master of Sinanju. Power is earned by deeds and works. The President of the Hausa has learned something today. He has learned that the Loni no longer hate him because he is a Hausa. They have hated him because he has been unjust. Today he is going to become a great leader because he will now bring the Loni into the palaces of government to build again a great land. The Loni will not be sergeants and servants; they will be generals and counselors." Chiun looked down at Obode whose eyes met his. They locked momentarily and Obode nodded in agreement, then looked away, back at the head of Princess Saffah who still ministered to his burned feet, her long black silken hair splashing about his blistering ankles.

"To keep this new power, the Loni must be worthy," Chiun said. "And then soon there may be a new race of kings in this land. With the bravery of the Hausa, with the beauty and wisdom of the Loni."

He looked now at Saffah. She looked at him and then, with tenderness, at Obode, then nodded to Chiun. She smiled and reached out her hand and placed it on Obode's shoulder.

"People of the Loni, the legend is done. You may tell your children you saw the Master. You may tell them also he will return if ever man's hand is set unfairly against you people whom I protect."

With those words, Chiun dropped his hands and walked toward his hut. He picked Hillary Butler from the crowd, took her arm and led her inside with him.

Remo followed and found Chiun sitting on his prayer mat. Hillary Butler sat on the floor near him, just watching.

Chiun looked up, saw Remo, and said: "Where were you when I needed you?"

"You told me not to interfere."

"Ah yes, but would a worthy son have listened? No. He would have said, ah, that is my father, he is in danger, nothing must stop me from saving him. That is what a loyal son would have said. It is the difference between good breeding and being something the cat dragged in."

"Well, it didn't really matter anyway. It was just a trick. Nobody stands on hot coals."

"Come," Chiun suggested. "We will go out and walk the fire together. It is done often in the civilized sections of the world," meaning, Remo knew, the part of the world Chiun came from. "Japanese do it. Even some Chinamen."

"But how?" Remo said.

"Because they are at peace with themselves," Chiun said triumphantly. "They think of their souls instead of their stomachs. Of course to do that one must first have a soul."

"Bicker, bicker, bicker," Remo said. "It was still a trick."

"The stupid never learn; the blind never see," Chiun said and would say no more.

Remo turned to Hillary Butler. "We'll get you started on your way home tonight."

She nodded. "I want . . . well, I want to thank you. I don't really understand all this, but maybe . . . well, anyway thank you."

Remo raised a hand. "Think nothing of it."

Chiun said, "You may be grateful. The Master has done what he had to do. This one . . . well, he did the best he could."

Later, as they prepared to leave, Remo stood near the graying fire pit, and picked up a small chip of wood from the ground.

He flipped it out into the pit of coals. The chip of wood hit, seemed to break up the steady pattern of heat waves for a split second, then flared into flame.

Remo shook his head. He turned, and saw Chiun standing there, smirking.

"There is still time for you to learn the fire walk."

"Try me next week," Remo said.

Remo, Chiun and Hillary Butler left the Loni camp that night with a hundred-man Loni escort, fourteen of them with no other responsibility but to carry Chiun's luggage.

Saffah and Obode bade them good-bye, then Saffah took Remo to one side.

"Good-bye, Remo," she said. She began to say something else, stopped herself, said a word that sounded to Remo like "*nina-upenda*" and walked quickly away from him.

On the trail down the mountainside, Chiun said more to himself than to Remo, "I am glad we did not have to kill Obode."

Remo glanced at him, suspiciously. "Why?"

"Hmmm?" Chiun said. "Oh, there is no reason."

"There is a reason for everything you say," Remo said. "Why are you glad we didn't have to kill Obode?"

"Because the chief of the Hausa is to be protected."

"Who says? Why?" Remo demanded.

Chiun was silent.

"Two-faced sonuvabitch. I'm going to get Smith to get the Washington pollsters to take the soap operas off again."

Chiun considered this for a moment. "There is no need for you to punish an old man."

"Then talk. Why was Obode to be protected?"

"Because when my ancestor many years ago left the Loni and they were overthrown . . ." Chiun paused.

"Get on with it."

"He left to go work for the Hausa," Chiun said. "For more money," he explained brightly.

"Well, I'll be. Talk about double-dealers," Remo said. "Has any Master ever played anything straight?"

"You know not the meaning of such words," Chuin answered.

"Yeah? Well, try this. *Nina-upenda*," he said, repeating the Loni word that Saffah had spoken to him.

"Thank you," Chiun said and Remo had to find out later from one of their guards that the word meant "I love you."

It made him feel good all over.

THE DESTROYER
Assassins Play-off

He who plays with the sword shall succumb to him who works with the willow branch.
—HOUSE OF SINANJU

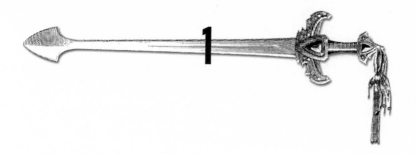

HE had paid $8,000, all that was in his family's savings account, and had promised $12,000 more in three years of monthly installments to be sitting in the drafty main room of this Scottish castle in the drizzly, bitter chill autumn of the highlands, his knuckles on the floor, his weight on his knees in a position of respect.

They had remodeled the room, they said. A new wooden floor, polished to a high gloss. New rice-paper tapestries with the symbols of Ninja—the night fighters—of Atemi, the fist methods; of Kung Sool, the archery; of Hsing-i, the boxing; and many others he did not recognize.

But they had not taken away the draft from Kildonan Castle, north of Dundee and south of Aberdeen, inland from the Firth of Tay. Only the Scots, thought William Ashley, could create a structure that was drafty without being ventilated.

And even the Koreans couldn't overcome it.

The large room smelled of pungent sweat mixed with fear and perhaps it was the chill that made Ashley's knees ache and his back feel as if someone were tightening a garrote on his spinal column. Not since he was a novice in the little commercial karate dojo in Rye, New York, had Ashley felt the pain in the position of respect, knees on floor, hands extended outward so that you rested on both feet and hands. It was in that little dojo after work that he learned respect for himself in the conquest of his body. Learned to control his fears and his passions, learned that it was not the yellow belt or the green belt or the brown belt or even the highest—or what he thought was the highest then—the black belt, that was important; no, what was important was what he became with each step taken toward a perfection far off in the distance.

And it was precisely this striving for perfection that had brought Ashley to the highlands with his family's savings and his three-week annual vacation.

He had initially thought that perfection was an unattainable goal, a thought that kept men rising and improving, a goal that when you were closest you realized was farther away. A place and a thing beyond where you would ever be. It was a direction, rather than a destination.

Which is what he had said in the Felt Forum of Madison Square Garden last month. Which was why he was here, $8,000 poorer and telling himself, like all those who really understand the martial arts, that body pain must eventually diminish.

He had made the remark about perfection being unattainable to a Korean who had come to the annual martial arts exhibit and who had commented somewhat complimentarily on Ashley's performance.

"Almost perfect," said the Korean, who wore a dark business suit with white starched shirt and a red tie. He was young but somewhat fleshy around the jowls.

"Then I am happy," said Ashley, "because no one is perfect."

"Not so," said the Korean. "There is perfection."

"In the mind," said Ashley.

"No. Here on earth. Perfection you can touch."

"What school are you with?" asked Ashley, who himself was karate but knew of kung fu, aikido, ninja and many other fighting methods of the body.

"Perhaps all schools," said the Korean. Ashley looked at the man more closely. He could not be older than his thirties, and such arrogance in one so young surely meant ignorance rather than competence. He reminded himself that not all Orientals knew the martial arts any more than all Americans knew rocketry. The man had obviously come to the Felt Forum to see what the martial arts were about and just as obviously was a windbag. There were Orientals who talked through their hat, too.

The Korean smiled.

"You doubt me, don't you, William Ashley?" he said.

"How do you know my name?"

"Do you think your name is a secret?"

"No, but I am surprised that you know me."

"William Ashley, thirty-eight, computer programmer for Folcroft Sanitarium, Rye, New York. And you think because you are a grain of sand on the beach, I should not be able to tell you from any other grain of sand on the beach, and you are surprised that I know you."

"Very," said Ashley who knew what to do in situations like this. He was supposed to call Folcroft Sanitarium and report it because the information he worked with at the sanitarium was top security. The sanitarium walls were just a cover. He, along with two other National Security Agency programmers, had been sent there seven years before, and so secret was their work that no one man could tell, even if he were forced to, about the scope and nature of any project he worked on.

But something about this Korean made Ashley hesitate.

"If you are surprised, you have a very poor memory."

Bill Ashley slapped his thigh and laughed.

"Of course. I remember. Last year. Just before Christmas. You had been in some sort of accident, with crude oil, I think, and had suffered skin burn. Severe, if I remember. You came to our dojo and you were recuperating and our sensei said you were a great master. Your name was, don't tell me, I remember, I remember, I remember . . ."

"Winch."

"Right. Winch," said Ashley. "How do you do, sir. It is an honor to meet you again. Oh, I'm sorry." Ashley put his hand down. He remembered the man did not shake hands.

Together then, they watched an exhibition of monkey fighting, a peculiar form in which much leverage was claimed, but Winch pointed out to Ashley that there was no leverage at all, just the illusion of power.

When one of the fighters knocked the other off the mat, Ashley said that looked like plenty of leverage to him.

"Only because they were both monkey style, balancing on a single foot, instead of thrusting from that foot. Anyone with feet wide apart who got close so that he could see the little lines on the teeth could, with a push, make any monkey fighter look like a fool."

"I believe it because you say it, but they are both fifth dan black belts."

"You do not believe it, but you will," Winch said and rose from his seat. In a language Ashley assumed was Korean, Winch spoke to several of the monkey fighting masters who looked shocked, then angry.

"Put on your gi," said Winch. "You will make the monkey boxer look like a fool."

"But they are all very famous here in the New York area," said Ashley.

"I have no doubt. Many people are famous here. Just keep your feet wide apart and get very close and push."

"Perhaps a more forceful attack?" said Ashley.

"A push," said Winch.

"What did you tell them?" asked Ashley, nodding past Winch toward the black belt experts who were staring at him.

"What I told you. That you will make any monkey boxer look like a fool and that they should be ashamed that true Koreans would lend their presence to such silliness."

"Oh, no. You didn't," gasped Ashley.

"Go," said Winch.

"What about humility?"

"What about truth? Go. You will shame that monkey boxer if you do as I say. Do not box. Do not attack with feet or slashing or chopping blows. Get close and push. You will see."

When Ashley, in his two piece gi, entered the ring, he heard snickers from the black belts. He saw several smile. The monkey boxer chosen to take care of Ashley smiled. He was about the same age as Ashley, but his body and even his skin was harder, more alive, for he had been training since he was a child. Ashley had started when he was twenty-eight.

Ashley bowed his respect before the match, but the monkey boxer, apparently angered by Winch's derision, stood rocklike, unmoving, ungiving of respect. A low murmur went through the crowd around the ring. This was not to be done. This was twice that tradition had been broken. First with the open insult from Winch, and then with the monkey boxer's failure to honor his opponent.

It was then that Ashley, looking at his opponent's face, knew the man meant to kill him. It was a smell as much as anything, his own body emitting something that told him he held his own life in his hands and he did not want it there.

Ashley desperately wanted to assume some known form of defensive position he had learned, but a greater force took over. His mind. He knew he should not be on the mat with this expert in the first place. Nothing he had ever learned would be good enough to compete with this man staring hate from his brown slanted eyes, the face twisted, the teeth bared, the body rising on the tips of the toes, and then one foot leaving for the spring. Only something Ashley had never tried before might work. He was committed to what Winch had told him.

The lights were hot overhead and the crowd seemed to disappear as he forced his unwilling body to approach the master, as he forced his feet wide for a solid stance—and then, as he saw the flash of the monkey boxer striking at his eyes, he also saw the tiny lines of ridge on the man's teeth, and Bill Ashley pushed forward, his hand coming to the boxer's chest.

Later he would tell people he did not know what happened. But there, in the heat of the center of the mat, he felt his hand go into the hard chest of the monkey boxer, and the boxer's blow forced his own body around Ashley's hand like the spoke of a wheel moving around the hub, and the monkey boxer hit the mat with a thwack. Ashley's hand was still out there in front of him. The boxer twitched and a drop of blood reddened the white mat under the dark black oriental hair.

"I just pushed. Not hard," said Ashley.

A few hands clapped and it became applause and a doctor ran up into the ring, and Ashley kept telling everyone he had just pushed. Really, that was all he had done.

He bowed to the ring, now full of desperate nervous men.

"He'll live," said the doctor. "He'll live."

"He'll live," announced the chairman of the event.

"It may just be a concussion," said the doctor. "Stretcher. Stretcher."

And that was how it had begun. Ashley had dinner with Winch and learned about a new concept in perfection, frightening in its simplicity.

William Ashley had, all his life, simply believed the opposite about what perfection was. He had believed it was something martial artists moved toward. But it was the other way around. Perfection was what they all came from.

As Mr. Winch explained, there was a method, a way, that had to do with the way things moved and were, that was perfect execution of the art. There was one martial art at the beginning, in the deep, deep past of the Orient. From this one art came all the others with all their codes and all their disciplines. And, inasmuch as they differed from this sun source, they were less.

"Could I learn it?" asked Ashley. They were eating at Hime of Japan, a restaurant on the other side of Manhattan from Madison Square Garden that served a more than passable teriyaki. Ashley maneuvered his chopsticks with skill, creating little crevices with his rich brown meat and vegetables to catch the pungent sour sauce. Winch had only a spoonful of rice, which appeared to take forever for him to finish.

"No," said Winch, answering Ashley's question. "One cannot put the ocean into a brandy snifter."

"You mean I'm unworthy?"

"Why must you make a moral judgment? Is a brandy snifter unworthy of the ocean? Is it not good enough for the ocean? Is it too evil for the ocean? No. A brandy snifter is a brandy snifter and will take a brandy snifter full of salt water. If you must moralize, it is good enough for a brandy snifter of the ocean. But for no more."

"I have a confession to make," said Ashley. "When I saw the monkey boxer first strike canvas, I hoped he was dead. I kept saying that I only pushed, but I had this sort of fantasy, well, that I had killed him, and I honestly hoped I had killed him, and that it would make me famous."

Mr. Winch smiled and leaned back in his seat. He placed his

stubby yellow hands with the slightly long fingernails on the table.

"Let me tell you about perfection. All these forms that you have learned come from the killing forms. But they are not a game, as you and the others make of them. A man who makes a game of these things will succumb to a child who does things properly. You were right in your feelings, right to wish that the monkey boxer were dead, because that is what the sun source of the martial arts was designed to do. To kill."

"I want to learn perfection."

"What for? You don't need it."

"I want to learn it, Mr. Winch. I need it. I need to know it. If I have but one life and I do one thing in it, then I would know this perfection."

"You have not listened, but then you are a brandy snifter, and I know brandy snifters and what brandy snifters will do. So let me say now, the cost is high."

"I have savings."

"The cost is very high."

"How much?"

"High."

"In money?"

"In money," said Mr. Winch, "twenty thousand dollars. That is the money price."

"I can give you nine thousand now and pay off the rest."

"Give me eight thousand. There is some traveling to do."

"I can't go out of the country without clearance. It's sort of a job requirement."

"Oh. Are you in the CIA?"

"No, no. Something else."

"Well, then, brandy snifter, we'll have to forget it. Just as well, too. There is a very high price."

"Couldn't you teach me here?"

"That's not the point," said Mr. Winch. "The point is I am not doing it here. I teach at a place in Scotland."

"Out of the country. Damn. Still, it's this side of the Iron Curtain and maybe, just maybe, my people will think Scotland is secure."

"They will, brandy snifter, they will. English-speaking peoples have a well of trust that is bottomless. For other English-speaking peoples. I will see you at Kildonan Castle with your eight thousand dollars, brandy snifter."

Bill Ashley did not tell his wife about the $8,000, and he hid the savings book so that she would not find out. He did not know what he would say when he eventually told her. He would have to tell her, he knew, but he would take care of that after he had seized his share of perfection, as much as he could absorb.

The job was something else. While the National Security Agency only used Folcroft as a cover for the information bank Ashley worked on, he still had to get vacation permission from the director of the sanitarium, Dr. Harold W. Smith.

Ashley was always careful to maintain his cover precisely when talking to the crusty old New Englander who thought the information banks contained data on some sort of mental health survey. Ashley always read from the looseleaf notebook on what he was allegedly supposed to be working on before he entered Dr. Smith's office.

One thing had always struck him as odd, though. Dr. Smith, who was not supposed to be that concerned with what his staff was specifically doing, had a computer terminal to the left of his desk, and unless the NSA had done some clever short-circuiting, that terminal appeared as if it could get a readout from every computer core in the sanitarium.

Ashley was sure however that NSA was not about to do some

dumbass thing like let the cover know what it was covering. Still, it was disconcerting to see it there, disconcerting to just entertain the possibility that the director of a sanitarium might have access to highly classified secrets, information so sensitive that no single programmer had access to work outside of his own, and no two were allowed to socialize.

"So you wish to take a vacation?" said Smith. "Early, I see."

"A bit. I feel I could use it, sir."

"I see. And where are you and your wife going?"

"Well, I sort of thought I'd go alone this time. A real vacation. I need it."

"I see. Do you often take vacations alone?"

"Sometimes."

"Oh. When was your last vacation alone?"

"In 1962, sir."

"You were a bachelor then, weren't you?"

"Yes. If you must know, sir, I'm having trouble with my wife and I just want to get away from her. I've got to get away for a little while."

"Do you think your work will suffer if you don't?" asked Smith.

"Yes, sir."

"Well, I see no reason why you shouldn't get a rest. Let's say at the end of the month."

"Thank you, sir."

"You're welcome, Ashley. You're a good man."

Bill Ashley smiled when he shook hands, for how would Smith know if he were a good man or an atrocious misfit? Peculiar fellow, that Smith, with his fear of the sun. The only other one-way windows Ashley knew of were at the Langley headquarters of the CIA and Washington headquarters of NSA.

With the Smith formality taken care of, Ashley put in the

proper forms to his real boss in Washington. The answer was yes.

As was custom, he was taken off sensitive matters right away and just did garbage work waiting for his vacation. On the day before departure he transferred his savings account into his checking account. He would have liked to have given Mr. Winch the cash directly, but if his real boss got word—and they had people who would give them the word—that Ashley had withdrawn $8,000 from his savings in cash just before his vacation out of the country, there would be more government people around him than ants on a piece of sugar. He was sure Mr. Winch would take a check. He would have to. That's all Ashley had.

"Brandy snifter," said Mr. Winch when Ashley was shown into the coldest heated room this side of outdoors—the lord's chambers of Kildonan, it was called—"you must first wait until your check clears. A check is a promise of money. It is not money."

When the check did clear, Ashley quickly wished it hadn't, so badly did his back and arms hurt from waiting in the position of respect on the cold wooden floor. And for $20,000 he wasn't even getting a private lesson. There were three others in the class.

They were a bit younger than Ashley and a bit more athletic and much more advanced. Mr. Winch made Ashley watch. Their strokes seemed familiar, yet much simpler. The circling motions were much tighter than Ashley had seen anywhere else, not so much a fixed circle but the forcing of a turn around an opponent.

"You see, Mr. Ashley, you were trained to practice your circling motions around an imaginary point," Winch explained. "Your method was learned from someone a long time ago who watched this method in practice, probably against someone who didn't move. Sometimes it works, sometimes it doesn't. That is because it is derivative. All the derivative arts have their flaws because they copy the externals without understanding the essence. And there are other reasons. Witness the kung fu masters who attempted to fight Thai boxers. Not one survived the first round. Why?"

Just to relieve the building pressure on his back from the fixed position, Ashley raised a hand. Mr. Winch nodded.

"Because they had not been trained to fight but to pretend to fight," said Ashley.

"Very good," said Mr. Winch. "But more importantly, the boxers were hard men winnowed from the soft. The boxers had used their skills for their living. The boxers were at work; the kung fu at play. Up, Ashley, on your feet. Assume a position."

"Which position, Mr. Winch?"

"Any position, brandy snifter. Stand or crouch or hide. You'd be better off with a gun, probably, and perhaps two hundred yards distance. That is, if you had a gun, which I wouldn't give you."

"What am I supposed to be learning?"

"That a fool and his life are soon parted."

Mr. Winch clapped his hands and a large, blond, crewcut man, with a hard face and ice blue eyes and hands with knuckles meshed together, danced forward and came into Bill Ashley hard. He also came fast. Ashley didn't see the blow, and he knew he had been hit only when he tried to move his left arm. It wouldn't.

The next man, a big bear of muscle and hair, giggled as he took out Ashley's right arm. It felt as if his shoulders had two hot knives attached to them, and suddenly Bill Ashley realized he needed his arms for balance. It was very hard to stand, and then it was even harder when the left leg went and he was down on the floor writhing and moaning his agony, after the third trainee had delivered the leg blow.

And then the right leg went when Mr. Winch immobilized it with a disdainful kick.

Ashley screamed when they took off his white gi. The bones must be broken, he thought. This was wrong. You didn't break someone's bones in training. That was wrong training. He saw a rice paper banner flutter from the ceiling, and he knew by the cold at his back that someone was opening a window. It was not his imagination. It was getting colder. He knew his clothing was off, but he could not look. His head had to stay exactly where it was or his joints felt incredible pain, as if someone were shredding his ligaments with a rasp.

He saw the banner on the ceiling float down, a lopsided upside-down trapezoid with a vertical line through it. A simple symbol he had never seen before.

"Why? Why? Why?" moaned Bill Ashley, softly, for loud talk made his arms move slightly.

"Because you work at Folcroft, brandy snifter," he heard Mr. Winch say. It was too painful to turn his head to look at Winch.

"Then it wasn't for my money."

"Of course it was for your money."

"But Folcroft?"

"It was because of Folcroft, too. But money is always nice, brandy snifter. You have been poorly taught. From your very hello to the world, you have been coming to this day because you were poorly taught. Goodbye, brandy snifter, you were never made for the martial arts."

There was one blessing to the chill that overcame his bare body on the new wooden floor in the lord's chambers of Kildonan Castle. It was going to make everything better. Already, his pain was numbing and soon it would all be gone. The temperature fell further at night and Ashley slipped into a deep darkness, only to be disappointed by weak light in the morning. But when the room was most light, about the time of the high sun, Ashley slipped again into the deep darkness, and this time he did not come out.

He was found six days later by a detective from Scotland Yard acting on a tip from a telephone caller who would later be described as having a "vaguely Oriental" voice.

The yard also got Ashley's New York State, U.S.A., driver's license in the mail without a note. Since it was addressed to the detective who got the tip, he assumed the body belonged to William Ashley, 38, 855 Pleasant Lane, Rye, N.Y., five-feet-ten, 170 pounds, brown eyes, brown hair, mole on left hand, no corrective lenses.

It not only checked out, it became known as the "Kildonan Castle Murder," and the detective appeared on the telly describing the gruesomeness of the death and how the yard was looking for a madman.

Ashley had died of exposure, not of the broken limbs, each shattered at the joint, he said. No, there were no clues. But the murder scene was horrid. Frightfully horrid. Yes, he could be quoted on that. Frightfully horrid. Never seen anything like it before.

It was when he had finished his second daily press briefing that the man from British Intelligence had all those questions.

"Did this Ashley fellow take long to die?"

"Yessir. He died of exposure."

"Were any papers found on him?"

"No sir. The bloke was stark raving nude. Exposure will kill faster than thirst or hunger."

"Yes, we're well aware of that. Was there any indication that he was tortured for information?"

"Well, sir, leaving a person with four crushed limbs naked on a bare, cold floor in a drafty highland castle is not exactly a comfort-inducing experience, wouldn't you say, sir?"

"You don't know, is that right?"

"Correct, sir. Was this chap important in some way?"

"Really, now, that's not something you'd expect me to answer, is it?"

"No, sir."

"Did you find out who had title to the castle?"

"British government, sir. Castle was abandoned for taxes years ago. Owner couldn't keep it up, so to speak."

"Which means what?"

"Unoccupied, sir."

"I see. Are you telling me ghosts did it?"

"No sir."

"Very good. We'll get back to you. And forget you spoke to me, would you please?"

"Forgotten already, sir."

The report by British intelligence to the American Embassy in London was brief. Ashley had come to England as a tourist, had proceeded directly to Scotland, spent one evening at a small inn and was then discovered more than a week later in a condition of semidismemberment.

It was a closed coffin funeral in Rye, New York. Which was an excellent idea since the body was not that of William Ashley but a derelict from the New York city morgue. The Ashley body was in a medical school just outside Chicago where a doctor who thought he worked for the Central Intelligence Agency was examining the limbs. The blows, more than likely, had been made by some sort of sledgehammer. The joints were too shattered for the human hand to have inflicted the damage. Ashley had indeed died of exposure, contracting pneumonia with the lungs filling and causing death somewhat akin to drowning.

In Rye, New York, an agent who believed he was working undercover for the FBI, posing as an agent of a federal reserve board, saw to it that the $8,000 missing from the Ashley savings account was redeposited with no record that it had ever been withdrawn.

And the only person who knew exactly what all these men were doing and why sat behind a desk in Folcroft Santarium, looking out his one-way windows at Long Island Sound, hoping Ashley had indeed been a victim of robbery.

He had ordered the $8,000 put back into the account because the last thing this incident needed was more international publicity with Ashley's wife crying about missing money. The National Security Agency had been a bit lax in not having reported the transfer of Ashley's funds from savings to checking, but by and large it was the most thorough and accurate of all the country's services.

Dr. Harold Smith, the man whom Ashley thought was his cover, was the only man who knew what Ashley did for a living. Including Ashley.

He reviewed the man's program files. Ashley had been in charge of storing information on East Coast shipping. He had thought he was heading an information sorting, which tried to detect foreign penetration of national shipping, always a key spot for espionage. But Ashley's real function, which he could never see because he only performed half of it, was tabulating real shipping incomes versus ladings.

It was part of an overall formula Dr. Smith had worked out years before that showed, when ladings began to exceed income, that organized crime was gaining too much control over the waterfronts.

Smith had found out years before that he could not end crime's influence on the waterfront, which included everything from loansharking to the unions. But what he could do was to keep crime from controlling shipping. When the formula showed that that was becoming a danger, a district attorney would suddenly get proof of kickbacks at the ports or the Internal Revenue Service would get xeroxed copies of bills of sales for a shipping executive who bought $200,000 homes on a $22,000 a year salary.

Ashley never knew this. He just worked on feeding the computer core. His terminal couldn't even get a readout without registering it up in Dr. Smith's office. Smith checked the records. The last time Ashley had requested a readout of the computer was six months before, and that was merely to check the accuracy of some data he had fed in the day before.

Going over it for the last time, Smith had to conclude that if William Ashley had been tortured to the last secret hiding place of his mind, he could not tell his captors what he did for a living. He simply could not know.

No one in the organization knew what it was that he did for a living—no one, but two.

It had all been carefully arranged like that years before. It was the essence of the organization, formed more than a decade before by a now dead president who had called Smith to his office and told him the United States government did not work.

"Under the Constitution, we cannot control organized crime. We cannot control revolutionaries. There are so many things we cannot control if we live by the Constitution. Yet, if we do not extend some measure of control, they will destroy this country. They will lead it to chaos," said the sandy-haired young man with the Boston accent. "And chaos leads to a dictatorship. As surely as water falls over a dam, a lack of order leads to too much order. We're doomed unless . . ."

And the "unless" that Smith heard was an organization set up outside the Constitution, outside the government, an organization that did not exist, set up to try to keep the government alive.

The organization would last for a short while, no more than two years, and then disappear, never seeing public light. And Smith would head it.

Smith had a question. Why him?

Because, the President had explained, in his years of service, Smith, more than any other manager in the Central Intelligence Agency, had showed a lack of prideful ambition.

"All the psychological tests show you would never use this organization to take over the country. Frankly, Dr. Smith, you have what can be uncharitably described as an incredible lack of imagination."

"Yes," Smith had said. "I know. It's always been like that. My wife complains sometimes."

"It's your strength," said the President. "Something amazed me though, and I'm going to ask you about it now because we will never see each other again, and you will of course forget this meeting . . ."

"Of course," Smith interrupted.

"What puzzles me, Dr. Smith, is how on earth you could flunk a Rorschach test. It's in your aptitude records."

"Oh, that," Smith said. "I remember. I saw ink blots."

"Right. And in a Rorschach test, you're supposed to describe what the blots look like."

"I did, Mr. President. They looked like ink blots."

And that was how it had started. The organization was supposed to be an information-gathering and -dispensing operation, providing prosecutors with information, letting newspapers get stories to embarrass corrupt officials. But early on it became apparent that information was not enough. The organization that did not exist needed a killer arm. It needed a killer arm the size of a small army, but small armies had many mouths and you didn't very well convince a hit man he worked for the Department of Agriculture. They needed an extraordinary single killer who didn't exist—for an organization that didn't exist.

It was really rather simple at first.

The organization had found the man it wanted working in a small police department in New Jersey, and it had framed him for a murder he didn't commit, and it had electrocuted him in an electric chair that didn't work, and when he came to he was officially a dead man. Such was his nature, which had been scrupulously checked out before, that he took well to working for the organization and learned well from his Oriental trainer, becoming—but for a few small character flaws—the perfect human weapon.

Smith thought about this as he watched a storm brew darkly over the Long Island Sound. He fingered Ashley's file. Something did not fit. The method of killing was so insane, it just might have a special purpose and meaning.

Everything else about the case had seemed orderly, even to the withdrawal of the money. The killing came after the check had been cashed through a Swiss bank account in the name of a Mr. Winch. Smith examined again the report from British intelligence. Ashley had been killed on a freshly finished wooden floor. So heavy machinery had not been used to crush his limbs because its marks would have showed on the floor. Perhaps light machinery? Perhaps the killer was a sadist?

For a man who not only did not believe in hunches, but could not quite remember ever having one, Dr. Harold W. Smith felt a strange sensation when thinking about the Ashley death. There had been a purpose to the way he was killed. Smith didn't know why he thought that, but nevertheless he kept thinking it.

Through his evening meal of codfish cake and lukewarm suc-cotash, he thought about it. Through his perfunctory goodnight kiss to his wife, he thought about it. In the morning he thought about it even while processing other matters.

And since it was beginning to interfere with his other duties, which could lead to disruption in the entire organization, it therefore demanded an answer.

And it had to be quickly because, of the two men who might be able to answer the riddle of Ashley's death, one was on an as-signment and the other was preparing to return home to a small village in North Korea.

HIS name was Remo and the fresh snow fell on his open hand and he felt the flakes pile up. At the edge of the tall pine tree, across the three hundred yards to the yellow light coming from the cabin, was fresh, white, even snow, not even drifting in the windless late autumn evening in Burdette, Minnesota.

Remo had walked to the edge of the clearing, circling the cabin until he was sure. Now he knew. The perfect clearing in the Minnesota woods was an open field of fire. The assistant attorney general had made sure of that. If he didn't see anyone coming, then his dog would smell them, and from that cabin, anyone coming across that open blanket of white, by ski, by snowshoe, foot by foot, anyone would be almost a stationary target in the yellow light cutting the November night.

For some reason, Remo thought back to a night more than a decade before when he was strapped into an electric chair, when he thought he had died, and then had awakened to a new life as a man whose fingerprints had gone into the dead file, a man who did not exist for an organization that did not exist.

But Remo knew something that his boss, Dr. Harold W. Smith, did not know. He *had* died in that electric chair. The person who had been Remo Williams died, because the years of training had been so intense that even Remo's nervous system had changed and he had changed, so that now he was someone else.

Remo noticed the snow melt in his hand and he smiled. When you lost concentration, you lost it all. If he let the whole thing go, he would next feel chill in his body and then, out here in the freezing Minnesota snow, he would surrender his body to the elements and die. Cold was not a fixed point on a thermometer but the relationship between the body and its environment.

An old children's trick was putting one hand under hot running water and the other hand under cold water, and then plunging both hands into a bowl of lukewarm water. To the hand which had been hot, the lukewarm water felt cold. To the hand that had been cold, the lukewarm water felt hot. So too with temperature's effects on the body. Up to a certain point, it was not the temperature of the body, but the difference between the outside temperature and the body's temperature. And if the body temperature could be lowered, then a man could stand subfreezing weather in a light white sweater and white gym pants and white leather sneakers, and a man could hold a snowflake in his hand and watch it not melt.

Remo felt the quiet of the snow and saw gusts of sparks come out of the chimney of the yellow-lit cabin far off.

Snow was very light water, water with more oxygen in it, and if you let your body into it, moving level with the ground and it was all around you and you were part of its whiteness, not an intrusion on top of it, but every portion of your body moving through it, then it became light water and you moved quickly, not breathing, but with fingers darting forward and flattened palms pushing back and the body going level and quickly toward where the cabin had last been seen above the snow.

Remo stopped and his knees automatically lowered, packing the snow beneath them. He lifted his head above the opaque whiteness and smelled the fresh burning hickory and the heavy, fatty odor of meat cooking. Two figures moved behind the steamed windows. One jerky and the other with the hollow float of a woman, probably young. The assistant attorney general did have a girlfriend, Smith had told Remo, and of course there could be no living witnesses. From what Remo had gathered, the assistant attorney general had the incredible misfortune to come into certain cases prepared badly. Prosecution witnesses wound up proving a defendant's innocence; legal procedures fouled up so that so many criminals' rights were violated that they never went on trial.

Many, many mistakes which Assistant Attorney General Dawkins would blame on the courts for being too soft. And while other lawyers grew rich by preparing their cases, James Bellamy Dawkins became even richer by not preparing his.

It was when a mousy title clerk who thought she earned her side income from the National Real Estate Annual filed her yearly report with the magazine—which somehow rarely published anything she sent—that James Bellamy Dawkins was on his way to targethood.

A computer in a Long Island sanitarium on Long Island Sound spit out these coupled facts: Lost cases increased riches. In the instance of James Bellamy Dawkins, the worse he did in court, the more land he owned.

It was put to him somewhat gently at first. Perhaps, having two more years to serve and having already accumulated a sizeable fortune, he might want to devote his full energies to convicting certain perpetrators. He was shown a list that remarkably coincided with his benefactors.

He rejected the suggestion with a warning that should anyone attempt to remove him from office, he would immediately indict everyone on that list for abundant crimes they could not have committed, and when the charges were dropped, let them sue the state of Minnesota silly.

Better yet, indict them for murdering his caller and once they were acquitted, they could go out and do the real thing because a man couldn't be tried for the same crime twice.

In brief, Assistant Attorney General James Bellamy Dawkins was not going to change his ways nor was he going to resign, and God help the state if anyone tried to push him out.

That response ultimately reached the Folcroft computer and gave all those facts to Dr. Harold W. Smith, who decided immediately that America could do without James Bellamy Dawkins.

So Remo's eyes rose above the snowline and he saw the two figures and smelled the cabin smells and lowered his head back into the whiteness where his knees rose and he moved forward, not packing the very light water in which he went, but moving through it as if he belonged to it.

Remo heard the dogs bark and the cabin door open crisply and a man's voice say, "What is it, Queenie?" And Queenie barked.

"I don't see anything, Queenie," came the voice again.

And just because he felt like it and just because he had seen a horror movie recently and possibly because it was Halloween, Remo poked a little hole up through the snow and moaned:

"James Bellamy Dawkins, your days are numbered."

"Who the hell is that?"

"James Bellamy Dawkins, you will not live through the night."

"You there. Wherever you are. I can blow your head off."

"Trick or treat," said Remo.

"Where are you?"

"Trick or treat," said Remo.

"Go get him, Queenie."

Remo heard the barking approach and Dawkins, a paunchy man with hollow face and a . 30-30 rifle at rest in front of him, saw his bull mastiff streak through the snow, her body leaving a beveled path, her feet churning cones spaced at the outside of the bevel. When Queenie grabbed hold of whatever it was, she would get a good piece of him and Dawkins would shoot away the rest. The man obviously had come to kill him and all Dawkins had to do to show self-defense was to make sure a weapon was found on the body. If it didn't have one, he would supply it. The man was already on his property and that would suffice as circumstantial evidence supporting intent. The weapon would do the rest.

But a strange thing happened to Queenie, who had already devoured her fill of fall rabbits and had even come out on top against a family of raccoons. The path she made suddenly ended and she disappeared in the snow. Vanished.

Dawkins raised the gun to his shoulder and blasted around the area the dog had silently disappeared into. He heard a moan and he fired the lever action rifle again and the next shot showed the snow darkening and he chuckled to himself.

"What the hell are you shooting at, Jimmy?" came a woman's voice from inside the cabin.

"Shut up, honey," said Dawkins.

"What you shooting at this time of night?"

"Nothing. Shut up and go to bed."

Dawkins aimed at the spot where the red darkness was beginning to spread and he saw a small convulsion under the snow. Somehow the man had made his way under the fresh snowfall, but he saw no declivity leading to the blood, just Queenie's trail.

He watched and the snow was still, and then he tramped out from the cabin to inspect his kill. But when he was almost to where Queenie had gone out of sight, he felt something tugging at the back of his pants and he found his body sitting down. Then a hand was smacking snow into his face and he could not hold onto his .30-30 and he tried desperately to get the snow out of his face.

He tried to stand, but just when a foot seemed to get firmness underneath it, it somehow slid out. When he tried brushing the snow from his mouth, his hand seemed to go out in strange directions. Then the horror of it overtook him.

He was going to drown in snow and he could neither stand nor get the cold air-draining stuff out of his mouth. Then, in one last desperate life-grabbing thrust, he threw his whole body away from the force that seemed to be holding him down. And he moved nowhere and swallowed another handful of snow.

Everything became white and then he was no longer cold. Only his body was. When he was discovered the next morning by his horrified mistress, the county coroner labeled his death suicide. As he figured it, Dawkins had "flipped his giggy," shot his dog, then rolled around swallowing snow until he drowned and froze.

In Minnesota, the incident made immediate headlines:

ELECTED OFFICIAL DEAD IN LOVE NEST

By the time the story was in print, Remo's plane had landed at Raleigh Durham Airport in North Carolina where he took a taxi to a motel outside Chapel Hill.

"Out all night?" winked the desk clerk.

"Sort of," said Remo.

The desk clerk chuckled. "You must have spent it indoors. Nights can get chilly here in late autumn."

"I wasn't cold," said Remo honestly.

"Oh, I wish I were young again," said the clerk.

"Young has got nothing to do with it," said Remo, taking three keys because he had rented three adjoining rooms.

"There was a call for you from your Uncle Marvin."

"At what time?"

"'Bout ten-thirty this morning. Funny thing happened. The phone went dead almost as soon as I rang your room. I went to your door and yelled that there was a phone call but all I heard was the television on inside, and I didn't push it."

"I know you didn't push it," said Remo.

"How's that?"

"You're breathing, aren't you?" said Remo and when he slipped into the middle room he was very quiet because a frail, elderly Oriental with a wispy beard sat on the floor in lotus position, golden kimono draped immaculately around him.

The television set with the taping device to catch the other channels and then run the concurrent shows consecutively so that not one second of one soap opera would be missed was on.

Remo sat down quietly, not even rustling the couch. When Chiun, the Master of Sinanju, was enjoying his daytime dramas, no one, not even his pupil Remo, disturbed him.

In the past, some, by accident, had thought this was just an old man watching soap operas and had failed to treat this moment with reverence. They were no longer among the living.

So Remo sat as Mrs. Lorrie Banks discovered that her young lover loved her for herself and not her new face lift operation performed by Dr. Jennings Bryant, whose eldest daughter had run away with Morton Lancaster, the noted economist, who was being blackmailed by Doretta Daniels, the former belly dancer who had purchased the controlling shares in the Elk Ridge Cancer research hospital, and was threatening to close it down unless Lorrie disclosed where Peter Malthus had parked his car the night Lorrie's eldest daughter was run over and crippled for weeks, during the night of the flood when Captain Rambough Donnester had run away from the dark incident in his past, leaving the entire city of Elk Ridge exposed to the elements without the protection of the Air National Guard.

Lorrie was talking to Dr. Bryant, wondering whether Peter should be told about his mother. It occurred to Remo that just about two years earlier the actress was discussing whether someone else should be told some other gloomy thing about a relative, and what made these dramas different from reality was not so much what happened but that everyone was so all fired concerned about it. To Chiun, however, this was beauty and, as much as anything could be, a justification for American civilization. He was further convinced that this was the epitome of American culture when, in an exchange program with Russia, America had sent the New York Philharmonic—as Chiun said, "keeping the good things home." In exchange, Russia had sent the Bolshoi Ballet, which Chiun knew was also second-rate because their dancers were clumsy.

It was four-thirty in the afternoon when the last commercial on the last show was finished, a movie came on, and Chiun turned off the set.

"I do not like your breathing," he said.

"My breathing is the same as yesterday, Little Father," said Remo.

"That is why I do not like it. It should be quieter within you today."

"Why?"

"Because today you are different."

"In what way, Little Father?"

"That is for you to understand. When you do not know how you are each day, then you lose sight of yourself. Know this, no man has ever had two days alike."

"Did we get a phone call from upstairs?"

"There was a rude interruption, but I did not hold it against the maker of the telephone call. I endured the rudeness and the callousness and the lack of consideration for a poor old man enjoying the meager pleasures in the quiet twilight of his life."

Remo looked for the telephone to return the call. He found a hole where the cord had been snapped clean from the wall. He looked for the detached phone and not until he saw a dark hole in the white wood dresser did he realize where the phone had gone. The cracked body of the instrument was imbedded in the back of the dresser, welding the entire piece of furniture to the wall.

Remo went into an adjacent bedroom and dialed a number. This number did not activate a telephone directly, instead it sparked a series of connections across the country, so that there was no single line making up the connection by the time a phone finally did ring in the office of the director of Folcroft Sanitarium.

"Hello," said Remo. "Uncle Nathan called."

"No," said Dr. Smith. "Uncle Marvin called."

"Yeah, right," said Remo. "I knew it was somebody."

"I tried to reach you before, but we were disconnected and I thought you might have been clearing something up at the time."

"No. The phone rang while Chiun was watching his shows."

"Oh," said Smith heavily. "I have sort of a special problem. An accident happened to someone in a rather strange way and I thought you and Chiun might be able to shed some light on it."

"You mean he was killed in a way you don't know and you'd figure Chiun or I would know."

"Remo, please. There's no such thing as a completely secure telephone line."

"Whaddya going to do? Send me a matchbook with invisible

ink on it? C'mon, Smitty, I've got more important things in my life than playing security games."

"What is more important in your life, Remo?"

"Breathing correctly. Do you know I'm breathing the same today as yesterday?"

Smith cleared his throat and Remo knew it was the sound of unhappiness, that Smith had heard something he did not wish to deal with because he was afraid that further answers might confuse him more. He knew that Smith had recently given up trying to fathom him and was beginning to accept Remo like Chiun. An unknown quantity that served well. It was a major concession by a man who loathed anything he could not put in some order, well-labeled and perfectly filed. Mysteries were anathema to the head of the organization.

"On second thought," said Smith. "Send your Aunt Mildred a birthday greeting. She's fifty-five tomorrow."

"That means I'm supposed to meet you at O'Hare Airport information at three in the afternoon. Or is it three in the morning? Or is it Logan Airport?"

"Morning. O'Hare," said Smith dourly, and Remo heard the receiver go dead.

On the flight from Raleigh-Durham to Chicago's O'Hare Airport, Chiun suddenly marveled at the hidden skills of Americans. Chiun acknowledged that he should have known that there must be other areas of excellence.

"Any nation that could produce As the Planet Revolves or The Young and the Daring must have other isolated pockets of worth," said Chiun.

Remo knew that Chiun thought airplanes were very close to soundly designed flying objects, so he commented that America was the leader in aircraft and that he had never heard of a Korean-designed plane.

Chiun ignored that comment.

"What I am talking about," he said grandly, producing two torn pieces of white paper between his long graceful fingernails, "is here. This. And in America, too. What a pleasant surprise to find such an art so well performed in a place so far away as America."

Remo looked at the sheets. They were filled single space with sloppy typing.

"This, one can trust. I sent him my birthday and place and time of birth to the exact minute, and I sent him yours."

"You don't know for sure when I was born. Neither do I," said Remo. "The orphanage records weren't that exact."

With a flurry, Chiun's hands dismissed Remo's reservations as inconsequential.

"Even with an inexact date, such excellence of accuracy," said Chiun.

Remo looked closer. On the other side of the papers were circles with strange signs in them.

"What is it?" asked Remo.

"An astrology chart," said Chiun. "And in America, too. I am most pleasantly surprised that the great art, so poorly practiced by so many, is done well and in, of all places, America."

"I don't buy that stuff," said Remo.

"Of course, because in America little machines do everything in quantity. But you forget that men of brilliance and insight still exist. You do not believe in the forces of the universe because you have seen fools and charlatans represent them. But there is in America at least one true reader of the planets."

"Dippy dong," said Remo and winked at a passing stewardess, who almost dropped her tray in pleasant surprise. Remo knew he should not have done that because invariably the stewardess would be at him all trip for coffee, tea, milk, pillow for his head, magazines, and anything else that would get her close to him. At New York's Kennedy, two years before, a Pan-Am lassie had followed him from the plane crying that he had left a Kleenex in the seat.

"You may say that," said Chiun, "but let me read to you in your own language the keen insights of this reader of the forces of the universe."

And Chiun read in the manner of story-telling with his voice rising on the significant points and lowering at the serious ones.

"You," read Chiun, "are in tune with the gentleness and beauty of your world. Few realize your wisdom and kindness that is concealed by your desire for humility. You are troubled by the incessant badgering of those close to you who cannot publicly acknowledge your awesome magnificence."

"Pretty good," said Remo. "And what did he write about you?"

"That is me," said Chiun, and he read from the other paper: "You have a tendency to self-indulgence and are wont to function on whatever thought passes through your mind. You do not think things through, but run through days as if you have no tomorrow."

"That's me, I take it," said Remo glumly.

"To the letter," said Chiun. "Oh, does he know you. There is more. 'You do not appreciate the great gifts given you and squander them like duck droppings.'"

"Where?" said Remo. "Let me see where he said that. Where did he say 'duck droppings'?"

"He didn't say that exactly. But he would have if he knew you better."

"I see," said Remo, and asked for the two papers. True. All but the duck droppings was there. But Remo noticed something else. Chiun's chart started under the heading "positive" and then was torn off midpage. Remo's began under "negatives" and did not have a top of the page.

"You took my negatives and your positives," said Remo.

"I kept that which was correct. There is enough misinformation in the world. Let us be grateful that, in a country like this, we have found at least what is half correct."

"Who is this guy?"

"He is the Ke'Gan of the mountains. The mountains always have the best seers. A Ke'Gan. Here in America. That is why I first chose to write him, telling him of our birth signs." Remo looked at Chiun's chart which still had the astrology service's masthead.

"Ke'Gan?" he said. "The guy's name is Kegan. Brian Kegan. Pittsfield, Massachusetts."

"The Berkshire Mountains," said Chiun.

"Pittsfield. You've still got that post office box there, don't you? What are you doing with a post office box in Pittsfield, Massachusetts? What does a Master of Sinanju need that for?"

But Chiun folded his hands and was silent. The post office box had been rented long before, when Chiun had been ready to take up job offers, so that his assassin's profession could continue to support the aged and the weak and the poor, of his little village of Sinanju in North Korea. But the job crisis had ended and Chiun continued working for Dr. Smith, but he kept the post office box and refused to tell Remo what mail he received there.

The stewardess was back. No. Remo did not want coffee. He did not want tea. He did not want an alcoholic beverage or *Time* magazine.

"Sir," said the stewardess. "I've never said this to a passenger before, but I bet you think you're something special. I bet you think every woman is just dying to fall in bed with you, don-cha?"

Her pale cheeks flushed red and her blond shortcut bobbed in anger. Remo could smell her delicate perfume. He shrugged.

"I wouldn't have you on a bet, buddy. Not on a bet."

"Oh," said Remo. She left with her pillow and magazines but was back momentarily. She wanted to apologize. She had never talked to a passenger like that before. She was sorry. Remo said it was all right.

"I'd like to make it up somehow."

"Forget it," said Remo.

"I dearly would. Is there any way I could? Just tell me and I'll do it. Whatever you say."

"Forget it," said Remo.

"Screw you," she said. And Chiun, seeing passengers stare, raised a graceful hand, the fingernails a symphony of delicacy.

"Precious blossom, do not belabor your gracious heart. One cannot expect the rodents of the field to appreciate the precious emerald. Do not offer your gracious gift to him who is unworthy."

"You're damned right," said the stewardess. "You got a lot of wisdom there, sir. You really do."

"What did I do?" said Remo, shrugging.

"Go back to your cheese, mouse," said the stewardess. She left with a triumphant smile.

"What came over her?" asked Remo.

"I have given the best years of my life to a fool," said Chiun.

"I didn't want to bang her. So?"

"So you took her pride and she could not leave until it was given back to her."

"I'm under no obligation to service every woman who comes along."

"You are under an obligation not to hurt those who do you no harm."

"Since when is a Master of Sinanju a spreader of love and light?"

"I have always been. But light to a blind man can, at best, only mean heat. Oh, how the Ke'Gan knows you."

"Let him try turning off your soap operas one time. He'll get your love and light."

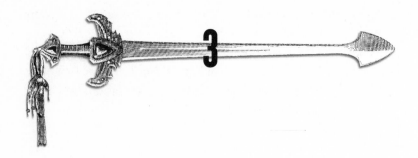

SMITH was looking at his watch and waiting like any other piece of dry furniture when Remo and Chiun arrived at the seat opposite the Trans World Airlines ticket counter.

"You're on time," he said to Remo, and to Chiun he gave a curt nod which might be interpreted as a small bow if one did not know that Smith was completely devoid of bows or any other sort of pleasantry. Courtesy required minute amounts of imagination and was therefore impossible for Dr. Harold W. Smith.

The Donsheim Memorial Hospital, perhaps the most modern in the entire Chicago area, was on the outskirts of the city in the pleasant suburbs of Hickory Hills, away from the knifings, shootings, and muggings of the inner city, which desperately needed a supermodern facility like Donsheim and therefore, by the laws of nature and politics, had no chance of ever getting one.

Smith walked around the hospital on the neat, grasslined concrete walk until he came to a gray door without a handle. It had only a lock, and Smith produced a key from a large keychain.

"One of your outlets?" asked Remo.

"In a way," said Smith.

"Everything is in a way," said Remo.

"The emperor knows the emperor's business," said Chiun, to whom anyone who employed the House of Sinanju was an emperor, as they had been in ages past. It was a breach of propriety that an assassin should talk openly to an emperor, which Remo understood to really mean that an emperor should never know what his assassin was thinking, a practical code worked out over centuries of experience.

Yet Remo was an American and Smith was an American, and just as some things of Sinanju might always remain a mystery to Remo, this openness between Remo and Smith was just as strange to Chiun.

The sharp smell of a hospital corridor brought back memories of fear to Remo, fear he had learned before he knew how to use his nerves for his own power. Smith counted doors, seven in all, and entered the eighth with another key. It was a chilly room, and Smith turned on the lights and buttoned the top button of his coat, shivering. Remo and Chiun stood still in their light autumn clothes. Eight large metal squares with handles stood neatly stacked against the wall. A sharp yellow fluorescent light cast a foreboding glare against the metal.

In the center of the room with white tile floors, smooth for easy scrubbing, were three bare tables, seven feet long and three feet wide with white plastic tops. The disinfectant could not hide it, the constant scrubbing could not hide it, nor could the chill eliminate it. The room smelled of the rot of death, that sickly sweet richness of fatty nodes decomposing and bacteria-heavy intestines dissolving themselves.

"He's in the third one up," said Smith.

Remo rolled out the drawer to the center table.

"William Ashley, thirty-eight, died of exposure," said Smith, looking at the bloated corpse. Facial hair had grown a stubble of beard through the slick dead skin. The eyes bulged under lids that reflected the fluorescent light above. The shoulders bulged as if Ashley had a giant's muscles there, and the hips swelled as if they wore football padding.

"We found through X-rays that all four main joints, shoulders and legs, were damaged. Victim's lungs had filled with fluid caused by exposure. Was found on a bare floor of a chilly Highland castle, unable to move because of joint injuries. In brief, gentlemen, he drowned from his own lung fluids," said Smith. He thrust his hands into his pockets for warmth and continued. "He was one of our employees. What I want to know is do you recognize the method of killing?"

"Cruelty has many forms and many faces. It is unfair to blame the House of Sinanju," said Chiun. "We are known for quietness and swiftness, nay, even for mercy in the speed with which we perform our duties. Kinder than nature we are and have been and always will be."

"Nobody was accusing your house," said Smith. "We want to know if you recognize the manner of death. I know that our methods of concealment and secrecy are confusing to you, but this man was one who worked for us and did not know it, like most of our employees."

"It is very hard to teach servants to know their job," said Chiun. "I am sure that, with the wisdom of Emperor Smith, within but a short time the laggardly servants shall know what they are doing and for whom they work."

"Not exactly," said Smith. "We do not wish them to know for whom they work."

"A wise idea. The less an ungrateful and stupid servant knows, the better. You are most wise, Emperor Smith. A credit to your race."

Smith cleared his throat and Remo smiled. Remo was the only man who bridged the gap between the two older men.

Remo understood that Smith was trying to explain that there was a force America was ashamed to admit existed, while Chiun believed an emperor should always remind his subjects what forces he had, the stronger the better.

"In any case," Smith said, "this matter bothers me. The strangeness of the death raises some questions and I'd like some answers."

"One cannot blame the House of Sinanju for every cruelty that happens," said Chiun. "Where did this occur?"

"Scotland," said Smith.

"Ah yes, a noble kingdom. A Master of Sinanju has not set foot there for hundreds of years. A fair and gracious people. Like yourself. Of much nobility are they."

"What I'm asking is do you recognize the manner of death? You'll notice the skin hasn't been broken but there has been incredible damage to the joints."

"To three joints," said Remo, "and that was because they didn't know what they were doing."

"I have X-rays," said Smith. "But the doctor who examined the body said all four joints were crushed. I remember that."

"He's wrong," said Remo. "Both shoulders and the right hip are crushed. Sloppy hits. The left leg was the way it should have been done. The leg was taken out without destroying the joint."

Smith set his lips tightly and took a plain gray envelope from his pocket. The X-rays had been reduced in size to look like . 35 millimeter film. Smith held the film strips up to the overhead light.

"Gracious. You're right, Remo," he said.

"He has been taught well," said Chiun.

"So you recognize the manner of death?" asked Smith.

"Sure. Somebody who didn't know what he was doing," said

Remo. "He got in a good lucky shot on the left leg, and then botched the job on the right hip and both shoulders."

Chiun was looking down at William Ashley's body, and he was shaking his head.

"There were at least two people who did this thing," he said. "The one who was correct in the left leg, and whoever else did the other work of butchery. Who was this person?"

"An employee," said Smith. "A computer programmer."

"And why would one wish to disgrace this whatever-you-said?"

"Computer programmer," said Smith.

"Correct. That is the word. Why would one wish to disgrace him?"

"I don't know," said Smith.

"Then I know nothing about the way of death," said Chiun.

"That doesn't help, Chiun," said Smith with a slight trace of exasperation. "What should we do?"

"Watch everything closely," answered Chiun, who knew that Americans liked to watch their disasters to give them a good headstart, until even the most dense person in the land realized something was wrong.

And then Chiun brought up something that had been bothering him. He had been promised a visit to his home. He knew it was a difficult journey and that it would cost much to deliver him to Sinanju. All was in preparedness even to the special boat that would slip him into Sinanju Harbor from under the water. But he had not gone at the time it was first ready because of his loyalty to Emperor Smith, long might he reign in the glory that was uniquely his.

"Yes, the submarine," said Smith.

Humbly, Chiun requested that he leave now for his visit. Korea in the late autumn was beautiful.

"Sinanju is freezing, windy ice in late Autumn," said Remo who had never been there.

"It is home," said Chiun.

"I know that is the home of the House of Sinanju," said Smith, "and you have served well. You have done wonders with Remo. It is a pleasure to assist you in returning you home to your village. But we will have difficulty in sending your shows to you. You might have to do without your television shows."

"I shall not be in Sinanju long," said Chiun. "Just until Remo gets there."

"I'd hate to have both of you out of the country," said Smith.

"Don't worry, I'm not going," said Remo.

"He will be there by the next full moon," said Chiun, and he said no more until the next day when he was preparing to board a plane that would take him to San Diego where his special ship would take him home.

Chiun waited until Smith had gone to a booth to buy insurance on Chiun's life, before he told Remo:

"That manner of death, Remo, it is very strange."

"Why strange?" said Remo. "A duffer with one lucky hit and three bad ones."

"There is a custom in Sinanju. When you wish to disgrace someone, to show that he is not even worth the killing, the ancient custom is to deliver four blows, then walk away and let your opponent die."

"You think that's what happened here?" Remo.

"I do not know what happened here, but I tell you to be careful until you join me in Sinanju."

"I'm not coming, Little Father," insisted Remo.

"By the next full moon," said Chiun, and then he signed the insurance form Smith put in his hands with a complicated ideograph that looked like the word IF drawn between two parallel lines.

As Chiun's plane took off, Smith said, "A mysterious man."

"Mysterious is just a western term for rude and thoughtless," said Remo as he felt the chill from nearby Lake Michigan whip over the guard rail at O'Hare.

"Mysterious is my term for what you and he are able to accomplish, what you do. For instance, without using guns."

Remo watched the white painted 707 with the stripes of red thrust into the air, its jets bellowing heat and smoke.

"It's not that complicated when you know," he said. "It makes a lot of sense. It's simple when you know, but in its execution it can be complicated. Especially in its simplicity."

"That's not really clear," said Smith.

"Look at him," said Remo as he saw the plane circle. "Look at him. Just going home like that. Well, I guess he's got a right to."

"You didn't say why you didn't use a gun."

"A gun sends a missile. Your hands are more controlled."

"Your hands are. But it's not karate, is it, or one of those?"

"No," said Remo. "Not one of those." Chicago was a cold and lonely place.

"Why you? Why Chiun? What makes you different?"

The plane too quickly became a speck. "What?" asked Remo.

"Why are you two so effective? I've had comparison readouts done with the martial arts, and once in a while there is an isolated instance of one of the things you do, but by and large it's just nothing like what you do."

"Oh, that," said Remo. "The guys with the wooden boards and their hands and stuff like that."

"Stuff like that," said Smith.

"Well, I'll try to explain," said Remo, and he explained as well as he could, as well as he had tried to explain it to himself. For he had not learned it in terms of almost anything he had known before meeting the Master of Sinanju.

First, the main difference might be the simple comparison of a professional football player and a touch football player. An injury that would send a Sunday touch passer to the sidelines wouldn't even be felt by a linebacker in the National Football League.

"The pro does it for his living. It's beyond those levels of entertainment or even ambition. It's survival. The pro lives by what he does. There's no comparison. The second is Sinanju itself. It was, like, born out of desperation. I've heard it from Chiun. Farming and fishing were so poor in that village that they had to drown their own babies."

"I know that the Masters of Sinanju supported their village by renting themselves out," Smith said. "Frankly, with the communists in North Korea I thought that might end."

"Well, it might end in fact, but where Sinanju started, the method and the thought, was every Master knowing it was the life of his target or the life of his village's children. Every Master. For thousands of years. Down to Chiun."

"Okay," said Smith. "For them, survival. But why your high competence?"

"Well, in learning, the Masters of Sinanju found out that most human muscles were on their way to becoming vestigial organs like the appendix. They learned that most everyone uses maybe ten percent of his strength or intelligence or what have you. Chiun's secret is teaching the muscles and nerves and stuff to use maybe thirty per cent. Or forty."

"That's what he does? Forty percent?"

"That's what I do," said Remo. "Chiun's the Master of Sinanju. He does one hundred per cent. On his bad days."

"And that's the explanation?"

"That's the explanation," said Remo, turning from the guardrail. "As to whether it's the truth, I don't have the vaguest. It's the way I explain it."

"I see," said Smith.

"No, you don't," said Remo. "And you never will."

WHEN Hawley Bardwell killed his first man with his hands, he knew he had to kill another. It was not like his first tackle in a football game where he heard the knee of the halfback pop in his ear. That was good. But to see a man going to die when you hit him with just your hand was beyond satisfaction.

It was like discovering you had this tremendous need only when it had been filled, and then, in a rush of feeling so good, Bardwell had stepped back on the bare, new polished wooden floor of that drafty castle and watched the black belt guy spin backward, reaching to support the shoulder that would never move again.

It was so simple it was laughable. The guy, named Ashley something, Bill Ashley or Ashley Williams or whatever, had taken that *sanchin-dachi* stance and had made a simple block, and then the left blocking arm itself was used to crack back into the joint. With the first pain of that, Bardwell had his second stroke right into the joint, and that was the beginning. Of course, he didn't have that guy all to himself. He had to share him, but he knew it was his blow that started it and when they left the guy squirming on the floor, that cold floor, pinned by the pain in his own joints, Bardwell knew football, karate, even three years boxing professionally, was like 3.2 beer compared to white lightning. It just didn't compare.

So when Mr. Winch promised him his own kill, personal, no-body else to share, Hawley Bardwell almost fell down and kissed his instructor's feet. Mr. Winch was what he had always wanted as a coach or as a commander in the Marines. Mr. Winch understood. Mr. Winch had given him the power. No matter how tempting so far, Hawley Bardwell, six-feet-four of hard knotted muscle and chilling blue eyes and a face that looked as if it were hacked out of a stone wall, kept his hands to their purposes assigned by Mr. Winch.

And when he had to wait by the cemetery in Rye, New York, and when a man who looked like his hit, but really wasn't, came to pay respects to one of the graves, that William Ashley, Hawley Bardwell held back. It was not the man. He was almost six feet tall with high cheekbones and deepset brown eyes, but he didn't have those thick wrists. So Hawley Bardwell waited his week as Mr. Winch had told him, and then drove down to New York City, parking his car in one of those incredibly expensive garages his wife had warned him about, and went to the Waldorf Astoria where he asked for Mr. Sun Yee as Mr. Winch had instructed.

Mr. Sun Yee was, of course, Mr. Winch, who said that he took many names, "Winch" being closest to what his name really was.

"Good afternoon, Mr. Winch," said Bardwell to the shorter man who met him in a shimmering green kimono.

"Come in, Bardwell," said Winch. "I take it you did not see your target."

"Right. How'd ya know?"

"I know many things," said Winch and smiled.

Bardwell felt uneasy about the smile, like a tickle in his stomach. If Lynette had not been so specific when they had started their journey to Scotland about Mr. Winch being the best thing—next to her of course—in Hawley's life, he might, even with his great respect, be suspicious of Mr. Winch. Great man, but that smile was something else.

"Well, let's see how much you have remembered," said Mr. Winch and Hawley Bardwell assumed the stance he had been drilled in and then redrilled in, and redrilled in. Knowing enough about the martial arts he knew there were other stances, but Mr. Winch had always said he must get this one right and feeling a hand on his spine, he knew he still didn't have it down perfectly.

This was the stance from which he had struck the blow in the castle. You stood with your weight within yourself, not rested on any foot, not so much evenly distributing the weight, but keeping the weight inside yourself, and being within yourself, you struck from the inside of your weight. From the outside, it looked like someone standing with feet slightly apart, almost slouching, and the blow came pop, first pushing the left-hand block back into your man's shoulder, then following. It sounded like *po-pop* when done right. Standing in the hotel suite, Hawley remembered the delicious sound of his hit's shoulder going *po-pop*.

Mr. Winch clapped and Hawley's big right arm slapped out first flat for the block and then instantly turning into the nukite hand sword it was supposed to be.

"Good," said Mr. Winch to Hawley Bardwell who stood with arm outstretched as if shaking hands with someone he didn't wish to get close to. "Very good."

"But this sort of leaves me open, don't it? I mean my whole body is open now. I've been practicing, and everytime I do this stroke, I think how open I am at the end of it."

"To add some protection to you," Mr. Winch said, "would make you less effective. Against the man who will be your target, your defensive blocks would become shattered bone. Of course, if you do not trust me . . ."

"I trust you, Mr. Winch."

"Good. Because now I will give you your man."

"Where will I find him?"

"He will find you," said Mr. Winch. He outlined a plan under which, if Hawley Bardwell followed it faithfully, he would not only have his man but $15,000 as well. And the $15,000 came first.

There were many strange things he did not understand, but to Hawley Bardwell this plan was a delight. Not only would he realize money, as Lynette always said he would if he stayed with Mr. Winch, but he would have his main target, and others, first, to practice on.

Yes, he could kill them if he first practiced the shoulder stroke, and no, there was no chance of his being caught by anyone, except the man who would be his ultimate target.

Bardwell was so excited he wanted to tell Lynette that the place he was going to take the $15,000 from was the very place she worked as a teller. But Mr. Winch had not said he could discuss it, even with his wife, so on the evening of his plan he just told her he was going for a little walk. The way he said it must have warned her, for she said, "Watch your ass there, Hawley," and he responded, "Sure enough," and then he just moseyed out onto the main street of Tenafly, New Jersey, with the shops closing and the police sleepily cruising the dwindling traffic and the crisp wetness of winter upon the New Jersey city waiting for the grace of snow.

As Mr. Winch had explained it, the whole operation was an extension of the stroke. Your protection was your offense.

Down the street he could see lights on in the second story of the Tenafly Trust and Savings Corp. He had two hundred dollars on deposit there, the most he and Lynette could put away on his gym instructor's salary. As she had said so many times, at least they weren't getting in the hole if they could put away even two dollars a week. Lynette always had such good reasoning. Perhaps that was why, of all the wives of his pupils, Mr. Winch seemed to favor her.

Bardwell moved on the street behind the bank. Mr. Winch had warned him not to cut into the narrow alley behind the bank until he was just opposite that building. Police were always checking for burglars in the back of the smaller shops and he should cut his alley time to the minimum. For the police, the bank was the one building that needed the least night supervision. It had the modern time-lock safe, the kind that had put safecrackers out of business. All the money went in there at five every night and was not available to human hands until 8:30 A.M. The illusion of safety was their biggest weakness, Mr. Winch had said.

Bardwell saw the high white concrete ledge of the bank roof rising above the yellow two-story frame house of this residential street just behind the main thoroughfare. He moved quietly down the driveway across a well-mowed yard and over a fence and he was in the alley. He could smell the rich pungent odor from the delicatessen and hear his feet make a small splash as he walked through a puddle left by that afternoon's rain. The bank had three doors, two of them with alarms and bars and wire mesh, for they protected the entrance to the main floor and vault. By financial logic, the third door needed no expensive alarm system for it led only to the executive offices of the president, the senior vice president, and the comptroller. It was secure because there was an effective alarm seal between their offices and the money below, a single inside door.

So Bardwell's hand closed on the key Mr. Winch had given

him, and he took it out of his pocket and felt for the lock. He paused and listened. A footstep crushed a tin can. A flashlight sent a terrifying yellow beam down the alley. Bardwell pushed himself into the doorway as he felt the key click. He could disappear into the door but Mr. Winch had told him that at night movement, not objects, attracts attention. So he fought his instinct to put the door between himself and the light, and he kept stillness within him as Mr. Winch had taught. The light continued and the steps came right behind him and he expected a billy stick in his back. It was so close he could hear breathing. But the steps went on also, and when they were a good hundred feet down the alley, Bardwell eased himself into the alcove behind the door and, with a relieving click, shut the door between himself and the outside.

It was dark and he ran his left hand against the wall. He felt a linen-type wallpaper whose ridges were glossy smooth to the fingertips. His left foot bumped a solid vertical. The toe eased up until it was at the first level of the first step and then pushed forward until it hit another vertical. He pressed down on the foot and lifted the other, and slowly he began to climb the back steps. It seemed that the door came on him suddenly, bumping him in the chin.

"Hold it," he heard a man's voice. "Someone's at the door."

"Rubbish," came another man's voice.

"I heard something. I told you I heard something."

"You heard your losing streak. Shut up and deal."

Bardwell pushed open the door and stepped up into the lit office, a plush, beige-carpeted expanse of modern furniture and hanging chrome lights, leather couches, and a shining mahogany table in the shape of a hexagon. Five men looked up from their cards and chips. It was this room's light he had seen from Main Street. It was from this room that he would rob the bankers, despite their time-lock vault downstairs that would be as useless as marbles in a microscope.

"It's Hawley Bardwell," said the senior vice president of Tenafly Trust and Savings. He had his thickfingered hands over his cards, his sludgy gray eyes glancing from Bardwell to the man on his left, whose cards were tilted forward, an absent-minded exposure obviously caused by Bardwell's entrance.

"Who?" said a flaccid-faced man with crowning silver hair whom Bardwell recognized as the president of Tenafly Trust and Savings. His cards had been lowered beneath the table.

"Lynette Bardwell's husband," said the senior vice president.

"Who?" said the president, adjusting his sleek horn-rim glasses.

"Assistant head teller. Won 'employee of the year' award," said the senior vice president and the president's face squinted in fruitless mental search. The vice president leaned across the table and whispered:

"The blonde with the nice ass, sir."

"Oh. You're the gym teacher they fired for some sort of brutality, Bardwell."

"I was the football coach."

"Oh, well. What do you want? We're having an important meeting, as you can see. Tell me what you want, and after that you can tell me how you got in."

"No meeting," said Bardwell. "It's a card game."

"This is our regular Thursday night meeting, and sometimes we end it with cards," said the president of Tenafly Trust and Savings. "It's also none of your business, Mr. Bardwell. Now, what do you want?"

Hawley Bardwell smiled a delicious smile and he could taste his joy, just looking at the five men. He could no longer resist. He took the closest, whose head was twisted around looking at him and popped him right square in the forehead with the heel of his right hand. The skull whipped back like a giant lead sash had yanked it and the neck snapped like stretched cellophane punctured by a toothpick. The head hit the table, startling the chips in the center with a shock wave.

Before anyone could adjust to the kill and realize this was something more than a fistfight, Bardwell moved left into the president of Tenafly Trust and Savings, who was raising himself in indignation. Bardwell lowered him with a stroke face center with the fingertips of his flat hand, splitting the jaw like an over-stuffed sausage casing. The eyes blinked, the head lowered, and Bardwell flipped the unconscious man across the room and charged into a man backpedaling away, holding his cards in front of his face and wincing. As funny as the fan of cards seemed, they obstructed a solid stroke and Bardwell would not risk his flesh against the celluloid edges. The burly comptroller was across the table swinging at Bardwell from his knees, planted on the pile of chips, and this gave Bardwell his shoulder stroke. The man's left-hand punch was blocked, then his shoulder popped, and Bardwell's right hand drove to the nerves and was back. The comptroller shrieked in pain. Then the senior vice president, who had known Lynette had a nice ass, did a very foolish thing. He went toes centered into the *sanchin dachi* and Bardwell got his second shoulder shot this time with even more help from the blocking elbow. The senior vice president spun as if he were on a cord, and Bardwell moved back into the man, who now cringed in the corner. Bardwell got the cards down with a light kick into the groin and then from a close position, well-centered within himself, used the shoulder stroke skull center. Perhaps it was the wall corners, holding the head square like the inside of a triangle vise, but there was no pop of the neck. Bardwell saw his fingertips surrounded by bloody forehead up to his knuckles.

His fingertips felt warm gush, and he knew his nails were in the man's brain. He eased his hand from the moistness and it struck him as odd that it felt like Lynette's vagina. He wiped the reddish gook off on the comptroller's white shirt. Then at his leisure and pleasure, with foot and chairleg, he finished the comptroller, the senior vice president, and the president of Tenafly Trust and Savings, and took from their persons $14,375.

"There's $625 missing," thought Bardwell, but he would not delay longer looking for it. Like almost every employer, these bankers thought their secrets were safe because no one dared mention anything to them. As Mr. Winch had said, "A servant is a person who knows the most about his master and tells him the least." So their secret Thursday night poker game was a secret just to them. Others knew, and men as brilliant as Mr. Winch could find out, about bankers who knew most of all that a check wasn't nearly as good as cash, especially in a gambling game. Bankers who wouldn't trust their colleagues for a temporary loan, bankers who every Thursday night brought $3,000 apiece to a poker game and shielded the game from the street with only their minds, not even bothering to draw drapes. Bankers who thought there was nothing safer than a bank. Dead men.

That night, when Lynette lusted, Hawley Bardwell turned away from her in the bed. How could he tell her he had already been totally satisfied that evening, and just sex with a woman would be a pale letdown, something akin to masturbating after spending a weekend with a sexy movie star.

He not only had what he wanted, but, as Mr. Winch said, he would have more. It was all to get the man he wanted. His target.

When the target was notified of what the press called "the horror at the bank," he thought the call from upstairs was notification that Chiun was returning from Sinanju, or had changed his mind about going.

"No, Remo," said Smith. "Sub left on schedule. He's gone. But I would suggest you read carefully a very interesting story out of Tenafly, New Jersey. I think we've been given a break."

"Why?"

"You don't know what happened in Tenafly? It's the biggest story in the country today. It has all the gruesome and irrelevant facts that the press loves. But there's something in it for us, too. I'm surprised you didn't catch it on a newsstand."

"I haven't been out today."

"It was in yesterday's papers, too. I thought you would be in Tenafly by now."

"Wasn't out yesterday either," said Remo. "Or the day before."

"Well, I think you should get out now and look at the story. Particularly the way the men died."

"Yeah. Right. Right away," said Remo. He hung up and watched the light on the taping machine that indicated Chiun's programs were being recorded for his return. The machine would turn off automatically by three-thirty P.M. that afternoon, but Remo watched the light anyway for the whole afternoon. By four P.M. he had a sock on and by seven P.M. he had the other sock on, and by ten o'clock he was in his shorts with trousers, and by the time it was all put together with turtleneck sweater and tan loafers, it was eleven-thirty P.M., so Remo postponed the trip until the next morning when, wearing the clothes he had slept in, he left the motel at four-thirty A.M. because he couldn't sleep anymore.

The clerk at the motel outside Raleigh-Durham Airport asked where Remo's friend was because everyone had taken a liking to him even though the old Oriental didn't go out much, and Remo answered:

"I don't need him and I don't even miss him."

"Oh sure, sure," said the clerk. "Just asking if he was going to come back, sort of."

"I couldn't care less," said Remo.

"Sure," said the clerk.

"You got newspapers here?"

"Just yesterday's."

"Fine," said Remo.

"When will you be back?"

"Couple of days or so. Don't touch my television."

"Sure. What should I do if the old fella comes back while you're gone?"

"He won't," said Remo, and he heard his voice crack. On the plane, which landed at Newark, he read about the "the horror at the bank."

He took a taxi to Tenafly, a rather long and expensive trip, and when he got to the bank there appeared to be no police lines.

"In back," said a passerby. "It happened up there on the second floor, but everyone is in the back."

In the alley behind the bank, Remo found a police cordon and a small crowd hanging around in front of it. He checked his wallet, leafed through cards identifying him as an FBI man, Treasury agent, representative of the Food and Drug Administration, and a freelance magazine writer. Unlike other cover identifications, every one of these cards were real. There was a listing in every one of these organizations for a man named Remo Pelham or Remo Bednick or Remo Dalton or Remo Slote. The organizations never saw him because he was always on special assignment, but he would always be vouched for if someone checked.

"*Pinnacle Magazine,*" said Remo, flashing the card to a patrolman at the cordon. "Who's in charge?"

It was a dull twenty-five minutes as he listened to the deputy chief of police, who three times repeated the spelling of his own name, explain the gruesome five-man murder. The deputy chief wasn't sure if the motive was robbery because $625 in cash was found in the center of the table under a pile of chips. But it could have been robbery because everyone knew the five bankers always brought $3,000 apiece to their regular Thursday night poker game. It was a thing people didn't talk about much. There were, the deputy chief explained, at least three instruments used in the mass murder. He personally believed one of the instruments was a blunted spear. A chair leg was another of them. They couldn't get prints from the chair yet but don't write that, said the deputy chief.

"The horror of men's minds always astounds me," said the deputy chief and asked Remo if he wanted an eight by ten glossy of the deputy chief taken upon his promotion to that rank.

"You say these guys were hit in the head, shoulders and chest?"

"Right. One guy's skull was cracked clean through. That's where I got my blunted spear theory. You might want to call this the blunted spear murder case. Did you get my name correctly? I don't see you taking notes." The chief looked at the crowd on the other side of the police lines and waved. "Hi, Hawley, c'mon over," he shouted with a wave, and in a lower voice said to Remo: "Used to be our football coach. Good one, too. Fired him because he wanted to make winners out of spoiled brats. You know, New Yorkers coming over here. Afraid their little Sammy's going to get his big beak broken . . . don't quote me . . . well, hello, Hawley."

And the deputy chief introduced Remo to the man, who stood a good four inches above Remo, a broad-shouldered, well-muscled man whose walk aroused Remo's curiosity. It had a certain familiar balance, not quite the way Remo or Chiun walked, but a hint of similar principles.

"This is Hawley Bardwell. Wife works in the bank and he's worried about her safety. Comes here every day since the incident. Hawley, this is Remo Slote. He's a magazine writer."

Bardwell offered his big hand to shake and Remo noticed the man's eyes focus on his wrists. It was a strong handshake and Remo wiggled out of it by collapsing his palm and thrusting his hand into his pocket.

"You don't have to worry, Hawley. Whoever did it is a thousand miles away by now," said the deputy chief.

"I guess you're right," said Bardwell. He was smiling.

"Can I see the bodies?" asked Remo.

"Oh, two were buried right away. Religious thing, you know. The other three are still at the funeral homes. Their burial's tomorrow."

"I'd like to see the bodies."

"Well, that's sort of delicate. The families are having closed coffin funerals. But we have pictures back at headquarters."

"Not as good as the bodies," said Remo.

"I'm a close friend of one of the families," said Bardwell. "Maybe I can help."

"I didn't know that," said the deputy chief.

"Yeah," said Bardwell. "That is, before everyone started forgetting they knew me when I was fired."

"I always supported you, Hawley. I thought you did wonders with what you had. Always supported you."

"Not publicly," said Bardwell.

"Well, not exactly out in the open. I've got my job."

"Yeah," said Bardwell. "C'mon, Mr. Slote," he said to Remo. "I'll show you the bodies that are still above ground."

"You shouldn't take it so hard, Hawley. You'll get another job," said the deputy chief.

"I expect so," said Bardwell. All the way to McAlpin's Funeral

Home, he explained to Remo how it must have been a dozen men who killed the bankers, because of the terrible injuries.

"Uh-huh," agreed Remo.

McAlpin's was a dark-carpeted, quiet private house, transformed with some neat carpentry into a funeral home.

"They'll be waking tonight. But we can get a good look now because no one's here in the afternoon," said Bardwell.

"I thought you knew the family."

"That's just something I told the chief. He's got balls of tapioca."

The coffin was white ash, polished to a high gloss, and Remo wondered at all the fine furniture that was made just to be planted with an occupant who couldn't care less. The room smelled of Pineclear air freshener, and the two walked up the aisle of dark folding chairs. Bardwell opened the coffin. A man's skull was waxed down the middle with skin-colored wax powdered over. Remo pressed down on the wax to see how wide the cavity was. His thumb collected powder and he rubbed it away with a forefinger.

"They had to scoop out some of the brains, I hear, just to get the head closed again," said Bardwell. Remo saw perspiration form on his forehead. Saliva collected in a small pool at a corner of his lips.

"I heard there were some people with their shoulders hurt," said Remo. "That's what the papers said. That they were immobilized first at the shoulder and then killed."

"Yeah," said Bardwell in a heavy breathy gasp. "Whadddya think of that head, huh? Isn't that the worst thing you've ever seen? Huh?"

"No," said Remo. "The guy should have used a gun instead of his hands. If he's going to use his hands that way, he might as well use something wild as a gun."

"What wild?"

"You don't need that much in the central forehead. The hand must have gone into it up to the knuckles. You only need a break and a minimum of pressure inside the brain for an instant kill. Sloppy. I bet it was some karate idiot on a spree."

"But don't you think it's fantastic that somebody with a bare hand could do that? Don't ya? Huh? Don't ya?" said Bardwell.

"Inferior," said Remo and he noticed Bardwell smiling and centralizing his balance, and then because he had been trained to, Remo did something wrong because his body did something right. Bardwell's right hand shot out at Remo and Remo took it, but in doing so, he felt a small direct pressure on his left shoulder and Bardwell's hand kept going through and into the shoulder. An insane stroke. A stroke of such incredible, suicidal stupidity that Remo had never seen it before. And what made it so insane was that the power and accuracy required training, but no one would ever train for something like that. It was suicide against anyone with a serious level of competence.

Bardwell's right hand was into Remo's shoulder while at the same time his face, whole head, throat, and heart were open as a gift to Remo's right hand or right leg. It was a here-I-am-kill-me thrust, and Remo's right hand had but a half a foot to go to catch Bardwell's throat, splitting the thorax and driving pieces of it back into the vertebrae. Bardwell had set himself up for his own death just to get in a cheapie shoulder shot. Remo felt the pain in the left shoulder and wiggled the fingers of his left hand. He could still do that. But the arm would raise only slightly.

Bardwell could raise nothing. He lay at the foot of the coffin, his tongue lounging out of his mouth, forced out of his jaw by the pressure from the throat.

"Shit," said Remo. He had found the man who could talk about the death of William Ashley, and he had killed him because he had reacted automatically. It was almost as if the man had been set up so Remo would have to kill him. Now Remo had not only stifled his possible explanation of why Smitty's man was killed, but he also had a body to get rid of. He worked with his right hand, letting his painful left shoulder hang limp.

Underneath the comptroller with the patched-up forehead, underneath the white silk and the styrofoam red rosary, was bedding, the final support for a body that needed no support. Remo pushed back the white ash lid and with his right hand grabbed the belt of the corpse and deposited it on the other side of the lid. He paused and listened. No movement. No one was coming. He whistled a moving tune he had heard Aretha Franklin sing, remembering only the "needya, baby, baby, needya, baby."

He took the fine seam out of the silk covering at the bottom of the coffin and found cheap cardboard supports. He ripped the cardboard down to bare unfinished wood and placed it in a pile at his feet. His one hand worked like a flashing blade as he picked up the rolling beat of the song and lost the tune so totally he would never find it again.

He grabbed a handful of Bardwell's muscled stomach and hoisted the corpse up into the bare bottom of the coffin. He flattened Bardwell for a better fit, eliminating the bumps of the chest and head without breaking skin. Then, crushing the cardboard at his feet, he reconstructed the well sides around Bardwell and covered it again with the white silk, carefully tucking in the edges.

"Perfect almost," muttered Remo. "Needya, baby, baby."

He took the comptroller of the Tenafly Savings and Trust Company off the lid and put him gently into his final resting place and stepped back to examine his work.

"Shit." The comptroller was three inches too high. Maybe he

could get an inch and a half off him and this time he cracked the corpse's spinal column, put a hairline midchest, and pressed down on the groin area, for the comptroller had been well padded in the posterior. Where Bardwell was slim, the comptroller was fat and vice versa. So it worked.

Remo stepped back again.

"Nice fit," he said. Of course, by the time the wake became active, with people coming by to pay last respects, the release of Bardwell's sphincter muscles might cause an unnerving smell, but for now, a nice job. Remo heard someone and quickly touched up the powder on the comptroller's cold face.

"Baby, baby, needya, baby," sung Remo and from behind him a whiny voice called out:

"You there. What are you doing with the deceased?"

Remo turned and saw a man in black suit, white shirt, and black tie with a very pale face, pale because he used the same powder on himself as he had used on the comptroller.

"Just a friend of the deceased."

"The wake's tonight. I know who you are. I know your kind. If you've played with that man's privates . . ."

"What?" said Remo.

"Sick," said the man. "You're sick. Sick. Sick."

"I was just saying goodbye to a friend."

"I bet, sicko. I know your kind. Hang around funeral homes trying to get jobs but you'll never get one in mine. You know why? You're sick is why. That's why."

"If you say so," said Remo.

"Glad I caught you before you could get to anything."

"Thank you," said Remo, taking it as a compliment for his work.

At the bank he saw the deputy chief again, who introduced him to the head teller, who pointed out Lynette Bardwell. She had a strong, elegant face with a faint almond shaping to her gray eyes and neat, bouncy blond hair, streaked with just the right touch of darker blond. Her lips were full and moist and she carried herself with a calmness. Even under the formal stiff white blouse and tweed skirt, Remo could sense the beauty of her body. He wondered what she had seen in Bardwell.

He waited until the bank was closed to customers and then, with the head teller's permission, took her into one of the private rooms where customers examined safe deposit boxes.

"Why do you want to interview me?" asked Lynette. She was only in her early twenties, yet she seemed unflustered by the interview.

"Because your husband is the man who slaughtered those bankers upstairs."

Lynette Bardwell lit a filter tip cigarette and exhaled.

"I know that," she said. "What do you want?"

"I'm interested in his friends, who might have taught him what he knew about handling himself in a fight."

"And just who are you?"

"I'm the man your husband confessed to."

"That dumb bastard," said Lynette, and her composure disappeared as she surrendered to teary sobs. "That dumb bastard."

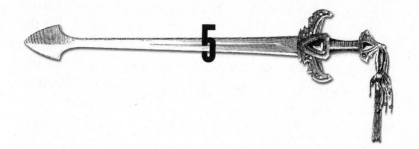

As he watched her weep, Remo realized he had overestimated Lynette Bardwell's toughness. He had listened to that nasal bray that New Jersey women called human speech, and had been fooled by it. Lynette Bardwell was just a woman, soft and yielding. He decided not to tell her that her husband was dead.

Lynette blotted her eyes with a tissue and looked up. "If you want to talk all night, you've got to buy me a sandwich."

"Don't you think Hawley will mind?" asked Remo not really caring. For Hawley Bardwell to mind would involve his raising himself from the dead, getting past one body, and out of a sealed coffin. Remo wasn't worried.

"Suppose he does?"

"He's a pretty fast guy with his hands, I suppose. He might light into you pretty hard."

"Hah. That'll be the day," said Lynette. "Look, big magazine writer, are you on an expense account or not?"

"Yes."

"Then no sandwich. Dinner. A real dinner."

Lynette Bardwell's idea of a real dinner was a cinder block structure outside the city that had changed from diner to restaurant by adding wood paneling, tables instead of booths, and turning down the lights. No one apparently had bothered to tell the chef of the change in status because the menu was still built upon one-plate meals, most of them seeming to specialize in chopped meat.

Lynette ordered salad—"it's nice and crisp here all the time"— to which Remo did not comment, contenting himself instead with the thought that so was birchbark. She wanted Thousand Island dressing, sirloin steak rare, baked potato with cheese mixed in, asparagus tips with hollandaise sauce, and a Tom Collins in a tall glass to start everything off.

Remo asked for a glass of water to start things off, and rice, if the cook had long-grained wild rice, with no seasoning, no salt, no pepper, no monosodium glutamate, and if they did not have long-grained wild rice, he would settle for just the water.

Which he did, because the chef had never heard of wild rice and if it was made by Minute Rice he would have known about it. The waitress snapped her gum as she told Remo this and delivered the water. He sipped it. It was good to be back home in New Jersey where the water contained trace elements of every one of the known elements, including macadam.

Lynette sipped at her Tom Collins, carefully replacing it on the paper napkin between sips, and asked Remo suddenly:

"What's wrong with your shoulder?"

"Why?"

"It looks like you're holding it funny," she said. "Like it's hurting."

"Touch of arthritis," said Remo, who thought he had been disguising the immobility of his left arm. "Where did Hawley learn his karate?"

"Oh, he's been at it for years. There are places in Jersey City that he goes to."

"You know the name of them?" asked Remo, putting the water aside for when he might really want it, like after a thirty-day trek in the Sahara.

"Not really. I don't pay any attention to that. I don't know what kick some men get out of hopping around in pajamas."

"You prefer men hopping around without pajamas?"

Lynette giggled. "Well, maybe not hopping," she said. She raised the glass to her mouth and looked over the top of it at Remo. "What makes you think Hawley killed those bankers?"

"He told me," said Remo.

"Just like that? He told you? 'I killed the bankers and stole their money?'"

"Almost," Remo said. "He kind of bragged about the different strokes used on them. He talked too much about it not to have done it."

"Did you tell him you knew?"

"Yes."

"And then what?"

"He said he was going on a trip."

"Somehow I don't believe you," she said. "If Hawley knew you knew, then I think he would have smacked you around, too."

"Maybe he was afraid of me. Maybe I look like another guy who hops around wearing pajamas."

Lynette shook her head. "No, no. Definitely not. You're not the pajama type."

"How did you know he did the killings?" asked Remo.

"He told me." Remo waited for her to fill in the blanks, but she said nothing more.

"Have another drink," said Remo.

Lynette Bardwell did. And another. And another. That was before the steak (well done and stringy), the baked potato (burned to a crisp), and the asparagus tips (not tips but spears).

She did not seem to mind. She ate doggedly through it, reveling in the dim lights and the canned music by two hundred and two violins, and she had yet another drink and leaned on Remo heavily as she lurched with him toward her car.

"Suppose Hawley's home?" said Remo. "Maybe I should stop near your house and you can drive home yourself?"

"He won't be," she said with some confidence. "Home, James."

She snored a little bit. She woke up near her house, sat upright, and snapped her fingers. "I just remembered," she said thickly.

"What?"

"There's a guy Hawley practices with. Another karate freak."

"What's his name?"

"Fred Westerly."

"Where do I find him? I'd like to know more about all this karate stuff."

"He's a cop. I remember now. A policeman. A lieutenant or something. I think he's in the training school. Hawley mentioned him once. Yeah. Jersey City. He trains cops in Jersey City."

"Fred Westerly, huh?"

"Thass right," Lynette said, and her head dropped onto Remo's shoulder and she was asleep again.

Getting out of the car, she lurched heavily against Remo's left shoulder, forcing him to grit his teeth against the explosions of pain that sounded inside his skull. Biting hard on his lip, he sleepwalked her upstairs to the bedroom in the Bardwell's tiny frame Cape Cod on the edge of town.

She put up no resistance as Remo undressed her and put her under the covers. Before he left, Remo did a thing to the nerves under her left armpit and whispered in her ear, "Dream of me. I'm going to be back."

She smiled in her sleep.

As he walked away from the house, Remo saw a small light click on in the upstairs bathroom.

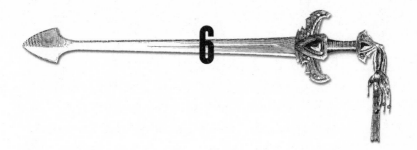

CAPTAIN Lee Enright Leahy of the U.S. Submarine *Darter* had made this trip before. Five times in five years and each time he understood it less. Because of the destination, he couldn't embark from Japan. Russia and North Korea got copy on any ships leaving through the Sea of Japan and especially submarines, and anyone making port at Taiwan or the Ryukyu Islands might as well forget it. You could add China, too. So much for normal secrecy for normal trips.

For this trip, you had to start evasive action at San Diego, spreading the word you were heading for Australia, letting crew wives know their husband's next port was Darwin. You crossed the Pacific practically at flank speed, entering the East China Sea submerged between Miyako and Naha Islands. Then you headed north into the East China Sea, risked the China coast within a hundred miles of Shanghai, and kept on the China side as you entered the Yellow Sea, because if the Chinese did get copy on you, there would be a delay, hopefully, before they would inform North Korea. At latitude thirty-eight and longitude one twenty-four, you veered north by northeast into the West Korean Bay and then, in that infernal joint where North Korea and Communist China meet, you let out a team of SEALS (Sea Air Land) boys, the descendants of frogmen, Rangers, OSS, and every other whacko group that the military was forced to use on missions on which they would not send the sane.

And all this to deliver a tiny purse of gold to an old woman who would meet them on the coast, just outside the village of Sinanju, at three A.M. every November 12.

What puzzled Captain Leahy was that the bag contained less than $10,000 in gold, and it cost hundreds of thousands of dollars to deliver and risked millions plus an international incident. He had wondered why the CIA (he was sure it was the CIA) couldn't find a safer and cheaper contact route, or at least deliver three years' gold at once, thus eliminating two risky trips.

So when the *Darter* turned north into the East China Sea, only to surface later that evening, Captain Leahy thought he would visit with the passenger. This time they had a passenger who was not only bringing the gold, but clumsy bolts of cloth, boxes of jewels, a clumsily framed, autographed picture of an insignificant soap opera actor, and three outsized lacquered trunks. How they were ever going to fit into the rubber rafts, he didn't know. But he was grateful that he had gotten away with refusing to surface and carry electronic gear that would pick up, of all things, television shows that some idiot in the Pentagon was thinking of beaming to the Pacific just for the *Darter*.

At that suggestion, Leahy had popped his apple.

"Dammit. There are safer and saner ways to transmit information than through television," he had said.

"It's not exactly information," said the admiral who coordinated CIA-Navy relations.

"Well, what is it?"

"Television shows."

"You mean newscasts or something?"

"Not exactly. The shows listed are, minus commercials, twenty-one minutes and fifteen seconds of *As the Planet Revolves,* thirteen minutes and ten seconds, minus commercials, of *The Young and the Raw*, twenty-four minutes and forty-five seconds, minus commercials, of *The Edge of Life*. Total transmission time would be under an hour."

"I'm supposed to surface between China and North Korea, with Russia looking on, to pick up soap operas? What's happened to you people?"

"We got the commercials knocked out," said the admiral. "With commercials, it would go an hour and fifteen minutes."

"What is this thing anyhow?" asked Captain Leahy.

"We're not in the habit of letting everyone be privy to the broader picture, Captain."

"Is anyone privy to the broader picture?"

"Well, frankly, Captain, I don't know either. This one's so supersecret I'm not even totally sure it's CIA. Do you want me to put down an absolute 'no' on the surfacing for television shows?"

"Like slightly," said Captain Leahy.

"You're refusing the mission if you have to surface for the shows?"

"I am refusing."

"Can't say as I blame you. Let me see if we can get the shows bumped."

By sailing time, the admiral was beaming triumph. "I went to the wire and we won," he said. He was wearing civilian clothes and standing on the conning tower of the *Darter*. "You're down to three steamer trunks in the rubber rafts."

"You ever try to paddle a steamer trunk in a rubber raft in the West Korea Bay in November?"

"You don't have to succeed," said the admiral with a broad wink. "All you've got to do is try. Good luck, Lee."

"Thank you, sir," said Captain Leahy. Now he remembered the admiral's wink as he passed the steamer trunks lashed to the bulkhead and knocked on the door of the passenger's compartment.

"It's Captain Leahy."

"Yes," came the squeaky voice.

"I want you to know we're entering the Yellow Sea," said Captain Leahy.

"Then you are not lost. Is that what you are telling me?"

"Well, not exactly. I wanted to talk to you about debarkation."

"Are we at Sinanju?"

"No. The Yellow Sea. I told you."

"Then there is no need to discuss whatever-it-is-you-said."

"Well, your trunks are sort of heavy and I'm not sure the SEALS can paddle them in."

"Oh, how typical white," came the voice from inside the compartment. "You have the only ships that cannot carry things."

"We could carry in a whole city if we had to, but not into old Kim Il Sung's North Korea. The premier is not one of our most ardent admirers."

"Why should he be when you are such a defiler of the arts? Do not deny it. It was you who refused to give an old man the simple pleasure of a daytime drama."

"Sir, we might all have gotten ourselves blown out of the water if we surfaced to pick up those television shows. I refused for your own good. Would you want to be captured by the Chinese?"

"Captured?"

"Yes. You know, taken prisoner. Thrown in a dungeon."

"The hands that can do that have yet to be put on human wrists. Away, you imitation sailor."

"Sir, sir . . ." But there was no answer and the passenger did not come up on deck or respond to knocks until the *USS Darter* finally surfaced off the coast of Sinanju. All the men were bundled in cold weather gear, their eyes peering out of cold weather masks; the decks were icy and the wind was tossing ice spears at their backs.

"Here he is," said one of the sailors, and the deck crew stared in disbelief, for a frail old man, barely tall enough to see over the bridge, climbed down to the deck in only a dark gray kimono whipped by the China winds, his wisps of beard fluttering, his head uncovered, his hands in repose beneath the kimono.

"Sir, sir," shouted the captain. "The SEALS can't get your trunks into the rubber raft. They won't fit and even if they did, in this sea, you'd capsize."

"Do you think the Master of Sinanju would entrust his treasures to an imitation sailor, working for an imitation Navy? Bring the trunks to the deck and lash them together, end to end like a train. You have seen trains, have you not?"

And thus it was done upon the boat of the white men with the round eyes, and the three trunks of the Master of Sinanju that would float were bound together. For the Master had rightly thought to bring only those trunks that could sustain themselves, knowing this in all clarity: A sailor who cannot haul simple baggage for something as precious as a drama of beauty and truth is a sailor to whom one could not entrust the wealth of a village.

And wrapped in skins and clothes of nylon, their tender faces covered from the home winds that were strange to them, the white sailors lowered the trunks that had been carved and welded by Park Yee, the carpenter, the trunks which had lasted in the new land discovered by the grandfather of Chiun in the year of the dog—the year before the good czar sold the bridge of the North Peninsula called Alaska to the same Americans that Yui, the grandfather of Chiun, had discovered.

And the trunks in the home sea floated behind the flimsy yellow boats of the white men. Now, know it that all the white men were not white in color. Some were black and some were brown and some even yellow. Yet their minds had been destroyed by whiteness so that their souls were white.

Chiun, the Master of Sinanju, himself rode the last boat near the trunks, which were tribute for his people. And lo, upon the darkened shore, he saw standing a beautiful young maiden, upon the rocks above the large cove. But alas, she was alone.

"Ever see such a pig?" asked a bosun's mate, nodding toward the fat-faced Korean woman squatting on the ugly outcropping of rock.

"Yeah. In a zoo," said the other paddler.

"At least she wears heavy clothes. The old gook must have antifreeze for blood. This wind'd numb a yak."

The radio on the raft crackled with a message from the sub, surfaced six hundred yards offshore. A column of lights was approaching from Sinanju. Heavy vehicles. Possibly tanks.

The squad leader of the SEALS informed his passenger of approaching trouble. "You can return to the sub with us. But we have to go now. Right now."

"I am home," Chiun said to the young man.

"That means you're staying?"

"I will not flee."

"Okay, fella. It's your ass."

Chiun smiled and watched the frightened men scramble back into their rafts and paddle back toward the ship that bobbed on the waters of the bay. The girl climbed down from the rocks, approached, and bowed deeply. Her words were like music to Chiun, the words of his childhood and of games in which he had learned the secrets of the body and mind and of the forces of the universe. The language of home was sweet.

"Hail, Master of Sinanju, who sustains the village and keeps the code faithfully, leader of the House of Sinanju. Our hearts cry a thousand greetings of love and adoration. Joyous are we upon the return of him who throttles the universe."

"Graciously throttles the universe," corrected Chiun.

"Graciously throttles the universe," repeated the girl, who had been practicing all week and had worried only about "adoration," because that was the word she had forgotten most. "Graciously throttles the universe."

"Why are you alone, child?"

"It is not permitted anymore to practice the old ways."

"Who does not permit?"

"The People's Democratic Republic."

"The whores in Pyongyang?" asked Chiun.

"We are not allowed to call the government that anymore."

"And why do you venture here, child?"

"I am the granddaughter of the carpenter by the bay. We are the last family who believes in the old ways."

"My cousins and my wife's cousins and my wife's brothers and their cousins, what of them?"

"They are of the new way. Your wife is long since gone."

In the way the girl said this, Chiun knew there was something she was hiding that was painful.

"I knew of my wife's death," said Chiun. "But there is something else. What is it?"

"She denounced the House of Sinanju, Master."

Chiun smiled. "Such is the way of her family. Such always was her nature. Do not weep, my child. For in all the universe, there never was a harder heart nor more base family."

"The People's Government forced her," said the girl.

"No," said Chiun. "They could not force what was not there. Her family was always jealous of the House of Sinanju and she came to it with bitterness. And she led me to the great mistake." Chiun's voice broke on the last two words as he remembered how he had taken in the son of his brother, at his wife's continual urging, and how that son of his brother had left the village to use the secrets of Sinanju to gain power and wealth. And such was the disgrace to Chiun that Chiun, whose name had been Nuihc, reversed the sounds and became Chiun, leaving the old name of Nuihc for disgrace. And the disgrace had sent Chiun forth from the village to sustain it by his labors and talents, at a time when he should have enjoyed the golden years of his life in comfort and respect.

"She said, O Master, that you had taken a white to teach. But my grandfather said, no, that would be the debasement typical of your nephew and your wife's family."

Above the dark ridge, Chiun saw a procession of lights making their way to the cove.

"That was a courageous thing for your grandfather to say. I hope the tribute sent to the village has softened the hearts of some toward me."

"We never got the gold, O Master. It went to the People's Party. They were here this year also to collect it, but when the collectors saw that you came yourself they ran back to the village for help. I alone stayed, because I have learned this speech every time this year on the possible occasion of your return."

"You held to the old ways with no payment?" asked Chiun.

"Yes, Master of Sinanju. For without you, we are just another poor village. But with the tradition of your house, we are the home of the Masters of Sinanju and yea, though the world spins through chaos or glory, Sinanju is something because of you and your ancestors. This I have been taught. I am sorry I forgot 'graciously.' "

Hearing this, Chiun wept and brought the girl to his bosom.

"Know you now, Child, all you and your family have suffered will be but memories. Your family shall know glory. This I promise you with my life. The sun of this day shall not set without your exaltation. Be despised in the village no longer. For among all the people, you alone are pure and good."

And by way of a joke to ease the burden of the girl's heart, Chiun noted that usually "adoration" was forgotten.

And now the people of the village were upon them, and the man called Comrade Captain, who had been a fisherman, accosted Chiun, the Master of Sinanju, standing before his tribute in the cove. Surrounded by men and the armaments of war, Comrade Captain showed bravery.

"In the name of the people of Sinanju and for the People's Democratic Republic of Korea, I claim the tribute."

And behind the captain, people yelled and cheered and applauded and some raised guns above their heads and others banged on a large tank which they had brought with them to show their new power.

"If you claim it," said Chiun, "then who among you will lay hand on it? Who will be first?"

"We will all do it at one time."

And the Master of Sinanju smiled and said: "You think you will all do it at one time. But one hand will be the first and I will see that hand and then that hand will move no more."

"We are many and you are but one," said Comrade Captain.

"Hear you this. Cow dung is many but the cow is few, and who does not trample dung with contempt. This I feel for you. Yea, though the shores were covered with you, I would but tread distastefully through you. Only one among you is worthy. This child."

And they jeered the Master of Sinanju and cursed the granddaughter of the carpenter and called her all manner of unclean things. And Comrade Captain said unto the people of Sinanju, "Let us take his tribute for we are many and he is but one."

And they rushed forward with a joyous shout, but at the trunks which had floated in along with the Master, no hand moved to touch, for none wanted to be first. And the people were still. Then the captain said, "I will be first. And should I fall then all will descend on you."

And as he touched the first trunk of tribute, Chiun, the Master of Sinanju, said to the people he would also see who would be first to lay hand upon the Master and that person would perish.

And with that, he slew the captain before the trunks, and Comrade Captain was still in death, and the people moved not. Then an old woman, from north of the village where the tradesmen lived, said they had more power than Chiun, the Master of Sinanju. They had a tank which was all powerful. And the people made way for the trunk, all but the

granddaughter of the carpenter, who had been re-
viled. She alone stood with the Master of Sinanju.

But when the tank was upon the Master of
Sinanju, his great hands moved with their awesome
skill and one tread popped and then the other so that
the tank was mired with its own weight and could
not move, like a man numbed by wine.

And upon this helpless tank climbed Chiun and
sealed the top hatch. And with such awesome leverage that no man had, he made the turret still and
cracked from its front the guns that could kill many.

Now beneath tanks were other hatches, but this
tank had settled into wet sand and the hatches could
not open.

"Those in here I leave for the tide," said the Master
of Sinanju, and there was moaning and crying from
within the tank. For these soldiers, although they
came from Pyongyang, knew the tide would soon be
upon them and would drown them, and they begged
for mercy.

But Chiun would hear none of it, and he called the
people close around him and he said to them: "But
for this child, none of you would see another day.
You have made light of the tribute and desecrated the
name of the House of Sinanju in its own village."

But the child begged that Chiun not be harsh with
the people for they were in fear of the whore city Pyongyang and the evil ones who lived along the Yalu
and the corrupt in the large cities like Hamhung
where people wrote things on paper for common
folk to perform. She begged him that he share the
tribute with all, and the Master of Sinanju told her

that even though none was worthy, they would share because she asked. And those inside the tank asked if they too could be spared.

But Chiun would hear none of it, and he called for them anyhow. The old woman from the tradesmen's quarters said if it were not for the evil ones in Pyongyang they would have greeted the Master properly in the first place. So it was agreed to leave them.

The granddaughter of the carpenter said those inside the tank were doing what they were told because of the same fear and that they should be allowed mercy also, but Chiun said "Pyongyang is Pyongyang and Sinanju is Sinanju."

All knew he meant that those in the tank did not matter, and upon reflection the granddaughter agreed that the Master of Sinanju was right. They were from Pyongyang.

So with many praises, the villagers carried the trunks back to the village with the girl high among them. And many said they had always loved her but were afraid of Pyongyang, and many offered marriage to her and placed her with great honor. All this before the sun rose.

There was great rejoicing in the village, but the Master of Sinanju showed no joy. For he remembered the white man, dead of the many blows of contempt, and he knew a great battle was yet to come in Sinanju, and the man who had to win it was another white man.

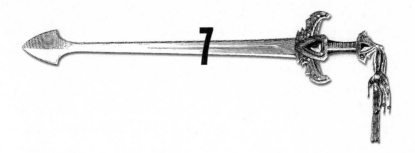

No, no, no!"

The two men facing each other on the tumbling mats froze in place.

"You two shits are hopeless," bellowed the man who walked onto the mats between them. He was a burly man with lumps of muscle for shoulders and the bristly mustache of a British sergeant major. He wore a white karate uniform with a black sash that was slung low and tied down in the area of his groin. He raised his hand to his face and the overhead lights glinted off his manicured fingernails.

"This isn't a frigging dance," he yelled again. "You, Needham . . . you're supposed to be killing this man. Trying to choke him. You ain't squeezing with enough power to wrinkle a grape."

He turned around. "And you, Foster. He's supposed to be a killer and you're supposed to take him out. Fast. Christ help the public if you two ever get out on the street."

Needham, a tall thin man with a wiry brush-cut who looked like an upside-down broom, grimaced at the back of Lieutenant Fred Wetherby. He thought he had been squeezing hard enough to hurt. Foster, an athletically muscled black man, said nothing, but let his eyes bespeak his contempt for the mustached police lieutenant. A dozen police recruits, sitting on the floor around the mats waiting their turn to wrestle, saw the look. So did Lieutenant Wetherby, who turned back to Needham.

"Needham. Step forward."

The thin man moved forward, his slowness betraying his unsureness.

"Now try it on me," Wetherby said. Needham put his two hands up to Wetherby's thick sloping neck. As he was doing it, he decided that perhaps he was not really cut out to be a policeman. He was not happy with hand-to-hand combat.

He could not get his hands around Wetherby's neck, but he squeezed as hard as he could, keeping his muscles tensed for the throw he knew was coming.

"Squeeze, goddammit," Wetherby roared. "You don't have no more strength than a girl. Or a pansy."

Needham clenched the throat tightly. His thumbs found Wetherby's Adam's apple. He pressed in with his thumbs in a flash of anger. He felt a numbing blast hit his right forearm. He tried to keep squeezing but his fingers lost control. He knew that his right hand was slipping loose. He felt a duplicate of the first blow hit the inside of his left forearm. He willed himself to keep squeezing. Keep squeezing this bastard. Rip his throat out. He tried, but the left hand, too, slid loose, and then he felt a sharp pain in the pit of his stomach. He had forgotten, in his anger, to keep those muscles tense to absorb the impact of the blow, and then he felt himself going over Wetherby's back and he hit hard onto the mat. Over his head he saw Wetherby's face, his long thin lips pulled tight in a grimace of hatred, and he saw Wetherby's foot raise up over his head and then come slamming down toward his nose. It was going to hit his nose. He knew it. It was going to mash his face in and make him bleed and shatter and blast his nose bones into his nasal passages.

Needham screamed.

The callused bare heel of the big man touched his nose.

And stopped.

Needham could see the spaces between Wetherby's toes, only a few inches from his eyes. He could see the hard, tanned calluses on the bottom of the lieutenant's foot.

Wetherby stood still a moment, the ball of his foot still touching Needham's nose, and then his thin lips opened and his widely spaced teeth showed in a smile, and he took a deep breath. "Okay, Needham," he said. "You were squeezing hard that time but you forgot to fall right. Remember, roll and slap your arms to spread the impact out."

He nodded. "Okay. Off the mat." Needham, who would realize only later that his fears about being killed in front of a class of fellow police recruits were irrational and groundless, rolled over and moved, sorely stiff, off the mat.

Wetherby turned back toward Foster who had watched the action with a fixed grin.

"Now that's the way to do it," Wetherby said. "No pattycake. Break the hold, throw the man and stomp. Is any of this seeping in through that concrete barrier you call a skull?"

His eyes met Foster's and he saw a glint of anger in the black man's. Wetherby did not bother to show any emotion. He did not like blacks; he thought they destroyed any police force they served on; he especially disliked them when they were cocky as Foster was.

"Do you think you can do it now?" Wetherby asked.

"Oh, I can do it, Lieutenant," said Foster. "Don't you worry about it."

"I never worry."

Foster stepped forward into the center of the mat.

"Ready?" asked Wetherby.

The black recruit bounced up and down in place, light athlete's movements to distribute his weight evenly and make sure his balance was proper.

"Okay," he said. "Go on . . . sir," he added in a verbal sneer.

Wetherby slowly raised his hairy thick arms and took a light grip on Foster's slick brown neck.

"Go!" he shouted and squeezed.

Foster felt the sudden shock of pressure on his throat. He felt the pain of thumbs pressing into his Adam's Apple. He did as he had been taught.

He curled his left hand into a fist and punched upward toward the ceiling, between Wetherby's two arms, then slammed his left arm outward. The force of the blow was supposed to force the strangler's right arm to let loose. But, instead of the crash of bone and muscle against bone and muscle, he felt Wetherby's right arm collapse, retreating, absorbing the pressure of Foster's blow by bending before it. And all the while the burly lieutenant kept the death grip with both hands on Foster's neck.

Foster tried the same stroke with his right hand, but with the same result. Wetherby allowed his arm to absorb the impact of the blow by moving his arm backward slightly, but not enough to dislodge his own grip on the black man's neck.

Foster looked into Wetherby's eyes. There was a smile in them. They crinkled at the corners with amusement. Shit, thought Foster, this man's crazy, this crazy honkey is going to strangle me.

Foster's eyes widened in panic. He felt his chest start to ache as the air was slowly being cut off from his lungs. He tried to gasp and suck in air. He could not. He repeated the hand maneuver, both hands punching up, simultaneously this time, but Wetherby pulled him forward by the throat so that Foster's fists struck his own forehead.

The black man brought a knee up hard, trying to strike Wetherby in the groin, anything to make him loosen the grip.

But his knee contacted only air. Help, he tried to shout. Let me go, motherfucker, he tried to say but no words came out of his throat. His eyes felt as if they were clouding over. He felt no more urge to attack. He tried again to breathe, but he could not and then he felt a lazy softness pass over his muscles and his eyes closed, as much as he tried to will them to stay open, and then the class saw that he was hanging like a rag doll from the hands of the lieutenant.

Wetherby held on, squeezing, a few seconds longer, then he released his grip and Foster, unconscious, dropped back heavily onto the mat.

The watching rookies murmured.

"Don't worry, he'll be all right," said Wetherby. "But that's a new lesson for you. Don't get fancy, because the minute you do, you're going to meet somebody who's better than you. Do whatever it takes to take your man out and do it quickly and with no regrets. Otherwise, you're going to end up like him." He looked down contemptuously at Foster, who was starting to regain consciousness with some gasping groans. "Or worse," said Wetherby. "If you can imagine that."

He toed Foster. "Okay, Shaft. Up and at 'em."

Still groaning, Foster slowly rolled over from his back onto his stomach, then lifted his knees until he was up in a crawling position. No one moved among the watching recruits until Wetherby nodded. "Give him a hand, somebody," he said.

He looked over the heads of the recruits at two men walking through the door. He felt a tingle in his hands and he sucked a breath deep into the pit of his stomach. Now. At last. It was now.

"All right, men," he said. "That's it for the day. See you to-morrow."

He walked toward the door where he was met by the deputy chief in charge of police training.

"Fred," the man said. "This is Mr. Slote. He's a magazine writer doing a piece on police training procedures."

"Good to meet you," said Wetherby, extending his hand to shake the other man's.

Nothing exceptional, he judged. Thick wrists, but barely six feet tall and slim. He gave away four inches to Wetherby and probably seventy-five pounds, and thick wrists or no, strong for his size or no, it wouldn't be enough, because a strong and good big man beat a strong and good smaller man every time.

Well, almost every time, Wetherby corrected in his mind. There was one little man who was so good that Wetherby would never fool with him. It was strange to think about. Here he was a policeman and dedicated to the law, and somehow he had been pulled outside the law. At first he had told himself he had done it because he wanted the combat secrets the little man had promised him, but now he knew there was another reason, an overwhelming reason. Lieutenant Fred Wetherby did what the little man said because he was afraid not to. It was that simple. And because it was that simple, Wetherby did not have to have any second thoughts about it and he could just stand back and enjoy what he had been told to do. Like kill this puny little Mr. Slote who stood in front of him.

"I'll be glad to show you around," said Wetherby. "We're unusual in police training in that we put so much stress on hand-to-hand combat. Do you know anything about hand-to-hand combat, Mr. Slote?"

"You can call me Remo. No, I don't know anything about it."

"I'll leave you two alone," said the deputy chief. "If you want anything when you leave," he told Remo, "just stop in my office."

"Sure thing, chief. Thanks."

He turned to watch the deputy chief go. Wetherby said, "What happened to your arm?"

Remo put a hand gently up toward his left shoulder. "Talk about clumsy. Would you believe a garage door closed on it?"

"Not really," said Wetherby, meaning the words, but smiling to take away the insult of them.

Remo, annoyed because he had thought he was moving well despite the left arm which he could not move at all today, said, "I've heard a lot about you."

"Oh?"

"Yeah. Fellow in Tenafly. Hawley Bardwell. He said he studied with you."

"Bardwell. Bardwell. I don't know any Bardwell," said Wetherby.

Remo covered his surprise, while deciding that Lieutenant Fred Wetherby was a liar. Lynette Bardwell had name, rank, and serial number. She couldn't have been mistaken about Wetherby.

He said nothing and allowed himself to be shown around the now empty gymnasium. He had started his new life in a gymnasium much like this one. A gym at Folcroft Sanitarium. He had just recovered from an electrocution that wasn't on the level, and someone had put a gun in his hand and promised to let him go if he could shoot an aged Oriental skittering across the gym floor. And because Remo was cocky and young and sure of himself, he accepted the offer and wound up eating splinters from the gym floor.

Wetherby was showing Remo training posts, padded two-by-fours used to teach hand blows, when Remo asked, "Do you find your trainees ever use this knowledge?"

"Sure," said Wetherby. "Think how many times a policeman has to throw a punch to defend himself. How much better is he if he uses something better than a punch?"

"But don't you feel upset about turning men out into the streets who have this terrible weapon in their hands?"

Wetherby smiled at the faggy liberal bleeding heart reporter, and wondered how this Remo Slote had managed to get so much on the bad side of Mr. Winch. He locked the inside gym door as he strolled past the practice posts.

He showed Remo toward the practice mats. "We train recruits for forty full hours in hand-to-hand combat."

"Forty hours," said Remo. "Wow, that's a lot."

"Not nearly enough to get good," said Wetherby.

"By the way," said Remo, touching the mat with his right toe, "you didn't tell me where you had trained with Bardwell."

Wetherby stood on the mat facing Remo. They were five feet apart. "I told you, I don't know any Bardwell. Probably just another amateur."

"And you're a professional?" asked Remo.

"Right. Here's why."

One moment, Wetherby was standing, talking. The next moment, he was in the air, heading toward Remo. His right leg was cocked underneath his flying body. Remo recognized the move. The right leg would come into the top part of his body. As Remo fell backward Wetherby would land, and the next step would be a killing hand-blow to Remo's temple.

That was if it was done right.

To be done right, it could not be done to Remo.

Wetherby's leg lashed out. The foot took Remo heavily in the right shoulder.

But there was something wrong with the technique Wetherby had been taught. He could only land the next blow, the killer to the temple, if his opponent went down and didn't strike back.

Remo did not go down. He struck back. He stepped backward one step, saw Wetherby's midsection as open as a church collection basket, and put his own foot into the policeman's solar plexus.

It was over that fast. Wetherby's blow. Pop. Remo's response. Splat.

The look of killing hatred on Wetherby's face changed immediately to a look of puzzled query. His eyes opened wide as if in surprise. He dropped onto his back on the mat. His eyes stayed open.

"Crap," said Remo. "Crap and double crap." Another suicide pilot dead in an attack and Remo still had no information.

And now he had another worry. The fire in his right shoulder, where Wetherby's foot had landed, was spreading through the upper part of his body. He tried to lift his arm. It raised slowly with almost no power. But at least he could still move it. By the next day, he feared he would not even be able to do that. But as long as it worked, he had to use it. He couldn't just waltz out of police headquarters, leaving the dead body of the training officer in the middle of the gym floor.

Slowly, with his right arm held stiffly, he dragged the burly man's body to a supply room at the end of the gym. With every step he took, the pain throbbed more in his shoulder. He felt like screaming now. Another suicide attack. And why?

It was while he was stuffing Lieutenant Wetherby's body into the bottom of a barrel filled with basketballs that he finally understood what it all meant.

He left the gym, disgusted. He had found out nothing, and yet he had found out everything. He was being subject to the traditional Sinanju attack of disrespect.

Two more blows were yet to come.

But he knew no friends of Bardwell, no friends of Wetherby's, and he did not know when or where the third attack might come.

He would have to back go to Lynette Bardwell and try again, look for another name.

But he knew now whose name was already signed to the fourth blow that awaited Remo.

The name was Nuihc. Chiun's nephew, who had vowed death to both Remo and his Korean master.

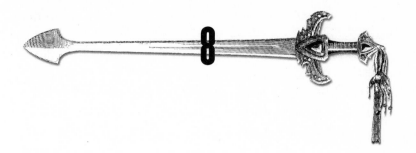

IN Pyongyang, the loss of a people's tank was put before Kim Il Sung, premier of the People's Democratic Republic.

Sung was not from Sinanju, nor was he a believer in the old ways. He was a leader of the new way and he was called comrade by peasant and warrior alike, for he said they were all equal. Still, Sung always wore his warrior uniform with general's boards on his shoulders and a stiff black leather belt.

Sung nodded when he first heard the story. He had heard of the Master of Sinanju, he said. A fairy tale designed to cover the activities of a horde of bandits and cutthroats, he said, and sent a follower named Pak Myoch'ong to go look into the story, for it had been believed that the Masters of Sinanju were of the past, and not a thing for a People's Democratic Republic to worry about.

The first person Pak Myoch'ong took himself to was the governor of the province in which Sinanju was located. The governor had anticipated and dreaded the query because it was he who had instructed the soldiers to confiscate the tribute sent every year by the Master of Sinanju to his own village.

"Why do you question me such?" asked the governor. "Do you doubt that I can rule this province?"

"If the premier doubted you could rule, you would not be governor," Myoch'ong said. "No, I merely ask who are these men who destroy a people's tank with their bare hands."

"It is not I who say so," said the governor. To Myoch'ong it was a denial that any Master of Sinanju existed, so he asked "If not the Master of Sinanju, who?"

"The Americans," said the governor. He pointed out the ship that had been sighted near Sinanju just the week before. And were they not capitalists? And did they not hate the People's Democratic Republic of Korea, and were they not schemers and doers of all manner of evil things?

Myoch'ong said nothing, for he was a wise man and he knew that while it was good for the people that their hatred should be aroused and directed toward someone outside of Pyongyang, nevertheless everytime he heard the word "American" he suspected it was a way of claiming innocence for failing to do one's duty.

So he took himself to Sinanju where there was rejoicing and he said to a child:

"Who is this man called the Master of Sinanju? I would meet with him."

The child took him to a large house at the end of the village's main street. The house was old but made of wood and ivory and stones from other lands, not the weak wood of the Korean countryside.

"How long has this house been here?" he asked the child.

"Forever," said the child, which to Myoch'ong meant only a long time because he knew children. But such was the look of the house, the mix of styles from many lands and cultures, that he said to himself, yes, this house is very old. It is the history of many races; it is the history of man.

Even though Myoch'ong was a server of the new way from his youngest days, when he entered the house he bowed and took off his shoes in the old way, which his people had taken from the Japanese. He bowed to an old man with a white beard whose hands had fingernails grown long in the manner of the ancients, and the old man said:

"Who are you that I have not seen you in the village?"

Myoch'ong answered that he was from Pyongyang and served Kim Il Sung, and asked if the old man were truly the Master of Sinanju "of whom many wonders are spoken."

"I am the one of whom you speak," said Chiun.

"I have heard that with but your hands you are more powerful than the people's tank."

"That is true."

"How can it be true? Steel is harder than flesh."

"The greatest weapon is the human mind. A tank is but a tool and no better than the mind that uses it."

"But fools can destroy wise men with it."

"I say unto you, young man, that there are wise men and there are wiser men. But the wisest among them has learned only that he has not uncovered the true strength of his mind. Even a fool who uses his mind is stronger than a wise man who does not."

Myoch'ong admitted his confusion and Chiun said:

"You seek a man of miracles. Yet the greatest miracle is man himself. And this I know and this you do not know and this your Pyongyangers in the people's tank did not know and now they sit in the sand like empty shells."

"I still do not understand," said Myoch'ong. "But perhaps our premier will. I would take you to him."

Chiun waved his hand in dismissal. "Sinanju does not come to Pyongyang. Return to your loose women and wine."

But Myoch'ong was not ready to leave.

"If you have such great wisdom, why do you not seek to share it with your people? Why do you sit here in this house alone, with none but this serving girl?"

"Can an ocean fill a teacup? Can the sky fill a bowl? So it is that Sinanju cannot be given everyone."

"But it is given many."

"Few," said Chiun.

"I am told that you are not the only Master of Sinanju."

"There is a pretender named Nuihc who calls himself Uinch or Winch or Chuni. All these are the same. He is one man, the son of my brother."

"See. So you share with him."

"That share will soon be removed," said Chiun, "and removed so thoroughly its remover will be white. This I say to you. The heart is the first home of the House of Sinanju, and when I found none of ours worthy, I gave it to a white man."

"An American?" said Myoch'ong, disclosing his worst fears.

"One I found eating hamburgers and drinking alcohol and other poisons. Weak in mind and body, but his heart was good. To him I have given all. From a pale piece of pig's ear, I have made him Sinanju."

Myoch'ong glanced about the room and saw a photograph of a pale-faced man, framed in gold, with western handwriting across the photo, and he asked Chiun if this were the white man of whom he spoke.

"No," said Chiun. "That is an artist of great skill. That is Rad Rex who in the daytime dramas of the Americans performs with genius and brilliance in a great drama called *As the Planet Revolves*. That is his signature on the picture. In America, I have many important friends."

Myoch'ong thought quickly, then again asked if Chiun would not come to Pyongyang to see Premier Kim Il Sung himself and receive an autographed picture of the premier which the whole village could appreciate and put in a place of honor.

But Chiun answered: "When has Kim Il Sung ever worried

about Mary Lambert's operation at the hands of the illegitimate son of Blake Winfield's stepdaughter, the one who discovered that Carson Magnum, the mayor, was addicted to heroin and had taken payoffs from Winfield himself never to expose the abortion ring which had almost killed Mary when she was pregnant with the child of the unknown father?"

"It was not his fault," said Myoch'ong. "If Kim Il Sung had known of these things, he would have worried too."

"It is a ruler's duty to know many things," said Chiun, dismissing Myoch'ong with a wave of his hand and setting his face toward the window, beyond which was the sea.

Myoch'ong puzzled over those things that night and finally summoned seven soldiers of great strength to his side. "Whoever slays the Master of Sinanju will be made colonel if he is major and general if he is colonel," he said.

The soldiers nodded and grinned, and armed with guns and knives set off for Chiun's house, because each wanted to be the one to win promotion.

In the morning, none had returned to Myoch'ong, so he went himself to Chiun's house to see what the seven had done. Entering the house, he saw not a tapestry or trinket disturbed. Chiun sat upon his cushion, unharmed, and told Myoch'ong: "That which you have sent has returned to the earth. Go now and tell your master in the whore city Pyongyang that the Master of Sinanju will see him if he will bring tribute."

"What kind of tribute," Myoch'ong asked.

"First, take all Pyongyangers from this province. Second, chastise the evil governor who has usurped the tribute due this village. Third, a message should be sent to America that the great dramas will be happily received. There are ways to do this and Americans know them. Your premier should invite such men as can do this to Korea. He should treat them well, for if they are treated well perhaps even Rad Rex himself may come. These things are possible."

And Myoch'ong left with heavy heart for he knew Kim Il Sung would not invite Americans into his land again. When he appeared before the premier, he told him of what he had seen and of the seven men who were no more. The premier was angered and purposed the sending of an army against Sinanju, but Myoch'ong bade him delay for he had heard tales of how neither wall nor steel nor human arm could stop the Masters of Sinanju, and that through the ages their special talent had been the elimination of heads of state. Or, he added shrewdly, of those who would be heads of state.

And King Il Sung paused and thought, and then he asked where Myoch'ong heard these things. And to this, Myoch'ong answered he had read of them in old manuscripts that told of Sinanju.

"Reactionary feudal fairy tales designed to suppress the aspirations of the masses. Sinanju has always been a home for bandits and murderers and thieves," said Kim Il Sung.

But Myoch'ong reminded him of the seven soldiers and of the people's tank and disclosed to him the corruption of the governor of the province.

Yet this did not dissuade the premier. But when Myoch'ong said that the Master of Sinanju had taught his secrets to a white, an American, and might teach more Americans these things, the premier dismissed everyone from his conference room but Myoch'ong.

And quietly, so that even the walls could not hear,

he said to Myoch'ong: "I would see this bandit. I shall go with you to him. But this I warn you. Should he be but another lackey of the imperialists, you will be denounced before the presidium and the politboro."

"This one is not a lackey of anyone."

"Good. On the way you will tell me what he wants of us, should there be such demands."

Now Myoch'ong was not a fool, and every time the premier asked what the Master of Sinanju desired, Myoch'ong saw a pleasant field to look at, or wondered about the strength of the people's army, or brought up the Japanese whom everyone hated.

And again Myoch'ong returned to the house of the Master of Sinanju and asked permission to enter. And Kim Il Sung, seeing Myoch'ong bowing in the old manner, spat upon the floor.

"A den of feudalism," he said.

"Pigs and horses dribble on floors. That is why they are kept in barns," said the Master of Sinanju.

"Do you know who I am, old man? I am Kim Il Sung."

"And I am Chiun."

"Watch your mouth, Chiun."

"It is not I who drivels on floors. You get your manners from Russians."

"You are a bandit and a lackey of imperialists," said the premier without caution, for he was angered greatly.

"Were you not the premier of our people in the north," said Chiun, "I would slay you like a pig for dinner. Yet I withhold my hand for I would reason with you."

"How can a lackey reason?" said the premier. "All his reason serves his white masters. I serve Korea."

"Before you, young man," said Chiun, "Sinanju was. During the Mongol invasion, Sinanju was. During the Chinese lords, Sinanju was. During the Japanese lords, Sinanju was. During the Russian lords, Sinanju was. They are all gone and we are here as we will be here after Kim Il Sung was. But I would speak with you for, lo, after these many years Korea has a leader who is of her own. And that is you, although you are but a Pyongyanger."

And hearing these words, Sung sat. But he neither bowed nor did he remove his shoes as in the old ways. And Myoch'ong listened with great apprehension. But when Chiun spoke, he knew all would be well for there was much wisdom in the Master.

"You come here seeking the wisdom of Sinanju, otherwise why would a premier come to this poor village?" said Chiun.

And Sung agreed.

"You call me lackey," said Chiun.

And Sung agreed.

"Yet who is the lackey? Have I joined Sinanju to the Russians? Have I made compacts with the Chinese? Do I on every occasion support Arab and African and even whites just because they profess belief in one form of government?"

"They are our allies," said Sung. "The Russians give us arms. The Chinese fought Americans for us."

And Chiun smiled.

"The Russians gave arms because they hate the

Americans. The Chinese fought because they hate the Americans. Lucky are we that these two hate each other for they would sit in Pyongyang and not you. As for Africans, Arabs, and whites, they are far away and not even yellow. The Japanese are greedy, the Chinese despicable, the Russians swine, and as for our own southerners, they would sleep with ducks if birds had big enough openings."

At this, Sung roared in laughter.

"This man has a proper outlook," he said to Myoch'ong. "Who is responsible for calling him a lackey? Who has given me such misinformation?"

And Chiun spoke again. "But we must look with more sympathy upon our southern brothers because they are of the south and cannot help themselves. This is their nature."

Myoch'ong gasped. For never had anyone dared say any kind thing about those beneath the thirty-eighth parallel.

"I too have often thought such. They cannot help being what they are," said Sung.

"And Pyongyang is not the nicest of places. It is where good people go wrong," said Chiun.

"I was not born in Pyongyang but in Hamhung," said Sung.

"A fine village," said Chiun.

"Sinanju is fine also," said Sung.

"I am of Paekom," said Myoch'ong.

"But he has risen above it," said Sung.

"Some of our best friends come from Paekom. They transcend their origins," said Chiun.

Now Kim Il Sung was satisfied that here was a

man of good heart and proper thinking. But he was troubled.

"I hear you teach Sinanju to whites. To an American."

Now Chiun knew this to be a great offense, one that could not be laid before the premier with all honesty, so he was careful with his words, and he spoke with slowness and with caution.

"In my own village, in my own family, none I found was worthy. There was laxness and sloth and deceit. Among ourselves, we can admit these things."

Sung nodded for he too knew of the problems of governing.

"There was ingratitude for what was offered," said Chiun.

How well did Sung know this also.

"There was backsliding and lack of discipline," said Chiun.

Oh, how truly did the Master of Sinanju know this, proclaimed Sung.

"The son of my own brother took the preciousness given him and used it for selfish gain."

How well did Sung know this trait. He looked somberly at Myoch'ong.

"He acted like a southerner," said Chiun.

Sung spat and this time Chiun nodded approval. For it was a proper moment for such things.

"And so I sought another, that this knowledge of our people should not die."

"A wise thing," said Sung.

"I would have chosen one of us. But in all the village, in all the North, I did not find one with a Korean heart. I did not know you at the time."

"I had my problems," said Sung.

"So I sought a Korean heart like yours. One of us."

"Good for you," said Sung, placing a strong hand on the shoulder of the Master of Sinanju by way of congratulation.

"This man of our heart happened to have suffered a misfortune at birth. A catastrophe."

Sung's countenance became exceeding sad.

"What was this misfortune?"

"He was born white and American."

Sung gasped at the horror.

"Each morning he had to look at his round eyes in the mirror. Each meal he had to eat hamburger. Each day, naught but others with that same affliction for company."

"And what did you?"

"I found him and saved him from the Americans. From their thinking and ill manners."

"You did well," said Sung. But Myoch'ong, being of a suspicious nature, asked how Chiun knew this was not just another American but a Korean heart in an American body.

"Because he learned correctness exceeding well, and to prove the point he will demonstrate what he has learned when he comes to honor his heritage here in Sinanju."

"How do we know," asked Myoch'ong, "that it is not just an American to whom you have taught all of Sinanju?"

"An American?" said Chiun with a scoffing laugh.

"Did you not see Americans in the great war with the south? Did you not see Americans when you had them with their ship? An American?"

"Some Americans are hard," said Myoch'ong. But so taken with the words of the Master was Kim Il Sung that he forgot his own truth and looked at Myoch'ong with scorn. Of course, this white man has a Korean heart, he said.

"His name is Remo," said Chiun.

And thus it was that evening, in the large People's Building in Pyongyang, when the name Remo was mentioned again to the premier, Kim Il Sung recognized it. He was told a message had been received that an American named Remo would be disgraced in the village of Sinanju, and that he would be disgraced by a man named Nuihc.

And the sender of this message was himself Nuihc and he pledged the devotion of his soul to Kim Il Sung and the People's Democratic Republic of Korea. And he signed his message in this fashion:

"Nuihc, Master of Sinanju."

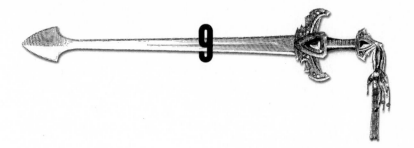

I 'D like a million dollars, lady, in singles. Don't count it, weigh it."

Lynette Bardwell looked up at her teller's cage and smiled at Remo.

"Hiya," she said. "Missed you last night."

"You were among the missing last night," Remo said. "But I thought there's always tonight. You almost done here?"

Lynette looked at the clock in the center of the bank lobby, high up over Remo's head. The craning of her neck caused her bosom to rise.

"Ten minutes more."

"Dinner okay? Your husband won't mind."

"I guess he won't," said Lynette. "I haven't heard from him. I guess he did go away for a while."

Remo waited in front and Lynette came boobily bobbing out in precisely ten minutes.

"Take my car?" she said. Remo nodded. In her car in the parking lot, she leaned over to brush his cheek with her lips. The top of her body pressed against his right shoulder. Remo grimaced.

"What's the matter? You hurt your shoulder?"

Remo nodded.

"How'd that happen?"

"Would you believe I ran into a barrel of basketballs?"

"No."

"Good. Don't."

Lynette drove and Remo picked the dinner spot this time, an even darker restaurant than the night before, but one that looked as if it could cook rice.

It could, and Remo joined Lynette in eating.

"Did you see Wetherby?" she asked.

"Yes. But he couldn't help."

"Couldn't help you what? You know I don't know what it is you're after."

"I'm doing a book on Oriental fighting. Your husband, Wetherby, they all have some special training, something unique. I know enough about it to know that. But they won't tell. I think I've stumbled onto some new training secret, and, well, I'm stubborn."

"I wish I could help," she said, picking over a piece of crabmeat. "But it's not my bag."

"What is your bag?"

The crabmeat vanished into her mouth without a trace. "I'm a lover, not a fighter."

Over her brandy, Lynette confided that her husband had never stayed away at night before. "You didn't scare him away, did you?"

"Do I look like I could scare anybody away?"

Remo picked slowly at his rice, first using his right hand, then his left. The pain in his shoulders was growing, and each time he brought the fork to his mouth he could feel the burning heat of injury moving through the shoulder joint, throbbing its pain into his consciousness. If only Chiun were in the States, instead of gallivanting around in Sinanju, he might be able to help. Someplace in that memory of his would be a way to make Remo's arms work again, someplace a way to stop the pain and the weakness.

And these were just the first two blows. He knew now that he had been targeted by Nuihc, the nephew of Chiun, who sought Chiun's title and had vowed Remo's death. Already Remo's arms were gone, worthless. What was next?

Finally eating wasn't worth the pain, and Remo just let the fork drop from his fingers. He found himself nodding at Lynette without hearing what she was saying, and soon they were driving toward her house and he heard himself accept her offer to stay in her upstairs spare room so he could rest.

And he felt so badly he no longer tried to maintain any pretense by asking if her husband might object. The husband was dead, and fuck 'im, he had hurt Remo's arm and he couldn't rot in that coffin fast enough to suit Remo.

Lynette helped him upstairs to a big bedroom in her house and he let her undress him. She did it slowly, trailing her fingers over his body and she put him naked under the covers. She was soft but efficient and Remo thought it rather marvelous how she had learned to hold her liquor much better than she had the night before. That was funny. Funny, funny, Remo thought. Look, look, look at funny Remo.

He could not move his upper body. The pain surged through his shoulders and down his arms, numbing his fingertips, into his chest where it seemed to attack each one of his ribs, into his neck where it made movement painful.

Hurt, hurt Remo. Look, look, look at hurt, hurt Remo.

He was hallucinating. It had been so long since he had suffered pain, real pain. For most people, pain was a helpful warning sign that something was wrong with the body and the owner should take care of it. But Remo was one with his body, it was not a belonging but a being, and he did not have to be reminded when there was something wrong with his body, and so there was no need for him to feel pain. He had almost forgotten what pain felt like. He had felt pain when he sat in the electric chair. They had failed to fry him, but at least they had given him a quick braising. That was pain. And so was this. In between those two times, in all the ten years, there hadn't been too much other pain to remember.

Look, look, look, funny Remo. He was losing control.

Look, look Remo, look at the beautiful lady walking through the door. Look at the white nylon gown she's wearing that you can see through.

Look at the soft swelling of the highrise breasts, look at the smooth round outlines of her body, silhouetted against the hall light. Look at the long tan legs. Look how she smiles at you, Remo. The lovely lady likes you, Remo. She will make you feel all better. Remo wanted to feel all better. He smiled.

Lynette leaned over him in the bed. "I will make you feel better," she said.

Remo kept smiling, because it hurt to stop. "Make me feel better. Want to feel better. Arms hurt."

"Where do they hurt, Remo?" Lynette asked. "Here?" She touched his left shoulder through the strand of muscles in the front and Remo groaned with the pain.

"Or here?"

She touched his right shoulder with her fingertips and pressed and Remo screamed.

"Hurt. Hurt," he shouted.

"There, there. Lynette will make you feel better," she said.

Remo opened his eyes narrowly. The tall blonde woman he had made a widow was standing next to the bed, and then with a smooth practiced swoop she was lifting her negligee over her head.

She held it in her fingertips at arm's length, her eyes seemingly fastened to his by wires, and then she dropped the negligee into a soft fluttery mound on the floor.

She moved closer to Remo, ran fingers down his cheeks, trailed them down his neck, and then pulled the blanket down from his unclad body.

No, he wanted to say. No. No sex. Don't feel well. No sex.

But Lynette Bardwell was moving her fingers all over his body now, and he found that if he concentrated on something other than his shoulders, the pain was not so severe, so he concentrated on that part of the body that Lynette was concentrating on and then Remo was ready. Lynette smiled and moved up onto the bed and was over him and then on him and then surrounding him, swallowing him with her body.

She knelt over Remo looking down at him and her face was smiling but there was no mirth in the showing of her teeth, which looked as if they were about to bite, and there was a glitter in her eyes, a kind of merciless sparkle, and she began to move her body and it helped, it helped, it helped if he moved his a little, and he stopped thinking of his shoulders and thought only of himself and Lynette and their junction.

He wanted to move his hands up to her, to reach her body, but he could not. His hands and arms were straight at his side, pinned there by her thighs straddling him, but he still had some movement in his fingers and he used them to touch the insides of her thighs where there were large clusters of nerves, very delicately throbbing.

His fingers brought her to life. Her eyes opened wider and she began moving on him faster, wilder, and it was better, better than the pain in his arms, and he wasn't thinking of the pain anymore. The pain had come from two people who had tried to disable him before killing him, and the next blow would be someone coming after one of his legs, but he couldn't, he wouldn't think about that now.

Lynette was sitting up straight, and she threw her head back and laughed, a loud rolling laugh, and then she looked down at him, and for the first time Remo focused on her eyes and saw the meaning in them, and she let her body fall forward, her head toward his face, but she caught herself with her two hands, slamming them against his shoulders, like an athlete doing pushups.

The pain shot through his body and Remo screamed. And she twisted her arm muscles and the hard heels of her hands ground into his shoulder joints. She laughed again and leaned her face close to his.

He felt his face was wet. She was crying? No, he was crying, crying in pain.

"You killed my husband," she said. It was not a question.

"And you killed Wetherby," she said. She twisted her hands again into his shoulders.

Hurt. Hurt. Have to get away.

"But they damaged you. And I'm going to damage you worse. And the little bit that's going to be left of you will go to Nuihc. In a bag."

Nuihc? She knew. Lynette was the third kamikaze. The third shot was hers. Did she know that Nuihc planned for her to die? That Remo was supposed to kill her? But he couldn't kill her. He couldn't move.

"You know Nuihc?" Remo gasped.

"I serve Nuihc," she corrected. "Hawley was a fool. Wetherby was a brute. But Nuihc is a man. He loves me. He said the best blow in Scotland was mine. I was the best."

She continued moving the lower half of her body up and down, using Remo as an instrument for her pleasure and his pain, and all he could do was keep his fingers going inside her thighs.

"Mr. Winch is a man," she said.

He felt her voice soften and her muscles begin to tense, then relax, in an unconscious rhythm she could not control.

"The kind of man you might have been. Ohhh. Ohhhh."

She was bucking on Remo now like a bareback cowboy on a crazed horse. He was pinned and powerless and in pain from her hands on his shoulders. She screamed a heavy gasping scream of pleasure and said "Oh, Nuihc, Nuihc," and when she stopped, she said, "You could have been a man, too. If you had lived."

And then her creamed wet body moved up off Remo and he could feel the blessed relief of her small fists withdrawing from the points of pain on his shoulders and he could open his eyes again. He saw her standing on the bed, looking down at his body below her bare legs, and he saw her curl her left leg up under her, standing as if she were a flamingo, and then she drew the other leg up, too, and her body crashed down, aimed at the long rope of muscle in the front of his right thigh, and even before she landed, Remo could sense what the excruciating pain would be like, and then her body hit, and it seemed to land in slow motion. First there was the touch of contact, then pressure, then pain as her weight and skill tore open the long lifting muscle of the thigh.

"First you," she yelled, "and after you, the old man."

Purely by reflex, purely by training, purely by instinct, knowing it meant nothing because he was going to die, Remo rolled his left leg toward the far wall, so the knee was pointing outward, then with all the effort and strength he had left, he rolled the knee back inward toward his own right leg, toward Lynette Bardwell, who knelt on his right leg, her face exultant with the glow of victory, and he drove the knee across his own body and heard the crack as it found her temple bone.

Lynette still smiled. She looked at Remo, smiling, and then, for just a brief second, the smile turned into a look of pain, and in that moment Remo knew that she suddenly suspected that Nuihc, whom she thought loved her, had guessed that she would die here, and then she could no longer worry about things like that because her thin temple bones were driven into her brain by the force of Remo's driving knee, and the smile and the look of pain both withered, like a time-lapse photo study of a flower's life and death, and Lynette fell forward onto Remo's chest and died.

He felt the warm sticky ooze from her head drip onto his chest. It felt warm. Warm. And warm was good and he wanted to be warm, so he didn't have chills. And the pain in both shoulders and the pain in his right thigh all hurt, and he closed his eyes and decided it would be nice to sleep.

And if he died that would be nice, too, because then he would always be warm. And he wouldn't hurt anymore.

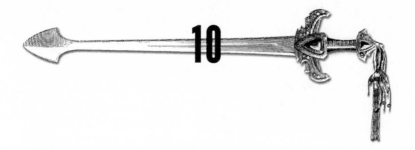

REMO woke.

He had slept to forget something, and now he remembered it. The pain in his shoulders and arms.

And there was something wrong with his legs.

A weight was on them. He looked down toward his legs, but he couldn't see them. Right under his chin, grinning up at him, was the wide-eyed, open-mouthed, bloodied head of Lynette Bardwell.

Remo remembered.

"Hi, toots," he said. "Read any good karate books lately?"

Carefully, Remo slid his left leg out from under the woman, then with his left leg he pushed her. Her body rolled down from his right leg onto the bed, then slipped onto the floor where it hit with a brittle, cold thump.

Remo swung his body around, extended his legs to the floor, stood up, and collapsed onto the gray tweed rug as his right leg buckled under him.

And just that much effort brought back the pain, like a toothache that seems to have been cured by a night's sleep, but starts throbbing before you get out of bed.

Remo crawled toward the wall and then using the wall as a brace managed to get himself into an upright position. Trying to put no weight on his right leg, using it just for steering, he hobbled to the bathroom and, hammering with his powerless arms, was able to get the shower turned on.

He hoisted himself into the shower and stood there a long time, unable to soap himself, but letting the water wash Lynette Bardwell's dried blood off his body.

The warm water washed away some of his pain, too, and Remo was able to think. Nuihc was coming after him. The next attack, the fourth blow, would be deadly.

He got out of the shower, leaving the water running. He stopped in front of the bathroom mirror and looked at his own image. "You're kinda young to die," he told the face that looked back at him. But the face didn't seem frightened; it seemed puzzled as if it were trying to remember something. Looking at the face was like looking at a stranger, and that stranger was puzzled. There was something in the back of his mind, some tiny memory that he knew he should remember. But what was it?

Remo dragged on his pants and congratulated himself on wearing a button-front shirt because at least he could slip his arms into it. Yesterday's pullover would have been out of the question.

What was it?

Something Lynette had said. Something.

What?

What?

"After you . . ." After Remo, what? What?

"After you," she had said, "After you," and then he remembered as the words jumped back into his ears as if someone were shouting at him.

She had said:

"After you, the old man."

Chiun.

Remo hobbled to the telephone. He was able to cradle the

phone between left ear and shoulder and, thanking God for pushbutton dials, banged out an 800-area code toll-free number.

"Yes?" came the lemony voice.

"Remo. What time is it?"

"It's two-twelve P.M., and this is an unauthorized time for you to call. Don't you remember that . . ."

"I need help. I'm hurt."

In Folcroft Sanitarium, Dr. Harold W. Smith sat up straight in his chair. In ten years he had never heard those words from Remo.

"Hurt? How?"

"Muscles torn. I can't drive. Send someone for me."

"Where are you?"

"Home of Lynette Bardwell. Tenafly, New Jersey. You can tell me from Lynette 'cause I'm still alive."

"Are you in any danger of compromise?" asked Smith.

"That's it, Smitty. Good for you. Up the organization. Worry about security."

"Yes," said Smith noncommittally. "Is there any danger?"

"I don't know." Remo sighed. It hurt to talk and now the telephone was hurting his shoulder where it rested. "If the security of this operation depends on me, start looking for a new job."

"Stay where you are, Remo. Help is coming."

Smith listened. There was no joking, no wisecracking in Remo's voice this time, as he said: "Hurry."

Smith rose, carefully buttoned his jacket, and walked from his office. He told his secretary he would be gone for the rest of the day, which announcement she greeted with open-mouthed astonishment. Dr. Smith, in the past ten years, took off only every other Friday afternoon, and on those days he arrived early in the office and worked through his lunch hour, so he had already put in his full eight hours before leaving for his golf date at the nearby country club. A date which, she had one day learned, he kept with himself, playing alone.

He boarded a medical helicopter on the sanitarium grounds and was flown to Teterboro Airport in New Jersey where he rented a Ford Mustang, even though a Volkswagen was cheaper and there would be one available in just an hour or so and he liked the Volkswagen's gas economy.

With the help of a telephone directory and the driver of a mail truck, he found the Bardwell house. He parked behind a brown Ford in the driveway and went to the side door leading to the kitchen. No one answered his knocking. The door was unlocked.

Smith entered a kitchen filled with plastic clocks that looked like fried eggs sunnyside up, cooked too long, and with ceramic spoon rests that looked like smiling babies, and with coffee, sugar, and flour canisters that looked like overgrown soup cans, and a room in which everything looked like something else.

Smith had no mind for philosophy so it did not occur to him that a vast portion of America made its living by making things look like other things, and that this was a little strange because it might have been better to make the first things good-looking enough so that they had no need for disguises.

The lean pinched-face man moved quietly through the first floor of the house, efficiently searching the rooms, the kitchen, dining room, the living room, the bath, the television room in the back, decorated with a shelf holding a collection of plaques and trophies from karate competitions, set up in rows, that looked like nothing so much as an advancing army of Oriental men and women fighting their way through unfriendly air to reach their enemies.

He found Remo upstairs on the floor of the bedroom, lying next to the bed. Next to him was the body of a naked blond woman, her face and head caked with dried brown blood.

Smith knelt quickly next to Remo and put his hand inside Remo's open shirt. He saw Remo's mouth move into a grimace of pain. Smith looked at his watch. He counted the heartbeats for fifteen seconds. Twelve. He multiplied by four. Remo's pulse was forty-eight.

If that had been Smith's pulse rate, he would have rushed to a cardiologist. But Smith, who read his medical bulletins on CURE personnel like a financier read the stock market tables, knew that for Remo a pulse of forty-eight was in the normal range.

"Remo," he said.

Remo's eyes opened slowly.

"Can you walk?" Smith asked. "We've got to get out of here."

"Hi, Smitty. Keep an eye on the paper clips. Every time you turn your back, someone's stealing them."

"Remo, you've got to get up."

"Get up. Right. Got to get up. Can't go lying down on government time."

He closed his eyes again.

Smith put his left arm under Remo's thighs and his right arm across the top of Remo's right arm and under his back and hoisted Remo into his arms. He was surprised, despite himself, at how light Remo was. He had weighed two hundred pounds when the organization had found him ten years ago, and Smith had known that his weight had come down some forty pounds, but like all gradual weight losses it had not been visible.

Leaning backward to counteract Remo's weight in his arms, Dr. Smith descended the steps to the first floor. Every time he reached his foot down to touch a new step, the slight jar to his body brought a squint of pain into the corner's of Remo's closed eyes.

In the kitchen, Smith deposited Remo into a chair at the

kitchen table, then went outside to start the car's motor and drive it up as close as he could to the kitchen door.

He opened the passenger's door. When he got back into the kitchen, Remo's eyes were open.

"Hi, Smitty. Took you long enough to get here."

"Yes."

"I must have called you hours ago and here you are, taking your time about things, while I'm feeling rotten."

"Yes," said Smith.

"How'd I get to the kitchen?" asked Remo.

"You probably walked," said Smith. "Just as you're going to walk to that car outside."

"I can't walk, Smitty."

"Hobble then. You don't think I'm going to carry you, do you?"

"Not you, Smitty. That's laborers' work. Do you WASPs go to a school where you learn to be obnoxious?"

"When you finish feeling sorry for yourself, I'll be out in the car," Smith said coldly. "I suggest you hurry up."

Smith waited in the car, an unusual feeling of disquiet within him. He wished that he could have told Remo he was concerned about him, but he did not know how. Years of training, years of service, years of administration in that strange government underworld where a man who was your friend for years one day just stopped coming around, vanished, swallowed up, gone, and no one ever spoke of him again, as if he had never existed in the first place.

It was just too long-standing a tradition for Smith to be able to violate.

He watched as Remo came out onto the small kitchen porch. He tried first to hold onto the stair railing with his right hand, but he winced and gave that up. He put his right hip against the railing, then hopped down a step, landing on his left foot. Then he leaned sideways, right hip against the railing, until he was balanced and ready for his next lunge down.

Remo made it, hopping, to the car, and slid in through the open door. Smith reached across him, pulled the door shut, and backed carefully out of the driveway. He drove as quickly as the speed laws of New Jersey permitted, out of the town, onto Route 4, heading for the George Washington Bridge.

Only when he was on the highway did he ask Remo what had happened.

"There was a girl in the upstairs bedroom . . ."

"I saw her."

"Right. She disabled my right leg."

"And your arms?"

"Shoulders, Smitty. Two other guys did that."

"But how?" asked Smith. "I thought you were trained to stop that sort of thing from happening."

"Suicide attacks," said Remo. "Anyway, I need something."

"Yes. A doctor," said Smith.

"I need a submarine."

"What?"

"A sub. I'm going to Sinanju."

"Why? Remember, you're supposed to be checking out the death of one of our programmers."

"Remember the blows he suffered that mashed his joints?"

"Yes."

"I've had three of them so far. The fourth is due in Sinanju."

"I don't understand," said Smith.

And because Remo did not understand either, did not know how he knew what he knew, he said, "You don't have to. But Chiun is in danger and I've got to go to Sinanju."

"What good are you going to be to him? You can't even walk."

"I'll think of something. I'd rather be near him."

Smith drove on mechanically, not distinctively enough to be called good driver or bad driver.

A few minutes later, he said:

"Sorry, Remo, you can't go. I can't allow it."

"I'll pay for the gas myself, Smitty."

"Chiun is different," Smith explained. "He's a Korean. But you're an American. If you're captured in North Korea by the government there, it can cause an international incident. Not to mention blowing our whole apparatus. We'll have to close down."

"And what do you think you'll have to do if the *New York Times* gets a letter tomorrow listing locations, places, dates, killings, government interference? There was that business in Miami, remember? And the labor union. What will happen to you then?" asked Remo.

Smith drove on glumly.

"That's blackmail," he said.

"Company policy."

"Extortion," said Smith.

"Company policy."

"A naked unprincipled threat," said Smith.

"That's the biz, sweetheart," said Remo.

Smith pulled off the highway at a motel outside White Plains and, with a key from a ring in his pocket, opened the door of a room the organization rented year-round. He helped Remo into the room, located in the back of the building, secure from the street, helped Remo onto the bed, then left. He was back in twenty-five minutes with a man in a business suit, carrying a leather medical bag.

The doctor examined Remo carefully.

Remo would not cooperate. "I don't need all this," he told Smith in a hiss. "Chiun can fix me up."

The doctor called Smith into a corner of the room for consultation.

"This man belongs in a hospital," he said softly. "Both shoulders are separated. The major muscles in the right thigh are actually ripped. The pain must be excruciating. Frankly, Doctor, I think you overstepped yourself by removing him from the scene of the accident. He should have been carried by ambulance from the wreck."

Smith nodded as if he agreed with the lecture. "Patch him up as best you can until I convince him to get to the hospital, please."

The doctor nodded.

Despite Remo's total lack of enthusiasm, he bandaged Remo's shoulders, restricting his arm movements even further, but guaranteeing that the separated muscles would have time to knit before being abused. He also bandaged Remo's right thigh heavily. His last act was to reach into his bag and withdraw a hypodermic syringe.

"I'm going to give you something for the pain," he said.

Remo shook his head. "No, you're not."

"But the pain must be terrible. This will just help to relieve it."

"No needles," said Remo. "Smitty, remember that hamburger that put me in the hospital? No needles. No drugs in the system."

Smith looked at the doctor and shook his head. "He'll deal with the pain, doctor. No injections."

Smith escorted the doctor to the door and outside on the walkway thanked him for his assistance.

"Don't mention it," said the doctor, who had not come willingly, but only because his hospital director had told him if he did not go on this case he might find someday that he had trouble in obtaining his specialty licenses. The medical director of the hospital had said this because he had been advised that it would be beneficial in the ongoing review of his income tax returns to make sure that a doctor was available for a motel call, in exactly three minutes.

When Smith reentered the room, Remo was sitting up on the bed.

"Okay, Smitty, where is it?"

"Where is what?"

"My submarine."

"One thing at a time."

"Anybody who can get a doctor to make a house call won't have any trouble getting a submarine to sneak me into North Korea."

And with that, Remo closed his eyes and lay back to rest.

He would soon be on his way to Sinanju; he had done all he could; the next thing was to warn Chiun about the danger from Nuihc. It was only as he drifted into sleep that he allowed himself to remember that it was Remo himself who had drawn the first three blows from Nuihc's kamikazes, and the next blow, under the ages-old tradition of Sinanju, would mean Remo's death.

And after Remo, Chiun.

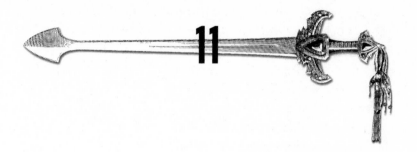

CAPTAIN Lee Enright Leahy of the U.S. Submarine *Darter* thought it was all very funny. Sneaking into enemy waters, putting ashore a man old enough to be Confucius, sneaking away, and what kind of a man was the old Oriental? A man who wanted to watch soap operas and was annoyed that Navy submarines did not have TV reception facilities for *As the Planet Revolves*.

Captain Leahy thought this all very funny, so funny in fact that he was in the process of telling it to his fellow drinkers at the officers' club bar at Mindanao, where the Navy maintained a small base to refuel submarines.

But he had not gotten quite to the good part, the part about the soap operas, when he was tapped on the shoulder by a chief petty officer.

"Cap'n, sir."

"What is it?" Leahy said, his voice surly at being interrupted.

"Phone call, sir."

"Tell them I'll be there in a minute."

"It's Washington, sir."

The CPO's voice was insistent.

The moment was gone; the officers who had been listening with rapt attention were now turning back toward each other, picking up the threads of their own conversations. Damn, thought Leahy. Aloud he said, "Probably another ferry run for another old gook who likes soap operas," but the comment did not get the rise he had hoped for and Captain Leahy went to the phone.

There he was told by an official in the Navy Department that he would be presented with a passenger who would have sealed orders. Leahy would follow the orders. He would not mention this to anyone as the orders were top secret and so was the mission.

And he was directed to return to his ship immediately to await the arrival of the passenger.

Annoyed, without even time to finish his drink, Captain Leahy, jaw set, marched out of the officers' club and walked the hundred yards to the pier where the *Darter* had been refueled and made ready for another voyage. The long oil and supply hoses that were used to revitalize the sub's innards had been dropped from the feeder holes as the sub lay tied up at dockside. Refueling, resupply was over.

Captain Leahy clambered up the gangway to the deck of the sub where he was met by his executive officer.

"We've taken aboard a passenger," the exec said.

Leahy shook his head. "Another Charley Chan?" he asked.

"No, sir, this one's an American. Young. Or I think he's young. He seems to be injured. He walks with a cane. I've put him in my quarters, sir."

"All right, Lieutenant. I'd better go see what nitty-witty the U.S. Government is up to tonight."

Captain Leahy went down the forward hatch and knocked on the door of the passenger's compartment.

"Yeah?"

"The captain."

"What do you want?"

"I'm coming in to talk to you."

"If you want to."

When Leahy opened the door, the new passenger was lying on the built-in bunk, wearing jockey shorts. Both shoulders were heavily bandaged, his right thigh was wrapped around with bandages. A cane leaned against the small built-in writing desk. The passenger's clothes were strewn on the floor.

"Don't tell me," Leahy said. "We're taking you to the Rusk Institute for Physical Rehabilitation." He smiled at his own joke. He was the only one who did.

"No, actually you're taking me to Sinanju." The passenger nodded his head toward the desk. "It's all in those orders over there."

Leahy opened the sealed envelope marked "top secret." The orders were identical to those he had received for the old Oriental.

"Is your luggage aboard?" asked Leahy.

"I don't travel with luggage."

"That's a novelty."

"And I don't like soap operas," said Remo.

"That's a novelty, too."

"And another novelty is that I don't like company, I don't feel like chit-chat, I won't complain about the food because all I want is rice unseasoned, and I won't complain about the air or the noise or the boredom as long as we get out of here and get to Sinanju as quickly as possible."

"My sentiments exactly."

"See you there," said Remo. "I'm going to sleep."

And that was the last Captain Leahy saw or heard of his passenger until they were in the West Korean Bay and he had to go to the passenger's cabin to tell him they were soon to surface.

"I'll need a raft and a man to row me ashore," said Remo. "My shoulders aren't up to rowing. Or swimming."

"Right. Will you need any help ashore?"

"I don't think so," said Remo. "I should be met."

"I rather doubt it," said Leahy. "We're way ahead of our estimated arrival time. You may have to wait ashore a long time for whoever it is is supposed to meet you."

"There'll be someone there," said Remo stubbornly, working one toe against the other heel, trying to get on his soft Italian leather slip-ons.

So Captain Lee Enright Leahy was not totally surprised when his submarine moved in close to the shore and he popped up the periscope and scanned the shoreline and saw, standing on the sand, looking out toward the USS *Darter,* the aged Oriental, wearing a bright red brocaded robe, pacing back and forth, obviously oblivious to the cold.

"Of course, he's here," Leahy mumbled to himself. "We left him here, he's been here ever since, and this other looneytoon is going to get off here and the two of them are going to wait and I'm going to come back twice more with two more people until they have a full table for bridge. The whole country's going nuts."

"Beg pardon, sir," said the executive officer.

"Surface and let's prepare to put our cargo ashore," said Leahy. "Before he decides to become a teapot."

"Aye, aye, sir," said the exec. Turning away, he mumbled "Teapot, eh?" and decided that Captain Leahy would have to be watched.

So this is it, huh?" said Remo as he limped through the shallow rock-bottomed water onto the shore. Behind him, the two sailors in the rubber raft used their oars to push the craft away from the shoreline and to hustle back to the waiting submarine.

Chiun stepped toward Remo, a smile lighting his face.

"Yes," he said. "This is it. The Pearl of the Orient." He waved his arms dramatically right and left. "The Sun Source of the World's Wisdom. Sinanju."

Remo's eyes followed Chiun's arms to the left and right. To the left was barren, rockstrewn desolation; to the right was more barren, rockstrewn desolation. The waves broke white, bubbling, and cold on the shore.

"What a dump," said Remo.

"Ah, but wait until you see the fishing building," said Chiun.

Using his cane for support, Remo hobbled forward again toward Chiun. Water squished from his soaked loafers but he did not feel the cold. Chiun's face squinted up as he seemed to see, for the first time, the cane in Remo's hand.

"Aiiieeee." His left hand flashed sideways, almost glinting in the brittle November sunlight of Sinanju. The broad leading edge of his hand hit the cane. The wood snapped and broke. Remo got his weight off it just quickly enough to avoid falling into the water. He stood there, holding the curved crook of the cane in his right hand, the rest of the cane bobbing in the water behind his back, before seeming to fight its way over the waves and back out toward the sea.

"Dammit, Chiun, I need that."

"I do not know what they have taught you in America while I was gone, but no disciple of the Master of Sinanju will use a walking stick. People will look. They will say, look, there is the disciple of the Master, and how young he is and he walks with a stick and how foolish of the Master to have tried to train such a pale piece of pig's ear to do anything. And they will scoff at me and I will not have it in my own land. What is wrong with you that you think you need a cane?"

"Three attacks, Little Father," Remo said. "Both shoulders and right leg."

Chiun searched Remo's face to determine if he knew the significance of the three attacks. The thin set of Remo's lips showed that he did.

"Well, we must go on to my palace," said Chiun, "and there we will care for you. Come."

He turned and walked away along the beach. Remo, using his left leg to move, and dragging his right leg heavily, hobbled after him. But he could not keep up, as Chiun widened the distance between them.

Finally, Chiun stopped ahead of Remo and gazed around him as if examining the majesty of his kingdom. Remo caught up to him. Without a word, Chiun turned and continued along the path he had taken, but this time more slowly, and Remo was able to stay at his side.

Fifty yards farther along, they stopped atop a small rise.

"There," said Chiun, pointing off in the distance. "The new fishing building."

Remo looked where Chiun pointed. A shanty of old water-logged planks and rolled tarpaper roofing perched precariously atop a deck that itself was perched delicately atop wooden pilings. It looked as if one sardine over the legal limit would topple it into the bay.

"What a dump," said Remo.

"Ahhh, to you it looks like a dump but it is highly efficient. The people of Sinanju have built it just right, to do its work. They are not interested in things for show, for the sake of show. Function is important. Come, I will show it to you. Would you like to see it?"

"Little Father," said Remo. "I would like to go to your house."

"Ah, yes. The American to the end. Not wishing to look and to learn from the wisdom of other people. It would not be right for you to try to learn how to build fishing buildings. That would make sense. Suppose someday you are without work? You could say, aha, but I can build fishing buildings and maybe that would keep you from standing on line for charity. But no, that requires foresight, of which you have none. And industry, of which you have less. No. Fritter your time away like the grasshopper, which finds itself in winter with nothing to eat."

"Chiun, please. Your house," said Remo, who stood only with great pain.

"It is all right," said Chiun. "I am used to your laziness. And it is a palace, not a house," and he turned left and began trudging along a sandy dirt road toward a small cluster of buildings several hundred yards away.

Remo hobbled to keep up with him.

"Didn't you once tell me, Little Father, that every time you entered the village, they threw flower petals in your path?" asked Remo, noticing that the road to the village center was empty of people and that Chiun, for all the so-called majesty of his office, might have been just another golden-ager out for a walk.

"I have suspended the flower petal requirement," said Chiun officiously.

"Why?"

"Because you are an American. I knew you might be misunderstanding of it. It is all right. The people protested but in the end I prevailed. I do not need flower petals to remind me of the love of my subjects."

No one met them on the street. No vehicles were to be seen. There were only a few stores and Remo could see people inside them but none came out to greet Chiun.

"You sure this is Sinanju?" asked Remo.

"Yes. Why do you ask?"

"Because it seems that a town you support and that your family has supported for centuries ought to pay a little more attention to you," said Remo.

"I have suspended the attention-paying requirement," said Chiun. His manner, Remo noticed, was less official and sounded a little like an apology. "Because . . ."

"I know, because I'm an American."

"Right," said Chiun. "But remember, even if they do not come out, people are watching. I wish you would walk right and not embarrass me by seeming to be an old man, old before your time, older even than your western dissolution would seem to require."

"I will try, Little Father, not to embarrass you," said Remo and, by an effort of will, he forced himself to put some weight on his injured right leg, reducing the limp, and, even though each motion pained him, he forced himself to swing his arms from the shoulders almost normally as he walked.

"There is the ancestral palace," said Chiun, motioning ahead with a nod of his head.

Remo looked ahead. Into his mind flashed a building he had once seen in California. It had been created by its builder from junk, made of broken bottles and tin cans and Styrofoam cups and old tires and broken pieces of boards.

Chiun's house reminded Remo of a house built by the same craftsman, but this time with access to more materials, for in a village of wooden shanties and huts, Chiun's home was made of stone and . . .

And . . . glass and steel and wood and rock and shell. It was a low, one-story building whose architecture seemed to be American ranch as seen through an LSD haze.

"It's . . . it's . . . it's . . . really something to see," said Remo.

"It has been in my family for centuries," said Chiun. "Of course, I had it remodeled many years ago. I put in a bathroom which I thought was a good idea you westerners had. And a kitchen with a stove. See, Remo, I am willing to take advice when it is good."

Remo was pleased to hear that, for he had some additional good advice for Chiun—tear it down and start all over. He decided to tether his tongue.

Chiun led Remo to the front door, apparently made of wood. Only apparently, because the door had been totally covered over with shells of clams, oysters, and mussels. The door looked like a section of Belmar Beach four hours after a New Jersey rip tide.

The door was heavy and Chiun pushed it open with seeming difficulty. He looked at Remo almost apologetically.

"I know," said Remo. "You have suspended the door opening requirement."

"How did you know?"

"Because I'm an American," said Remo.

While Remo had considered the building's exterior as ugly, not even that had prepared him for the inside. Every available inch of floor space seemed to have something on it. There were jugs and vases and plates, there were statues and swords, there were masks and baskets, there were piles of cushions in place of chairs, there were low tables of highly polished wood, there were colored stones in glass jars.

Chiun spun around and indicated his domain with another sweep of his hand.

"Well, Remo, what do you think?"

"I am underwhelmed," said Remo.

"I knew you would be," said Chiun. "These are all the prizes of the Masters of Sinanju. Tribute paid us by rulers from all over the world. From the Sun King as you call him. From Ptolemy. From the shahs of those countless countries that make grease. From the emperors of China when they remembered to pay their bills. From tribes of India. From a once-great nation of black Africa."

"Who ripped you off giving you a jar of colored stones?" asked Remo, looking at a jar which stood in the corner of the room, a foot and a half high, filled with dull stones.

"How American you are," said Chiun.

"Well, I mean one of your ancestors got hustled."

"The jar was the agreed-upon price."

"A jar filled with rocks?"

"A jar filled with uncut diamonds."

Remo looked at the jar again. It was true. It was filled with uncut diamonds and the smallest was two inches across.

"But I would not expect you to understand that," said Chiun. "For you, for the western mind, all the world is divided into two categories: shiny and not shiny. For you, a piece of glass. But for a Master of Sinanju, diamonds. Because we can look under the dullness and see the value of the core."

"Like you did with me?" said Remo.

"Even Masters of Sinanju sometimes get fooled. Something that is supposed to be an uncut diamond may turn out to be just a rock."

"Chiun, I wanted to ask you something."

"Ask me anything."

"I wanted to know," and then Remo felt the strength draining from his limbs and he knew that his muscles had been extended beyond the point that they could be extended, and his right leg started to cave, and suddenly the effort of will ended, and his shoulders were blazing with pain. He opened his mouth to say something more, but he couldn't, and then he was falling toward the floor of the room.

He did not remember hitting the floor. He did not remember being lifted.

He only remembered waking up and looking around. He was in a small sunlit room, lying on a pile of cushions, naked, covered only with a thin silken sheet.

Chiun stood by his side and when Remo's eyes opened, he knelt. Carefully but quickly, his hands began to remove the bandages from Remo's shoulders.

"The doctor put those on," said Remo.

"The doctor is a fool. No muscle is helped by being strapped. Rest, yes. Imprisonment, no. We will make you well soon. We will . . ." but his voice trailed off as he saw Remo's right shoulder, as the last strand of bandage fell off.

"Oh, Remo," he said in a sad, pained voice. He said nothing further as he unwrapped the left shoulder and then he said it again, "Oh, Remo."

"The one who hit the leg was the best of all," Remo said. "Wait until you see it." He paused. "Chiun, how did you know I would come here?"

"What do you mean?"

"When you said goodbye to Smith, you said I would be here."

Chiun shrugged as he bent toward the bandage on Remo's right thigh. "It is written that you would."

"Written where?" asked Remo.

"On the men's room wall at Pittsburgh Airport," said Chiun nastily. "In the books of Sinanju," he said.

"And what does it say?" asked Remo.

Chiun deftly removed the bandage from Remo's thigh. This time he said nothing.

"That bad, huh?"

"I have seen worse," said Chiun. "Although not on anybody who survived."

He took a bowl from a small table near Remo's sleeping mat. "Drink this," he said. He lifted Remo's head and brought a cup to Remo's lips. The liquid was warm and almost tasteless except for what seemed to be a trace of salt.

"Awful. What is it?"

"It is a mixture from the seaweed that will start making you well again."

He let Remo's head down slowly. Remo felt tired. "Chiun," he said in a questioning voice.

"Yes, my son."

"You know who did this to me, don't you?"

"Yes, my son, I know."

"He is coming, Little Father," said Remo. His eyelids grew heavier as he spoke. It seemed as if his words were being spoken by someone else.

"I know, my son. He is coming."

"He may try to hurt you, Little Father."

"Sleep now, Remo. Sleep and heal."

Remo's eyes closed and he began to drift off. He heard Chiun's voice again. "Sleep and heal, my son."

And then Chiun's final words. "Heal quickly."

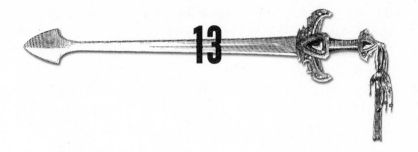

AND thus it came to pass that the Master of Sinanju did walk along the path in the village where he had once been of such honor.

His feet were heavy, as was his heart, because he knew that powerless, unprotected was the young disciple from the land across the sea, and because he knew that the evil force that would destroy that disciple would soon make its appearance on the rocky soil of Sinanju.

And the Master thus had no patience with the tongues of fools, and when people approached him on the path, to talk about the young disciple, about the leadenness of his step, about the infirmities that seemed as if they were of age, the Master had no patience with them and flailed about and scattered them as the barking dogs scatters the goose. But he did not harm the people who gave him such aggravation, because it has always been written, since the dawn of writing, that the Master must not raise his hand in anger to harm a person from the village.

And it was this very command that gave the Master such pain of spirit. Because the one who was coming to destroy the young disciple was of the village of Sinanju, yea, even of the blood of the Master, and the Master could find no way in which he might violate his ages-old vow and inflict upon that one the death he deserved.

Yea, as the Master walked alone, he thought that his disciple, injured as he was, defenseless as a babe as he was, that his disciple would be killed, and Chiun, the Master of Sinanju, could not protect him because of his vow never to hurt someone from the village.

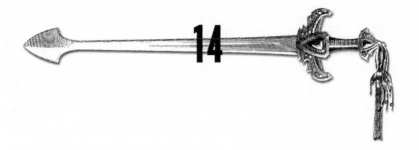

PREMIER Kim Il Sung was at the plain wooden desk in his office in the People's Building in Pyongyang when the secretary entered the room.

The secretary was a young captain of artillery. He affected a gabardine military uniform instead of the rough canvas-textured khaki that was official government issue, but Sung had never held this against him because he was a good secretary.

Communists could come and Communists could go; military styles could come and go; pride even could come and go, but good secretaries were to be nurtured.

Once, years before, Sung had been accused of turning into a reactionary rightwinger after seizing power, and he had explained in what he considered his gentle voice that all revolutionaries become conservatives after gaining power. "Radicalism is fine for revolution," he had said, "but conservatism is what gets the trucks out of the garage in the morning."

He had then displayed his continuing revolutionary zeal by throwing the insulter into a prison for two weeks. When the man was released, Sung summoned him to his office.

The man, a minor official from one of the provinces, had stood before Sung, humiliated, chastened.

"Now you know you cannot judge everything by appearances,"

Sung had said. "It was an easy lesson for you to learn because you are still alive. Many have not been so lucky."

So it was that Kim Il Sung rated his secretary by secretarial standards and not by any standard of appearance set for soldiers. And so it was that Sung rated the man his secretary ushered in to see him, not by his size or his clothing or his speech, but by a kind of internal fire that seemed to come through the man's eyes and that invested all his words with power.

"I am Nuihc," the man said, "and I have come to serve you."

"Why am I so lucky?" said Sung.

He saw immediately that the man named Nuihc had no sense of humor.

"Because it is through you that I can regain the hereditary title of my family. Master of Sinanju."

"Yes," said Kim Il Sung. "I have met the Master. He is a charming old rogue."

"He is a very old man," said Nuihc. "It is time for him to tend his vegetable garden."

"Why do you bother me with this?" asked Kim Il Sung. "Who cares what a small band of brigands does in one tiny village?"

He had chosen his words carefully and was rewarded by a small flash of anger in Nuihc's eyes.

"You know, my Premier, that that is not so," said Nuihc. "The House of Sinanju has for centuries been famed in the ruling palaces of the world. Now it is up to you to decide whether or not you wish the house to be run by a Westerner . . . an American. Because that is the choice. Who will be the new Master: Me? Or an American who represents the CIA and the other spy agencies of the government in Washington?"

"And again, I ask, why does it concern me?"

"You know the answer to that," said Nuihc. "First, our nation will be a laughing stock if this hereditary house becomes the property of an American. And second, the powers of the House are well known to you. Those powers could be put to use in your behalf, to the benefit of your rule. Not as they are now, working for the capitalists of Wall Street. Do you know, for a certainty, that the power of Sinanju will not be turned against you tomorrow or the next day? Whenever Washington wills it, Premier, you will pass into the pages of history for the dead, killed in office. You can prevent that."

Sung thought about those words for a long while before answering. He had met Chiun, and there had seemed to spring up almost a bond of friendship, but the old man had told him that he worked for the United States. This Nuihc might be right. One day, a word might come and soon Kim Il Sung would be dead.

On the other hand, what guarantee did Sung have that Nuihc would be any better? He looked carefully into Nuihc's face. His blood relationship with the old man was obvious; there were the same lines of face and body, the same feeling of coiled spring tension when the man only stood casually in front of Sung's desk.

"You wonder," Nuihc said, "whether or not you can trust me."

"Yes."

"You can trust me for one reason. I am driven by greed. The leadership of the House will give me power and wealth. Beyond that, I want our nation to rise high in the world; I want it to happen because at the side of Kim Il Sung is Nuihc, the new Master of Sinanju."

Kim Il Sung thought again for a long while, then he said, "I will consider it. In the meantime, you may avail yourself of the hospitality of my house."

It was almost dark when Chiun returned to his home. Remo still slept. The Korean girl who was Chiun's servant knelt by the white man's side, occasionally blotting up the sweat from his brow.

"Be gone," said Chiun.

The girl rose and bowed deferentially toward Chiun.

"He is very ill, Master."

"I know, child."

"He has no strength. Are white people always so weak?"

Chiun looked at her sharply but could tell she meant no disrespect. Yet here she was, Chiun's servant, the one loyal follower in the village, and even she could not hide her disappointment that Chiun had picked a white man to learn the role of the Master for that day when Chiun would rule no longer.

He struggled to keep his temper, then said softly, "Many are weak, child. But this one was strong, a giant among men, until he was brought down by the cunning attacks of a cowardly jackal's henchmen, a jackal too cowardly to attack himself."

"That is terrible, Master," said the girl, her face and voice ringing with the earnestness of someone who wanted desperately to believe. "I wish I could meet this jackal."

"You shall, child. You shall. And so shall he," Chiun said. He looked at Remo as if looking at a faraway cloud and then returned to the present moment and chased the girl from the room.

"Heal quickly, Remo," he said softly in the silent room. "Heal quickly."

Nuihc had not tried to leave the room that Kim Il Sung had provided for him in the palace. He was not worried by the guards he knew were outside the door, but he was waiting for an answer.

At dinner time, there was a knock on the door.

It opened before Nuihc could speak.

Kim Il Sung was there. He saw Nuihc sitting on a chair, looking out the window, toward the east, toward west, toward Sinanju. He smiled.

"Tomorrow we go to Sinanju," Sung said. "To crown a new master."

"You have chosen wisely," said Nuihc. He smiled also.

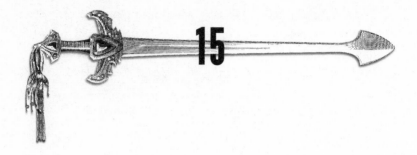

THE caravan arrived in Sinanju shortly after noon the next day.

There was a lead car in which sat Kim Il Sung and Nuihc, followed by a car containing the governor of the province and Sung's adviser Myoch'ong. Lesser party officials followed in other cars, and while their mission was to drive the hated American influence from the history of Sinanju, none of them thought it incongruous that they drove in Cadillacs and Lincolns and Chryslers. The motorcycle escort of soldiers, six in front, six behind, six on each side, drove Hondas.

The caravan was spotted more than a mile outside the city, on the paved road leading to the town which had grown up around the old village of Sinanju. Within minutes, word had reached the old quarter that the premier was coming, along with the real Master of Sinanju, and in only moments word was at the home of Chiun.

"Master," said the granddaughter of the carpenter to Chiun, who sat on a mat staring through one of the house windows toward the bay, "many men are coming."

"Yes?"

"The premier is with them. And so, they say, is one of your blood."

Chiun turned slowly on the mat to look at the girl.

"Know one thing, child. When trouble comes, it comes at its

own time, never at yours. Even now, how quickly comes the day of darkness."

He turned back toward the sea and folded his arms and seemed to gaze beyond the bay, as if searching for a land where the sun might yet be shining.

"And what shall I do, Master?"

"Nothing. There is nothing we can do." Chiun's voice sounded old and tired.

The girl stood for a moment, waiting for more, then walked slowly away, confused and not really understanding why the Master was so deeply depressed.

The caravan of cars skirted the main city of Sinanju, turned toward the shoreline, then followed a dirty sand road that led into the heart of the old village.

They halted in the square in the center of town, and Nuihc and the premier stepped out onto the street. The premier wore his military tunic, Nuihc a two-piece black fighting costume. In the custom of Sinanju, it was unbelted. Fighting uniforms were belted for demonstrations; for fights to the death, no belts were worn. This tradition dated back four hundred years when two of Chiun's ancestors had fought for the vacant title of Master of Sinanju. One of the contenders wore a uniform with belt. Five minutes later he had been strangled with the belt. Since that time, no Master had worn a belted uniform except in exercise, practice, or demonstration. But never in combat.

Nuihc looked up and down the streets. He could see people peering through their windows but afraid to come out onto the street until they knew more about this caravan and its meaning.

"It has been many years since I walked this ground," said Nuihc. A heavy breeze blew off the bay and swirled his long, shiny black hair about his face. His eyes were narrowed into slits that looked like knife-cuts in smooth yellow flesh.

Kim Il Sung saw Nuihc's eyes and the blood lust in them, and it was there as if it always belonged there, and for just a moment Sung again wondered if it were not just a matter of time before that lust was turned upon him.

Chiun's palace was at the end of the street, thirty yards from the square, and now Nuihc looked at it and his face broke into a smile.

"Let us do it," he said.

Without waiting for an answer, he stepped off through the dust and sand toward the house of the Master of Sinanju. Kim Il Sung remained standing alongside his vehicle. Purposefully, conscious of the eyes watching him, Nuihc strode to the front door of Chiun's home and pounded on the door with his fist. Under the hammering, shells cracked and broke loose and powdered the wooden step in front of the door.

"Who is there?" answered a young woman's voice after a long pause.

"Nuihc is here," said the long-haired man in a loud ringing voice. "Descendant of the Masters of Sinanju, himself the new Master of Sinanju. Send out the American weakling and the senile traitor who has given him our secrets."

There was a long pause.

Then the woman's voice again.

"Go away. No one is home."

Nuihc pounded upon the door again. "There is no hiding for you, old man, not for you or for the white lackey you would impose upon the people of this village. Come out of there before I come in and drag you out by the scruff of your scrawny neck."

Another pause.

The woman's voice again.

"It is not permitted to enter the Master's house without the Master's permission. Be gone, urchin."

Nuihc paused as it seeped into his head what Chiun's game was. Nuihc was protected in anything he said to Chiun because the old man, as Master of Sinanju, was not permitted to raise a hand against another from the village. But that protection ended should Nuihc enter Chiun's home uninvited, and Chiun could have the right to deal with him as just another burglar. Nuihc did not like the prospect. Still, how to get the old man and the American out of the house?

He walked back, jauntily, toward Kim Il Sung. His mind was clicking and he knew the answer.

He spoke to the premier, and then Sung and his entourage followed Nuihc back to the house.

Again Nuihc pounded on the door. Again the woman answered: "Go away, I told you."

"The premier is here," said Nuihc, raising his voice to be sure both Chiun and the villagers heard.

There was a pause.

The woman's voice again.

"Tell him he is in the wrong place. The nearest brothel is in Pyongyang."

Nuihc spoke out crisply. "Tell the old man that unless he and the imperialist white swine come out, the premier will order this house destroyed by explosion for being what it is: a spy's den giving comfort to an enemy of the state." He turned and smiled at Sung.

Another pause. Longer this time.

Finally the woman's voice again: "Return to the village square. The Master will meet you there."

"Tell him to hurry," ordered Nuihc. "We do not have time to waste on the doddering of the ancient." He turned and walked alongside the premier, back the thirty yards to the village square, where they waited by the premier's Cadillac. Now they were not alone. The people of Sinanju, who had been watching and listening from inside their homes and shops, now stepped out onto the old wooden sidewalks and, as the premier and Nuihc passed, they cheered.

Inside his home, Chiun had heard Nuihc's final ultimatum and now he heard the cheers and knew what they were for. He stared out toward the bay. After all these years, after all his service, after all the centuries of tradition, it had come to this: a Master of Sinanju, humiliated in his own village by one of his own family, with the village citizens cheering the intruder.

How pleasant it would be to do what should be done. To step out into the square and to reduce Nuihc to the pile of flesh and bone chip that he should be. But the centuries of tradition that had given him pride also gave Chiun responsibility. He was disgraced now before the villagers, but he would be disgraced in his own eyes if he should strike Nuihc.

The younger man knew that, and the knowledge of his freedom from attack had emboldened his tongue.

It should have been Remo, Chiun knew. It was for Remo to meet this challenge, to destroy Nuihc for once and all. So it had been written in the books ages before. But Remo lay asleep, his muscles unable to work, more helpless than a child.

And because neither Remo nor Chiun could raise an arm against Nuihc, the title of Master of Sinanju was going to pass, for the first time in unremembered centuries, into the hands of one who would not wear it with pride and honor.

Chiun rose from his mat and went into the main living section of the house and he lit a candle. From a chest, he took a long white robe, the robe of innocence, and a black fighting uniform. He fingered the black uniform fondly, then dropped it atop the chest. He would wear the white robe, the color of the unspoiled. The color of the chicken.

He donned the robe quickly then kneeled before the candle and prayed to his ancestors. In that moment was crystallized all the training of Sinanju, because its root was: to survive.

And Chiun had made his decision. He would give up the title of Master. He would trade it for Remo's life. And then one day, when Remo was well, there might be a chance for Remo to reclaim that title.

It would do Chiun no good. He would, by that time, have been marked in history as a disgrace, the first Master ever forced to give up his title. But at least the title might one day be wrested from Nuihc, and that was some small measure of consolation.

Chiun reached forward a delicate long-nailed finger and extinguished the candle flame by squeezing the wick between thumb and index finger. He rose to his feet in one fluid movement that left his robe still and unswirling.

"Master?" said the girl, appearing next to him.

"Yes?" said Chiun.

"Must you go?"

"I am the Master. I cannot run."

"But they do not want you. They want the American. Give him up."

"I am sorry, child," said Chiun. "But he is my son."

The woman shook her head. "He is white, Master."

"And he is more my son than any yellow man. He shares not my blood but he shares my heart and my mind and my soul. I cannot give him up." And Chiun touched the girl lightly on her cheek and walked toward the front door.

In the square, the villagers crowded near the car where Nuihc and the premier stood. The motorcycle soldiers kept them at a respectful distance, but their voices spoke out clearly.

"The Master is too old."

"He betrayed us by giving the secrets to the white man."

"Nuihc will restore the honor of Sinanju."

Some felt they should say that Chiun's labors had always supported the village, that it was not given to mere villagers to know what was on the Master's mind, and that the poor did not starve and the elderly were not discarded and the babies were not drowned, sent home to the sea, anymore because of Chiun's efforts. But they did not say these things because it seemed no one wished to hear them, and instead all wished to heap praise upon Nuihc who preened himself and soaked up the adulation as he stood by the premier.

"Where is he?" asked Kim Il Sung of Nuihc.

His answer did not come from Nuihc. The crowd was silent, its humming babble stopped in midword. All eyes turned toward Chiun's home.

Coming down the street slowly, down the thirty yards toward the cars and the crowd and his tormentor, came Chiun, his face impassive, his steps slow but light, his hands folded within each other inside the voluminous sleeves of his traditional white robe.

"Where is the American?" one man called.

"The false Master still protects the westerner," said another in outrage.

"Traitor," screamed another man.

And then the voices rose above the tiny square, "Traitor! Traitor! Traitor!"

Back inside Chiun's house, the young woman who was his servant heard the catcalls and the hoots and her eyes watered with tears. How could they? How did they dare to do such a thing to the Master? And finally she realized the reason. It was not the Master they hated, but the white American. For the white American, the Master was doing this.

It was not fair. The Master's life destroyed because of the American.

The American would not escape the responsibility for his being. She went to the living room and from a pearl-encrusted scabbard withdrew a highly polished knife with a long, curved blade.

Holding it behind her, she went into the room where Remo slept. His eyes were still closed. She knelt down beside the sleeping mat. She raised her eyes to the heavens and offered up a prayer to her ancestors, to understand what she was doing.

She looked down on the hated white man. "Lift the knife up and drive it into his heart," a small voice whispered insistently inside her.

The white man's eyes opened. He smiled at her.

"Hi, sweetheart, where's Chiun?" he said.

She lifted the knife up over her head and willed herself to drive it down into Remo's chest, but there she let it drop from her hands and buried her face against Remo's chest, weeping.

WHERE is the swine American?" Nuihc's voice was a sneer as he looked across the two feet of space separating him from Chiun.

Chiun ignored him. To the premier, he said: "I see you have chosen a side."

The premier shrugged.

"How like a creature from Pyongyang," said Chiun. "To cast his lot with a trollop."

One of the motorcycle soldiers stepped forward. He raised his pistol over his head to club Chiun for his insult. Chiun did not move. The pistol poised and Kim Il Sung barked: "Cease."

The soldier let his hand down slowly, then with a look of hatred at Chiun he backed away.

"Do not be angry," said Chiun. "Your premier has saved you to die another day."

"Enough," said Nuihc. "Remo. Where is he?"

"He rests," said Chiun.

"I have challenged him. He is a coward not to be here."

"A coward. A coward. The traitor has given the wisdom to a coward," came cries from the crowd.

Chiun waited until the noise subsided.

"Who is the coward?" said Chiun. "Is it the injured white man? Or is it the cowardly squirrel who used three people to have him injured?"

"Enough, old man," said Nuihc.

"Not enough," said Chiun. "You fool these people now into thinking how brave Nuihc is. Did you tell them how you last faced the American? In the museum of the whale? And how he left you tied up, with your own belt, like a child?"

Nuihc's face flushed. "He had help. He did not do it alone."

"And did you tell them how you tried to kill the Master, in the oil fields of that faraway land? And how I left you to dry in the sun like a starfish?"

"You talk much, old man," said Nuihc bitterly. "But I have come here to get rid of the American for good. And then I, not you, am the Master of Sinanju. Because you have betrayed your people by giving the secrets to a white man."

"Traitor!"

"Traitor!" came the voices again.

"You have forgotten the legend of the night tiger," said Chiun. "Of the dead man whose face is pale and who will come from the dead and be trained by the Master to be the night tiger who cannot die. You have forgotten these things."

"Your legends are for children," said Nuihc with a sneer. "Bring on your American and we will see who cannot die."

"Where is he?"

"The white man . . . bring him forward!"

The voices raised in a roar and under them, Chiun spoke softly to Nuihc. "You may have Sinanju, Nuihc. Let Remo live. That is my price."

Loudly, so he could be heard by all, Nuihc answered. "I do not deal with the senile and the foolish. Remo must die. And you must be sent home." A hush fell over the crowd. In the old days, before the labors of the Masters of Sinanju had given the villagers sustenance, the old and the weak and the hungry babies were sent home—by being put into the cold waters of the bay to drown.

Chiun looked carefully into Nuihc's eyes. There was no mercy there, no pity, no flicker of humanity.

His final offer.

"I will send myself home," said Chiun. "But the man with white skin must live."

His voice was a tired plea for mercy for Remo.

His answer was a smile from Nuihc who said, "So long as he lives, Sinanju's secrets are not secrets. He has learned the ancient ways, now they must die with him. Now."

"Now!" came the cries.

"The American must die!"

And then it was that a voice rang over the shouts of the maddened townspeople. And so it was that they turned and cast their eyes toward the palace of the Master and a hush fell over them as there they saw, standing in the dust of the road, the white man dressed in a two-piece black suit without belt.

And his voice rang over the heads of the villagers like an alarm bell and they looked at each other in amazement because the white man spoke in the tongue of the villagers, and his words were the words of that land and its old ways, and what he did say was:

"I am created Shiva, the Destroyer, death the shatterer of worlds. The dead night tiger made whole by the Master of Sinanju. What is this dog meat that now challenges me?"

And the crowd was hushed, for their tongues were coated with the powder of fear.

Chiun was looking at Nuihc when Remo's voice sounded. The old man saw Nuihc's eyes widen with surprise and perhaps fear.

Kim Il Sung looked shocked, also frightened, but fright could be forgiven in one who was not of the House of Sinanju.

Chiun turned slowly. Had the gods heard his prayers and visited a miracle of healing upon Remo?

But the hope faded when he saw Remo, standing there heavily, most of his weight on his uninjured left leg, his hands and arms still hanging awkwardly close to his body, resting on his hip bones to take the pressure of their weight off his damaged shoulders.

When Chiun thought of the pain Remo had endured to dress and to walk down that dusty road to the village square, his heart filled with love, but also pity because now Remo faced Nuihc's murderous vengeance.

Nuihc saw too. He saw the wrists resting awkwardly on hips; he saw the weight resting heavily on Remo's left leg. With a smile that promised death, he walked from the small group of men toward Remo.

Remo stood there, his brain throbbing from the pain of his walk. Nuihc was supposed to deliver the fourth blow to Remo's left leg, the blow that would cripple or kill him.

He had a chance if Nuihc got careless. If he got close enough to Remo, the bigger American might be able to drag him down with his weight and get in some kind of blow. It was all he had. As he looked up and saw Nuihc's eyes meeting his, he knew it would not be enough.

Over Nuihc's head, Remo could see Chiun standing still, his face draped in sorrow. He knew the torment that must be in Chiun's mind now—his affection for Remo, and his refusal to disgrace the House by hitting a villager, even if that villager was Nuihc.

Nuihc stopped now. He was out of Remo's reach.

"So you still walk," he said.

"Get on with it, dog meat," said Remo.

"As you will."

Remo waited for him to come closer, to deliver the fourth stroke, the one to Remo's left leg.

Nuihc did not do it. His right leg flashed out and the point of his foot smashed into the knot of muscles at Remo's right shoulder. Remo screamed as the muscles reseparated.

His wrist dropped from its resting place on his hip. The weight of his arm could not pain any more than the shoulder itself did.

Slowly Nuihc moved around behind Remo, as if the American were a stationary object. Remo could not turn to see the blow coming. He felt it land, inside the muscles in the back of his left shoulder. Again he screamed with the pain, as he could feel the fibers of muscle tearing.

Still he stood.

Nuihc was back in front of him, his face contorted with hatred.

"So you are Shiva?" he said. "You are a weak white man, weak as all white men are weak, corrupted as all Americans are corrupted. How does this feel, night tiger?" he shouted and drove his left foot into the bunch of muscles in Remo's already injured right thigh.

Another scream.

Remo went down. His face hit into the dust. The powder coated his lips. His mind felt each muscle of his body and each one shouted its pain. He did not try to rise. He knew the effort was hopeless.

Nuihc stood over him. "I do not even need the fourth blow for you," he sneered. "I will save it for a few moments. Remember. It is coming."

He turned back to Chiun and Kim Il Sung.

The crowd cheered.

"Hail Nuihc. Hail the new Master. Look at the weak American." And they laughed as they pointed at Remo.

Nuihc walked away. Remo lay in the street, the dust on his lips, and he felt the dirt sticking to his face, and for a moment he did not know why it was sticking, and then he realized it was because he was crying.

And then even crying was too painful for him and he just lay in the street, hoping that Nuihc would kill him quickly.

Nuihc stood next to Chiun and Sung.

"There he is, eating the dirt of Sinanju. This is the one, the outsider to whom the ancient one gave the secrets because he said the white man was strong and wise. Look at him. Do you think him strong now?"

The townspeople looked again at Remo. One laughed aloud. And then another, and another, until all of them were laughing as they looked at Remo, face down in the dirt, not moving.

Nuihc joined in the laughter and when they stopped, he asked in a loud voice, "And what do you think of the wisdom of one who picked that white man for his strength? I say, Chiun is too old. Too old to be your protector. Too old to be the Master of Sinanju. Too old for anything except to go home again as the aged and the weak and the foolish did in the olden times."

And the crowd lifted its voices.

"Go home, Chiun. Nuihc is our new Master. Send the ancient one home."

And in the dust, Remo heard the words and knew what they meant, and he wanted to cry out, "Chiun, save yourself, these people aren't worth your spit," but he couldn't say it because he could not talk.

Remo heard the voices and then he heard another voice, a voice he had known for so many years, a voice that had brought him wisdom and had taught him at every step, but now it was a different voice, because all at once it seemed old and tired, and the voice said, "All right. I will go home."

It was Chiun but it didn't sound like Chiun's voice anymore. Chiun's real voice was different. It was strong. Once when he had been dying of burns, Remo had heard Chiun's voice and it had been strong in his head and it had said, "Remo, I will not let you die. I am going to make you hurt, Remo, but you will live because you are supposed to live."

And another time when Remo had been poisoned, through the mists he had heard the voice of Chiun, saying: "Live, Remo, live. That is all I teach you, to live. You cannot die, you cannot grow weak, you cannot grow old unless your mind lets you do it. Your mind is greater than all your strength, more powerful than all your muscles. Listen to your mind, Remo, it is saying to you: live."

That was Chiun's voice, and this old man's voice that had said it was going to allow itself to die, that wasn't Chiun's voice, Remo told himself. It was an impostor's voice, because Chiun would not die and Remo would tell him that. Remo would tell him, Chiun, you must live. But to tell him that he had to be able to move.

His right arm was flung out in front of him. He forced himself, through the pain, to feel the dust under his fingertips. He moved his index finger. He felt the dust and dirt slide up under his fingernail. Yes, Chiun, see, I am alive, he thought, and I am alive because my mind says live, and I remember it, even if you don't, and then Remo made his right middle finger move.

His left hand was under his head. The pain burned his shoulder like a white-hot poker as he turned his hand a fraction of an inch under his head. But didn't you always tell me, Chiun, that pain is the price one pays to stay alive. Pain belongs to the living. Only the dead never hurt.

He could hear their voices again, Nuihc's loud and triumphant, demanding no delay, demanding that Chiun march
now down to the sea and out into the bay until the waters covered him and he went home to his ancestors. And he heard
Chiun's voice, soft and sad and weak, the voice of a man who
has suffered a great loss, and he was saying he could not go
home until he had made his peace with his ancestors.

Remo felt the knot of muscles in his right thigh and he could
feel the separate tears in them, the tear that had first been
opened by Lynette Bardwell and then reopened by Nuihc who
had, in delivering the blow, done some new damage of his own.

Remo screwed his eyes tightly closed. He could feel the muscles, sense their existence, and pressing his lips together so he
did not scream, he tensed the muscles and the pain was worse
than any pain he had ever felt, but that's it, Chiun, isn't it, pain
tells you you're alive.

He heard another voice now, it must have been from the Korean official who stood with Chiun and Nuihc because Remo
did not recognize it. The voice said that Chiun could have a few
minutes before he would go home and the American would be
dispatched any way Nuihc decided, but his body would be sent
to the American embassy as a protest against spies infiltrating
the glorious People's Democratic Republic of North Korea.

His left leg still worked, Remo found, flexing the muscles
from thigh to calf. And the most important muscle of all worked.
His mind. His mind was the master of the muscles, the intellect
the ruler of the flesh, and he let them talk, he let them babble
on, and he knew what he would do. He licked his lips to get the
dust off them and he tasted the dirt on his tongue and it made
him angry at himself for failing, angry at Chiun for surrender-
ing, angry at Nuihc for always coming at them.

But mostly angry at himself.

He heard the voices talk on but he was not listening any more, he was speaking himself, speaking without sound, but speaking in his mind to his muscles and they were hearing him because they moved.

The crowd stilled, and there was a tiny babble of voices, and over them came Nuihc's voice issuing his final ultimatum to Chiun: "You have five minutes, old man."

And then there was another voice Remo heard and he was surprised because it was his voice. He heard it say, loudly, as if he was not even in pain, and he thanked the mind for making the body work, and the voice said:

"Not yet, dog meat."

And there was a scream from the villagers as they all turned and saw Remo standing again. His black uniform was coated with the dust of the street, but he was standing, and the villagers could not believe it, but he was standing, staring at Nuihc and he was smiling.

When Nuihc turned again to face Remo, he could not disguise the look on his face, a look of shock and terror.

He stood there, death-still, alongside Chiun and the premier. Remo, hurting in every muscle, in every tendon and fiber and sinew, made the only move he had left.

He charged.

Perhaps surprise or shock might stop Nuihc from moving fast enough, and while Remo could not walk to him, his charge might get him to Nuihc before Remo fell down again. And if he could fall with Nuihc under him, then perhaps. Just perhaps.

Remo was lunging forward now, his body moving lower and lower toward the earth, only the will of his forward motion preventing him from falling onto his face.

Three yards to go.

But Nuihc was in control again. He stood his ground ready to deal the final blow to Remo, and Remo saw it. When he was only a yard away, he let his body flip out to the right, and as he fell onto his damaged right shoulder he used all the power that was left in his body and concentrated it on his undamaged left leg and drove his bare left foot into the solar plexus of Nuihc. He felt the toe go in, deep, but he did not feel the crunch of bone, and he knew he had missed the sternum, he had hurt Nuihc but the blow was not fatal, and that was all Remo had left. As Remo lay on the ground, he looked up toward Chiun, in supplication, as if asking for forgiveness, and then he heard a scream and Nuihc's eyes bulged forward and he reached down with his hands to grasp his abdomen, but his hands never got there because Nuihc was pitching forward onto the ground.

He hit open mouth first and lay there, in a kneeling position, his eyes open, staring in death at the dirt of the street, as if it were the thing that interested him most in life and in death.

Remo looked at him carefully and realized that Nuihc was dead, and he did not know why, and he passed out because he didn't care.

Unconscious, Remo did not hear Chiun proclaim that Remo's courage was worth more than all Nuihc's skill and that Nuihc had not died of the blow but had died of fear and that now the villagers would know that the Master had selected wisely in choosing Remo.

And Remo did not hear the villagers proclaim undying allegiance to Chiun, and praise Remo for having the heart of a Korean lion in a white man's skin.

He did not hear the villagers drag off the body of Nuihc to cast it into the bay to feed the crabs, and he did not hear Chiun order the premier to have his soldiers carry Remo gently back to Chiun's palace, and he did not hear the premier promise that he would never again involve himself in Sinanju's internal matters, and that there would be an immediate end to the graft visited upon the tribute by the thieving governor.

Remo woke for just a fraction of an instant as he was being lifted by the soldiers, and in that fraction of an instant he heard Chiun's voice, strong again and demanding, order "gently," and before his eyes closed again, he saw that the fingernail of Chiun's left index finger was stained red.

Blood red.

And it was wet.